27 DECEMBER 2017

The old wooden hive stood at the edge of the orchard within sight of the big house. It was unnaturally quiet today, as if the bees had already heard the news, but he had to carry out his duty. In his hands Ezra Curnow held a piece of fragile black crepe that had been among his father's possessions. It had belonged to his grandfather, and no doubt to *his* father before that. Over a century of unbroken tradition of telling the bees the news of a death, even if the queen and her swarms had changed many times, just as monarchs came and went.

Laying the cloth across the roof-ridge of the hive, he knocked three times and said, 'I bring word from the human world to the Queen of Trengrose and her subjects. Miss Eliza's passed over, my lovelies, and left us behind. She lived so long we all thought she were immortal, but her time came at last. We will mourn her, but don't you take wing. We shall do all right together even though we'll miss her. Best you stay here, in Trengrose, where we all belong.'

He heard nothing but a whisper of sound at the threshold of the audible. Had the queen and her subjects heard him? Were they asleep? Already flown?

Anxiety gripped him. If the bees were gone, all would fail. He had kept a colony here for the best part of six decades: they were a part of his soul.

The world trembled on a precipice. Then a bee appeared at the lip of the hive and took to the air. Another followed, then a third. For a moment Ezra feared they might all come streaming out, but no, these were just scouts who buzzed lazily around him, then headed further into the orchard. He felt his nerves settle: they were simply heading out to search for sustenance. He knew there was butterbur in flower by the stream, and deadnettles and cow parsley too, and in his garden he had planted hellebores and cyclamen, and he left the spurge and periwinkle to run riot to ensure that all the bees – not just from his hive, but the wild bees too – had winter food.

He bowed his head in reverence, then straightened up with a grunt – it was cold, and the chill had got into his knees. After a moment he turned for home, missing his old friend already, feeling as bleak as the day.

2

April 2018

Ezra was taking a bath in the orchard with Daisy when the estate agent appeared. If he was surprised to see the man approaching through the trees, he didn't show it; the agent, on the other hand, gave a yelp of shock.

'Mornin',' said Ezra.

He ushered Daisy gently over the side onto the grass, where she shook out her feathers and then applied herself to giving each one a good fussing.

'Ah… good morning.' The man clutched his clipboard to himself like a breastplate. 'Are you aware that you're trespassing?'

Ezra leaned back in the bath. The water – brought from the house by watering cans and hosepipe and still being heated by the burning charcoal in a pit beneath the iron tub – had just been getting to a comfortable temperature, but now felt distinctly chilly. 'Trespassing, is it?' He eyed the intruder gravely and waggled his feet, which stuck out over the end.

'This is Trengrose land.'

'Ar,' said Ezra, frowning. He pulled his feet back in and began to lever himself out of the bath.

'No, no! Please stay where you are.'

'T'ent zackly relaxing being watched taking your bath.' Ezra stood up, water streaming off his knotted old body.

The agent stared fixedly at a point between the equally gnarly apple trees.

Ezra followed his gaze. 'Blossom's ansum this year,' he offered.

Daisy pecked experimentally at the visitor's shoes, but finding them of little interest, picked up her petticoats and strutted away into the underbrush. The agent stared at the retreating hen, then back at the old man. 'Ah yes, very "handsome",' he agreed, and when Ezra bent to retrieve his clothing, shuttled his gaze sideways. 'This is, I believe, part of the Trengrose orchard.'

Ezra said nothing. Deciding not to offer the man the entertainment of watching him struggle into his long johns, he used them instead to dry himself, then put on his corduroy trousers and secured them with a belt that must once have belonged to a larger man; the tongue hung down obscenely.

The agent set his jaw. 'You really shouldn't be here. I'm prepared to turn a blind eye on this occasion, but it would be better if you weren't to be found here again, Mr—?'

Ezra pulled on his huge wellies. 'Not from round here, are you?' he said, taking in the man's pristine Barbour jacket, yellow waistcoat and pressed suit trousers.

'Truro,' the agent returned defensively.

'There you go.' Ezra nodded, point proven. He made as if to leave, then turned back. 'Big house going on the market, is it?'

'I'm afraid that's none of your business. Not unless you have a spare million and a half in cash stashed away,' the agent said nastily.

'Million, eh?' Ezra sucked his teeth, then laughed. 'A million! Pounds, is that, or grains of sand?' Before the man could answer, Ezra picked up the watering cans and set off towards the quillet that he counted as his back garden, feeling the agent's eyes on him until he was out of sight.

Reaching the edge of the garden, he stopped briefly to appreciate the wildflowers – new ones every day as spring wore on – and felt his mind settle.

'Fumitory, alkanet, celandine, campion, forget-me-not, dog

violet, groundsel and three-cornered leek, mouse ear, scurvy grass, speedwell and oxalis, dandelion—' his Gram used to call it by its Cornish name – piss-a-bed – but he refused to saddle a fine plant with such a vulgar appellation, 'sow thistle and speedwell.' Sometimes at night, when sleep evaded him, he would list the plants he had noticed that day, and if sleep had still not claimed him by the time he reached the end of his reckoning, he would reorder them by colour category: pinks, blues, yellows.

He noted that today's newcomer was a tiny pink cranesbill and bent to examine it. When he straightened up, he found himself observed by a pair of dunnocks, blinking their handsome copper-red eyes at him.

'Careful, now,' he warned them. 'You may find you're trespassing.'

He wasn't the only observer of the little birds. Stretched out along a bough of the damson tree was a sleek shape, its patchworked coat of tabby, ginger and white a perfect camouflage among the sun-dappled leaves.

Bucca regarded the man lazily, knowing that he was unlikely to disturb his rest; knowing, also, that he had no greater ambition where the dunnocks were concerned than to spectate. He was comfortable, the warm light falling pleasantly upon his back and head, and the effort required to catch and defeather the little birds seemed in that moment beyond him, unless they foolishly wandered below and he could simply roll off the branch and crush them with his falling body. He yawned hugely, enjoying this fantasy for a fleeting moment, his eyes reduced to golden slits, then slipped lightly back into his doze.

Ezra deposited the watering cans in their accustomed place by the back door of the cottage, picked up the empty saucer there, and took it inside with him. He rinsed it under the tap and stacked it among his drying breakfast things.

Sharp spring light slanted across the framed photographs by the window, illuminating the dust that had fallen over their glass fronts during the winter. Ezra picked each one up and dusted it tenderly. Here his grandparents, Jude and Cecily, he tall and dark, towering over his tiny, pale bride, the sepia of their wedding photo faded so that their expressions were impossible to make out. Another, in a smarter gilt-edged frame, of Jude laughing into the camera, an old-fashioned pitchfork balanced on one shoulder, his dark hair full of straw as if he had just fought his way out of a haystack. It was a remarkably contemporary image, as if a modern photographer had staged it and doctored it to give the impression of age. He wondered, not for the first time, who had taken this candid shot. And there was his father, Ethan, the spitting image of *his* father Jude, with his long straight nose and sharp eyes and tumble of black curls, standing at the door of this very cottage, arm around Tamsin's waist. A picture of the twins in Tamsin's arms. Must be the summer of 1939. Those climbing roses were still going strong: Ma had always said they grew in enchanted earth. '"With sweet musk-roses and with eglantine, there sleeps Titania sometime of the night, lull'd in these flowers with dances and delight",' he murmured to himself.

Another photo lay behind the others, the image it bore imprinted on his memory like a scar. He left it there to gather dust and went to place Gram Cecily's copper kettle on the range to make a brew. Then, while the kettle came slowly to a boil, he went out to relieve himself. He sat in the outhouse, balancing more on one cheek than the other to avoid a nasty nip from the widening crack in the old Bakelite seat, and thought about the man with the clipboard. He'd been anticipating a visitation like this ever since Miss Eliza had died, had been lulled into a false sense of security when winter had passed into spring with no sign of change, and had begun to let himself hope that nothing would happen to alter the status quo. The world would go on along its natural track, and all would be well.

But a posh Truro agent in a yellow waistcoat mouthing the word 'million' was unexpected, and unwelcome. He experienced a rare moment of anxiety, a sort of inward creep of gooseflesh. A million. Who had that sort of money? And in cash? Gangsters, he thought. Gangsters and bankers. Same thing, really.

Pushing the thought away, he fixed his attention on the slice of his small domain he could see from his throne (the door to the outhouse being open): his vegetable plot, where the potato leaves had pushed up in neat, bright rows, the pea wigwams assailed by clever, twining tendrils, the flourishing rhubarb patch with its umbrella leaves, the early bumblebees progressing royally like mini Zeppelins. It was a timeless scene, one he made sure to enjoy every day. Only the seasons changed the view: blackthorn blossom, apple blossom, hawthorn blossom; golden sun, falling leaves, the grey light of winter.

But this year there had been snow. Snow this far south and west was a rare event: February was usually a wet month, too wet for snow to stick and stay. This February had been cold and dry, and one day when he had been cutting back brambles the noon sky had turned suddenly black, and snow had been dumped on the land as if someone up above had slit open a gigantic pillow and let fall its stuffing of cold, cold feathers. In less than twenty minutes everything had been white, the roads impassable for days.

The Beast from the East, the radio weatherman had dubbed this snowstorm.

Somewhere in the depths of his ancient Celtic soul, Ezra couldn't help but wonder if it had presaged doom.

3

The bicycle was Ezra's pride and joy: a Norman Roadster, a true antique. He brushed off the saddle – a proper old bum-cutter – gave the gears a brief blast of WD-40, settled his knapsack on his back, and pushed it out of the gate. Propping it against the drystone wall that bounded his cottage, he briefly admired the profusion of campanula and fleabane that had so thoroughly colonised it, latched the gate, and nodded with respect to the ancient stone cross on the other side of the lane. Then he swung a leg over the frame and pedalled down towards the road.

He was just looking right – where he could make out the sign for the Happy Paws Pet Cemetery up the road – then left, where a faded placard from last summer exhorted people to 'Visit Hockins' Farm Shop', when he heard a loud cawing. A small black bird detached itself from a tree and made a gliding fall from its perch to Ezra's shoulder. Crabbing sideways, it began to poke nosily into the old man's pocket.

Ezra laughed. 'Aright, Merlin, you old beggar? Yes, I got your favourites. Move yerself now.' He ushered the bird back onto his shoulder and fished something out of his pocket, holding his palm open to the bird.

The jackdaw turned its head sideways and applied its intense pale-blue gaze to the offering, then dipped and picked the mealworms up one by one with polite delicacy, before juggling them into its black mouth and despatching them greedily. Its shining ebony beak nuzzled Ezra's ear, nipping the lobe, then probed at the opening till the old man batted it away. 'No earwigs for you in there today, bird.'

But the daw wasn't giving up that easily. Where there were three mealworms there were certain to be more. As Ezra pushed off onto the road, it clung to his shoulder, its claws buried in the tweed of his jacket, and for half a mile or so man, bird and bicycle rolled along in happy symbiosis, the tyres caressing the tarmac, the air whistling through the wheel-spokes, the calm punctuated only by the occasional clunk of a gear change or Merlin's mimicry of the sound, followed by Ezra's appreciative chuckle.

Until they rounded a corner and found themselves suddenly confronted by an enormous four-wheel-drive vehicle spanning most of both carriageways. Ezra, who retained excellent reflexes despite his advanced years, applied his brakes fiercely. The driver was slower to react. Car and bicycle made a brief, uncomfortable acquaintance and Ezra, parting company with his seat and handlebars, landed unceremoniously on the sleek bonnet.

Merlin, who had perhaps foreseen the impending disaster, cawed a loud remonstration, safe from his position in the boughs of a holm oak.

From the interior of the vehicle there issued a piercing wail, a crumping sound, and then a muffled scream.

Ezra's mind – which, like the bicycle, had one moment been gliding serenely along, enjoying the blossom and the chatty comradeship of the jackdaw – now scrambled to make sense of his situation. Where had the attack come from? Was he hurt? Where was his gun? For a moment he was back on the hot backstreets of Limassol under insurgent fire. Instinct kicked in: he rolled to the ground and came up in a crouch, ready to fight, sweat breaking out on his back and his forehead, heart hammering with adrenalin. Where was his gun? He had no gun! And where was his brother? He had—

'Oh bollocks! For Christ's sake, Minty, calm down.'

English voice, possibly London, definitely not Greek Cypriot. Ezra reshuffled his thoughts, took in the car, his surroundings, and shuffled those painful old memories aside. He stood up unsteadily, feeling pain in his shoulder and hip.

The driver's door opened, and the man was suddenly in Ezra's face. 'What the hell were you doing in the middle of the road? Surely there are cycle paths for you people?'

'Twere you in middle of the road,' Ezra said slowly. 'In yer bleddy great tank.'

'I was driving with all due care and attention!' the man blustered.

Ezra looked away, rubbed his hip. It felt important that he didn't lose his temper.

'Toby! Toby! Is he all right? I can't see a thing.'

A woman's voice, indistinct, followed by cacophonous barking.

'For god's sake, Boris, will you shut up?'

Ezra glanced away from the irate driver – a man of middling years, soft in the middle, going thin on top (though trying to disguise the fact with a fancy haircut) – to the source of the second voice, and saw a giant white cushion where the passenger's head should have been.

'Bloody hair trigger on these airbag thingies.' He looked back at Ezra. 'Do you know if there's a decent Land Rover garage round here?'

Ezra snorted. He dropped to one knee to retrieve the Roadster, which had slid under the behemoth, dragged it out, inspected it for damage, and found the front wheel slightly out of true. The man, meanwhile, was examining the paintwork of his vehicle, making small sounds of distress. Ezra was gratified to see that something – probably his belt buckle – had scraped a fine silver line through the black paint of the bonnet all the way to the windscreen.

'Look what you've done!' the man said, indicating the scratch. His face was flushed: he looked as if he might cry. 'That'll cost a fortune to fix.'

The passenger door opened, and a figure crabbed out awkwardly. 'For heaven's sake, Toby, it wasn't his fault. You were going too fast.'

The man stared at the woman who had extricated herself from the vehicle. 'You never, *ever* concede fault,' he uttered through clenched teeth, and turned his attention back to Ezra. 'We should exchange insurance details.'

Ezra said nothing: there was nothing to say. He didn't have insurance of any kind – not vehicle insurance, buildings insurance, contents insurance or life insurance. He took each day as it came and hoped for the best. He looked up to where the jackdaw was perched and patted his breast pocket. With a chitter of delight, the bird launched itself, and sailed noiselessly down to land on Ezra's shoulder.

The dog, Boris – a rather foolish-looking Labrador – started to bark again, and the man took a step backwards.

'Wow, cool!' A lanky young man wearing headphones exited the back door of the Range Rover. He pushed the headphones back from his ears and grinned at Ezra. 'Is he your pet crow? I didn't know you could tame them.'

'He owns himself,' Ezra told the lad. 'No one owns a wild bird, do they, *biy*?'

The jackdaw dropped his head and burrowed into Ezra's pocket, emerging with another mealworm. His pale, intelligent eye regarded the lad for a moment, then he cocked his head back and swallowed the dried worm as if performing a trick.

'Wow! Did you see that, Mum? Did you see?' Before his mother could answer, he was approaching Ezra. 'May I stroke him?'

'It's him you should ask, not me,' Ezra said. 'He'm called Merlin.'

'Hello, Merlin. You're gorgeous. What a beautiful crow you are.'

'Jackdaw, not a crow. Crow's bigger, and don't have the grey head or the blue eye,' Ezra said.

'I'm Dom,' the boy said. 'Well, Dominic really, but everyone calls me Dom. Hey, Merlin, may I stroke your head?' He held an experimental finger out towards the bird, who regarded it steadily, then shuffled sideways in case he needed to take off suddenly. Dom's finger inched closer, then lightly touched the top of the jackdaw's head. There was a collective held breath. The finger moved down to the bird's shoulder. The jackdaw half-shut his pale eyes, looking dopey.

'He likes that.' Ezra beamed at the boy, whose cheeks were suffused with pink delight.

'Stop that, Dominic,' the man said, breaking the spell. 'It's probably got fleas. Get back in the car and control bloody Boris. We're going to be late.'

Dominic, deflated, ran a finger once more down the glossy feathers, gave Ezra a shy smile, then climbed back inside the car.

The man, having resumed control of the scene, gestured at the woman. 'Minty, get in the back with Dom till we get the sodding airbag sorted out.'

His wife shot him a furious look. 'Just one moment.'

She approached Ezra and touched his elbow in a way that felt almost intimate. She was a handsome woman, Ezra thought, not pretty, exactly, but striking: small-boned, elegant. Sharp green eyes, waves of chestnut hair, good bones. Maybe foreign. Well, most people in Cornwall were foreign these days – and by that he meant from past the Tamar.

'Are you sure you're not injured? You must be in shock. I'm so sorry about... everything, and I'm quite sure it wasn't your fault.' Her accent was refined, the sort of English voice you used to hear on the radio.

Ezra smiled at her. 'I'll be aright. Bike may need looking at, though.'

'Oh goodness, perhaps we should give you a lift—'

'Araminta, he's fine, just get back in the bloody car. I wanted to arrive before the agent so we could have a good deco, but now we're late.' Toby delved into his overcoat pocket and handed a small rectangle of white card to the old man. 'Call me on this number with your insurance details, there's a good fellow.'

Ezra glanced down at the card. No one had ever given him a business card before. He stuffed it in his pocket along with Merlin's dried mealworms.

Toby noted this with disgust, then asked, 'Are we on the right road for Trengrose?'

The name hit Ezra like a stone, but he rallied. 'Keep straight on, round the bend,' he offered. 'Over the hill, down the big dip, up t'other side, and follow the road right to the end.' (And off the bleddy cliff at Land's End, he thought, but did not add.)

With one foot on the ground and the other on the pedal, he negotiated the gap between car and hedge and cycled on, a little wonkily, towards Penzance.

4

From the back seat, Araminta Hardman stared at the rear of her husband's head and couldn't help but note a volcanic-looking pimple that had erupted on his neck. She had not noticed it this morning before they set out, or she would have dealt with it, as she dealt with all such unsightliness and imperfection. Minty was one of life's improvers. She wiped up spills, slid coasters under mugs, brushed away crumbs, kept touch-up pots of paint in every colour of the walls to deal with scuffs and smudges. She was teased by everyone she knew – called a 'neat-freak', which seemed unfair, though she *was* addicted to ASMR videos of sand being raked into intricate patterns, found objects being restored, or cleaners turning hoarders' kitchens from health hazards to sparkling perfection: she found such transformations soothing. They buttressed her belief in a perfectible world. The inability to banish Toby's spot right now made her feel queasy and displaced; and the encounter with the elderly gentleman had rattled her. The image of him shooting over his handlebars straight at the windscreen came back to her. They had almost killed him! The world could have changed shape in a few fateful seconds: a couple more feet, a less dry road, and Toby might have been up on a charge of reckless driving. Manslaughter, even. She imagined herself queuing to visit him in some filthy, dismal prison, being patted down for contraband goods or weapons, having to lie to her family, the neighbours; her clients. Or maybe, she thought with sudden, uncharacteristic, spiteful pleasure, she wouldn't visit him at all. It would serve him right.

But everyone was fine: all was back under control.

Taking a deep breath, she recalled the view from their room in Marazion that morning, resummoning the calming vista of sparkling sea and the mystical sight of St Michael's Mount – the steep island and towered house rising from the end of its causeway like a castle out of a Disney movie – and remembered why she had finally acquiesced to Toby's suggestion that Cornwall might be the answer to all their problems. Cornwall, with its wide-open spaces, its clean air and low population, the prospect of days on the beach, of bracing swims and coastal walks; and most importantly, the promise of a fresh start for all of them – particularly for Dom, but maybe also for her and Toby. Was their marriage fixable? Sometimes she wasn't convinced that she could rescue it. Usually she shut down that small voice of doubt, and she did just this now. They would be able to relax at a quieter, slower place, she told herself, and rediscover some of what had brought them together in the first place.

Except that Toby was still ranting about how 'the old yokel' was the one at fault, riding a pushbike (he made it sound as improbable as riding a giraffe) in the middle of the road. Her husband was an irascible man, especially when his pride was pricked, and Minty sighed. The way Toby lost his temper at the smallest things had alarmed her in the early stages of their relationship, but now she had learned to tune him out. She stared again now at the pustule and itched, simply itched, to lean forward and pop it, as brutally as possible. The idea of this gave her a strange joy, and she broke into a grin.

Toby caught her expression in the rearview mirror. 'I can't see what's funny about it. It could have been a disaster.'

'Well, darling, luckily it wasn't.'

Some minutes later, they passed a sign for St Buryan and

Toby swore. 'The old bastard! He gave us the wrong directions!' Swerving into a layby, he consulted the satnav, which had already proved not up to the job, since Trengrose didn't appear on it. 'What an arsehole.'

'Toby…' Minty said warningly, casting a sideways glance at their son. Dom was eighteen, and though it was highly likely he had heard and used such words many times before, hearing his father use such language would surely normalise this bad behaviour. She needn't have worried, for Dom's eyes were closed, one arm looped around Boris's neck, and his head nodded to the beat of whatever band was his current obsession.

Toby was equally encased in his own cocoon, one spun out of fury and frustration, trying to communicate with the vehicle's onboard computer system, telling it to 'Call estate agent!' but the car remained obstinately silent. He dug out his mobile phone and scrolled for the number, selected it, then cursed again. 'How can there be no mobile signal? What sort of place has no mobile signal?'

'Cornwall,' Minty said, with an inward sigh.

Toby put the car back in drive and roared up the next hill, bellowing as they reached the top, 'Call estate agent!' This time the Range Rover complied.

Half an hour later, they pulled into the lane to Trengrose House, after a close encounter with a standing stone at the bottom of the lane that Toby, in his temper, had grazed, adding yet another scratch to the paintwork of his beloved car.

The agent, who had been leaning against his flashy little BMW, shuffling through papers, strode across the gravel to meet them. He was used to buyers arriving flustered and late down here in West Penwith, so made sure he was particularly charming – especially to the woman who exited the back seat, having taken note of the deflating airbag. In his experience, no matter what power their partners thought they held, it was always the women who made the final decision on property purchases.

'I do hope no one was hurt.'

'Well, there was an elderly gentleman on a bicycle—' Minty began, but Toby cut her off.

'Everyone's fine,' he said curtly. 'Though your locals seem to think they own the road. And why is there a bloody great stone in the middle of the lane? Nearly took my wing mirror off.'

'I don't suppose anyone was thinking about accommodating Range Rovers when the lane came into being,' the agent said, with just a touch of daring sarcasm.

'If we buy the place, it'll have to go,' Toby growled.

The agent considered explaining the problems inherent in relocating an ancient monument, then decided against it. Selling properties was all about walking the tightrope between overt truth and hidden truth, and the old Celtic cross fell into the latter category. 'Well,' he said, flinging a hand in the direction of the property, 'here we are, and isn't it magnificent?'

Toby took in the soft cream stonework of the Georgian façade, the bank of neatly spaced windows, the wide stone steps leading to the central door, above which wisteria was budding with promise. Yes, there were cracked panes in some of those windows and clear signs of deterioration in the frames and sills; the corpses of last year's hydrangeas littered the flower borders, and the grand stone planters to either side of the steps boasted only a crop of weeds, but he began to feel the tension drain out of him. This was going to work. He slid a glance at his wife and saw the enchantment gleaming in her eyes.

Even Dom had emerged from the car, blinking in the strong sunlight, with an awestruck expression. The Labrador braided around his legs, tangling him in the lead. 'I bet this place has stories to tell,' he said.

Minty regarded her son thoughtfully: he was growing up. Stepping out onto the gravel, she had had the fleeting sense that she was getting out of a vintage car – with sweeping running boards and a long, sleek bonnet – to the sound of distant voices and snatches of music, clinking glasses and the scent of lavender.

Inside the house, however, the magic dissipated. Patches of damp stained the walls, plaster had fallen from the ceiling, and in one room, great chunks of cornicing decorated a threadbare Persian carpet. Gloomy pictures stared down at them; dark-wood furniture hulked like monsters. The whole place held a chill, and smelled of mildew, as if no one had taken care of it for a hundred years.

As her husband and the agent moved through the house and out of sight, Minty walked beneath the paintings, assessing. They were mainly uninspiring landscapes of the sort that were constantly turning up in auction houses, with big, carved frames and time-dulled colours: she moved quickly past those ones. Then there was a rather inexpertly executed still life. A couple of Victorian gentlemen in tall hats and stiff collars, austere and unengaging. Then she saw one that snagged her interest – the only woman depicted. More Samuel Llewellyn than Singer Sargent in style, but perhaps earlier than Edwardian. The subject had been painted in rather an unusual pose, half-turned from the portraitist, looking back over her shoulder as if surprised in the train of some intense task. How old was she? Hard to tell: no lines or wrinkles had been painted in, but that might have been more a result of the limits of the painter's skill, or a wish to flatter the subject, than any truthful reflection of reality. Fierce eyes under arched brows made sharp connection with Minty, dark hair swept back from aquiline features: quite severe, but softened by a sensual mouth, lips slightly parted as if she were about to rebuke an intruder.

Was she intruding? Minty found herself taking a step back, feeling suddenly as if she were being nosy. She turned quickly, but there was no one to be seen: Dom must have followed his father. When she looked back at the portrait again, she felt somehow that she was being mocked by the sitter. There was a glint in her eye that Minty hadn't noted before; more colour, more light.

How fanciful! She chided herself, then looked closer. Perhaps it wasn't a gleam in the woman's eyes that had caught her attention, but her *ear*: a discreet earring glowed there, a dark stone set in a curlicue of gold. Elegant, unusual: the sort of thing Minty herself might wear. She wondered how she had missed this detail. The touch of ornamentation softened the image, personalised it. Involuntarily, Minty's hand went to her own ear, where a similar gold-set pearl droplet hung. White, to the sitter's black. Enjoying the connection, she said aloud with a nod to the woman, 'Pleased to meet you'; then smiled at her own whimsy, before turning to catch up with the others.

She found them in the kitchen, where an immense antique iron range cooker dominated one wall. It looked as if the entire kitchen had been constructed around it. The cavernous space was lined with cream, brick-sized tiles, with a dark decorative green dado. It was like wandering into an unrenovated Tube station, like the old Angel Islington, or an immense urinal.

Toby, though, appeared undaunted. He and the agent were deep in conversation about refits and refurbs, and the agent was saying, 'Imagine oak parquet and underfloor heating, a modern cooker to replace that old Cornish range, units from floor to ceiling, stainless steel splashbacks, granite worktops and a long table against that wall with proper old carver chairs – there are marvellous auction houses down here where you can pick up all sorts of bargains.' He strode to the window. 'You could knock this through and have double bi-folds out onto the courtyard—'

'It's not listed, then?' Toby asked avariciously. He had scoured the particulars, but a listing that would preclude wholesale redevelopment was not mentioned.

The agent smiled widely. 'That's the beauty of this property. It's the house that time forgot. Been in the same family for generations, pretty much untouched, and so tucked away that it seems to have been passed over by everyone, including Historic England.'

He led them up a wide staircase to show them several vast bedrooms and two enormous bathrooms 'in need of a little updating' (an outrageous understatement), and finally up a narrow set of stairs into a long garret space illuminated by three small arched windows or, as the agent termed them, 'original swept-head windows, though it would be quite straightforward to convert them into dormers'.

Here, a sharp sense of well-being flowed over Araminta, which was odd, since of all the grand spaces within Trengrose House, this was the meanest of all. It felt like a retreat, a refuge. It smelled, faintly, of flowers. She found herself closing her eyes and centring herself within the enclosing space. Something about it felt welcoming. Something about it felt *right*.

Toby was still talking. 'A million and a half still seems a lot... especially *cash*...'

'The way of the world these days, when property moves so fast,' the agent said glibly. They didn't want to get bogged down in mortgage company enquiries about the complexities of curtilage and the lack of registered title. 'And of course, there's also the land and the outbuildings.'

'Even so, the refurbishment and upkeep...'

Her husband and the agent started back down the stairs and Minty caught the words 'other revenue streams' and 'holiday lets' as they passed from view. Instead of following them, she walked across the creaky floor of the garret to one of the little windows, but the glass was so covered in guano that it was hard to see out. With some effort, she wrenched it open. Oddly, the scent of flowers, rather than dissipating into the Cornish air, seemed to intensify.

Beyond lay the sweep of the gravel drive, then a swathe of trees, including one particularly handsome conifer. Further on were glimpses of the narrow lane leading to the main road. On the horizon stood a grey church tower, and white dots of houses set amid farmland. And even, she thought, squinting, a strip of blue-grey sea over the distant hills. It was a lovely view, one full of possibility. She imagined pools of golden light gleaming on polished floorboards, a Gillow library chair there in the corner, a reading light above it, Turkish carpets on the floor, bookshelves, a desk. This could be her hideaway; she could write that book about her Royalist ancestor in the English Civil War here, the one she'd held in reserve for a new phase in her life.

She saw herself sitting under one of the little windows at a little desk, Cornish sunlight falling warm upon her face as she tapped her teeth with her fountain pen, deep in thought, before dipping it into the inkwell and continuing to write.

Catching herself in this indulgent fantasy – an inkwell, for heaven's sake! – she laughed and went to shut the window. As she did so, she spied a rooftop towards the edge of the orchard, just before the lane. Funny, she hadn't noticed a building there when they drove in. Probably because she had been focused on calming Toby's anger after he scraped the stone cross. Might that be one of the outbuildings the agent had mentioned? She made a mental note to ask him.

She found her husband and son with the estate agent outside in a courtyard floored with cobbled setts and surrounded by tall, creamy stone walls covered in climbing vines.

Dominic gave a little whoop when he saw her. 'Look, Mum – grapevines!'

Minty was about to correct him, but when she looked closer, the unfurling, virid leaves were unmistakable. 'How amazing!' She turned to view the back of the house, which seemed warmer and more amenable than from the front.

'Just imagine if you stripped all this vegetation off and sandblasted the stonework,' Toby said loudly.

'I do believe there's a door in that wall, underneath all the plant-life,' the agent continued. 'Leads to an orangery.' He pulled strands of vine away to reveal the edge of a small door. Flakes of old paint furled away with the leaves, and he stopped excavating. 'We can get to it around the back.'

As they walked back through the house, Minty asked the agent if he knew anything about the paintings. He was surprisingly knowledgeable, holding forth about Cornish landscape painters of the eighteenth and nineteenth centuries, till at last she cut in impatiently and asked him about the portrait of the woman.

'Oh, that will be Miss Catherine,' he said, before correcting himself. 'Mrs Catherine Rosevear: quite the matriarch. Mother of Miss Eliza, who sadly passed in December last.'

'Not sadly for us though, eh?' Toby joked.

Minty winced. 'It's amazing, darling, but a million and a half?' she said to him quietly as they followed the agent outside. Cash, too: that had been emphasised. It would pretty much wipe them out, since the proceeds of the Chiswick house – her old family home, gifted to her by her widowed mother when she downsized to Old Amersham – would also need to cover a pied à terre in London.

Toby winked at her. 'Maybe,' he said, but she knew the word was a bargaining tool rather than an agreement, especially when, annoyingly, he brushed her hand away and addressed himself to the agent as they descended the steps outside. 'On the particulars it says there's – what – fifteen acres?'

'Yes, some farmland, an orchard, a small woodland. There's a certain amount of rental income coming in from the tenant farmer, unless you fancy taking on the running of a small dairy herd?'

Toby looked horrified. 'Ha ha, no thanks. And the woodland – is it productive?'

'It's very... well established,' the agent said carefully.

'What sort of fruit trees are in the orchard?' Minty asked.

The agent smiled tightly, the image of Ezra Curnow naked in the battered old bathtub with a chicken on his shoulder returning with forceful clarity. 'I couldn't tell you exactly, but let's go and have a look at the outbuildings, shall we?'

As Toby walked ahead with the agent, Minty and Dom went to examine the orangery – really a long greenhouse ornamented with white finials and wrought iron flourishes. The air inside was hot and humid: a jungle of plants was running riot in there. They picked their way through the greenery, exclaiming in amazement at their discoveries: strawberries like ruby jewels, citrus trees on which green fruit was burgeoning, their fallen blossoms still giving out a heady fragrance; pots of lavender and herbs, seed trays bursting with unlabelled life. An immense vine ran the entire length of the building, winding around the roof trusses, its hanging bunches of fruit in a more advanced state of ripeness to the exterior vines in the courtyard. They might even be, Minty realised suddenly, escapees from this monster, since she was sure she could see tendrils disappearing through the door at the far end.

Dom grabbed his mother around the waist in a sudden, unusual, display of affection. 'This place is incredible, Mum. We could even make our own wine!'

'You can put that idea straight out of your head,' Minty said wryly.

They caught up with the two men as they approached some piles of granite poking out of massive stands of nettles.

'Oh dear,' said Minty.

Toby grimaced. 'When you said "outbuildings", I'd at least expected them to have roofs. These are just ruins.'

'The important thing is that you have the *footprint*,' the estate agent said. 'It should be relatively straightforward to secure change of use. I might even know a couple of people on the planning committee…'

'Even so, a million and a half is already a bit of a stretch for us – we'd need an income stream immediately. All this—' Toby waved a hand back towards the house, 'is going to cost a fortune. New roof, new damp course, rewiring, replumbing, new bathrooms, new kitchen… honestly, I'm not sure what we'd be paying for.'

Minty looked away, used to her husband's negotiating tactics.

'Yes, yes,' the agent said (he too was used to such ploys), 'but imagine what the estate will be worth once the work is done. It's a spectacular opportunity, unique in my experience, with no listing, and with land and such potential.'

Minty remembered the question that had been hovering. 'What about the building between the orchard and the road? I saw a roof from the attic window.'

A shadow crossed the agent's face. 'There's a small cottage there,' he said shortly.

'Part of the Trengrose estate?' Toby pressed.

'Yeees, bit of a grey area.'

'What do you mean? Either it is, or it isn't.'

'It's within the bounds as I understand them,' the agent said carefully, 'but it's not in the particulars as such.'

'Surely you know whether it's part of the estate or not?'

'That's something that can be clarified with the legal team, I'm sure,' the agent said smoothly. 'All I know is that the cottage is occupied – old chap, been there donkey's years.'

'How old?' Toby asked ruthlessly.

'I can't give you his biography, but I don't imagine he'll be much of a consideration for any great length of time,' the agent lied, remembering the gnarled old body rising out of the bath – ancient, yes, but ancient in the way an old tree was ancient: tough, unyielding. 'I'm sure he'll be in need of more suitable accommodation soon.'

'Well,' said Toby. 'That's another complication we hadn't factored in.'

The agent spread his hands. 'I'm quite sure the Duchy will take such details into consideration,' he said.

'The Duchy?'

'The property is being marketed on behalf of the Duchy of Cornwall. The former proprietor expired intestate, so under the terms of *bona vacantia*, it all passed into the hands of the Duke of Cornwall.'

'That's most irregular.' Toby frowned.

'It occurs with remarkable regularity down here,' the agent replied. He wagged a finger playfully. 'If you buy down here, better make sure you leave a will!'

Minty and Toby smiled dutifully, but Dominic laughed out loud. 'It sounds like something out of *Game of Thrones*!'

Again, Minty thought of the castle on the island rising out of that glittering sea this morning. Clearly, things down here obeyed other rules, enabled unusual possibilities. 'I'm sure we can iron things out,' she said coolly, '*if* we decide to make an offer.' In the space of half an hour, her world had spun through one hundred and eighty degrees. She was beginning to fall in love with the prospect of Trengrose. It was the ultimate improvement project. She'd once thought this about Toby, but that hadn't gone entirely to plan.

As the agent lowered himself into his ridiculous sports car and drove off across the gravel and out of sight, Araminta Hardman embraced her husband. 'It's perfect,' she said, then took a step backwards. 'Almost perfect. Hold still, darling.' Her beautifully manicured thumbnail and forefinger neatly nipped the top off the unsightly pimple on the back of Toby's neck, eliciting exactly the yelp of pain she had anticipated, and squeezed the contents into a tissue. 'Much better,' she sighed, dabbing till the juices dried.

'Gross!' Dominic made a face. 'You're like a pair of chimpanzees.'

5

Ezra rode the bicycle up the lane towards the Hockins' farm shop. Its front wheel was still slightly bent, though it had got him the three miles to Penzance, where a kind chap at the repair shop had adjusted the gears and spokes and done whatever he could to set the wheel right. One look at Ezra's scuffed corduroys and holed jacket and he had refused payment, even though Ezra had gone through the ritual of patting every pocket, performing the gentle pantomime of searching for his wallet.

'Let's just say this one's on me, mate,' the young man had said. Was he young? Anyone under forty seemed impossibly youthful to Ezra. He reckoned this lad to be in his late twenties, maybe early thirties. Unruly black hair, deeply tanned face and hands – almost like a lost Curnow cousin – plain wedding band, probably married with children going through school; a gap-toothed smile as he added, 'Sure you'd do the same for me.'

Ezra had thanked him, but he wasn't entirely sure he would have done the same thing earlier in his life: at an equivalent age he had been a deeply unhappy person, not much given to acts of charity.

Now, he ran a hand over the bicycle's frame, documenting its new geography, the day's scratches and dents, remembering how it had come by the first of its many wounds...

★

The Curnow twins were fighting again. Ten years old, they were developing separate identities, and this often led to friction, even violence. Ezra had got Arthur down on the grass and was trying to pin down his brother's arms with his knees. An earthworm dangled from the fingers of one hand, twisting in the unfamiliar element of air.

'Open your mouth! Go on – if you think you're a blackbird, you got to eat worms!'

Arthur had been mimicking a blackbird's fluting call when his brother had leapt on him. Being twins, their fights tended to last until they both got bored, or one inflicted rather more pain than he had meant to.

At last, Arthur managed to get a knee up and lever his brother off him. They wrestled for the worm, Arthur crying plaintively, 'You'll squash him, put him down!'

Strong hands separated them. Ethan Curnow took the now rather squashed worm out of Ezra's fingers and examined it. 'Not sure this one's going to survive.'

Arthur scrabbled a hole in the flowerbed beneath his mother's favourite roses. 'Put him in here and cover him up,' he pleaded. 'Then he'll get better. The soil here is magic: Ma always says so.'

His father laughed and shook his head. 'I'm not sure even the magic of your mother's rose bed is going to save him, but let's give it a try. Then you're coming up to the big house with me.'

Ezra watched the palaver of the worm interment impatiently. The big house! Visits to Trengrose promised treats – lemonade and cake, or even pocket money earned for helping Miss Catherine and Miss Eliza in some task or another: sweeping the courtyard, potting up seedlings in the long greenhouse, collecting slugs and snails. His father seemed alert, energised; a little nervy. It was unusual for him to turn up in the middle of a work day, too. He made them wash their hands, and when Ezra turned it was to see his father running a damp hand through his hair in an attempt to flatten and control the dark curls, something he only usually did on going-to-church Sundays.

He scrutinised the pair. 'You be polite, like your ma has taught you.'

Arthur rolled his eyes at his brother, and Ezra mimed a gigantic yawn. Ethan laughed out loud, couldn't help himself. Little rascals.

'Mind your Ps and Qs, you hear me? Or you'll catch the flat of my hand.'

It was an empty threat, and both boys knew it. Even so, they followed their father meekly up the lane to the big house, not knowing what to expect, but full of anticipation.

It was Eliza Rosevear rather than her mother, Catherine – the mistress – who was waiting for them outside Trengrose's front door, strikingly pretty in her form-fitting tweed skirt and white cotton blouse, the sleeves rolled up to reveal her sun-gilded forearms. Her gaze flickered briefly, seriously, to meet their father's, then quickly away to rest upon the boys, for whom she had the widest smile. She came running down the steps and, taking each of the twins by the hand (highly embarrassing, but something they were willing to submit to because it was Eliza), led them around the house to the barn.

There, she went down on one knee before them and gave them each a solemn look. 'Now then, Arthur, Ezra, you must promise me you will not fight over what I'm about to give you. I wish I could have acquired two, but there was only one to be had, so you have to be good boys and share it. Will you promise me that? Cross your heart?'

They nodded eagerly.

'Say it out loud.'

'We promise!' they chorused. 'Cross my heart!'

'Because if you do fall out over it, I will ask your father to bring it back to me so that I can give it to someone more deserving. Now, stay here.'

She disappeared into the shadowed depths of the barn, emerging a moment later wheeling a man's full-sized bicycle.

The twins whooped. They ran towards Miss Eliza, or more properly, towards the bicycle, which they touched with reverent hands – the shining metal frame, the black leather saddle, the swooping back mudguard, the smart red-and-gold logo of a mail-clad soldier, and the word 'Norman' emblazoned on the down-tube.

'It came from the auction house, and it's rather big, but I'm sure you'll grow into it. And if your father needs to use it at any time, you must be sure to let him.'

Ethan looked away shyly. He urged his boys to thank their benefactress, and they gazed at her with shining eyes and formed polite words. They had always liked Miss Eliza, but the gift of the bicycle made her a goddess.

Their father took charge of the bike on the way back to the cottage, but as soon as they were out of sight of Trengrose House, he let them try out the monster, helping one after the other up in turn, adjusting the height of the saddle, steadying the handlebars till each found their equilibrium. Even so, they had to stand on the pedals, it was so tall. But by the time they reached the cottage, the twins had largely got the hang of it, and had even managed to ride it with both of them aboard.

They were shouting with such excitement that Tamsin came running out of the gate to see what all the commotion was.

'What's this then?'

'A present from Miss Eliza!' Arthur shouted, his cheeks red from effort and thrill.

'She bought it at the auction house for us,' Ezra added, worried that their mother might refuse them the gift.

Tamsin gave her husband a narrow look. 'Did you know about this?'

Ethan spread his hands. 'T'ent nothing to do with me. All Miss Eliza's idea.'

'Why would she do this? They ent *her* boys.' The planes of Tamsin's pretty face took on a martial aspect, and her fists balled.

Ethan put an arm around her and ushered her inside, calling back over his shoulder, 'Now, boys, you be careful with that bicycle!'

Two minutes later, fighting about who was going to sit on the saddle, and who was to stand and pedal, the twins bashed the bike into the standing stone across the lane, and in this way it sustained its first of many scrapes. It was with whispers and stolen shoe-blacking that they managed to camouflage the damage to the paintwork, an urgent shared enterprise that bound them in secrecy.

Must have been 1949 or '50, Ezra thought now. After the war the country's factories had gone from manufacturing weapons to making peacetime products, and this old Norman Roadster had been one such result. He shook his head. Where did all that time go? Nearly seven decades. It was all just numbers, though, wasn't it?

Now, here he was at Bob Hockin's, discussing more numbers.

'A million and a half?'

'That's what the agent said.'

The farmer's expression became as ruminative as that of one of his Friesians.

Ezra, used to Bob's need to absorb information slowly, allowed the silence to stretch out while the words sank in, and perused the shop's offerings. His gaze skimmed over the packs of beef and bacon and settled on a new batch of clotted cream made by Bob's wife Thurza, its buttery golden crust cracked and tempting. Every week, his mother, Tamsin, used to make her own, leaving it in the stove all day with the door open, so that the whole cottage was redolent with the smell of baking cream, before transferring it to the cellar to chill overnight and form its crust. The memory caught at him now, the promise of treats to come, and everything in order. Washing on Monday, shopping on Tuesday, pasties on Wednesday, cream-making Thursday, saffron cake Friday, scones on Saturday: a soothing calendar of never-changing routine.

Except that now change was in the air.

'A million and a half,' Farmer Hockin said again. 'Who'd spend a million on that old wreck?'

'A million and a half *cash*,' Ezra reminded him. 'T'ent a wreck though, tis a fine old place. Just needs a bit of care.'

'Not like you to be sentimental.'

'Just don't like the idea of it falling into the hands of people who won't love it for what it is,' Ezra said softly.

The farmer sighed. 'Wish I could conjure up the money.'

'Do you?'

'Ay, not really, no. Too big for me and mine. Davey's off to college in Plymouth, and I can't see Kerensa coming home any time soon. No jobs, she says, and she's not wrong.' He grimaced. 'Quite how I'm going to keep the farm going, I don't know, I ent a young rabbit any more, and Davey ent interested. Sides, all the youngsters leave Cornwall these days. No prospects, they say; and nowhere they can afford to live. Workers' cottages down the road are going for over two hundred and fifty: barely more than one up one down.'

'Sam says the same. I don't think he'm much enjoying London, though. Reckon he'd come back down here if he could scrape by. He could always live with me and work up at yours, but you know his mother.'

Ezra's great-nephew was a good lad, but he had a lot of ideas of his own, and his mother was a snob.

'A million and a half, though,' Bob said again. 'I suppose there's the land. But by my reckoning that's only – what? – a hundred grand tops. I'm renting some of it, not too dear, but the rest? Can't build on it, can't develop it, old mine workings and all.'

He picked at the offerings Ezra had brought him today – salad leaves, herbs, French beans, strawberries – far earlier than any other of his suppliers. The old man had green fingers, and that was the truth.

'I should have lemons for you in a week or so; basil, too.' Ezra picked up a small block of cheese, regarded the price sticker, put it down again. He needed tea, coffee, milk and butter: cheese might have to wait. But he could make do with tea brewed from mint and nettle tops, and that would eliminate the immediate need for milk. Also, it would help with the arthritis. He picked up the cheese again, then cast a loving look towards the clotted cream.

Bob Hockin followed his gaze. 'Better than supermarket. Melts on your tongue.' He looked over his shoulder. Thurza was due to take over in the shop any minute. Bob poked among the bunched herbs, but not having found what he sought, leaned over the counter confidentially. 'You haven't got any... you know... have you?'

Ezra grinned and opened his jacket, took a packet out of the inside pocket. 'Do you a deal?' He never liked to initiate these things, but he'd been hoping Bob would ask.

'Proper job.'

6

Ezra's cottage was situated a little way up Trengrose Lane, just opposite the Celtic stone cross. It was, in estate agent terms, a modest dwelling erected in the late nineteenth century, from granite blocks mortared with lime. It had thick walls and small windows, and a traditional scantle roof of Delabole slate that the occupant still maintained himself via a ladder, scavenged tiles and the odd slap of cement.

The interior consisted of a single living space featuring an original range where at any one time bread could be baked while a stew bubbled on the hotplate, and the whole residence might be heated gently or fiercely, by dint of opening the fire door. Beyond the living space lay two bedrooms, a small scullery and a cellar; and up a ladder a low loft space occupied at various times by bats, squirrels and spiders, and, upon occasion, Ezra's great-nephew Sam. Every inch of space in the cottage had been utilised: unexpected cupboards and shelves crafted to fit awkward spaces; beds and benches fitted boatbuilder-style. It suited Ezra perfectly, as well it might, since he had been born here, as had his father before him, and here he fully intended to die, in his cosy armchair, with his feet up on the footstool embroidered by his grandmother Cecily (whose initial was carved, along with the J, for Jude, of his grandfather, on the wooden table), with a cup of tea cooling beside him and a cat curled on the hearthrug, after a satisfying day in his vegetable garden or walking the byways to check on Nature's patterns.

He deposited his cheese, milk and cream in the kitchen, refilled the tea canister and put the bag of coffee beans in the cupboard, feeling he had done well out of the exchange with Bob Hockin.

Then he went out to inspect his greenhouse, where the plants were thriving so joyously that there was barely room for the tomato pots. Indeed, given that the tomato plants would probably cope with life outdoors now that the weather was warmer, it made sense to drag them out and let his main crop breathe. It was, after all, a false economy. The tomatoes were a luxury; the main crop was what funded him throughout the year.

He checked the irrigation system – a bit Heath Robinsonesque, made from an old hosepipe punctured at intervals and a spare car battery he'd got from Bob, bits of wire and clips and tubing – and was content to see that it was generating its usual satisfying drip, drip, drip and a humid air of fructuous abundance. The greenhouse was cobbled together out of a collection of old wood and windows, hinges and panes of secondary glazing foraged from skips between here and Mousehole, where second-home owners had a fetish for ripping out everything they'd just bought; along with pieces of driftwood, old fencing, a transparent plastic dome he'd found by the side of the road, bits of corrugated PVC sheeting and some lengths of old drainpipe he'd found abandoned in a hedge, it made for a very serviceable growing space. Five minutes in there would leave him sweating and a bit lightheaded, apt to chuckle at his own jokes.

After he had resituated the tomato plants and given them a gentle talking-to ('You'll do just fine out here, my lovers. All the better to talk to the bees.'), he pulled a few stalks of rhubarb and took them inside to stew for supper. He could make a fair crumble and would eat it with a bit of Thurza's cream. His mouth watered.

He was just taking off his boots when Stan the postman appeared.

'Letter for 'ee to sign for!' he cried, waving a long white envelope. 'Looks official.' He left a brief but significant pause. 'Like the last ones.'

Ezra took the letter and read the typed address:

Ezra Curnow, Esq.
The Lodge
Trengrose House

The Lodge? 'It were never called that,' he said softly, as he had said upon seeing this address before. It was always just 'the cottage'. Originally, Jude's Cottage; then Ethan's Cottage, now his own. And who would address him as 'esquire'? He became aware that the postman was hovering, avid to know the contents. Ezra didn't share his business with anyone. 'If you tell your secret to the flowers,' his mother had always said, 'don't blame them for telling the bees.' Stan wasn't much of a flower, but he was a terrible gossip. The local saying was that there was no need to wait till Thursday for your copy of *The Cornishman* – just ask Stan.

'Must geddon,' he said firmly.

He turned to open the door and almost stumbled over Bucca, who leapt past him and fell upon Stan with shameless adoration. Ezra had only recently discovered Stan's magic hold over the antisocial cat: the postman carried treats in his pocket to placate ferocious dogs on his rounds, and Bucca had developed a taste for them.

Ezra did not rebuke the cat for his bad manners; he did not see it as his place to do so. Bucca was – like Merlin – his own autonomous being. He came and went as he pleased, demanding food and comfortable quarters like a vagabond king extracting his due from his loyal subject. He would disappear for days on end, reappearing smelling of tar or tractor oil, with straw and burrs in his particoloured coat, and sometimes with a ragged ear or a bitten face, looking like a renegade. Never hungry, though. Cats knew how to get by. If they could be bothered to, they hunted; if not, they conned food out of people, then moved on when too much was expected of them. Ezra had known a few people like that, too.

He signed for the letter, folded it and put it in his pocket, much to Stan's obvious disappointment, then bent down and scooped up the cat, who wriggled in his grasp. 'Come on, you old demon,' he chastised. 'Leave poor Stan alone.' Then he turned and went inside, quietly but firmly closing the door.

He opened a tin of sardines for Bucca, one of a consignment that had – quite literally – fallen off the back of a lorry a couple of weeks before. He'd been nearing the bottom of St Levan hill when a delivery truck had overtaken him with such an aggressive swerve that its back door had come open and a crate fallen out, shattered, and spilled its contents all over the road. Ezra had waved his arms at the accelerating driver, who – obviously thinking the old man was making obscene gestures at him – had blasted his horn and disappeared over the crest of the hill in a cloud of exhaust fumes. On examining the rolling cans and packets, Ezra had found tins of sardines, baked beans, carrots and a dozen boxes of Mr Kipling Fondant Fancies. His rucksack was so heavy by the time he had gathered up this cornucopia it had been hard to swing it onto his back. Cutting off the road, he had taken an obscure footpath, in case the driver realised his error and came back. All the way home, despite the weight of his burden, he had chuckled and blessed his fortune.

Now, standing in his kitchen with the cat scoffing down the last tin of sardines, he stared at the letter in his hand, and felt that all his luck might have run out.

When Ezra needed to think, he needed to move. Sitting still was about peace, blending in with your surroundings, being at one with nature. When things bothered him, he felt the urge to take the disturbance to the sea so that it might dissipate into its vastness and not disrupt the gentle world that wrapped him. As Sam might say, *keep the bad vibes at bay.*

So the next morning he took up his old army knapsack, the exterior faded, the original khaki showing beneath the straps and buckles, and filled it with a thermos of tea, some day-old scones, some cheese, a couple of hard-boiled eggs and one of the last of the apples (its skin a little wrinkled, rather like his own), plus the damned letter and a small pair of binoculars, and set off down the lane.

Late spring flowers festooned the hedgerows. He knew each one by the time of its appearance in the wild calendar, by its old name and the uses to which it could be put. He saw his first foxglove of the season near Chyenhal and made a mental note of it. Reaching the junction with the main road, he decided against the easy route – it would likely be choked with emmets. It wasn't that he didn't like visitors per se; he didn't have too many feelings about them one way or another. He just didn't much like other people. Experience had taught him that people were a menace – to each other, to the environment, to the region; to the planet. The best were thoughtless, the worst downright malicious.

Hopping over a gate on the outskirts of Kerris with remarkable agility for one of his years and arthritic joints, he tracked a direct route to the overgrown stone circle no one else seemed to know or care about. It was smaller than the famous Merry Maidens a couple of miles further west. Already the grass and bracken were high. You'd never spy the stones unless you knew what you were looking for. Ezra had known them all his life.

He and Arthur had played forts here as children just after the war, when the world had been in flux and children had raised themselves like little savages, exploring the fields and dells, coves and cliffs of Penwith like the first settlers in a virgin land. Other children had been gathered up and sent to school, but their mother was a free spirit and didn't believe in children being herded together to catch one another's germs and have their heads filled with what she called 'identical nonsense'. 'We've been through a world war for our freedom,' Tamsin told them, 'and I'm not having my boys regimented by the state.'

Ezra laid his palms upon the rough granite of the first stone, feeling its crystals alive against his skin, then walked around the outside of the circle, caressing each stone in an act of respect, as well as of superstition. The ritual was calming. The stones had been here for millennia before Ezra and his problems, and they would remain here for millennia after both had passed.

As if in counterpoint to this thought, a pair of swifts sped past, arrowing away into the blue, twittering out urgent communications as to the whereabouts of insects on the wing. The warmth of the soil beat through the soles of his boots, boots that had once belonged to his father Ethan; he smelled the peppery scent of herb robert and the coconut of gorse as he plunged down the slope, emerging at last at a boulder beach below a stand of Californian cedars. There, he took off his boots, and the socks he had knitted for himself out of one of his father's old jumpers that the moths had got at, and stood with the cold water of the Celtic Sea lapping at his ankles, begging the waves to carry off his troubles.

What to do?

Ignoring the problem in the hope that it would go away had been unsuccessful. The first official-looking letter that had arrived he had put in the compost without opening. Out of sight, out of mind. The second one he had held over the spout of the kettle, allowing its billows of steam to unstick the adhesive flap, since it had struck him that being able to seal the contents up again with no sign of forced entry offered him a degree of plausible deniability.

His gaze had skittered across the words, snagging briefly on certain phrases: *Duchy of Cornwall... Legal status... Occupancy rights... Unlawful...* Caught by a kind of terror, he had thrown it right in the grate, where it had gone up at once and burned to ash. In his sack was the third letter, the one that Stan had made him sign for. Even if not in his own name.

Ezra stared out at the succession of waves and remembered when his days had been spent upon that roiling surface – at its mercy, driven by time and tide, by ebb and flow, by shoal and lack. He remembered the storms and the injuries: Paddy Jacks going over the side and bashing against the boat with his boot caught in the nets; dragging him back in half drowned by water from above and below. He remembered being flung from one end of the boat to the other, the bruises, the broken bones, the smash of gear, the lash of lines; the wild flapping of desperate creatures drowning in the air; the lean weeks when they caught hardly anything, the ecstasy of the rest of the crew when they struck lucky and went to blow their windfall in the Swordfish. Returning to Cornwall after his National Service, Ezra had spent some time as a fisherman working out of Newlyn, before the world had changed shape and he'd found himself back at Trengrose, working on the estate, as was the family tradition.

He took the letter out of his rucksack and held it between shaking hands. He'd survived flood, fire and other men's hatred, but bureaucracy terrified him more. He gritted his teeth and read, slowly, deliberately, masochistically:

Dear Mr Curnow,

I am writing to you as a solicitor acting on behalf of the Duchy of Cornwall regarding the cottage situated at Trengrose known as The Lodge. The Trengrose estate has, since the recent death of its owner, Miss Eliza Rosevear, passed into the possession of the Duchy. We understand that you have been residing in this property which is located within the curtilage of the Trengrose House estate currently being marketed by the Duchy. The purpose of this letter is to seek clarification regarding your right to occupy the aforementioned property, as certain aspects surrounding its tenure remain uncertain, the previous owner sadly having passed away intestate, leaving certain questions unanswered regarding the legal status of your residency.

Firstly, we require information as to whether The Lodge is designated as an agricultural tied cottage. If it is indeed classified as such, specific legal provisions may govern your occupancy rights, and we would like to enquire whether you have agreements pertaining to such an arrangement.

Furthermore, we require clarification on any rental agreement that may exist between you and the previous owner. If you have been paying rent or contributing financially towards the property's maintenance and upkeep, it is essential to ascertain the nature and terms of these arrangements, as they may impact your rights and obligations as a resident.

Lastly, we must address the possibility that your occupation of the property may be unlawful. If you are residing in the property without proper authorisation, we kindly request your cooperation in providing any relevant information or documentation that may assist us in clarifying this matter.

The Duchy of Cornwall, in its capacity as seller of the estate, aims to ensure transparency and fairness throughout the sale process. It is of utmost importance that the legal aspects of your residency are properly understood and addressed. We urge you therefore to seek independent legal advice and consult with a solicitor specialising in such matters.

We kindly request your prompt cooperation to the aforementioned enquiries. Your timely response will enable us to ascertain your rights and obligations in relation to the property, ensuring that your interests are protected throughout this process.

Please provide your answers within fourteen days from the date of this letter. Should you have any queries or require further clarification, please do not hesitate to contact us. We look forward to hearing from you and have enclosed a prepaid envelope in order to facilitate your prompt response.

Yours faithfully,

It was signed with a flourish and a name Ezra could not pronounce.

He read it through three times, but it didn't get any less shocking. *Your occupation of the property may be unlawful...*

He could feel the weight of the establishment bearing down upon him: inexorable, inexplicable, inescapable. He had the sense of being a tiny, unimportant creature beneath the sole of the ruling class who wielded all the law, all the tradition and powers they had acquired over centuries of control. They acted not with deliberate cruelty or malice, but simply as part of an age-old system, crushing everything and everyone who did not conform. Ezra had never thrived inside the system: he just didn't fit in, asked too many questions, thought too deeply about the world. It was these attributes that had landed him in trouble during his National Service in Cyprus.

Summer 1958. Lemon-coloured light slanting through the window of a stifling room. Private Curnow was not listening to the words of the military policeman, or those of the commanding officer he had defied. He was not anxiously scanning the faces of those who would pass judgment on him. No, he was watching the passage of a cockroach – not just any cockroach, but perhaps the largest one he had ever seen – as it made its determined way across the floor, in and out of the pools of light upon the scuffed tiling, rarely deviating in its course. It did not scuttle; it did not scurry. It walked, slowly but deliberately – front right, middle left, back right; front left, middle right, back left – feelers splayed out ahead of it.

When the officer shifted his foot, the cockroach paused, moved its antennae questingly, then made a minute course adjustment and carried on. Ezra could not help but feel admiration for its stoic determination.

Stoic determination was a useful quality in life. Ezra had endured Cyprus, with all its horrors. He had endured the hideous fallout from those events. Here he was, on the brink of his eightieth year on this planet, still occupying the cottage that had been in his family for generations, still working the soil, breathing the air.

He would try to take the lesson. Like the cockroach, he would continue on his path, and he would endure.

7

Toby Hardman came home early one afternoon to the family house in Chiswick, startling his wife, who was sitting at her laptop, ostensibly working on a new design plan at the kitchen table.

It was very unlike her husband to appear suddenly like this, especially midweek. Minty closed the lid quickly, before he could see that she had been checking through bank statements. *His* bank statements. And had come upon some very questionable entries.

'The solicitors still haven't managed to get hold of that bloody tenant,' he grumbled.

'Do we actually know he *is* a tenant?' Minty asked, nonchalantly picking up her teacup. 'Have they ascertained his legal standing?'

'Here, read this.' Toby hauled his own laptop out of its carry case, shoving Minty's papers to one side.

She firmed her lips and rescued her Macbook Air and the notes and look-books before he knocked her tea over them. One of Toby's clients – a Russian financier called Alexei Antonov – had bought a manor house near Great Missenden and had told Toby he was looking for someone he could trust to redecorate it for him. Toby had at once recommended his wife. 'The last fellow filled it with neon lights and Perspex furniture,' Alexei had said. 'If I buy an English country house I want English country house style, not some twenty-three-year-old footballer's idea of chic.' Despite his questionable background, Alexei was more English than the English, so of course he adored Araminta Hervey (she was astute enough to use her maiden name in her business life), with her impeccably understated taste and aristocratic pedigree. For her part, Minty tried to push from her mind the fact that Alexei had almost certainly become fabulously wealthy by highly dubious methods and probably by employing violent and dangerous associates. He was always charm personified in his dealings with her, so she had decided to adopt her mother's advice of 'handsome is as handsome does'. And so far, Alexei was doing – and certainly paying – handsomely and promptly, within days of receipt of each of her hand-delivered invoices, which he demanded 'for the tax authorities'. Quaint, rather like his vintage Gieves suits, but really, you couldn't beat the old ways of doing things.

She leaned towards Toby's laptop screen to read the email from Pidcock, Pratt & Jones Solicitors. It stated that the Duchy of Cornwall was open to offers for the Trengrose estate but advised their clients to bear in mind a number of provisos.

The Duchy indicates that no Land Registry entry is to be found for the property since the estate has remained in the same family for more than one hundred years. Because there has been no sale or change of ownership during that time, there has been no legal requirement to register title. You would therefore be advised to establish title and register the property as part of the conveyancing if you were to decide to proceed with the purchase.

Furthermore, it should be noted that a question mark remains over the ownership and status of the dwelling on the southern boundary of the estate, which is indicated in blue on the attached plan.

Minty opened the attachment and expanded the view, a task that had foxed Toby. Immediately, she saw the tiny square outlined in blue representing the cottage she had spied from the attic window of Trengrose House. Set back from the lane abutting the orchard: an exquisite position. She returned to the email.

It has yet to be clarified as to whether said property is tied to the main house as an agricultural dwelling, and whether the current occupant (Ezra Curnow, Esq.) has a legal right to live there. The Duchy solicitors have to date been unable to establish the nature, length or terms of this individual's tenancy. They have written to Mr Curnow requesting this information and requiring a response within fourteen days of receipt of their enquiry.

'Well, that's all rather complicated.'

'I say we simply go ahead and buy the place and just kick the old bugger out,' Toby replied. 'If he can't prove he's a legal tenant, he's got no right to be there at all.'

Minty bit her lip. 'That doesn't seem very fair on the old man. We should perhaps just wait for clarification?'

'Someone else will nip in and buy the place while we dither. I tell you, Minty, Trengrose is exactly what we've been looking for. Loads of development potential, we can put those hippie tents in the field – what are they called – yoghurts or something?'

'Yurts.' Minty snorted.

'That's right, tarted-up camping.'

'Glamping.'

'If we can get this thing settled quickly, we could even catch the tail end of this year's tourist season.' Toby's face was alight with enthusiasm. 'I bet the agent knows the right people to ask. It would certainly help smooth our way, financially.'

Minty sighed, and sipped tea that was now lukewarm. She knew they would need to finance themselves while they made the place habitable if they did buy Trengrose, but a curious sense of proprietorial selfishness had crept over her ever since she'd imagined herself writing her Civil War book in the lovely attic space. After bringing the place back from the dead, she didn't want a field full of campers: she wanted the place to herself.

'Have you gone off the idea?' Toby asked. For a moment the bluster went out of him. He gazed at his wife with what seemed to Minty an almost pleading expression. Silence stretched between them, and eventually he could bear it no more. 'I hope not, because, actually, I... er... I put in an offer.'

Minty sat up very straight, her teacup halfway to her mouth. Her hands were trembling, just a little.

Toby was never quite sure what it meant when she was quiet like this. It could (as he had discovered from time to time across their twenty-four years together) denote the calm before the storm, the controlled, icy politeness of the English upper middle classes, which was one of the things that had so attracted him to her in the first place. When they had met in London, she had seemed exotic and unreachable, like Annapurna or South Georgia Island, and he had been filled with the unstoppable urge to conquer her. She was studying art and design: he had just come to the bar at Goldsmiths College to see a band. An apprentice broker, Toby was already earning a small fortune at Goldfrapp & Mason.

Going out with Toby had been a sort of rebellion for the young Araminta Hervey. She remembered how scandalised her art school friends had been.

'He's just so... straight.'

'Even his jeans have creases ironed into them!'

'Jesus, Minty, he's completely unreconstructed!'

What they meant was that Toby Hardman was from a different world; more particularly, from a different social class. That he was too effortfully polite, that he pronounced long words incorrectly, that he was trying too hard with his smart shirts and pressed jeans and shiny shoes (even though their own costumes of porkpie hats, paint-spattered T-shirts and artfully ripped denim were consciously curated too). But Minty rather delighted in their bewilderment, and loved to bring Toby to their exhibitions, where installation art took such precedence over figurative art, and where he would ask wonderfully crass questions about the arcane daubs and contraptions, especially when the artists tried, often condescendingly, to explain the concept and meaning behind their work.

'But really, it's just bollocks,' he'd exclaim, to their outrage, and to Minty's secret delight.

Toby *was* unreconstructed: that had been a large part of his charm. He didn't pussyfoot around her like the students she mingled with daily, didn't try to seduce her with circuitous approaches or obscure attempts to impress with knowledge: he grabbed her and kissed her, ran his hands all over her body like a pioneer claiming territory. She loved this: it made her feel womanly and desirable. Plus, Toby was a project. She set about improving him at once, starting with his wardrobe and grooming, lending his East End brashness more polish. Gaining confidence all the while, Toby took her to fancy restaurants in Mayfair and Belgravia, and once, memorably, out into the Oxfordshire countryside to the Manoir aux Quat'Saisons. Minty's father had just died, and for all her arty bravado, she had been feeling rootless and adrift. Toby represented a sort of emotional stability. He treated her like a princess, and she had thrived under his appreciative gaze. Moving to a course in applied design was something she had done to win further approval, since Toby could not get his head around the concept of art for art's sake: once she began to use her aesthetics in more practical ways, she had felt empowered by being able to turn her talents to making money. It was an eye-opening discovery to Minty just how few people had any idea of how to make a house a home, how to optimise space and use colour and detail to instil personality into it. Improving the world, one room at a time, became her mission.

Toby, meanwhile, had been astounded to discover how much money there was to be made from buying shabby flats in unfashionable parts of London and setting his new wife to work on them. Together, they had done up and flipped a dozen properties, each three or four of these projects enabling them to move to a larger place themselves. The property market was money in the bank. They used what they had to leverage more money for investments and so their stock grew.

Having children had meant a hiatus in Minty's earnings, but Toby was more than happy to carry the weight of their growing family on his shoulders. First Miranda, then Dominic. Everything had seemed perfect, as he climbed the ladder at Goldfrapp & Mason, became a partner, and got headhunted to Blackmouth & Moller, where he currently worked.

But then there had been a huge family row (the less said about that the better) and Miranda had run away from home. Dominic, meanwhile, had rather more surreptitiously gone off the rails. Boarding school had not – as Toby had professed his wish – straightened Dom out: instead he'd been expelled for dealing drugs.

'Drugs? Dealing drugs?' Toby had stared at the phone receiver in disbelief.

'I'm afraid so,' the headmaster had said. 'I'm afraid it's not the first time—'

'Well, it's the first time I've heard anything about it!'

'The first time we found him to be in possession of an illicit substance, he said it was because he was still adjusting to the school, and we agreed to give him the benefit of the doubt,' the head had continued. 'He said it was for his own personal use, that he used it for anxiety. I confiscated it, but told him the next time, it would be the police.'

Toby had felt a chill run through him. 'And did you go to the police this time?'

There was a pause at the other end of the line. 'Not yet,' the head said carefully. 'It is still of course an option, but we thought it might be better all round if you were to take your son out of school and make other arrangements for his education. He is, I am sorry to say, proving to be quite a disruptive influence on the other boys.'

Toby was dumbfounded. Little Dominic, quiet as a mouse, fixated on his games and fantasy books, 'a disruptive influence'? 'You make him sound like a sort of gangster,' he had said, imagining corner-boys from *The Wire*.

'Weellll,' the head said, drawing out the single syllable into long, telling seconds.

'I'll come down and collect him tomorrow.'

'I'd rather you came today. Or we could put him on the train and charge you for the ticket,' the headmaster said starkly.

And so, Dominic had finished his A-levels under the aegis of a home tutor in the Chiswick house and the eagle eyes of his parents. But drugs were all around in London, and Dominic's behaviour was becoming even more concerning. It had been Toby's idea that they move out of harm's way.

'But, darling,' Minty had reasoned, 'you work in London, and most of my clients are based here, too.'

'We'll keep a pied à terre in town.' He was proud of the French phrase, picked up from an estate agent he'd been chatting to when he thought it might be prudent to keep a little bachelor pad. 'A place we can use for work, and trips up to the Big Smoke. And we can buy a beautiful family home in the country. Keep Dom out of trouble. Give you a project to work your miracles on.'

Minty had given him a suspicious stare. A brief paranoid thought had occurred to her, but was quashed: the idea had been seductive, as had traipsing around the country to view potential properties: little manor houses in Oxfordshire and Hampshire; Georgian vicarages in Dorset and Somerset; smallholdings in Devon... progressing ever westward until they had stumbled on Trengrose House, almost as far west as you could possibly go without falling into the sea.

Now, she set her teacup down in its saucer. For all the delicacy of the movement, it seemed somehow decisive. A curious urgency had crept into Minty's blood. For all its decrepitude and years of neglect, Trengrose had cast a glamour over her. She thought about it throughout the day – fondly, as if of a distant lover; she dreamed about it at night. She couldn't help but find her vision for Misbourne House, Alexei Antonov's much larger mansion, being overlaid upon the smaller, and potentially prettier, property. All the things she could do to revive its faded beauty, to bring warmth and light and spirit back to it. In her mind's eye she saw pools of honeyed sunlight gathered on the freshly polished wooden planking which had been lifted and relaid once the underfloor heating had been installed; patterns of leafy shadow cast on the back wall of the kitchen; bees drifting lazily around the walled courtyard among giant Tuscan terracotta pots spilling bright geraniums. She already knew the colour palette she would use to honour the history of the house – Boringdon Green and Tracery II, Linen Wash, Dimity and Hollyhock. The names hovered around her like magic charms, like Shakespearean phrases.

She allowed a smile to curve her lovely lips. 'Let's go for it, darling.'

8

Ezra settled himself beside the hive and, striking a conversational tone, said, 'Well, my lovelies, here we all are, all as busy as... well, bees. You'm all gathering your pollen and nurturing your young and laying down riches for the future, and as for me, I'm pretending everything is normal, that's what I'm doing. Ignoring things I can't do anything about, and letting the world turn. Eating, breathing. Enduring.'

He was, he told himself, embracing the stoicism of the cockroach.

He paused, then took a packet of Rizlas and a small leather pouch from his top pocket. Expertly, he crafted a neat rollie, twisted one end of it, dug in his pocket for his matches, lit it, and took a long, slow draw, holding it deep within till he felt the kinks ease out of his back and his mind. Then he breathed out a stream of sweet-smelling smoke.

The bees that were drifting around the hive seemed to quiver. Some landed, their antennae circling. One or two extended their tongues, as if to taste the air. Others emerged to line the entrance lip of the hive, like spectators. The mood was mellow, the moment shared.

'The way I see it,' Ezra went on after a long, satisfying silence, 'you and I belong to one another. We are part of the same place, the same little world of Trengrose. And so are the plants and the trees and the flowers. The worms in the earth; the birds in the air. And the stream that runs through the woods and carries our memories over the granite. And the air we breathe, and the soil we walk upon. As individuals, none of us matters much. Our joint effort matters, though, when we work together. So, when I plant sunflowers, it's because I know you and the finches love them, and those little dahlias that flower deep into November, I never cut them for the house because I know you need them more than I do. I'll leave the dandelions and clover and ivy alone when they bloom; and in return you visit my crops and pollinate them, and when those plants are done they go into the compost, which goes back into the ground; and around we go again – taking what we need and giving back what we can, as long as we are able.'

He took another long toke. Then he lay down with one arm pillowing his grey old head and gazed up into the pitiless blue sky.

'You don't care, though, do 'ee, busy old fool, unruly sun? You'd burn it all up, given half a chance. And there are plenty among us who'd help.' He closed his eyes, remembering. *People*, he thought. Most were nice enough if you got them on their own. But some... *Some people are pure hellers.*

Even your own brother.

Growing up with a twin hadn't always been a joyful experience. Ezra and Arthur, despite being identical in appearance and often able to deceive grown-ups, had been unalike in personality. As babies they had existed almost as a single unit, never apart without hysterical tantrums, sleeping curled together like baby dormice. But once the concept of separate consciousness dawned, their periods of unbreakable togetherness had been broken by loud, ferocious fights that sometimes drew blood and nearly always raised bruises.

Ezra usually won these bouts, goaded into sudden bursts of dispute-settling violence that left his twin howling. He'd once clouted his twin with such force that he'd scarred him for life. But it was the internal hurts that really stayed with you.

Gwen, ah, Gwen...

Growing up, Ezra had flirted with all the girls, stealing his first kiss from Dolly, the gardener's daughter, at the precocious age of eleven.

'I felt her tit!' he had boasted to Arthur as they lay in the bunks they shared behind the screen in their parents' room; their grandmother, Cecily, an embittered old biddy, occupied the spare room, from which she emerged only occasionally to eat and utter curses.

Dolly was thirteen, well developed for her age, and had reddish hair that she curled in cotton wrappers every night to make it wave. She'd wanted to look like Jane Russell, she told the other girls at the farm; and so Ezra, craftily, had said to her on that day, 'You look just like Jane Russell,' and Dolly had been so grateful that she had bent to kiss him on the cheek and called him a sweet boy... and he had taken the opportunity to cop a feel.

'It was—' he had struggled for the words that would convey the revelatory experience to his twin, 'as soft as one of Gram's loaves, just out of the oven.'

Arthur had been fascinated. Girls were mysterious and bizarre. They didn't behave like boys, and they weren't as straightforward as animals, whose actions and reactions he understood. Girls laughed at you for no reason, talked behind their hands, ignored you, looked through you one minute, wanted to be friends the next. But when you played games with them and they got muddy or hurt you'd think they were spriggans, the way they cried.

This incident had formed another separation point between the twins, with Ezra regularly seeking out female company, and Arthur retreating into solitary walks. And then, just shy of their eighteenth birthday, along had come Gwen.

It was the early summer of 1957 and Manchester United – the Busby Babes – had won the Division One title for a second successive season, much to Arthur's disgust. 'I don't care,' he'd said steadfastly when Ezra teased him about his team, Chelsea FC, finishing in the bottom half of the table. 'At least Aston Villa stopped you winning the double.'

They had been standing in the lane outside their home, arguing about football while they mended the chain of the Norman Roadster, when Gwen had walked into view.

'Walked' was an inadequate description. Maybe 'glided' or 'manifested' was more accurate. The sight of her took their breath. The sun was behind her, haloing her form and her light blonde hair.

'Oh my god,' Ezra had sighed. 'It's Marilyn Monroe.' (The previous year they had sneaked into the Savoy Cinema in Penzance to watch *Monkey Business* and had come away practising their best Cary Grant accents, secretly dreaming lubricious thoughts about the blonde bombshell.)

Arthur could not speak: it was Ezra who jauntily declared, 'Hey, you look like a zillion dollars!'

Arthur grinned, remembering the line. 'How much did you say?'

'A zillion – that's a million trillion!'

Gwen favoured them with a smile. 'Am I seeing double, or what?'

Ezra stepped forward. 'Double trouble: we're the Curnow twins. I'm Ezra, and he's Arthur: you can tell the difference, cause of this.' Ezra swept the dark hair back from his brother's forehead and pointed to the scar on his temple. 'That were me did that. I were always the best fighter,' he boasted.

Gwen sucked her lip, disturbed by the violence implied by this statement. Arthur, seeing her discomfort, said: 'It's okay: we often fight, but it doesn't mean anything. We live in this cottage.' He waved a hand at their home, just over the campanula-bright wall. 'Our father's the Trengrose estate manager.'

'I'm Gwen, here to answer Miss Eliza Rosevear's notice for employment as a maid.'

'Are you a maid, though?' Ezra had teased suggestively, waggling his eyebrows.

His brother, embarrassed on her behalf by his twin's teasing, offered, 'I'll walk you up to the big house, miss. I know where the mistress'll be.'

Ezra wasn't going to let his brother get away with stealing this beauty off him. Abandoning the bike against the old Celtic cross, he had insinuated himself between Arthur and Gwen and the three had set off up the lane. Rather than announcing themselves at the front door of Trengrose House, they had made for the meadow beyond the barns where Miss Eliza had set up an easel and camping stool and was painting.

They'd chatted as they walked. Gwen was from a fishing family in Newlyn. Her father had suffered an accident on a recent trawling trip, and they needed more money coming in, so she had given up her School Certificate, and here she was. 'I hope I'll get the job.'

Up close, she didn't look so much like Marilyn Monroe, Arthur thought: she had freckles, and her hands were callused from helping her father mend his nets. 'I'll be digging the taters next week,' she'd said gloomily. 'Ma's done her back in.'

'Ent you got no brothers?' Arthur had asked.

'Roddy's in the Army. He sends some money home, but he drinks most of it.'

'I want to join the Army.' Ezra puffed his chest out.

Arthur hadn't wanted to at all, yet the prospect loomed. They'd be called up for National Service soon, unless they could wangle a pass as agricultural workers. This had been the subject of heated family discussions. 'It'll be the making of the boys, love,' Ethan had argued with his wife. 'They'll learn some discipline, see a bit of the world, come back as men.'

'I don't want my boys brutalised by the British Army,' Tamsin had countered fiercely. 'Why should good Cornish lads be sent off to do another country's dirty work? Sides, they got a lifetime ahead of them to be men. Let 'em be boys a while longer. You'm the estate manager: you can get them exemptions.'

Ezra had plied Gwen with eager questions about her brother's time in the Army, growing ever more animated about the prospect of taking up arms and travelling overseas; but Arthur had stayed quiet.

'And what about you, Arthur?' Gwen had asked him eventually, looking up at him from under her eyelashes.

'I'd rather stay right here,' Arthur had said, his mind quietly made up: if there was any chance of being near Gwen, he wasn't going anywhere.

Gwen had landed the job at Trengrose: she was lively and ambitious, sharp as a tack, and suited Miss Eliza well.

The twins vied for her attention – Ezra by teasing and flirting, Arthur by bringing her posies of wildflowers and walking her home to Newlyn when there was no one to pick her up in the trap. 'It's me she fancies,' Ezra said as they toasted sausages over an open fire in the woods on one of their summer camping evenings. 'I can tell by the way she looks at me.'

Arthur said nothing: he and Gwen had kissed the day before and the memory of her warm lips parting beneath his own had stayed with him every minute since.

Taking his twin's silence for acquiescence, Ezra added, 'But I reckon we could share her. It wouldn't feel right to be getting my end away and you getting nothing at all.'

As twins, they shared everything: their clothes, their room, the bike. But the idea of sharing Gwen, and the coarseness of his brother's pronouncement, made Arthur's entire spine burn with suppressed rage. In that moment he wanted to pummel Ezra till there was nothing left that any girl would want to kiss or caress. But he said nothing, just got to his feet and walked off into the wood to listen for owls.

Soon it was hard to hide what was going on, especially after Ezra caught Gwen and Arthur holding hands in the glasshouse. After that, the twins fought like wolves and Arthur had surprised his brother with his unexpectedly ferocious defence, defence that turned into bruised knuckles and black eyes for both of them.

That was the trouble with being twins: they were too evenly matched.

Gwen had been appalled. 'How could you do that to each other?' she asked Arthur as they lay side by side among the straw in the old byre with swallows and swifts flying in and out above them. 'You're family, brothers – even closer than brothers. Don't you love each other?'

Arthur had turned to face her. 'I love you more, though, see?' He ran a finger down her cheek, where a tear glistened in the muted light. They had just made love for the first time – and it was the first time for both of them.

'More than your twin brother?'

It sounded awful, put like that; but at that moment it was true.

They couldn't keep their love affair secret for long, not being twins who were rarely apart, and their mother had sharp eyes and instincts, too. When her sons' call-up papers for National Service came through, Tamsin had overcome her previous objections, even though Arthur had begged to stay working on the estate.

'No, my bird, off you go. You're too young to settle down,' she'd said. 'It's just that she's your first: that's what makes it all feel so urgent. Go away and do your time and then come back and see how you feel.'

But Gwen got pregnant, almost as if she and Arthur had willed it to happen. 'Now we'll have to get married,' Arthur said when she told him. The thrill of creating a new life between them obliterated all the doubts and worries that would later crowd in. He made her an engagement ring of braided grass right there and then, and Gwen burst into tears of happiness.

Their families were less than thrilled. Gwen's father swore he'd thrash Arthur; Tamsin had stalked around the house tight-lipped and pale-cheeked until at last she had sighed and said she supposed it was nature's way, though she was absolutely not ready to be 'a bleddy grandmother'.

Ezra had refused to attend the wedding, indeed had gone

missing for two whole days, until he was tracked down by Ethan, wet and shivering in a makeshift shelter down at the little 'secret' cove where the boys swam in summer, where he himself had run away as a lad after a falling out with his parents, and been brought home, silent and sulky.

A week after the wedding, the twins had been sent to army training camp, and a short time after that had been shipped out to the British Crown colony of Cyprus on counter-insurgency duties, where local militants were trying to force the issue of independence by carrying out beatings, bombings, assassinations…

Ezra sat up now, shivering as he remembered again those violent times that had changed everything, for him, for his twin, for his whole family. Fighting fire with fire was what they had been taught in Cyprus, and such inhumanity stayed with you, no matter how you tried to gentle your soul and still your mind.

He reached out to his bees again, immersed himself in the reassuring thrum of the beehive. Life went on. Trengrose nurtured them all. His mother had always said the earth here was magic, that if you were kind to it, it would be kind to you: feed it with love and understanding and it would repay your care. And that was what he had tried to do ever since he had come home, putting the bad memories, the bitterness and sorrow away in a box in the back of his mind, doing his best to live in the moment, in the season, in harmony with the natural world. He avoided other people as much as he was able. But now change was coming, and with it threat and disruption.

He carefully put out the burned-down spliff and, with a creak of joints and the grunt any such effort engendered these days, levered himself to his feet and went off to see to the weeding.

9

Midsummer

Bucca watched from his hiding place – the tangle of undergrowth where hedge and orchard gave way to open ground – the annoying humans come and go, shouting and clattering and generally ruining his tranquility. He'd been slowly gearing up for some hunting, having patrolled his territory – the interzone between human spaces where prey was to be found – and picked up many interesting scents. There were voles nesting between the stones in the broken orchard wall, and baby rats had run along the base, fresh out of their nest. In the orchard, he'd made his regular visit to the chicken coop to check on its inhabitants, but the old man had closed the coop up last night and no one had disturbed the chickens during the night, though he sniffed fox scat – an extraordinarily pungent hit of stink. He had tried to close his nostrils as he passed it, but the smell had followed him anyway, taunting: *my patch, my patch, my patch.*

It made him want to retch; it made him want to fight. Nasty orange creature, sneaky, stinking thief. But the arrival of the rumbling vehicles – a team of them, like little white houses on wheels, with their human operators – had disturbed and distracted him. For a long time, as the sun wheeled overhead, he had watched as they staggered under the weight of huge, inexplicable objects, a stream of them moving endless items, like ants on a mission.

Then another vehicle had rumbled into view – big and black, but not as big as the wheeled houses – and, horror of horrors, a big yellow dog had come bounding out of it. The fur on Bucca's spine prickled, ready to stand on end. A *kie*, ugh. If there was one thing he could not stand, it was a dog.

He watched with contempt as the stupid, barking creature was constrained. Served it right. Imagine letting a human put a collar around your neck and pull you around on a rope, as if you had no will of your own. Bucca would like to see someone try that with him. Ha!

He flexed his claws now and chewed a loose sheath off till they were all gleaming and sharp. He imagined sinking them into the invading dog's nose, the satisfaction of hearing its feeble whine. Over his long years, Bucca had made many dogs squeal and run.

A man with a loud voice was instructing all the other humans carrying things, pointing to the house, or around the corner to one of the outbuildings that was one of Bucca's favourite hunting venues. Someone had blocked out the light in the broken roof with a big green sheet, though the darkness within did not bother Bucca. Darkness was his preferred medium. Now, he wondered what these things were that the people were ferrying to the ruined barn. He would check them out later when he carried out the evening patrol of his territory: the outhouses, the bordering fields, and sometimes the courtyard garden of the big house if anyone left the gate open.

There had been a time, in his youth, a hazily long time ago, when he had come and gone freely throughout the house and had been able to leap up the vine-covered walls of the courtyard to help himself to the nests of fat little mice that lived within. Creaky joints, a bit of extra weight and the general torpors of age had curtailed such athletic activity these days, but he still harboured fond memories of sweet, crunchy little bodies and scented pools of dappled shade, feeling himself at the centre of the universe around which all else turned.

He watched as the dog raised its head, scenting the air, taking in all the information it could about its new environment. Bucca knew it would smell him within that complex map of aromas, beyond the vegetal, the human, the rodent. He saw the thing's ears prick up and its head swivel in his direction. He took a step forward, out of the pool of shadow with which he had been indivisible, and into the open, where the June sunlight hazed his outline, making him appear larger than he was, and pulled back his black lips to show his sharp, white teeth to his foe.

He was Bucca, Lord of the Wilds, Spirit of the Night, Haunter of the Ways.

No kie held any fear for him.

Bucca was not the only one watching the Hardmans move their belongings into Trengrose House. Ezra had been just as disturbed by the noise of vehicles rumbling down the lane. He had watched in horror as the removals lorry nearly got wedged between the ancient cross and his garden wall, had to back up and park in the layby near the junction and decant the contents into a series of boxy vans summoned from Penzance. He had made his way through the orchard and spied the goings-on from the cover of the gnarled apple trees, no more than fifteen feet away from the particoloured cat who, after his gesture of defiance, had slunk back into the cloaking shade.

So, it was done. The old house had new owners. A centuries-long unbroken chain had been broken. Ezra's gaze roved across the overalled men, the dozens of boxes and crates and stacks of furniture, and had come to rest on the big black vehicle. This he recognised as the car with which he and his bike had made such unfortunate impact all those weeks ago. He remembered the large, red-faced driver, and his rudeness not only to Ezra, but his own wife too (who had an odd name that he couldn't quite recall), and to their lanky son, Dominic, the slow, dreamy boy who had been charmed by Merlin. Anyone who liked wild animals and birds was all right with Ezra: it usually meant they had a good heart.

Some humans had lost all instinctual connection to the natural world. If you had no contact with the land and the living things that grew upon it, occupied and flew over it, all you knew was humans, and that did no one any good. He supposed that was how money came to be so important to them. It became a competition when you saw other people at close quarters all the time. You had to show yourself better than them: have a bigger house, bigger car, better clothes. He looked down at his ancient corduroys and wellies, and grimaced. People down here didn't care for show, not in that way, not most of the ones he knew. They'd been raised to scrape a living off the land and out of the sea. Cornwall wasn't an easy place to live, for all its beauty. It took its toll for that. But even though it was as far as you could get from any big city down here, the wider world had inevitably muscled its way in.

10

Araminta Hardman stood in the wide hall of her new home and took in a long, slow, deep breath. Below the aromas of an army of cleaning products lay the faint natural mildew and mustiness of an old Cornish house that had long fallen into disuse. It seemed that nothing could quite shift that smell. She could only hope that by bringing new life – new lives – and new warmth into Trengrose, the balance would shift little by little in her favour, banishing the damp and neglect. She refused to resort to artificial means of masking the smells, loathing as she did the chemical lies of scented candles and diffusers, but she had placed great vases of roses and hydrangeas around the house, where they glowed in pools of sunlight and gave out their summer fragrance.

Lozenges of coloured light lay scattered at her feet, reflections cast by the stained-glass panels in the front door. One of her first actions upon moving in had been to take down the heavy old velvet curtain that would have been pulled across the door in the winter: underfloor heating and better draught exclusion should make such fusty old measures redundant. Minty did not hold with curtains or draperies in general: they were to her mind dingy dust-gatherers in which insects made furtive nests. This had been followed by the removal of every downstairs curtain – be it grey, moth-holed lace, faded chintzy cotton or sun-blasted figured velvet and damask – allowing light to flood in, to reveal all manner of horrors and a few pleasant surprises.

After a back-and-forth between agents and solicitors, the Duchy had, before the house-clearers came in, graciously allowed Minty to sticker items she wished to keep. The things she had chosen included a huge Georgian dining table that had probably been one of the first objects furnishing the house, the ten carver chairs that accompanied it, a fine, dark-wood Jacobean settle, a well-proportioned Victorian dresser that she planned to strip, paint and distress, then install into the redecorated kitchen, some bookcases, which always came in useful, and a couple of handsome bedsteads for the spare rooms, though not – and she had been very clear about this in her communications – the bed in which Eliza Rosevear had expired. After some discussion about its limited worth on the market, the portrait of Catherine Rosevear remained hanging in the hall. 'Where it should be,' Minty had said tartly.

She had also stripped out the window-dressings in her and Toby's bedroom (which had not been the old lady's chamber), from the spare bedrooms, and from Dominic's room – though he had for some unexplained reason asked to keep the fabric – leaving just the original wooden shutters. Now, she girded her loins and headed upstairs to tackle the remaining space: Eliza's room. Out of what might have been a mixture of deep-seated superstition and respect for the not-so-long departed, it appeared that the local house-clearance team had not wanted to disturb the old lady's space. Minty had had to bribe their own removals people to take away the bed, the wardrobes, the vanity and the horrible old carpet that remained.

Approaching the door to what had been Eliza Rosevear's room, where the old lady had died, she brushed away her own small voice of disquiet and pushed open the door. She stood there on the threshold for a moment as if awaiting permission, then stepped inside. No sense of Eliza's hovering presence, no sudden drop in temperature, no words trembling on the edge of the audible; just an ordinary room, long since vacated. Minty's shoulders – that she had not realised she held tensed – dropped, and she began to apply her professional eye to the space. Eliza's was not the largest of the bedrooms, which had surprised her on their initial tour of the property, nor even the most handsome. It would make a decent dressing room, she thought. It was next to the main suite, and the light was excellent. Strip the old wallpaper, paint everything in Dimity. Built-in storage down both side walls, though not covering the pretty fireplace (goodness, she'd have to clean that out: it was still full of ashes!), a chaise longue beneath the window, which would offer a lovely view over the courtyard and, behind the vined wall, the long Victorian orangery, then the outbuildings – not so lovely in their ruined form – and the farmland beyond.

She crossed the room, her heels sounding on the bare wooden boards, to open the sash window and take in the mellow vista that offered aspects of both the domestic and working life of the estate. The peppery scent of geraniums floating up from the courtyard piqued her nose and she gave a little sneeze, automatically apologising for doing so, and half-expecting the room to answer, 'Bless you'. The scent of geraniums was momentarily joined by that of lavender. Minty turned, as if to greet whoever had entered the room behind her, but of course the room was empty. Apart from a little desk standing on the far side of the room, against the wall, and above it, a picture. How had the removers missed those?

The picture was a sketch rather incongruously presented within a gilt frame, pencil and ink, unsigned. A bit amateur, to be honest, Minty thought. But there was something about it that drew the gaze, something vital and connective that made her think she had seen the subject before. It was the eyes, she thought, moving closer. They were dark, as was the skin, giving the man an almost Spanish or Arabic appearance, the lids a little hooded, with a fold of skin drawing down into the inner corner. He appeared to be young, with a head of black curly hair, a lopsided grin and a spotted kerchief tied jauntily around his neck. The word 'gypsy' rose in Minty's mind, before she immediately banished it for being politically incorrect. But there was something rather un-English about the chap, maybe in the teasing glance, which seemed to her unapologetically flirtatious, maybe even sexual. Minty took the painting down from its hook and turned it over, brushing years, probably decades, of gathered dust particles off its hardboard backing, which offered no information as to the provenance of the piece, no auction house sticker, no written title, artist or date. Still, valuable or not, Minty could see why Eliza Rosevear had hung it on her wall. It was, she decided, rather a delightful little portrait, one to cheer an ailing old lady. Indeed, Minty decided she would keep it herself for the writing room: a perfect companion for the attic space, one who would look on her ventures approvingly but without uttering any annoying interruption, criticism or advice; one that she could cast an appreciative glance at from time to time, knowing he would make her smile.

She turned her attention to the little desk. It wasn't a clunky old pedestal desk, designed to dominate a room, but a more delicate davenport, probably used as somewhere to sit and pen invitations and thank-you letters. It featured four drawers that opened on its right-hand side, she found as she examined it, and two curving legs to support the front of the gently sloping desk, with feet as dainty as little hooves. Along the back of the desk was a series of smaller drawers, a place to keep family correspondence, perhaps. Gripped by sudden curiosity, she pulled each of the larger drawers open, but if they had once contained papers, they had – much to her disappointment – been removed. Maybe, given the ashes in the grate, burned. Minty realised that she would dearly love to know more about the house's former inhabitants, particularly the woman who had hung a portrait of a handsome young man above her desk.

The little drawers along the top were more fiddly. She was

rattling at one of them when Dom's head appeared around the door, his expression twisted in disbelief. 'There's no internet!'

Minty gazed at him as if he had stepped out of a time machine. 'Sorry, what, Dom?'

Her son repeated his complaint, adding, 'There's not even a phone signal!'

'I know, darling,' she soothed. 'We're just going to have to rough it for a bit.'

His eyes became wild. 'What do you mean, "rough it"? And how long is "a bit"?'

Minty had been dreading this conversation. She had asked her husband to explain matters to Dom, but being a man, he had dodged the responsibility. 'The phone company is going to come out and set us up with a phone line and an internet connection,' she explained patiently. 'But it won't be immediately.'

'What's "not immediately"?' Dom demanded.

Minty sighed. 'A couple of weeks,' she lied. The phone company had given her the runaround, then sent out an engineer who specialised only in restoring an existing connection. When she had spent an hour hanging on the phone in a coffee shop in St Just, a few miles away towards Land's End, they had said the next possible appointment would be in at least three weeks. They were extremely busy installing superfast broadband in Penzance. 'But I don't need superfast,' she'd said plaintively, 'I just need any old broadband connection. I have to work.'

Neither wheedling nor attempted bribery had got her anywhere. If anything, she had ended up at the back of the queue, and indeed was cut off and had to repeat the entire conversation three times with three different people.

Dom was aghast. 'But how am I going to survive? My entire life is online!'

'Oh, come on, Dom, there's a whole world outside for you to explore. Places to discover, things to see.'

'But I don't want to do any of that! I want to play Invasion

Force Earth – it's the only way I can keep in touch with my friends.'

'Which friends, exactly?' Minty knew she shouldn't ask.

Her son threw her a furious look. '*Any* of my friends. All of them. It's not like you care, anyway – you've dragged me away from everyone I know!'

Minty forbore from rehearsing the same old argument. 'Look, darling, you're just going to have to be a little bit patient. Try reading a book or something—'

'Books are old technology!' He glared at her, then away. 'Sorry,' he mumbled. 'It's just… hard, you know.' He stepped into the room, saw what she had been doing.

'Hey, that's cool! Look at the little drawers.' He reached out and, by luck or knack, managed to open the first one he tried. He looked in, ran a finger around its depths and brought out the contents: a coin, which he examined curiously. 'Never seen one of those before,' he said at last, passing it to Minty, who laughed.

'Oh my goodness, a threepenny bit.' She turned the twelve-sided coin over and scrutinised the monarch's head. 'George VI, 1943. How fascinating: a wartime coin.' Minty gave it back to Dom.

'Do you think it's worth a lot of money?' he asked, and she laughed.

'Sorry, darling, no.'

That didn't stop him opening the rest of the drawers in search of treasure, but all he found were two sticks of red sealing wax and a personalised stamp with 'T R E N G R O S E' spelled out around its circumference, a Celtic cross at its centre.

Minty was quite charmed by this discovery – 'I mean, who uses sealing wax these days?' she said to Dom, who had no idea what it was.

When its function was explained to him, he too was enchanted. 'Shame it's not gold: that was the colour the Lannisters used to seal their letters.' Then he had to explain to Minty who the Lannisters were.

'Can I keep them?'

'Of course.' She was pleased at his enthusiasm, though rather less so when he pronounced he was going back to his room to experiment with melting the wax. 'Please be careful!' she called after his retreating back.

Minty sighed. It might keep him occupied for an hour or so, but then he'd be frustrated and bored again. This transition wasn't going to be easy. Of course, she had known it wouldn't be, but knowing something hypothetically and then experiencing every wretched second of it playing out in real time were two different things. Dom would need time to adjust and make new friends, discover new projects, get used to this unfamiliar environment. She should probably drive them both into Penzance later so that he could get online at the library or in a café for a while. Was that tempting fate? Should she even be encouraging him to stay in contact with his old friends? But then, how could she stop him?

Another idea struck her. Perhaps they should buy Dom a bike so he could cycle into town whenever he wanted. For about five whole seconds this seemed like a stroke of genius. Then she remembered the unfortunate accident with the old man on the day they'd first visited Trengrose. Maybe not.

That evening, she raised her concerns with Toby, who listened – unusually, since he was a great interrupter of conversations. Minty could see him building up to something even as she outlined Dominic's frustrations, until he could hardly sit still, like an eager little boy who knew the answer in class.

'I think I may have the solution!' he declared. 'I've been thinking about it for a while. The lodge cottage at the entrance to the estate, wouldn't it make the most brilliant project for Dom? I thought you might help him renovate that old place, and then he could set up a website for it as a holiday let, can handle the bookings, do the cleaning, welcome the guests, do the whole

Airbnb thing, put the profits into an account and I'll help him invest it. Put it towards a car, or whatever.'

Minty turned this over in her mind a few times before replying. Then she grinned. 'That's not a bad idea. It would certainly keep him occupied while he decides what he's going to do with himself, and he's good with detail and problem-solving. If it goes well, he could make quite a bit. I've seen the rents people are getting around here during the season – a thousand, fifteen hundred pounds a week! Mind you, we've got no idea what state the place is in, or what the legal situation is with it yet. Did the agents ever come back to you?'

Toby looked sheepish. The agents had not come back to him. The whole question of the cottage remained a moot point. He'd hastily agreed to acquire the estate while leaving the matter of The Lodge as a grey area in the contract with talk of 'promissory title' and the like. He hadn't wanted to spell out to Minty just how grey this area was: she was more punctilious than he. He tended to fly by the seat of his pants, to get a rough deal done and tidy up the loose ends afterwards. He was sure it would all work out, especially if he could win Minty over, and he really needed her to buy into his vision if his bigger plan were to fall into place. Apart from anything else, it would make it harder for her to criticise him if things went wrong; and she would be an unshakeable ally in the matter of getting Ezra Curnow out of his rat-hole.

When Araminta put her mind to something, she was unstoppable.

The old codger wouldn't stand a chance.

II

The old codger was in his greenhouse, making a repair to his ramshackle irrigation system, when he heard voices: a man and a woman.

'I hadn't realised quite how rundown it was,' the woman was saying.

'This bit of window frame just came away in my hand! These bloody roses are in the way: I can barely even see in.'

'Maybe if we go round the corner—' The woman again.

Ezra peered through the foliage. If they came around the side of the cottage they would surely spot him. Moving noiselessly undercover, as he had been taught to do by the regulars as a young serviceman decades ago, he stepped out of the greenhouse and into the shelter of the fuchsia bushes that had been allowed to grow to their natural size. Camouflaged by their branches, and with the sound of a carder bee buzzing loudly in one of the flamboyant, scarlet-skirted flowers beside his ear, he watched the couple approach.

The man was portly and wearing a striped rugby shirt so pristine it had clearly never been anywhere near a rugby pitch. He had paired it with red chinos and tasselled loafers.

Tassels! On a shoe! Ezra almost choked. He could feel the

comforting hot rubber of his trusty wellies against the bare skin of the backs of his thighs as he crouched.

'What's that over there? A garden shed?'

'Looks a bit small for that.' The man strode across to it and opened the door, exclaimed, 'Oh my god.'

The woman peered around him, recoiled sharply. 'Surely not? In this day and age? He must have a bathroom indoors, mustn't he?'

Toby recalled the East End terraced houses in which his relatives had lived – some of them had *shared* outdoor privies. He decided not to mention this: it was like putting himself on a social par with the old man.

The woman closed the door again quickly. 'I really can't believe it.' She shook her head. 'Good grief. If there isn't an indoor bathroom, the renovation is going to cost a bomb.'

They made their way around to the back of the cottage. 'Look, there's another door here,' the woman said.

'No letterbox in that one either. What's the matter with people down here? Don't they receive mail?'

'Perhaps that's why he hasn't answered any of the letters,' the woman said.

'Rubbish! They were sent recorded.' The man sounded impatient.

'Oh, you know, this is a pretty remote area, and one of the poorest in the country, and he's really old – he probably left school at fourteen back then to work on the farm, or whatever. It's entirely possible he can't read or write.'

Ezra could hardly believe what he was hearing. Can't read or write? He'd worked his way through the entire Shakespearean canon by the age of nineteen, including the sonnets and Apocrypha!

'I hadn't thought of that,' the man said. 'You're so empathetic, Minty.'

'It's nothing to do with empathy, just social geography,' she replied crisply.

'Look – you can see in from here.'

He watched as the pair shielded their eyes with their hands, the better to spy into his life. Rage built in him. How dared they invade his home like this?

'Goodness, it's like going back in time,' the woman – Minty – said. 'I didn't realise anyone lived like this any more. Look, there's even an oil lamp on the table.'

'It's like a museum!' Toby added. 'Perhaps we should just leave it as it is and charge an entry fee!'

Minty did not laugh at his joke. 'It's going to be quite a job, though, isn't it? A bit much for Dom, I'd say. For a first project.'

'I'm sure you'll hold his hand. Besides, visitors want a bit of *olde worlde* charm when they rent a cottage down here, don't they? They can play at being Cornish peasants for a week or two, roughing it in a hovel!'

'I don't think anyone's going to pay fifteen hundred pounds a week to "rough it",' Minty said tartly.

All this talk of peasants and hovels and illiteracy made Ezra so angry that his fury almost obscured the real import of the discussion. These incomers thought they were going to get their hands on his cottage... and then rent it out to bleddy tourists! It was all he could do not to come charging out of the fuchsias and lay about the nosy trespassers with a garden implement. He imagined dealing the man a blow with a spade and watching the blood seeping through the blue-and-white stripes of the rugby shirt. Red, white and blue: the flag of occupation! The Cornish flag – the flag of St Piran – was plain, a pure white cross on a black background. Simple, stark; uncompromising. The colour of granite and tin, representing the moment when the saint had struck rock and molten metal had flowed out.

The couple had moved back towards the front of the cottage now, and he had to strain to hear what they were saying.

'That ruddy great lump of granite on the other side of the lane will have to go!' the man declared.

'Honestly, darling, it's an ancient monument. You can't just go around tampering with stuff like that – it's probably a sacred stone. It'll be catalogued by the county archaeologist or whatever. I think it's rather wonderful to have a piece of ancient Cornwall marking the beginning of our lane.'

'If you recall, the removals lorry couldn't get through. How do you think caravanners are going to manage?'

'I hadn't really thought about that. Yes, I suppose that is a bit of a problem.'

Ezra could feel the blood beating in his ears. The cross! The very thing Trengrose was named for – Tre-an-Crowes: the farm by the cross. He was damned if he was going to let these wretched people take his cottage. It was his home, and it had been his father's home, and his grandfather's home before him. He and his brother had been born here – in the kitchen the man had referred to as museum-like, by the light of that very oil lamp that still sat on the table his grandfather had made as a wedding gift to young Cecily Johns, with their initials carved into the frame on either side of a heart. By all accounts, young Cecily had been a local beauty, voted May Queen three years in a row, till she married Jude. Ethan – his father – had been the only child (so much for fertility), as dark as Cecily was fair. The men in their family were all dark of eye and hair, and their skin tanned easily out in the weather. 'Touch of the tarbrush,' is what his mother used to say, in those earlier, less tolerant times, ruffling his hair. 'You Curnows – got some Spanish or summat back in the line.'

Spanish was okay by Ezra. But no one had ever called him a 'peasant'. The word burned in his mind. Who did this tuss think he was? Well, if these people thought they were going to oust him from his cottage, he would give them something else to think about.

He stood up out of the cloaking fuchsia bushes and strode out, ready for a fight. But they were nowhere to be seen.

A red mist had descended upon him. It must have been the woman's voice that did it, her sharp enunciation, the accent of the officer class. His memory dragged him, like a stoat hauling a baby rat through a hedge, back to those early days in the Army.

In the autumn of 1957, after two months of basic training, Privates Arthur and Ezra Curnow found themselves on a military transport plane to Cyprus. Neither had ever flown before, like most of the other squaddies.

Ezra clutched his stomach as the plane rose into the air; his brother's eyes went wide with astonishment. 'We're flying!' he whispered to his twin, and Ezra grinned.

The novelty didn't last long. It took over eight uncomfortable hours to reach El Adem, the RAF base near Tobruk, where they disembarked while the aircraft refuelled, and stood under the wide desert skies, blinking in the unaccustomed heat. 'Gawd, it's like walking into an oven,' Tubbs said. He offered Arthur and Ezra a cigarette apiece. Smoking was a newly acquired habit: they accepted gratefully.

'Never thought I'd set foot in Africa,' Arthur said in wonder. He brought a pinch of dust up to his nose. 'It even smells different.'

Cyprus was different again. They landed at RAF Akrotiri the next day to another sort of desert: sand and salt flats, the colours so bleached it was as if they had walked into an old photograph. The horizon was blurred by heat haze as the sun reflected off the salt pan, and strange pink birds crowded together in shallow pools of water.

'Flamingos,' Harry 'Ashes' Ashwood, the group's know-all, informed them. 'They go that colour from the stuff they eat.'

'Bloody hell,' said Private Bell, known as Belly. 'They better stop feeding us shit then.'

'Not much like Cornwall,' Arthur said wistfully, and Ezra knew he was missing Gwen: she'd be over four months pregnant now. He could imagine her sweet silhouette, gaining unfamiliar curves.

'We wanted to see the world, though, right?' Ezra said cheerfully. 'Well, here we are.'

There were tons of young men just like them in this problematic part of the colonies: Ashes had confidently claimed there were over seventeen thousand British servicemen out here, both the regular Army, and squaddies doing their National Service, and certainly the Polymedia camp was a desolate scene of Nissen huts, rows of tents stretching into what seemed infinity, and everything rendered of indeterminate colour by dust. There was not a living plant to be seen, and only a few scrawny dogs that had wormed their way beneath the barbed wire fence in search of scraps.

'It's almost like they're keeping us in rather than the enemy out,' Tubbs murmured.

The briefing the next day did little to enthuse them. 'You're here to maintain order,' the officer informed them in his upper-class accent. Where they were all in scratchy khaki, he was resplendent in white shorts, white shirt, white shoes, white calf-length socks.

'Doesn't look as if he's seen much of the nitty-gritty,' Will 'Baps' Baker said quietly.

'Course not, we're the mugs sent to do the dirty work,' whispered Ashes.

The man wrote large letters on a blackboard:

E O K A

He underlined this three times. Underneath it he wrote 'E N O S I S' and then a series of Greek letters. He tapped the first acronym. 'Ethniki Organosis Kyprion Agoniston – the National Organisation of Cypriot fighters – nationalist guerrillas or, as we call them, terrorists. These are the people we are fighting. Their aim is to end British rule in Cyprus and achieve—' he tapped the second word, 'Enosis – literally "union with Greece". You have been posted here as part of your National Service to ensure these insurgents are squashed like the cockroaches they are. They are sly, they are cunning, they hide in plain sight. Trust no one – not even women or children. We have an uneasy truce now, but it won't last. These people are determined, fanatical, unscrupulous. They have knives, they have guns, they have explosives, they have bombs, and your job is to stop them using these weapons, to protect civilians, to protect the Turks – who by and large are on our side – but first and foremost, to protect British interests.'

He paused to scan their faces.

'Last year, a young waiter working at Government House smuggled a bomb into the residence by concealing it inside the woman's corset he was wearing beneath his uniform.' Tittering broke out around the room and the officer glared at them. 'It was no laughing matter! This man managed to infiltrate the Governor's private bedchamber. He planted the device, but by great good fortune it was spotted and detonated. That bomber is still on the run.

'Men like him have murdered soldiers and police, burned shops and businesses, terrorised villages, sabotaged depots, fired factories and warehouses, blown up supply lines and government property. It may be quieter now, but it won't stay that way. Your arrival coincides with Governor Harding resigning his post, so we're in an interregnum until the new one comes. You can be sure EOKA will take advantage of this situation. Intelligence tells us they have training bases in the Troodos Mountains, so once you've gone through specialist training here, you will be assigned to support British Army regulars and deployed on operations there. You are untried and unproven: raw clay that must be moulded and fired till you're hardened and competent. Believe me, in a short time, you will either be unbreakable or dead.'

Ezra had rolled his eyes, but Arthur looked horrified.

Training consisted of yet more drilling and being yelled at. Then they were split into groups and put under the charge of men experienced in what they called the S list: Subterfuge; Stealth; Sly; Savage; Sound; Speed; Shadow; Shape; Senses – everything they would need to master successful covert operations. They learned how to fight with knives (underarm slash, overarm slash, stabbing front and back), how to silently garotte an opponent, how to camouflage themselves, techniques to bamboozle and bemuse, to lay traps and deflect attention. They were taught the 'Perfect 3' of the kill point exploit: Surprise, Aggression, Speed.

'You may succeed in your objective with just two of these three,' Sergeant Gunn told them, 'but if you manage only one, you will fail, maybe even die.'

The twins rather enjoyed these activities: it was like being kids again, since they often found themselves pitted against one another, being the exact same height and weight; and just as when they were children, they fought ferociously and sometimes had to be separated because of their violence.

In their free time, they were released into Limassol, where there were markets, and other pleasures to be bought. They had each been issued with a thick rubber condom and sternly lectured on the necessity to wear it to avoid disease, but also about the need to show respect to the local women and only to use the brothels in town.

'I'm not doing any of that,' Arthur said. 'Not with Gwen waiting for me back home.'

They'd scragged him for that, wrestled his shorts off and shoved him in the latrine, his brother being the instigator. Arthur was too bookish, too quiet and thoughtful. He made the others feel guilty about cheating on their girls back home. Ezra just enjoyed being the dominant twin.

The night before they shipped out, they lay jammed together like pilchards with the other four in their six-man tent – Tubbs, Ashes, Tails and Alphabet (his moniker earned by the fact that his given name was Andrew Brown, and his brothers were Charlie and David).

'I don't know about you lads,' Ezra said into the anxious

darkness, 'but I can't wait to get out of this place and see some action.'

'Surely anything's better than being here,' Alphabet said.

Terrorists had launched an audacious raid on the airfield and destroyed five jets with their incendiary bombs: too close for comfort.

There was a scuffle and a yelp, and Ashes wailed, 'What the hell was that?'

Tubbs clicked his trusty Varaflame cigarette lighter to life. The flickering glimmer had illuminated Ezra's gleeful expression as he returned to his position.

'Surprise! Aggression! Speed!' he declared, and they had all laughed.

Their levity did not last long.

Standing out in the open in his threatened domain now, Ezra was resolute. If these fancy London people were going to try to winkle him out of his cottage, they would come to regret it.

Surprise! Aggression! Speed!

Three invaluable attributes in a fight.

To these he would now add another the long years had taught him: endurance.

He would embrace surprise, aggression and speed; and he would endure.

12

Dear Mr Curnow,
Rather than going through the solicitors, I thought I would
write to you direct, since I have tried knocking on your door
twice, but you are never in...

Toby sucked the top of his pen, a childhood habit. He couldn't remember the last time he had handwritten a letter but had been forced to put pen to paper because he couldn't get the bloody printer to talk to his laptop.

'That's because, darling,' Minty had patiently explained for the umpteenth time, as he never seemed to listen, 'we still don't have an internet connection.'

Toby didn't really 'do' detail, and certainly nothing as humdrum as contacting the phone company and endlessly chasing them when they missed yet another appointment or sent the 'wrong' sort of engineer. At work, he had assistants to handle this sort of thing. He sighed and bit down on the end of the biro. God, this was hard. Talking to people face to face was what he was good at, particularly over a drink...

Perhaps that was the key. Catch the old bugger around pub opening time and take him for a beer or three, get him pissed? Surely he'd agree to anything then. This plan was somewhat hampered by the fact that there didn't appear to be a local pub. Certainly, nothing within easy walking distance, and he didn't fancy getting caught over the limit by the local police. Toby was a man of natural excess and prided himself on it. 'Life is for living!' was one of his mottos; also, 'You only live once', and 'Let tomorrow take care of itself'.

He balled the piece of paper up and started again.

'Dear Mr Curnow—'

Too formal. Another sheet.

'Dear Ezra—'

Was that how you spelled it? It looked odd, made up. He checked the solicitor's letter. What a weird name. Was it foreign?

Now he worried that using the old man's first name was too personal. But surely it was better to start on friendly terms when you wanted to get something out of someone. It was what Jonty Moller had taught him: 'Look them in the eye and use their name as often as you can. Make contact. Make it personal and they'll find it harder to say no to you.'

'I wanted to introduce myself personally, since we are now neighbours.'

He stared at this sentence for a while before swearing and consigning this sheet, too, to the wastepaper bin. Christ, he was using up a sodding forest, just trying to get an ancient peasant to go for a drink.

Grinding his teeth, he wrote, *'Dear Ezra,'* then stopped. Saying 'we are now neighbours' struck the wrong note, placed them on an equal footing. So he scrawled, *'I just wanted to introduce myself, as the new owner of Trengrose.'*

Much better: this gave him the upper hand, the higher status.

'I have tried to find you a couple of times at—' he was about to write 'your' but caught himself just in time, *'the dwelling that is known as The Lodge, but managed to miss you on both occasions.'* He read this through and, satisfied, continued: *'I was told by our solicitors that the firm acting for the estate of Elizabeth Rosevear...'* He double-checked this and was relieved

to find he'd got the name correct, or almost. It said 'Eliza', but that must be short for Elizabeth. He wondered whether to mention that they were acting for the Duchy of Cornwall rather than for the old dear's estate, but that all felt too complicated to get into. He resumed, '... *had tried to contact you a number of times but had not managed to get an answer to their queries.*'

Did 'queries' have a double 'e'? He stared at the word till it became nonsensical. He could ask Minty, but she'd give him that look of hers, somewhere between amused and pitying, so no, he wasn't going to do that. Poor old boy wouldn't notice, he told himself. He'd probably have to find someone to read the letter to him anyway.

His mind circled back to Minty. Even though their marriage had survived some turbulence over the past couple of years, he felt that he had lost her respect. Sometimes when he spoke, he sensed that she was – just out of view – rolling her eyes at him. He shook the thought away. 'Onward and upward' was another of his bywords, or sometimes 'the best way out is always through'. He remembered how impressed Minty had been when he had first said that to her. 'Oh, Robert Frost,' she'd said, and he hadn't had a clue what she meant. He had just grunted, then gone to Google the name, where he learned with some disgust that the man was a poet; a dead poet to boot, and not even English.

He was distracted from his letter-writing by a stunning carnal memory and felt a jolt of electricity bordering on pain run through him. Chrissie never made him feel inadequate.

With a groan, he hauled himself back to the task at hand, reading through the few lines of the letter once again, before adding, '*so I wondered whether we might meet up for a—*' He had been going to write 'a drink', before remembering that Minty had told him a lot of Cornish people were teetotal because they were Methodists, which sounded bloody medieval. So, he simply wrote, '*cup of tea or something stronger*', which added a slightly jokey tone that he rather liked. He imagined the old boy chuckling at that and thinking that the 'new people' might not be so bad after all.

He finished the letter with a cheery, '*Do pop up to the house whenever you're free, or give me a call on—*' and he'd added his mobile number, before remembering with something approaching fury that there was no mobile signal at Trengrose. This fact in itself made him want to howl. In the end, he simply signed it *Toby Hardman*, then stowed it in an envelope and strode off to deliver it by hand.

13

Bucca was in a particularly foul mood. The morning's hunt had been spectacularly unsuccessful; the stupid kie from the big house had interrupted his patient vigil just as the mice had got used to his presence and thought him no more threatening than a rock. They were about to emerge into his sphere of attack – he was sure of it, could sense the tremor of their intent twanging on the etheric net that connects the consciousness of all natural things – when the yellow dog had bounded into the barn, yipping like a fool. It wasn't even being aggressive – that was possibly the most irritating thing of all – for its tail was wiggling and slapping in a stupid, uncontrolled way as if it wanted to leap and chase and play and be his friend.

Idiot.

Bucca had arched his back, peeled his lips away from his sharp, white teeth as a sign of his displeasure; and when this hadn't deterred the kie, had danced on his toes, emitting a combination of hisses and wails that should have made the creature run like a craven with its tail between its legs.

This kie, however, was remarkably dense, for it had kept coming, bouncing along as if all of life was a game. Eventually, Bucca had snarled out an unforgivable insult, then stalked off to the other side of the barn, not deigning to look back, just sinking on his hocks to slide beneath the gap in the wall there. But the encounter had rendered him furious. He felt he had lost face and that his favourite hunting venue had been ruined for him. And so he had slunk back to the cottage for some peace and quiet and slipped in through the cat-flap in the back door.

He could hardly quite believe it when he picked up the scent of the dog again, coming towards him, along with the smell of the man from the big house. Their scents came closer and closer, and he heard the man speak to his enemy, telling it to be quiet, stop jumping up. Bucca went to the front door and projected his hatred fiercely outwards.

Go away! Go away!

The intruders did not retreat. Bucca lay down along the bottom of the door like a furry draught excluder.

You shall not pass!

There came a knock at the door. The old man wasn't in – Bucca knew that: he'd seen him wheeling his bicycle out onto the lane – but the intruders clearly didn't. The man knocked again, called out, 'Mr Curnow?'

The deep, malign silence being directed towards them should have driven man and dog away in terror; but the next thing Bucca knew, something was poking into his flank. He could hardly believe the gall of it! He leapt to his feet to find the corner of a flat, white object protruding beneath the door. He glared at it, but it did not recede: indeed, another bit of it inched inside. This was too much!

Bucca dug his claws into the thing and stopped it dead. The object buckled as resistance increased on the other side of the door. Calculating, Bucca retracted his claws from the paper – just for a moment – allowing half of the intruder to enter the cottage in a rush before setting about it with all the pent-up fury from his aborted hunt. He gnashed his incisors into it, ripped it with his claws as he would have disembowelled his prey, chewed it in a fervour of repulsion at the taste of man and dog. Then he shoved the tattered remains outside again and flattened himself with intent against the gap, as he did so acquiring the weight of a planet, as all cats can do when they put their mind to it.

Toby stared down at the mauled letter that he had spent hours writing and rewriting. Half of it remained (almost) pristine; but the other half was so punctured, shredded and slobbered on that it appeared to have been subjected to demonic attack.

'Hi! Can I help you?'

Toby had been so lost in his speculations that he gave a small yelp. Standing before him was an immensely tall young man with a mop of curly brown hair and startlingly blue eyes. He had an open, friendly expression, and Toby couldn't place his accent.

'I, ah...' He indicated the injured letter. 'I was just trying to deliver this to Mr Curnow.'

The young man held out a wide hand. 'I'll take it and give it to him if you like.' His gaze dropped to the envelope. 'Looks as if it's suffered a bit of a mishap.'

'I was just trying to slide it under the door...'

The young man considered this, then grinned broadly. 'Oh dear, it's been Bucca-ed.'

Toby misheard this and frowned. 'You could say that, I suppose.' He paused. 'I don't think it'll be legible now. I'll have to go home and write it out again.' The prospect of having to do this made him want to scream.

'Or you could tell me what was in it, and I could tell Ezra. To save you going to all that trouble?'

As Toby hesitated, stuffing the letter into his pocket, the young Adonis moved his hand forward in a clear gesture of greeting, and Toby found himself reciprocating. They shook, and Toby did not try to intimidate the taller, younger man with one of his 'business' handshakes.

'Samuel Rivers,' he said. 'You can call me Sam. Ezra is – I was going to say my grandpa, but more accurately, I'm his great-nephew. I'm staying with him for a few days.'

Toby digested this. The positive part of this statement was that the giant didn't live here full-time, and 'great-nephew' sounded like a pretty remote relationship. On the negative side, he'd rather been hoping to deal with this matter quickly and quietly, without the interference of any other player. The idea that the decrepit old man had family around added a layer of complication. He flashed his most disarming smile. 'My name is Toby Hardman and I've just bought Trengrose—' he hiked a thumb in the direction of the big house, 'and this is Boris.'

They both looked down at the Labrador, which was regarding Sam with hopeful eyes – Boris associated all humans with food – but all the young man did was to bend and rub a large hand over the dog's head, flopping his ears this way and that.

'I was wondering if your great-uncle would like to meet me for a chat and... well, a drink.'

'That's kind of you. Very neighbourly,' Sam said. 'He's a bit of a loner, Gamps, but he is getting on, so it's great that there'll be someone keeping an eye out for him when I'm not here.'

Toby opened his mouth to correct this odd assumption, then thought better of it. 'Well, maybe just ask him to come and knock on my door in a day or two' – *when you leave*, he thought silently – 'because I'd love to get to know him and... ah... ask him some questions about Trengrose.'

Sam brightened. 'Ask me. I've spent a lot of time here. Well, until I went up to London, that is.'

'London, is it? I'm a Londoner myself.' For a moment, Toby felt a sharp pain of homesickness at the very mention of the city he loved. 'What are you doing up in town?'

Sam sighed. 'Studying. Doing a bit of delivery work to get by. Mainly missing Cornwall.'

'But, *London!*' Toby's eyes were lit from within. 'It must be incredibly exciting being up in the Big Smoke after this—' He swept a hand around in a gesture that took in the rundown cottage, the overgrown garden, the broken gate, the dusty lane beyond.

Sam shrugged. 'It was exciting to begin with, you know: bright lights, big city and all that. But god, it's so expensive. I could hardly afford to eat, so I had to take on a load of part-time work – really shitty stuff – and then there's the course.' He looked away, unhappy. 'That's to say, I'm not sure it's the best fit for me.'

'What are you studying?'

'A business degree.' Sam's mouth twisted into a complicated expression. 'Mum was thrilled when I got accepted for it, but you know, I'm finding it pretty dull.'

'Business, eh? Best way to learn is on the job. All that theory is great, I'm sure, but you never really understand the game till you're in it up to your elbows. We've had some pretty gormless graduates through our doors.' Toby laughed expansively, on sure ground now. 'Maybe you should can the degree and start getting your hands dirty.' He paused, then added, 'My firm is always looking for bright new interns. I could put in a good word for you...'

Sam grinned. 'You've only just met me.'

'You strike me as a capable young man. I have good instincts about these things.' What he was really thinking was, *Let's get this lad out of the picture and in my debt*. Also: *perhaps this is a bit of a gift*. Ostentatiously, he pushed his cuff back to consult his Rolex, making sure Sam had an unimpeded view of the complicated face of the Yacht-Master Everose. 'Look, it's coming up to lunchtime; why don't you just come back to The House with me—' He capitalised the words. 'Have a bite to eat? We can talk about it a bit more.'

Sam smiled shyly. 'Are you sure?'

'Of course. I'm just being – what was it you said? Neighbourly.'

'That's really nice of you. It's been ages since I've been in Eliza's—sorry, *your* house. Seems weird to think of her not being there any more, though.' A wistful expression crossed his face. 'She's been a fixture throughout my life. You know, like a landmark or a lighthouse or something: safety in the storm.

I always thought I'd come back here and work for her. Bit of a family tradition, being an estate manager at Trengrose.'

Toby raised his eyebrows. 'Doesn't look as if anyone's been managing it for a long time.'

'It's a real shame,' Sam said, but didn't elaborate.

Back at Trengrose, Toby let Boris off the lead and led his guest through the house, weaving between teams of workers and into the kitchen, which was in a state of some chaos. The old units had gone, and only the ancient range remained, the malignant resident spirit of the house. The honeyed old oak had been removed in preparation for the installation of underfloor heating, and duckboards had been laid in places to give access to the dining room and courtyard.

Sam stood in the eviscerated space, staring around. 'It's so much larger than I remember.' His gaze fixed on the old range. 'Ah, there she is.'

'We decided to keep it,' Toby said, though in fact it was Araminta who had decreed this, much to his annoyance. He thought it was a hideous thing, but she'd said something about honouring the history of the house. 'You know, to honour the history of the house.'

Sam nodded. 'That's nice,' he said quietly.

Toby washed his hands and opened the vast American-style fridge. 'Can't cook you anything, I'm afraid – we're practically camping. Cold cuts and cheese? Maybe a beer?'

Sam grinned. 'Sounds perfect.'

They ate at a table in the walled courtyard, sitting in huge, cushioned rattan chairs. Sam luxuriated. It was hard to find furniture to fit his tall frame and he was feeling replete, slightly buzzed, and a little guilty that Ezra would come home and find him gone, the cottage occupied only by a bad-tempered Bucca. He remembered the semi-destroyed letter and couldn't help but grin. That cat was a monster: grumpy, smelly and probably flea ridden, but he was also very much himself, a proper spirit of place – mercurial and chancy – and Sam respected that.

'So,' Toby said, handing a second chilled bottle of Peroni to Sam, 'tell me about your great-uncle Ezra.'

Sam coughed as the beer went down the wrong way. 'What do you want to know?' he asked at last.

Toby tried to appear casual. 'Has he always lived at The Lodge?'

Sam frowned. 'I've never heard it called that.'

Toby raised an eyebrow. 'Really? I'm pretty sure that's what it was called on the deeds.' This was an outright lie. No one had yet unearthed any deeds that showed the cottage by this name or any other; he was just testing the water.

'Oh, okay,' Sam said hesitantly. 'Gamps has lived there pretty much all his life. It's been in the family for ages.'

This was discouraging. Toby frowned. 'How do you mean "in the family"?'

'Passed down for generations,' Sam said carefully. 'You know – his father Ethan, and *his* father Jude – way back, really. They worked for the estate.'

'So it's a sort of tied cottage?' Toby asked, trying not to sound too eager.

A tied cottage was a known quantity, much easier to contest: it usually meant that the occupant worked for the landowner and in return was given or rented accommodation for the duration of their service. That put the cottage within his purview, gave him power over the occupant. And if he wasn't employing Ezra Curnow – and in all honesty, how was such an old man in any way employable? – then Ezra could make no case to stay. The matter began to feel cut and dried. He took a long, satisfying swig of his beer and thanked his lucky stars that he had chanced upon this young man.

Sam, however, was not paying Toby any mind. His guileless blue eyes were wide and inattentive. Toby turned and realised why. His daughter Miranda, just down from London, had appeared in the doorway, holding out her mobile phone, shaking it, interrogating the screen.

'The signal's hopeless here,' Sam said.

Miranda looked up from her phone with a little jolt of shock. 'Oh god, sorry, didn't see you out here!' She ran a hand through her hair, which was escaping from what had already been a messy bun, and laughed. 'Good job I was only swearing silently in my own head.'

'Wouldn't have bothered me,' Sam beamed, and she grinned back at him.

He put down his beer, rose from his chair, crossed the courtyard and held out his hand in a curiously old-fashioned gesture. For a moment, Miranda stared at it – at his big, wide palm and long, strong, tanned fingers – as if it were an alien object. Then she laughed and shook it heartily.

'Ran,' she said.

'Ran?' Sam thought he'd misheard.

'Short for Miranda.'

'Wow, okay.'

'If you ever call me Randie, I'll kill you. How about you?'

'Oh! Sam, short for Samuel.'

They stood there, gazing at one another, still connected by their right hands until Toby cleared his throat and said, 'Actually, I was just discussing the lodge cottage with young Sam here.' Implied in the statement was, *You interrupted at just the wrong moment, please go away.* Of course, his tone had no effect on his daughter, who swung a chair out from the table, sat down and scavenged the remnant bread, cheese and olives.

'Do you live in the cottage?' she asked Sam between mouthfuls.

'Wish I did. I'm up in London studying.'

Miranda leaned forward. 'What are you studying? I was at Goldsmiths, doing anthropology.' She wrinkled her nose. 'Mum was keen – it's where she went, and the course was great, but can I get a decent job in London? No chance: just slave labour.' She shrugged. 'I thought I'd go travelling, but you know, money.'

Sam felt a warm flush run through him at this. She was in London!

'Well, that's one thing you can't blame *me* for,' Toby drawled. 'You could've been working at Blackmouth & Moller, making a packet.'

Ran rolled her eyes dramatically. 'As if. Anyway, it's not all about money.'

An awkward silence fell in which Sam could feel the stirrings of an old family argument, and he said quickly, 'Business. At the LSE. I bloody hate it.'

'But London's great, isn't it?' grinned Ran.

Sam made a face. 'I'd rather be down here.' And then in case he was showing himself up as a hapless yokel, added nonchalantly, 'The bars are good, though.' In truth he didn't venture out much, never really had the inclination, let alone the spare cash. He was working weekends for a food delivery company, zipping around Balham on his friend Will's borrowed scooter. For the use of the vehicle, Will took half of whatever Sam earned and expected a free pizza on Sunday night. This was rank profiteering, but on the one occasion Sam had tried to complete his night service on a pushbike, he had soon realised that nothing else was feasible.

'Yes, really cool,' Ran agreed. 'Do you have a favourite place?'

Pinned like a trapped insect under her mesmerising gaze, Sam searched desperately for a name but came up empty. 'Oh, you know, Soho generally.'

'We should go out for a bar crawl one evening,' Ran suggested.

'Hey!' Toby wagged a finger. 'I didn't pay a fortune for your tuition fees and rent for you to be gallivanting around town getting drunk with young men.' He winked at Sam, as if to give the lie to this sentiment, but Miranda immediately turned sulky.

'You should talk. Besides, it's my life.' She turned her attention to Sam.

Lord, those eyes: an almost turquoise blue, fringed by the longest black lashes.

'Give me your phone,' she demanded, holding out a hand. 'I'll put my number in.'

Sam shrugged. 'Sorry, haven't got it with me. Never use it down here, not at home, anyway – there's no signal!'

'God, how do you cope? It's driving me crazy!'

'Just tell me your number. I'll remember it.'

She stared at him. 'Are you some sort of genius?'

He laughed. 'Hardly.'

She gave him her number and he repeated it and nodded. 'I'll text you soon as I've got signal. Then you'll have mine.'

'So, Sam,' Toby interrupted, 'I was asking about your great-uncle. It's good to know your neighbours, I think.'

Sam beamed. 'Oh, he's one-of-a-kind. Proper Cornish, with his roots sunk deep into the land. He won't be any trouble as a neighbour: all he wants is to potter around, doing what he does, and be left alone to get on with it.'

'I'd have thought it was a bit hard for him living on his own off the beaten track like this—' Toby began, but Sam cut him off with a laugh.

'It's not really off the beaten track. We're only three miles or so from Penzance – that's an easy enough walk or bike ride. Ezra's got a right old boneshaker: you'll often see him pedalling into town.'

Christ: Ezra Curnow must be the old man who'd run into him. What a bloody shame he hadn't been going a bit faster... 'He's rather elderly, isn't he, to be cycling on these roads? Just how old *is* he?'

A slight crease appeared between the young man's brows. 'I don't actually know.' His expression went vague for a moment, then he said, 'I reckon he's coming up seventy-nine.' He brightened. 'Yes, that's about right: he was born the year the Second World War broke out.'

'Seventy-nine, eh? Goodness me. It must be hard at that age to keep The Lodge well maintained. And how does he heat it? I can't imagine he's got central heating in there. There's no gas supply here, and I didn't notice an oil tank—'

'He heats it the way it's always been heated – he's got an old Cornish range. He collects firewood and burns that.'

Toby leaned forward. 'Where does he get his firewood from?' he asked with sudden interest.

'Oh my god, Dad, stop interrogating Sam!' Ran exclaimed indignantly. 'Why on earth do you want to know how the old man heats his cottage?'

'I... just wanted to help. Maybe offer to get the place... ah... modernised.'

His daughter's beautifully arched eyebrows shot up. 'That sounds remarkably altruistic! Cornwall must've softened you up.'

'I just thought,' Toby ploughed on, 'maybe if Mr Curnow were to move out for a bit we could help do it up for him. I mean, it's part of the estate, so I feel we have some responsibility here, even if it's not necessarily a formal responsibility.' He watched for Sam's reaction to this deeply insincere offer and to his casual annexation of the cottage.

'That's very kind of you,' Sam said. 'But I don't think Gamps would want that. The cottage is a bit ramshackle, but it's watertight and warm, and he's made it his own. Plus, he's got his own responsibilities – you know, to his chickens, and bees, and cat and—'

'And his crow!' Dom appeared suddenly at the kitchen door, where he must have been listening. 'He's got a crow called Merlin,' he informed his sister. 'It's amazing: it flies down and sits on his shoulder.'

'A crow?' Ran stared at her brother in surprise. 'He's got a pet crow?'

'Yes!' Dom cried, at the same moment as Sam said, 'No!' He went on, 'It's not a pet. Just a wild bird he knows really well, a jackdaw. Gamps has all kinds of friends like that.'

Dom remembered this now, the old man telling him the difference between a jackdaw and a crow. 'What sort of friends? Like eagles and wolves and things?'

Sam laughed, but kindly. 'Not quite. He gets visited by hedgehogs and badgers, and foxes and rabbits, too. Actually, the rabbits are a bit of a menace because they eat his veg.'

Dom's eyes were wide. 'Do they come when he calls them, like Merlin does?'

'Not even Merlin comes when called,' Sam grinned. 'They're all still as wild as wild can be, it's just that…' he paused, thinking. 'They recognise one of their own. Gamps is – it sounds a bit mad saying it out loud – but he's just as wild as they are, in his way.' He grimaced, seeing the look of disbelief, or possibly revulsion, on his host's face. 'Sorry, that makes him sound a bit weird, and he's really not. He just loves natural things, and they love him back.'

'Sounds like a bloody tree-hugger!' Toby said. Typical: they'd been landed with some superannuated old hippie. No wonder the cottage was in such a foul state.

'I think he sounds amazing,' said Miranda.

'Like he's Radagast or something, you know, the wizard with mice in his cloak and nests under his hat,' Dom said in awe, then had to explain who Radagast was to his father and sister, who were rather less well versed in Tolkien's lore. He finished by saying, 'The elves called him Aiwendil, which means "bird-friend" in Quenya,' which made Ran groan.

Dom was used to her disdain for fantasy. He fixed Sam with an intent gaze. 'Can he talk to them? You know, and make them understand? Not like Doctor Dolittle, like actually talking but, you know, communicating.'

Sam laughed. 'Well, sort of. They know he means them no harm, and that he fits into their world. I can't really explain it any better than that.'

'Cool,' said Ran.

After a few more pleasantries, Sam excused himself. 'I have to earn my keep when I'm staying with Gamps. He can't abide a slacker.'

'How long are you staying down here?' Ran asked. There was a light in her eyes, Toby noticed with a trace of alarm.

'Oh, just for the rest of the week,' Sam said, and the corners of his mouth turned down. 'Then I'm back up to London.'

'What on earth do you do for a *week* down here?' Ran wanted to know. 'I've only been here a day and I'm already bored to tears.'

'There are loads of lovely walks and places to explore,' Sam said. 'I'll show you a way down to the sea tomorrow if you like.'

She sucked her bottom lip, looking dubious. 'I haven't really got the right footwear.'

They both looked down at her sparkly flipflops.

'Maybe next time, then,' said Sam, feeling that the footwear thing might just be a polite excuse.

'It's okay,' Ran said quickly. 'Mum and I have the same size feet. I'm sure she'll have something I can borrow.'

'Tomorrow, then? Nine okay?'

Ran looked appalled. 'You must be joking! How about eleven?'

'Can I come?' Dom interrupted with uncharacteristic enthusiasm.

'Absolutely not,' Ran replied.

'I'll take you on one of the more adventurous walks one day, shall I?' Sam offered, seeing how crestfallen the lad was by his sister's sharp refusal of his company.

Dom perked up. 'I'd like that.'

Toby raised an eyebrow. Maybe his son was going to embrace Cornwall after all. But right now his concern was that Miranda was embracing it rather too much.

'Right,' Ran said firmly. 'I'll meet you down by the cottage at eleven.'

'Proper job!' said Sam, delight making him go all native.

14

By the time Ezra got home that evening it was to find his kitchen spick and span, a cat well fed and dozing by the range, and the smell of something delicious bubbling away in a big old iron pot. His great-nephew was sitting at the table with his brow furrowed, poring over a folder of printed notes.

Sam looked up as Ezra came in through the open door, and relief replaced his frown. 'I wondered where you were – I was beginning to worry.'

Ezra waved his concern away. 'Put the kettle on. I could murder a cup of tea.'

He pottered around the little space, transferring items from his knapsack into cupboards and the fridge. Sam supposed he'd been into Penzance, or to barter items at the farm shop. He didn't ask: Gamps could be close-mouthed about his comings and goings: 'Least said, soonest mended,' he'd say. Or, 'If you don't know, you can't tell.' Sam knew perfectly well what this referred to, and it always made him smile. Ezra obviously still thought he was just a boy.

'Been up the big house,' Sam said, when they both had hot mugs of tea in their hands.

'Ar?' The single syllable contained a world of suspicious enquiry.

'Met the new owner in the lane.' Sam decided not to explain the circumstances in full – the nosy neighbour enquiring about the 'lodge cottage', the mangled letter; the malevolent cat. 'Invited me up for a bite to eat.' He didn't mention the beer, either: it felt like fraternising with, not exactly the enemy, but something close.

Ezra's face had composed itself into granite lines, as redoubtable as the rock formations of Carn Kenidjack or Dr Syntax's Head. When Sam was a boy and had spent his holidays down here, his great-uncle had taken him climbing all over the Penwith cliffs – up Terrier's Tooth and Demo Route, Seal Slab and Little Brown Jug. He had loved every minute of it, even down to coiling the brightly coloured ropes, and oiling the carabiners afterwards to save them from salt corrosion. It was all second-hand kit donated by the local climbing club, but Sam cherished every nut and wire of it, every faded climbing shoe and battered old hex. Climbing represented freedom and escape: from the strictures of Home Counties life in his mother Sylvie's immaculate house, where plastic tracks led across acres of cream carpet, from her endless rules and one stepfather after another; from her general disappointment with life and, it seemed, him in particular.

Soon, he had been the one leading Ezra up climbs – exhilarating multi-pitch faces on Bosigran and Chair Ladder, or tricky little masterpieces like Saxon Direct and Peapod. Ezra would come puffing over the top with an enormous grin on his face before berating Sam for not putting in enough gear or protecting a traverse properly. Sam had happily taken the criticism: they were climbers from different eras, but they shared the same joy in the upward dance of movement, in sitting on a sunny belay with their feet dangling over the edge, looking down on the backs of the gulls, watching the waves sparkle till they were hypnotised; then back at the cottage after thumbing a lift home, rehearsing the day's dramas and triumphs over a pot of bean chilli. Sam missed those times; but Ezra had hung up his boots when

Sam went away to college and they hadn't ventured out since. It was his arthritis, but they didn't talk about it.

'He was okay I suppose, the new guy,' Sam went on after a long silence that made it clear that Ezra was not going to participate in the conversation. 'I'm going for a walk with Miranda – their daughter – tomorrow.'

Ezra raised an eyebrow, then said, 'Oh, brave new world…'

'Pardon?'

'Nothing.' The old man drained off his tea and got to his feet. 'Things to do,' he announced unceremoniously, and headed back outside.

Sam frowned, made to feel guilty somehow. The new owner had seemed pretty genuine and concerned. Plus, his daughter was very pretty.

Over supper later, the subject of the new people at the big house was not returned to, and Sam knew better than to try to revive it. Once Ezra had a bee in his bonnet about something, it was hard to dislodge it. Sam's mother, Sylvie, had always said that Ezra was a bloody-minded old man, best avoided, but given how difficult and snobbish his mother could be, this hadn't stopped Sam wanting to get to know his great-uncle – quite the opposite. When he ran away from boarding school, Ezra had taken him in as he would any young stray, letting him bed down in the room in which he stored his climbing gear and books, which suited Sam just fine. Even now when he came to stay, it always smelt the same to him – iodine and WD-40, a touch of papery mildew, and wood-ash from the fire in the grate. Tonight, he fell asleep as easily as he always did in Ezra's cottage, despite being full of anticipation for the walk with Miranda.

Sam was ready and raring to go immediately after an early breakfast. He roamed around the cottage like a caged lion, until Ezra could stand it no longer. 'Get out from under my feet!' he growled. 'If you've energy to burn, take the bike up to Bob

Hockin's and fetch me back some tea, flour and butter. You'm eating me out of house and home! I'll make a batch of scones for later.'

So Sam pedalled frantically up to the farm shop, got into an argument with Bob Hockin about Brexit ('I warned you it would be a disaster,' he groaned, as the farmer started complaining about rising prices and the inability to get hold of any pickers for his broccoli, the Cornish term for cauliflowers), paid for the tea, flour and butter out of his own pocket because he felt guilty about being a burden, and added a packet of extremely expensive fudge as a special treat, and to make amends for baiting the farmer. Then he pedalled back like a Tour de France racer, just in case Miranda turned up early and found him missing. He didn't trust Gamps not to engage her in the sort of conversation that would have her running back to the safety of the big house.

When he got back, however, Ezra was gently hoeing out weeds between his infant leeks and flowering chives, humming to himself and the bees that buzzed around him. Sam knew he could and should probably help with the weeding, but since eleven o'clock had come and gone, instead found his feet carrying him up the lane.

When he got within sight of Trengrose, he saw a figure coming down the steps from the house, dressed in rolled-up jeans, a shapeless plaid shirt much like his own, and a man's cloth cap. The long hair, though, gave her away. Melting quickly into the shadow on one side of the lane, Sam retraced his footsteps speedily back towards the cottage and hung nonchalantly around the gate, pretending to attend to its rusty hinges, keeping his gaze averted as he heard Miranda approach.

'I was worried you'd go without me!' she said breathlessly. 'I'm so sorry, my phone was out of charge, so I had no idea what the time was!' As if clocks didn't exist.

Sam put down the oily rag and wiped his hands on his cargo pants. 'No, you're all right,' he said gruffly. 'I'll just get my pack.'

Miranda, he saw, had come out without anything at all, so

in the kitchen he filled a bottle with water and grabbed a few edibles, and hurried back outside.

Too late. Gamps had slipped stealthily from the vegetable plot to the gate upon which he was leaning like a proverbial yokel, chatting to Ran. Seeing him through a stranger's eyes, Sam took in his filthy old cords and holey shirt with dismay. 'Ready?' he called hurriedly to Ran.

Ezra turned and cast a sardonic eye over his great-nephew. 'Now why would you deprive your old Gamps of the company of this charming young maid? "Summer's lease has all too short a date".'

Ran laughed aloud at the compliment, and Bucca came eeling out of the shelter of the blackcurrant bush, beneath which he had been contemplating the complexities of effort versus reward on a hot day, and blinked his gold-green eyes at the visitor.

Ran dropped to her haunches and started expertly rubbing the cat beneath his chin in just the way he liked best. 'Oh, I just love him!' she exclaimed. 'He looks like bits from three different animals have been stitched together – Frankenstein's Cat!'

Ezra grinned. 'He is a monster, right enough.'

Out of nowhere Bucca's giant purr came rumbling. Sam and Ezra exchanged a shocked glance. Bucca didn't like *anyone*, unless they came bearing food, like Stan the postie.

'Okay then, Gamps,' Sam said, breaking the spell. 'See you later.'

Ezra moved away to let him pass through the gate, but caught his arm as he went through, and whispered, 'Mind thee take her to the stones, let 'em work their magic.'

Ran swung her arms as she walked. She spun to face Sam when explaining something enthusiastically, her face radiant and her eyes clear. Before they had gone even a mile, he was a lost soul.

'They had a matrilineal culture,' she was saying as they reached the first stile onto the footpath, which was steep and a bit tricky.

Sam was unsure as to whether to offer a helping hand or to leave Ran to get over it herself. What were you supposed to do? He'd been brought up to politely open doors for women, but sometimes they gave you a dirty look, or worse, told you not to patronise them. But he needn't have worried: despite the borrowed footwear – a pair of pristine turquoise Converse trainers borrowed from her mother – Ran was as nimble as a goat, not even pausing her anthropological monologue as she tackled the granite and leapt down into the next field.

'That means all the wealth in the family passes down through the women, and the bloodlines are traced down the female side of the family, through mothers and aunts. For a boy, the most important male relationships would be with his mother's brothers. That's because you always know someone's mother for sure, but you can never be entirely certain about the father. In times of war, or with men travelling for work, women were left to their own devices: loads of children were born to men who weren't actually their fathers, but the women held the power. Plus a lot of these cultures revered goddesses and other female spirits.'

Sam's brows knit. 'How on earth did women go from being in such a powerful position to being owned and sidelined?'

Ran laughed. 'The Abrahamic religions have a lot to answer for. A lot of organised religion is more about patriarchal control than, you know, actual worship.'

Sam nodded. Was he part of the patriarchy? He used to go to Sunday School; he had written 'Church of England' on any number of forms. He didn't feel very powerful, though.

'And once they got hold of the wealth that was that, really. Women couldn't own their own property or inherit an estate; they had to marry and give everything into the hands of their husbands. Money gives people a lot of power. Men, I should say.'

Sam shook his head. 'Money's just a faked-up system. I don't know why we all go along with it, really: it's purely notional, if you think about it. A sort of make-believe people have agreed to subscribe to.'

She shot him a mischievous look. 'You're a bit of a hippie on the sly!'

'The rich get all the power and keep getting richer.'

'Yeah, but, it's not a closed system, is it? There are lots of ways to improve your financial standing. I mean, look at you, taking an MBA. You'll be able to get a great job once you've got that. The world is your oyster.'

Sam thought about mentioning her father's offer of interning but decided not to: it felt presumptuous, and probably had just been a throwaway remark. Instead, he ploughed on. 'But we don't have to be part of the system, do we? Look at Gamps – he's pretty much self-sufficient, living off the land, at one with his surroundings, happy as Larry.' Although, now he came to think about it, Ezra had not been himself this week. Something was clearly preying on his great-uncle's mind.

'Is he, though?' Ran said. 'I mean, it's pretty much impossible to exist outside the system these days, you know, with electricity and council tax, bills and benefits, and he must be getting a pension of some sort?'

Sam realised he didn't really know just how Gamps got by, and felt guilty, recalling Ezra's comment about eating him out of house and home. 'I think there are ways of coexisting with other people without being a part of their world. You know, just as we coexist with the natural world.'

'I don't really believe in the natural world,' Ran said.

Stunned by this pronouncement, Sam stopped and gazed at her in disbelief. 'What? We're standing in it.' He waved his arms, taking in the meadow flowers, the distant black-and-white cows, the wild Cornish hedges under the bowl of blue sky.

'It's not actual wilderness, though, is it?' she went on, sounding madly reasonable. 'Everything's been created by humans, by farmers. People have been farming down here for thousands of years. They divided the land up into fields—'

'We call them quillets,' Sam interrupted.

'Okay, quillets, then. That's a nice word. Quillets – like a patchwork quilt!'

'I don't think so—' Sam said, but she cut across him.

'And those farmers erected boundaries between the fields, and those walls and hedges have largely stood in the same place ever since, unless people took the stones from them to build houses. They say the West Cornwall field system is one of the most ancient artefacts in the world.'

Sam nodded slowly. 'Okay. But look – it's been left to go wild, in places at least. That's what I mean about coexisting with nature. You can't just take and take from the land: you must let fields lie fallow for periods of time or they'll be less and less productive. And if you keep intensively farming every scrap of the earth, all you do is deplete it and drive the wildlife to extinction, especially if you try to make up for the depletion by using chemicals – fertilisers and insecticides. There's an ecosystem, and we're all part of it, and if we upset the balance we all pay the price.' He pointed. 'Look at that bumblebee over there: she's out foraging for her hive. She's probably come from a larger than usual hive because she's out in the middle of the day – or maybe she's found some favourite flowers. She won't go to flowers that have already been visited by other bees – see how she skimmed that stand of oxeye daisies, then carried on? She's looking for a better source that hasn't already been collected. But what happens if someone cut back that hedge or bit of meadow and planted a non-flowering crop there? She'll have to go further afield, or maybe she won't find anything at all. She might die – her hive might fail. And if bees die, we're all in trouble: they pollinate our crops. So you see, it's a matter of balance. We've got to be mindful of the natural world and look after it, or it won't look after us.'

He ground to a halt, feeling embarrassed for his fervour, but Ran appeared to be listening intently, so he went on, 'Gamps loves bees. He grows plants especially for them, so they don't starve and don't have too far to go. I suppose some people might look at his garden and call it scruffy, but everything in it is there for a reason.'

Ran took this in. 'You know my dad thinks the cottage is part of the estate?'

Sam walked on, not taking this in at first. When he did, he turned and stared at her. 'What, you mean he thinks it belongs to him?'

Ran made a face. 'I don't think it's clear cut—'

'I should say not!' Sam said hotly. 'It's been in our family for generations.'

'Okay, calm down. He probably just needs to get that formalised somehow. Anyway, Dad's got plenty of other projects on the go to occupy him – you know, the glamping field, and getting the outbuildings renovated.'

The very word 'glamping' made Sam's teeth grate. 'As if we need more tourists,' he said grumpily.

'But you do, don't you? I mean, that's what Cornwall's all about – tourism. There'd be no jobs at all otherwise – you know, in hotels and restaurants, for cleaners, in shops and garages, and all.' She paused. 'It must be awful down here in winter.'

Sam took a deep breath. 'Actually, tourism only makes up a small percentage of the Cornish economy, but it's hollowing out our communities. Some places it's almost all holiday homes now – you can walk around in winter and hardly even see a light on or a fire burning. Incomers only ever see what suits them.'

Ran shot him a look. 'Oh, so it's incomers now, is it? Might as well go the whole hog and call me a grockle.'

'Emmet,' Sam corrected. 'It means ant.'

'Whatever.'

They didn't speak for a while after this, and Ran started to lag. Or maybe Sam had begun to stride out as if to put a greater distance between them. When he glanced back, she was looking down, her face shadowed. He had been rude.

'Sorry,' he said, walking back to her. 'It's just that visitors can treat us like slaves, put here to service their holiday fantasies. They come down here and think because we don't have much money that we aren't worth anything. But I didn't mean to include you among people like that.'

'I can see that would be bloody annoying,' she said slowly. Just as she did so, a pair of swifts skimmed past, on the hunt for flying insects, so close that they felt the air their wings stirred as a touch of breeze on their faces.

'Wow, swallows!' Ran cried. 'Magic!'

'Swifts,' Sam corrected, unable to help himself. 'Swallows have a red patch under their chins, and ribbon tails.'

'They're so fast!'

'Well, they are swifts...'

They both burst out laughing, then turned to watch the birds soar and swoop, flitting ecstatically across the field. Entranced, Ran started to spin, her arms spread wide, and her face tilted up to the sun, so fast that her cap flew off and Sam had to retrieve it. Then he too began to dance and spin, till the pair of them were whirling dervishes, channelling the life of the land up into the light of the sun through the tapers of their bodies.

At last, giddy, they fell down amid the meadow grass, and lay there gazing up into the shiny air as it was scythed through by swift wings, more and more of them.

'They're amazing birds,' Sam said after a while. 'They've come all the way from Africa, thousands of miles, hardly ever stopping. They even mate on the wing.' He remembered one of Ezra's old stories. 'The Ancient Greeks called them "footless" – I can't remember the actual word in Greek. They used to think they had no feet because they never saw them land.'

'I love that,' said Ran.

'They're on the red list now, though,' Sam added. 'That means as a species they're globally threatened.'

Ran didn't take her eyes off them. 'You're quite the mood-killer.'

'Sorry.'

'I don't understand. Who would want to kill a swift?'

'It's not even that we mean to kill them. It's to do with climate change and losing habitats. We keep knocking down or renovating the buildings where they like to nest – you know, like old barns and outhouses...'

'Oh, right,' Ran said. 'Like the ones at Trengrose. That my dad's about to do up.'

'Lots of swifts nest there,' Sam said quietly.

'They do? I haven't seen any.' She sat up, brushing the grass seedheads out of her hair. 'Though I didn't know what I was looking for until now. Till today, birds were just birds. But you know,' she said, changing the subject, 'they have to make some money out of the estate. God, why is life so complicated?' She pushed herself to her feet and they got up and walked on in silence.

Sam and Miranda came to a fork in the footpath, and he remembered what Gamps had said about the stone circle, so instead of ploughing straight down the hillside towards the sea, he climbed the stile into the next field and waited for Ran to join him. When he moved out of her line of sight so that she could see the circle, Ran gazed in amazement.

'Wow! Oh my god, how many times have I said "wow" today?' she laughed. 'I wasn't expecting this. Or the swifts.' She turned back to grin at him. 'How many more magical experiences have you got up your sleeve, Mr Wizard?'

Sam coloured. 'I can't really take credit for any of it... it's just... here.'

She skipped away from him to the nearest stone, laid her palm upon it, caressed it; bent to pick something, sometimes stepping away from the circle before returning to salute the next megalith. Sam saw that she had placed a different wildflower on each stone, as if performing a rite.

'Do you think it will grant my wish?'

So that was what she was doing. Sam laughed. 'I'm not sure that's what it's for.'

She pursed her lips. 'Spoilsport. What's it called? It looks like no one ever comes here.'

'Gamps calls it the Fox Dance. Up over there towards Boleigh,' he pointed north and east, 'is the Stone Dance, better known as the Merry Maidens. All the visitors go there: it's bigger and easier to get to. Hardly anyone knows about this one.'

'Well, I love it,' she said, giving him a serious glance. 'Thank you for showing me.' She thought for a moment. 'What about the stone down near The Lodge? Is that ancient?'

'I think that's a Celtic cross,' Sam said. 'But it could be pre-Christian. You should ask Gamps: he'll know. Why?'

'Oh, something Dad said.' She looked thoughtful.

They followed the footpath down through the woods, where sunlight dappled the ground and added a sense of the liminal to their journey: this was an in-between place, neither open nor closed, neither wild nor curated, a passage between the land and the sea, which they could hear lapping away down below, sucking at the beach pebbles, then releasing them in a rattling gush. This time, Sam did help Ran to make the transition down the steep, rocky defile to the cove below, and once they both stood with their feet on the damp shingle, she looked around and grinned so hard that her blue eyes became shining slits.

'W— No, I can't say "wow" again! But this is spectacular. So pretty, so private!' She turned to Sam. 'Do you bring your girlfriends down here for an alfresco shag?'

Sam went red right to the tips of his ears. Did she think that was why he had brought her to the little beach?

'I... ah... no?'

'What – no girlfriends, or no shagging?'

He stared at her, unable to find a witty response, indeed, any response, and wished he could just run right into the waves and swim away from her. Then he thought, *that's exactly what I'll do!*

He dropped his rucksack, shucked off his trainers and stripped off his T-shirt and cargo pants – but maybe not his knock-off

Calvin Kleins, he thought, though he had often skinny-dipped here, alone, and with girlfriends before or after they had, yes indeed, made love on the shore. Perhaps that was what had stung him: old memories, not always happy ones. Or perhaps it was her casual language that offended his romantic soul. He dashed into the waves – bitingly cold, straight off the Celtic Sea and thence the Atlantic – and submerged himself in a thrash of white water that made him gasp in shocked exhilaration.

The next thing he knew, there was a wet brown head next to him, long hair spread across the surface of the water like floating kelp.

'Oh my god, this is fantastic!' Ran kicked, then lay back with her arms flung wide, silver sun slicking off her bare breasts and belly and – Sam saw as an electric jolt ran through his groin – her neatly trimmed pubic hair. Having given him a good eyeful, she flipped like a dolphin and all he saw was the shining flash of her bum, followed by the soles of her feet, and she was gone.

Despite the chill of the water, he struggled for a long time to control his body's reaction sufficiently to be able to exit the sea with any degree of dignity. When he did, he charged straight up the beach and flung himself down on the hot pebbles with his plaid shirt over his lap and tried very hard not to stare at Ran as she walked out of the waves like some gorgeous siren. It was difficult not to think of the tale of the Zennor mermaid, who took such a liking to poor Mathey Trewella that she waited for him outside the church and enticed him down into the sea with her to drown beneath the waves so that she might keep him forever in her watery kingdom.

'That was great!' Ran declared, drying herself vigorously with her shorts, before stepping into her underwear and pulling it up over skin that was beginning to make goose bumps in the breeze. She hugged her knees to her still-naked chest. 'You know, wild swimming is brilliant for your immune system?'

Sam couldn't help but laugh. 'Wild swimming? We just call it swimming, and that wasn't much more than a dip. Sometimes,

I swim around the headland to Lamorna and back again. You can get some tricky currents around here, though. But you can also get dolphins and porpoises, and that's just magic. Once, I swam with a basking shark...'

'You swam with a shark?'

'Basking sharks are the second largest sharks in the world but they're harmless,' he grinned. 'All they eat is plankton and stuff – they open their mouths to sieve the seawater.' He measured the distance from pebbles to sky with his arms. 'I had to float and tread water and not make any fuss – I didn't want to frighten it.'

'*You* didn't want to frighten *it*?' Ran laughed.

'They're gentle creatures, and also endangered.'

'Well, Sam, you've given me a right good tutoring about the natural world today.'

'Sorry, didn't mean to preach.'

'That's okay. I like to learn, especially from experts.'

They ate their picnic, lay back in the sun and even dozed a little. At last, Ran sat up and looked around. 'Is the way we came the only way in here?'

Sam nodded. 'Yes. You'd never find it if you didn't know about it. I call it the Secret Cove.'

'Not so secret any more – I could tell anyone!'

'But you won't?'

She chuckled. 'No. I like that it's a secret between us. Where do most visitors go when they want to go to the beach?'

'Porthcurno,' Sam said without hesitation. 'It's big and gorgeous and sandy, and it's got a car park right by it. Though you'd hardly know it sometimes, the way tourists park all the way up the road, blocking people's drives and farmers' gates at the height of the season. That's the honeypot effect: attract people to one place to save the rest.'

'The what?'

'If you want to control tourist traffic and preserve wild areas, you encourage people to visit places close to the road or car parks, like wasps to a honeypot. It keeps footfall light in more fragile environments, the places that should be kept secret.'

'What, and then you charge people a mint to park? Sounds like the Cornish have got ripping off down to a fine art.'

Sam squirmed at the accuracy of her observation. He knew shops that put their prices up in the summer, or just for visitors, ferry crossings that doubled in price during the tourist season. 'People have to make their money however they can, whenever they can,' he said.

Miranda laughed. 'I was only teasing. Sounds as if you could put your business skills to work down here.'

Sam stared at her. After a long beat of silence, he said, 'I guess I just don't see Cornwall as a business. It's who I am, where I come from, where I belong.'

'But if there's no business, how do you get by here?'

Sam looked away. 'That's the dilemma.'

He seemed so wistful suddenly that Ran wanted to give something back to him for all he had given her. 'But it's just so beautiful. Don't you want to share that beauty with other people? You know, give them a bit of happiness to take home with them – lovely memories of a lovely place?'

Sam's jaw firmed; then he met her eyes. 'Honestly? No. No, I don't want really to share it. The Cornwall I love most is wintry and wild, when all the visitors have gone away. The way it was when I was little. I'd like that Cornwall back. It's selfish, but it's how I feel.' Even as he said it, he knew he sounded both obstinate and graceless.

Miranda shook her head sadly. 'That Cornwall's gone, Sam. Maybe it never even existed. There have always been tourists down here, and people who have housed and fed them and cleaned up after them and driven them around. You know that. Think of all those lovely old pre-war posters advertising the Cornish Riviera.'

Sam shook his head, at a loss. 'Maybe it's time to get back,' he said. He felt suddenly mournful on this lovely summer's day, alone in this idyllic cove, with the prettiest girl he'd ever met. As with his dreams of homeland, his nostalgia for a past that had never really been what he wished it was, Miranda was her own person, with a lot more thoughts and opinions than he had been ready for. It would take him a while to sort through them, on his own, quietly under Ezra's roof. He knew some of what she said was right – if you took a slice of the county, placed it on a slide beneath the merciless eye of a microscope and examined it objectively. But it was hard to be objective when you loved a place so much that it hurt – physically hurt – when you went away from it. When he was here, his mind felt free of the cage that life in the city imposed on it. He knew this was why he was finding it so hard to settle in London, why he fled from it at every opportunity. But if he tried to explain any of this to this forthright, urban young woman she would think him soft in the head; besides, his feelings were too inchoate for him to explain in any way that didn't come out sounding resentful, hostile, even xenophobic.

They packed up in silence. The swifts were no longer to be seen as they crossed the top meadow, and a chill was starting to fall that presaged the approaching autumn.

15

Sam went back to London a few days later. Ezra was sorry to see him go; even though he was used to his solitary life, he found his great-nephew easy company.

That had not, however, been the case during the tail end of his visit, ever since his walk with the girl, Miranda, from the big house, and Sam had been quieter than usual. Ezra hadn't probed. What – after all – did he know about women? The only woman he had ever known for any length of time was Miss Eliza, and she was hardly typical of the species. Miranda had probably knocked the lad back. It was probably for the best. Her father – not to put too fine a point on it – was a complete tuss.

The tuss appeared while Ezra was repairing the gate and hung around awkwardly, making surreptitious coughing noises, till Ezra finally lost patience and demanded, 'What you want?'

'Good morning. I'm Toby Hardman, your new neighbour.' He held out a hand.

Ezra ignored it. 'I know who you are.' A man may smile and smile and be a villain.

'I thought you might like to join me for a pint,' his new neighbour said.

'Busy, ent I?' Ezra shot back. He had no wish to go for a pint with Toby Hardman.

'Come along now, man: the gate can wait, surely? It's a lovely day. I could drive us to the King's Arms, or down to the Ship at Mousehole.'

Ezra shook his head. 'Got things to do.'

Toby put his hand on the gate. Ezra stared at it. It was a large hand, as one would expect from a large man, but with short fingers from which hair sprouted dark at the knuckles, and the flesh of his palm spread over the top rail. Soft, Ezra thought. A soft hand for a soft city man. 'What is it you want to talk about,' he asked, 'that you feel the need to take me out and get me plastered?'

Toby looked crafty. 'Nothing like that. Just a neighbourly gesture. Get to know each other a bit, you know?'

'Oh, I know,' Ezra said, bending to the hinge again. 'Well, tis a nice gesture, but you've made it now. Thank 'ee kindly.'

Toby felt dismissed and it made him angry that this lowlife should treat him so: him, Toby Hardman, rich and successful, the new master of Trengrose. He tamped the anger down. Make out you're not bothered, find a good starting point for the coming negotiation. 'Let's start again,' he declared with false bonhomie. 'Come and have a beer up at the house, then?' he added. 'See what we've done with the place.'

Ezra shook his head again. 'I have warm memories of the old place.' He didn't want them overwritten by whatever atrocities the Hardmans were perpetrating up there.

'Splendid,' said Toby. 'I'm sure you'll love to see how we're bringing it back to life. It was in quite a state, you know; unloved and falling apart.'

'It were never unloved,' Ezra said quietly, but Toby spoke over him.

'We've installed a wonderful kitchen and are keen to show it off. My wife Minty – Araminta Hervey as was, that's her professional designer's name, you may have heard of her – has worked miracles. You should meet her.' His eyes wandered over the rotten frames and peeling paintwork of the cottage.

'Already did,' Ezra said shortly.

'Did you?' Toby frowned, the ghastly accident on the day they had first viewed Trengrose all but forgotten.

Ezra bit his tongue, wishing with all the force of his being that this lumbering idiot would clear off.

'I really would like a chance to chat,' Toby ploughed on, seemingly oblivious to Ezra's hostility. 'There's a lot to discuss – the widening of the lane, the security lights, the signage... the status of The Lodge.'

Ezra applied a few final aggressive turns of his screwdriver to the hinge and straightened up. 'Say that again?'

'We're going to be widening the lane to make it more accessible,' Toby said. 'We'll have to take out a few of the trees along the drive, and that big old stone, and lay a better road surface. I don't want to be liable for insurance claims!'

'Why don't you get a smaller car?' Ezra asked.

'Oh, it's not just for us! It's for the campers – or glampers as my wife insists on calling them. Some will stay in the pods, but others may bring their own motorhomes in. Depends on the licence from the council, of course, but best to be prepared. As it is, the poor removals chaps and the builders all had a bit of a nightmare getting up to the house. I'd love to be able to work to a longer timeline – you know, spread the costs – but it's probably best to bite the bullet now. No one wants to come stay on a campsite while there's construction work going on, do they?'

Ezra took this in, seething silently. Campsite, eh? A load of emmets rumbling up and down the lane at all hours of the day and night. And no doubt the signage was to do with that. But all that was of secondary concern: he knew the conversation Toby Hardman really wanted to have was about the cottage, all those legal letters asking if he was a tenant, paid rent, worked for Miss Eliza... He ground his molars, feeling a twinge run through his jaw and right down to his bad hip. 'You got anything to say about my home, best come out and say it here and now,' he growled at last.

Toby took a deep breath. 'I'd rather do it sitting down. Might we—?' He gestured towards the cottage.

Over my dead body, Ezra thought, but didn't say. 'Out with it!'

'Well, Mr Curnow, you haven't answered any of the letters from the estate's solicitors, or from mine. They can't all have got lost in the post. Indeed, some of them were signed for. I checked.' He paused. 'Once apparently by Desperate Dan.'

Ezra said not a word.

'I need to know by what right you are inhabiting The Lodge,' Toby said bluntly, provoked by the old man's mutinous expression.

'Same right as my father, and his father before him.'

'They were Trengrose estate managers, weren't they?'

'Ar.'

'So, I'm guessing The Lodge was something of a grace and favour dwelling under the terms of their work contract.'

'Contract!' Ezra chortled angrily. 'Who has work contracts down here?'

Toby felt a shiver of excitement. No paperwork, no proof of right to tenancy: excellent. 'So, you're saying your father and grandfather lived here on an understanding? With the owners of Trengrose?'

'Ar, folk understood each other much better in those days,' Ezra said. He looked down and saw that he was holding the screwdriver like a weapon, his knuckles white. With a conscious effort, he relaxed his grip. Mustn't show the enemy weakness, and anger was weakness.

'So,' Toby pressed, 'there are no legal documents to prove your status to occupy the premises?'

Ezra sighed. 'Legal documents,' he echoed. 'Not everything works like that here, but you do your digging. You'll get nothing more out of me. This cottage is where I was born and it's where I shall die.' And he gathered up his tools, turned his back on Toby Hardman, and stalked back inside his home, shutting the door firmly behind him.

Toby stared after him. How dare that ancient squatter snub him? It was all he could do not to barge through the half-mended gate, storm up the dandelioned path, and batter the door down. He had to take several deep breaths to calm himself, as Minty had tried to teach him over the years. Even so, fantasies of bludgeoning the old bastard kept breaking through the imposed calm. 'Slowly, slowly, catchee monkey,' he muttered to himself at last. He'd encountered men like Ezra before. They came over hard and obstinate, but they were brittle. He just had to find a crack in the old man's defences. Toby had never knowingly been bested in a deal. Even if he'd had to cheat, or resort to violence, to come out on top.

He marched back up to Trengrose House. On the way, out of nowhere, something stung him on the neck. He felt the tickle of tiny feet on his skin and crushed the intruder with a slap, too slow to prevent the sting, or perhaps drawing it by his action, and stared at the creature, dying, curled and vibrating, on his palm, before throwing it away in disgust.

Bloody wasp! he thought, though it was in fact a bee, Minty later corrected him. *Filthy insect!*

His neck throbbed for hours.

Ezra sat at his kitchen table, tremors of rage rippling through him. So much for all those slippery words about neighbours and beer and cosy chats. That bastard was after his cottage. His home. Toby Hardman had sniffed an opportunity: money to be made, a kingdom to be expanded. Well, he'd soon find out – if he hadn't realised it already – that a Curnow man was not one of those soft city types this so-called Hardman was used to dealing with. He was not going to roll over and surrender. He would damn well see him off. Not an emmet, this one, Ezra thought, but a bloody cockroach.

Surprise.

Aggression.

Speed.

Endurance.

Ezra considered his strategies as he went about his daily chores. Seeing off a tuss like Hardman wouldn't be easy. The authorities always sided with the rich and influential, even down here, where you'd hoped there might be more leeway in interpreting the law. When he was growing up, matters had been different. Gangs had run the fishing villages. Anyone stepping out of line would soon have community justice meted out to them – being hung by the ankles over the seawall, slapped around by local enforcers; or in extreme cases, disappeared, either off oceangoing vessels or down remote moorland mineshafts.

Ezra had never been a part of the community in this sense, but on the outside looking in, at a remove. He preferred it that way. Trengrose and its environs were all he needed: the deep peace of the woodlands and meadows, the quiet rhythms of the seasons, keeping his distance from the rest of the human race, which he'd learned to distrust.

Which was why he'd ended up alone, with no other company than a bad-tempered barn cat named for a demon, his bees and his chickens, and the wild creatures who visited for food. And occasional visits from Sam.

Giving up human company had, for much of his life, seemed a decent bargain for not losing his soul. But isolation could leave you vulnerable. He would employ watchful waiting. And he would be ready.

Ezra noticed the surveyors arriving a few days later: two men in suits worn with wellington boots, carrying tripods and measuring equipment, clipboards and cameras. He leaned on his gate and watched them go past, then slipped into the orchard and shadowed them as they moved up the drive, staying out of sight. He watched as they measured and sighted and discussed, and then made markings on various trees, spraying them with white symbols. Several of the marked trees stood on the edge of the orchard. His orchard.

Ezra waited until the men had left, then went back to the cottage and gathered a few items.

He returned from a foraging expedition a couple of days later with a bagful of samphire, some sea beet and field mushrooms, to find a small crane and two workmen in neon jackets moving the Celtic cross opposite his cottage. Ezra dropped his knapsack and ran towards them.

'Oi! You can't do that!'

The men exchanged a glance. 'Authorisation from the council,' one said, tapping his jacket pocket.

Ezra glared at him. 'That's an ancient monument!'

The man shrugged. 'It's just an old stone that's in the way.' His accent was not local.

Ezra looked to the other workman and narrowed his eyes. 'Ent you Dan Jago's youngest?'

The second workman looked uncomfortable. 'Jem, yeah.'

'And you think it's okay to dig up a bit of Cornwall's history just so some rich tuss from upcountry can widen the bleddy lane for tourists?'

Jem shuffled his feet. ''Tis a shame and all...' he said lamely.

'I'll say it's a shame. I'll say money's exchanged hands!' Ezra was outraged.

'Now then, mister,' said the other man. 'Can't go around making allegations like that. If you want to see the permissions, you can go to the council website and look through planning. It's all there in black and white. "Removal of stone gatepost on Trengrose Lane".'

'T'ent a gatepost!' Ezra fumed. ''Tis a Celtic cross, been there a thousand years. Don't you know why Trengrose is called Trengrose?'

'Nope, and don't care.'

'Farm of the cross – that's what it means.'

'Well, it's in the way and we got orders to shift it and that's what we're going to do.'

'What you going to do with it?' Ezra asked belligerently.

Jem shrugged. 'All we been asked to do is take it down and move it out of the way.'

'It's a sacred stone. You lay hands on it you'll likely be cursed.' Ezra's regard was as dark and cold as agate.

Jem looked fearful but the other man scoffed. 'Come on, lad, job to do.'

An hour later, they were gone, and the ancient stone lay unceremoniously among the nettles and brambles like some wild piece of the landscape rather than an artefact fashioned by reverent human hands. Ezra knelt beside the fallen monolith and ran his fingers gently across its etched and pitted surface, but if he had been expecting a sensation of disrupted energies from the granite, he was to be disappointed. It was just a bit of stone, toppled and discarded, like so much of Cornwall's ancient past.

He went to his hives and sat quietly beside them, gathering his words and the calm to deliver them, and then he told the bees how part of their world had irrevocably been changed, their boundaries disturbed. He ended his speech with a warning: worse was to come.

A low rumble rose up like a sound wave within the hive, then dropped away, like sadness.

16

The next day Ezra's peace was shattered by the sound of chainsaws, followed by the distant crump of a fallen tree.

He wandered up the drive, at the head of which he saw a pair of tree surgeons. One gestured at him to go back. He pretended not to understand. The man shouted. Ezra cupped a hand to his ear as if he were deaf. The tree-feller signed to his partner to stop work and they both turned off their chainsaws and removed their ear defenders.

The silence after the barrage of noise was eerie, as if the world had come to a sudden halt. Then, with a clatter of wings, Merlin swept down over their heads, landed on Ezra's shoulder and began tenderly to groom the hair above his ear.

'Well, would you look at that?'

The tree surgeons seemed delighted by the bird's appearance. 'My uncle used to have a tame jackdaw,' one said. 'Called him Jacko. What's yours called?'

'I don't know the name he gives hisself. I call him Merlin.'

'Proper job.'

They came close to examine Merlin, and one dug in his overalls pocket and brought out a piece of cheese, which the jackdaw scrutinised with each of his pale-blue eyes, tilting his head this way then that, before snatching it neatly and swallowing it down. He eyed the man's pocket speakingly.

'He'll have the entire sandwich off you if you aren't careful!' said the other man, and they all laughed.

'Widening the track, eh?' Ezra asked innocently.

The tree surgeons exchanged a glance. 'I guess so,' the first one said, 'though I must say it seems a bit skewwhiff to me.'

'Skewwhiff?'

'Well, put it this way, if I were going to widen this lane, I'd be taking out trees on that side to make a smoother sweep.' He indicated some of the orchard trees that overhung the lane. 'But the surveyors marked out those sycamores and that big old pine up there.'

'Shame about that,' the second tree surgeon said. 'It were a lovely tree, Corsican pine. I'm surprised it didn't have a TPO on it.'

'A tree preservation order,' the first man explained to Ezra. 'Must've spoiled the view from the house, taking that one down.'

The sight of someone heading towards them down the lane interrupted their conversation. Knowing what was coming, Ezra turned quickly and melted into the orchard, but just within earshot.

He could've gone further: Toby Hardman's voice would have carried for a mile.

'What the hell do you think you're playing at?' he thundered.

'Sorry?'

'Felling that… that…' He floundered, not knowing what sort of tree it was. 'The big conifer. I didn't order that one to be taken down: are you totally incompetent?'

'It was clearly marked with the surveyor's symbol,' one of the tree surgeons said. 'We took photos before we started in case there were any questions.' He removed an iPhone from his pocket, tapped it and showed the image to Toby.

'It seemed a shame to fell that old Corsican pine,' the other man said. 'But I gather you're widening the road—'

'You can barely get a bicycle up this blasted track: but that pine was part of our bloody view!' Toby marched a few paces away and tried to make a phone call. They all heard him swear loudly.

'You'll get no signal here,' one of the tree surgeons offered helpfully.

Ezra crept back towards his cottage through the cool shade of the orchard. He felt profoundly sad about the old pine coming down, though once they examined it more closely they would find that it had a form of needle blight that meant it would eventually have had to come down before it spread. He'd reported as much to Eliza the previous year.

'It'll outlast me,' she'd replied. '*Après moi le déluge.*' She'd patted Ezra's hand. 'Though I'm no Louis Quinze.'

'And I ent no Madame de Pompadour!'

They had both laughed uproariously, but Ezra had come away feeling miserable. She looked so frail, was as tiny and fragile as a little bird, where in her youth she had fizzed with life and energy. And now she was gone, and so was her favourite tree. The pine had been a towering, dignified presence in the landscape for the whole of his life, like Miss Eliza herself.

Araminta Hardman, having come off a videocall to Alexei Antonov's site manager about the Misbourne House project, had escaped upstairs and was now arranging the notebooks and papers on her desk, running her hand over the smooth, beeswaxed surface, inhaling its woody scent. Already it felt like an old friend.

After discovering it in the bedroom downstairs, she and Dominic had wrestled the davenport up the narrow staircase to the attic with great difficulty, despite removing the larger drawers to lighten the load.

'Bloody hell, Mum,' Dom had sworn, puffing, 'what's this thing made out of, lead?'

'I think it's walnut, darling,' she'd said. 'It's quite a dense hardwood: that's probably why it's so heavy.'

It had taken a lot of searching through local antique shops to find exactly the right chair to go with her desk, but in the end Minty had found its perfect partner. She drew it out now, patting the soft leather seat she had restored with saddle soap, sat down, and pulled it in so that she was tucked squarely into the space, with her feet neatly set on the floor.

She picked up her pen – a Pilot gel pen rather than the traditional fountain pen she had fancifully imagined she would use here, but no mind – and opened the handsome Moleskine Extra Large notebook, an investment that made the project feel less of a hobby and more of a professional venture. This was also one reason why she had decided to write her draft in longhand rather than on a laptop. It felt like a more personal commitment to her subject to put pen to paper in the time-honoured tradition, connecting her to her forebears and their history in a way that tapping on the keyboard could never.

She already had the first line of the book in her head, had done for weeks in delicious anticipation of the time when her attic study would be finished and her writing space ready to accept her. Taking one look around at the eau de nil panelling, the Gillow library chair and the polished floorboards, she uncapped the pen and wrote the words, *'The year 1627 would prove to be a fatal one for the Hervey family...'* when somewhere outside, at a distance, but still too close for comfort, she heard a mechanical roar and whine, followed by the sound of an immense crash.

A jolt of pain shot through her. Minty sat there, her heart thudding in a way that frightened her. She thought she heard a woman's voice cry out, *oh no, oh no, oh no!*

Was it her own voice? The memory of her friend Jess's sudden collapse came back to her now – a heart attack last year, seemingly out of nowhere, though she'd been under a lot of pressure. Jess was fine now, on pills and with a stent, but still, she had been alarmingly young to have such a thing happen. Minty's frantic mind now ran through the checklist for heart attack symptoms for women. Pain – yes, a sharp brief pain in her chest, but she couldn't feel it now. Nausea? Lightheadedness? She didn't think so, but what would happen if she stood up? She let her breath out slowly, to control her racing heart. Another breath in, to check for pain in the ribs, down the arm, in her neck and jaw. Nothing. She held another breath, breathed out. With her palms flat on the desk, she pushed herself to her feet.

No dizziness, good. What was it, then, that she had felt? If it were not something within her, might it be something outside she had misconceived as pain?

Minty went to the window and stared out. For a moment, the world seemed much as it had. For long seconds, she stared at the familiar scene, until she registered an absence. The cedar, or whatever it was, that tall, dignified presence at the head of the drive that defined the view so beautifully, was gone. That couldn't be right. She shook her head and stared again. Yes, there was definitely a gap where it had been! She felt the strangest sensation of loss that blossomed into a sudden sharp, floral smell like an olfactory hallucination.

It was then that she spotted the two men in orange work jackets and helmets, chainsaws ported over their shoulders, walking away down the lane.

Minty howled. She hauled at the window that she herself had recently painted, in such a hurry that she had painted over the catch. Swearing, she twisted the brass fitting till at last the paint gave way and pushed the sash up to yell at the retreating backs of the two workmen. 'What are you're doing? Have you cut down my tree?'

They gave no sign of having heard her.

Why was this happening? Was it vandalism? And then she remembered what Toby had said the day before, about the people coming to widen the drive. Anguished by this sudden realisation, she began to pull at her hair, an old childhood habit that occurred only when she was under great stress. Why, why, hadn't she paid better attention to what he'd been saying? Why hadn't she double-checked the plan, and overseen the surveyor? Toby could be so reckless. She blamed him at once. All the same, guilt prodded at her: she knew she hadn't been listening because she had been so preoccupied by the anticipation of finally starting her book.

By the time she had fled down three flights of stairs, hauled on some outdoor shoes and run down the steps outside, it was to see Toby storming across the drive, no doubt on the way to make things worse.

'What was that noise?'

She turned, and there was Dominic, looking sleepy and dishevelled.

'They're felling trees to widen the lane for access,' she said tightly.

'Oh, right. For the *glampers*.' He enunciated the word with disdain.

'Yes, for the campsite.' The permissions had come through from the council with remarkable speed, just as the estate agent had promised.

'Does that mean they'll be driving past the house all the time?'

'Don't exaggerate. The site will only be open for the summer months. We must make some money, you know, if we're going to keep you in trainers and energy drinks!'

Dom scowled. 'I'd rather go without.'

'For god's sake, Dom, I'm sure you'll manage. We'll screen the lane. You'll hardly know they're there.'

'Yeah, but then there're the barns and stuff,' he said darkly. 'Honestly, Mum, what's the point of escaping the city if we come down here and build a new one?'

'It's hardly—' She turned back, but he was gone, headphones clamped firmly back in place. Minty sighed. She didn't really blame him. There was still no internet, and he was bored. She hoped Toby would get the lodge cottage sorted sooner rather than later. That would keep Dom occupied and should also bring in some income, much more than the glamping. Plus, it wasn't right on their doorstep.

Taking a deep breath, she went to inspect the damage done by the fallen tree.

Ezra watched the tree surgeons disappear out onto the main road. And he smiled.

He weeded the salad bed and introduced some ladybirds to the aphids on the rosebush, stood watching with satisfaction as the bugs grasped their prey between their maxillae and chewed contentedly, working their way methodically up the stem.

You had to have a plan, he thought to himself, *and carry it out steadfastly.*

Surprise. Aggression. Speed.

Then he went indoors, opened a drawer, took from it a pen and notepad, sat down at the kitchen table and found a clean page.

He paused contemplatively for a moment, then wrote the words:

CAMPAIGN PLAN

17

Minty surveyed her handiwork with no little satisfaction.

Trengrose Glamping

the sign read, in beautiful, bold red italics, the capitals gorgeously
looping. Even though it had been years since she had employed
her calligraphy skills, the sign wasn't half bad. She added a big
red arrow indicating the entrance to the lane and stood back. It
should be easily visible to anyone driving west down the road
from Penzance. She would put it up later, when the paint was
dry.

With permission for the site granted by the council, she had
arranged for the rental and delivery of half a dozen glamping
pods, rounded wooden cabins that looked rather like hobbit
holes, a prefab showerblock and portaloos, and had overseen their
installation. It was terrifying how fast they were haemorrhaging
money – she'd even dipped into her own savings, an account she
had kept carefully ringfenced ever since she and Toby had almost
split up a few years ago – but she had to see it as an investment
in their future down here, on the no pain, no gain principle. And
it was a pain, a lot of pain, to have to share her magical space
with strangers.

Of course, Toby was up in London, so she'd had to do everything on her own, apart from the rudimentary website, which had been created by a very sulky Dominic.

They had already had some bookings, although the logistics were something of a nightmare given that they still had no internet, so answering enquiries and taking deposits required Minty to drive into Penzance every day. Truth be told, she rather enjoyed the time on her own; was beginning to recognise local people and be recognised in her turn. Friendly nods and smiles, of which she had initially been suspicious, had gradually become greetings. She would return from the short jaunt with an increased sense of herself and her new life, a little more optimism about the future, a little more reinforcement of their choices. She also came back with new items of clothing picked up for a song from trendy little boutiques on Causewayhead and down Chapel Street. People here dressed rather differently to how Minty dressed, and she had become rather self-conscious at being quite so 'put together' (even her jeans were 7 For All Mankind, and she usually paired them with a fitted Chanel jacket and toning scarf, an outfit that would look casual but entirely suitable for a visit to Bond Street, but made people stare speculatively at her in Penzance). She bought patterned cotton shirts and linen trousers, thonged sandals and a pair of soft, flat leather ankle boots in a beautiful ochre that made no sound on the unclad stairs of Trengrose and were also sturdy enough for site visits to the glamping field. She put away her Roland Mouret dresses and Dior slingbacks, her spike-heeled boots and suede skirts, with a fleeting sense of regret. Surveying the scattered cables and holes in the floor left by the builders at the end of each day, the stacked radiators and light fittings, tubs of plaster, tools, tins of paint, and abandoned paint trays and brushes strewn around, like an explosion in a DIY shop, she began to wonder if she would ever wear anything elegant again. It appeared she was no longer Araminta Hervey, budding author, interior designer to the rich and famous; but Minty Hardman, wife, mother, cook, cleaner, laundress, building supervisor, penny-pincher and all-round dogsbody once more.

But – she reminded herself as she surveyed her excellent sign – all this would change. Money would come in, people would quietly occupy their glamping pods and enjoy spending time under the stars in the Cornish landscape, and they would have phones and internet, and the house would be fully habitable; Toby would have sorted out the lodge cottage and Dominic would have a project to occupy himself, and at long last, she would be free to get back to her writing.

Ah yes, the lodge cottage. It had come to symbolise the key to their future.

A key, perhaps, she could help to turn.

She would, she thought, look in on the old chap down at the cottage after installing the sign on the post set up for it at the junction and ask him when he was moving out – as Toby had assured her he would be soon. The old boy would probably be packing up and sorting through his meagre belongings. She would take him some of the cake she had brought back from Penzance as a peace offering. Perhaps he would even offer her tea and they would sit down in his grim little kitchen and then she could get a proper look at the place and start making plans – think about which walls to knock down, the layout of the new kitchen, colour scheme, that sort of thing.

Yes, that was what she would do. Boris needed a walk, and so did Dom. Perfect.

The old chap was not, in fact, packing up. Ezra was sitting in a secluded spot around the back of the cottage on an old wicker chair, having a smoke. His eyes were closed, and scattered sunlight filtering down through the leaves fell upon his beatific expression. In his lap was a volume of poetry and the remains of the ploughman's he had made for his lunch (a heel of the bread he had baked yesterday, some of the Cheddar he had bartered from the farm, a bit of last year's green tomato chutney, and some salad leaves picked from the vegetable patch and desultorily washed off in the rain butt).

Bucca lay a short distance away with the remains of the rat he had eaten for his brunch. He had found the creature meandering on the edge of the orchard where he had pounced upon it in epic fashion. Feeling heroic after the short but decisive battle and the subsequent heads-first feast, he now contemplated the gruesome remains, then, with one paw, pushed the half-eaten corpse into the long grass. He had gone off the idea of finishing the rat, having to shear off the annoying scratchy little claws, excise the bitter gall bladder, remove the scaly tail. It seemed like too much work right now. He would eat the rest of it later. Maybe. Or maybe he wouldn't. The sight of the twisted innards, and the remaining stiffening limbs, had reminded him of his own mortality. It was a fleeting thought, one that would surely be dispersed by a good nap. Bucca curled in on himself, tucked his nose under his tail, and immediately fell into a dreamless sleep.

Which lasted less than ten minutes. For suddenly there was snuffling, then barking, followed by the disgusting stench of dog.

He sprang to his feet, black lips drawn back in an evil grimace, all his hackles up.

'Hey, Boris, stop it!'

Bucca was across the grass before Ezra opened both eyes, just in time to see the feral cat bolt like ginger-and-black lightning into the shrubbery, leaving a bewildered yellow Labrador whining over the mystery of a clawed muzzle.

'Oh my god, what was that?' Araminta Hardman turned to see the leaves of the hebe quivering, and no sign of the attacker.

Ezra heaved himself to his feet, carefully setting aside his volume of poetry. '"I cannot bear the noise! For Nature's voice is never loud; I seek for quiet joys",' he quoted solemnly.

Minty stared at him. 'John Clare,' she said after a long moment.

This was a surprise, for them both, each suddenly regarding

the other in a slightly different light. Then Ezra said cryptically, 'Bucca is possessed of a wild spirit.' He crossed the yards between them and examined the stricken dog's wound, then bent and picked some leaves off a small plant, stuffed them into his mouth, and chewed.

Minty watched in a sort of disgusted fascination as he hooked the macerated results into his hand, prodded them into a loose wad, then applied the resultant paste to Boris's scratched nose. Boris bore this strange treatment in good part, even wagging his tail a little.

'That'll stop it getting infected,' Ezra said. 'It'd be better if your fella could chew them himself, since his own spit'll be better for him than mine, but knowing dogs, he'd prolly just eat it.'

Minty made a mental note to get Boris checked out by a vet tomorrow, then remembered that she had not yet signed him up with any local practice; besides which, tomorrow was Sunday, which meant emergency rates. 'What was that you put on him?' she asked, in case he took a turn for the worse.

'Just broadleaf plantain: it'll help un heal. Good to eat, too, if you find the leaves fresh and young. I put 'em in a salad or stir fry 'em like spinach.' He watched the woman's expression change from frank scepticism to curiosity. 'And, if you pick 'em at summer solstice, you can use them for divination.'

Now she laughed. 'It's just a weed.'

'Tis one of the nine sacred herbs, you know: blessed by the goddess.'

Oh lord, Minty thought now, *he's a nutter. I might have known.*

Despite Ezra's laconic disposition, once you got him on a pet subject, he could be surprisingly loquacious. He took her silence as an invitation to continue. 'There's an old tale about un.' He bent and picked another leaf and held it out to Minty, who took it gingerly, turned it over. It was wide and flat, with ribs that fanned out from the stalk. 'You find un everywhere, pressed low to the ground, in a rosette, with its seedhead held high. You can walk on it, take a pony over it, drive over it and still you won't kill un. They say that's because there was a maid in the early times fell in love with a wayfaring man who went on his way, as wayfaring men will. The goddess came upon the girl weeping by the roadside and transformed her into a plantain so she could spread across all the roadways of the world until she found the wanderer at last.'

Charmed despite herself, Minty asked, 'And did she? Find her true love?'

Ezra gave a shrug. 'Does anyone?' He looked away. 'You'll find plantain most anywhere you look: it'd be good to give un another dose later.'

Minty smiled. There was no way she was going to put some dirty old leaves in her mouth. Besides, if Dom came upon her chewing leaves, he'd think she'd found some illicit wild stimulant, and that would never do.

As if the very thought had summoned him, Dominic appeared. 'Was that your cat I saw, dashing across the lane?' he asked without preamble, grinning at Ezra.

'Ar, that'll be Bucca. But no one owns him. He owns himself.'

'Cool,' said Dom. 'I think I've seen him out hunting near our barns in the early morning.'

This surprised Minty, who had no idea her son ever got up before midday.

'Prolly,' Ezra agreed. 'He'm a good ratter.' His gaze slid towards the grotesque remains in the grass.

Minty, drawn to what he was looking at, gave an involuntary little scream, but Dom walked over and stared down with considerable interest. 'Wow, he's eaten exactly half of it.' He looked back at Ezra. 'Do they always eat the head first?'

Ezra loved this question. It was exactly the sort of question people who were genuinely interested in the natural world should ask. 'It's to do with the fur,' he said. 'It grows backwards from the nose, so if you start eating from that point, it goes down easier, with the grain, so to speak.'

Dom absorbed this. Then he said, 'He's chewed the feet off, too. I bet the claws would be scratchy if you swallowed them. Cats are clever, aren't they? Not like old Boris. You couldn't leave him to fend for himself for five minutes: he'd just stuff himself with cowshit and campers' rubbish.'

'That's because dogs have got too far from their natural selves,' Ezra said. 'Time was, they looked after themselves just fine. Most things will, given half a chance.'

'Not in my world, more's the pity,' Minty said with a bitter laugh. Then she added brightly, before her son took offence, 'I see you grow your own food.'

She cast an approving eye over the rows of salad plants, brassicas, beans and tomatoes, impressed by the orderliness of the vegetable plot: she'd expected it to be as ramshackle as what she glimpsed inside the cottage. Still, there was no point in vegetable beds at a holiday let, so they would have to go: visitors wanted a nice lawn they could laze around in, smart tables and chairs where they could sit with a glass of wine as the sun went down. And a barbecue; yes, you could pave the area where the old man had been sitting and build a smart outdoor kitchen there. Solar lights in the trees – she really could turn this into a bijou little haven.

'Ar. Between the garden and the chickens, I do all right.'

She thought she'd heard chickens on her walk down to the road. And the rooster had woken her some mornings. 'Do you eat them?' Minty asked. Meaning, *I suppose you'll have to kill them when you move into your sheltered accommodation.*

Ezra looked aghast. 'Never, no. Just the eggs.'

'I'd love to see the chickens,' Dom said. He looked around.

'Oh, they'm out and about, pecking and scratching.' Ezra thought it wisest to draw the conversation to a close, before the woman could ask about the orchard, and other things. He had seen how she had appraised his garden with a speculative light in her eye and remembered her remarks about his cottage. 'Well,' he said, 'best geddon.'

'Oh, of course,' Minty said automatically, her Home Counties politeness kicking in. 'Come along, then, Dom. Let's get Boris home and see to his nose.' She tightened the lead to the Labrador, who had been sniffing his way towards the half-rat carcass, then asked, 'I say, could you possibly recommend a local veterinarian?'

Ezra regarded her silently.

'I mean, which one do you take your cat to, for his shots and things?'

'Bucca? I wouldn't want to take *he* to any vet.'

Minty looked perplexed. 'But what about for flea treatments and the like?'

'Fleas? They don't seem to bother him much, and if they do, why I comb 'em out for him and apply a little oil of oregano.'

Minty shuddered inwardly, imagining the cottage overrun with fleas, their eggs sequestered in the soft furnishings, in dirty corners, in the spaces between floorboards. They would have to get pest control in when they finally took back the cottage. She wondered if any fleas could have jumped onto her in the time she had been standing there, and suddenly became convinced that she could feel itchy bites around her ankles, around her midriff, down her back. Turning Boris away sharply, she called back over her shoulder, 'Nice to chat to you, Mr Curnow. See you soon.'

But Dom lingered. 'I'll see you at home in a bit,' he told his mother, but the dog had already pulled her halfway to the gate, and she was out on the lane before she remembered she had meant to ask Ezra Curnow exactly when he was moving out.

Dominic Hardman waited till he was sure his mother was out of earshot, then said to Ezra, 'Where d'you get your piff from?'

Ezra frowned. 'Beg pardon?'

'Your ganja. Hash. Pot. Grass. Weed. Wacky baccy…'

The old man narrowed his eyes, then looked away to where he had been sitting. There was no curl of tell-tale smoke from the butt of the spliff he had been enjoying before the intrusion, but the boy must have smelled it when he went to check out Bucca's leftover lunch; maybe it had still been burning down then. Well, there was no point in denying the fact of it.

'Enjoy a smoke, do you?' he asked.

Dom's face lit up. 'Oh yes! I used to grow my own at school! I constructed this geodesic dome in a wild bit of the grounds and grew some in that. It was brilliant!' His expression became wistful. 'But then I got chucked out and we ended up down here.'

Ezra regarded the boy steadily. 'At school, you say?' It was hard to gauge people's ages from the position of his advanced years. 'How old are you, lad?'

'Coming up eighteen,' Dom said defensively. 'Though I was sixteen when I started cultivating my weed.' He paused. 'And selling it.'

'Selling it, eh?'

Dom's eyes gleamed in the bright sunlight. 'Yeah, it was amazing! I made a mint. Could have made a load more if I'd been able to scale up production, but—' He spread his hands. 'Got caught and expelled. Mum and Dad went totally ape.'

Ezra nodded slowly, digesting this. 'I can see they might.' He mulled it all over a bit longer. 'And that's the reason you all came down here and bought Trengrose?'

Dom nodded. 'My parents pretend that's not the reason, but I heard them talking about it at night. They thought it would keep me out of trouble, being in the back of beyond.' He cast his eyes down. 'I miss my friends, though,' he said miserably. 'It's lonely down here.'

Ezra's expression softened. 'I'm sure it is.' He gestured towards his wicker chair. 'Why don't you sit for a while with me?'

Dom took a step towards the chair, then said, 'No, it's okay, I can sit on the grass.'

Ezra took his seat once more and Dom, careful to avoid the half-rat, sat on the ground beside and a little in front of him, and watched in admiration as the old man deftly rolled two small, neat spliffs.

'Really?'

'If you'd like to, and so long as you don't tell your parents. Deal?'

'Deal! It's been ages since my stash ran out. That's how I got to see Bucca hunting in the mornings. I get up before anyone else stirs to have a smoke and take the edge off things before everything kicks off, go and wander round the grounds and the greenhouse and stuff, keeping out of everyone's way. It's been pretty horrid up at the house, with Mum and Dad arguing all the time, and shouting at workers, and people coming in and out, making a big noise and a mess, and no internet or phone signal so I can't even game, or keep in contact with my friends.'

Ezra was, by choice, largely divorced from the modern world, but even he knew how people depended on these invisible forms of communication – you only had to be within thirty yards of the farm shop and hearing Thurza Hockin having a meltdown because they'd lost internet connection and she couldn't put a card payment through to understand a degree of the frustration Dominic was feeling.

And he knew what it was like to be a lonely young man, cast adrift from the rest of the world.

Remembering something Eliza used to say to him, he quoted, '"All shall be well, and all shall be well, and all manner of thing shall be well."'

'I've heard that before,' said Dom.

'Julian of Norwich,' Ezra said. 'A medieval mystic.'

'Shows how much *he* knew,' the boy said darkly.

Ezra smiled. 'She. Julian was a woman, a fourteenth-century anchoress.'

'A sailor?'

Ezra's smile widened. 'On the sea of thought, maybe.' He handed one of the spliffs to Dom and lit it for him, lit his own, took a puff, then at last spoke again. 'They say she shut herself away in a cell in order to comprehend the nature of the universe.'

He let his thoughts roam around the library of his mind till he found what he was looking for.

'"A hazelnut, lying in the palm of my hand, as round as any ball. I looked upon it with the eye of my understanding, and thought, 'What may this be?' And my question was answered generally thus: 'It is all that is made.'"'

'I don't understand.'

Ezra grinned. '"The fool doth think he's wise, but the wise man knows himself to be a fool."'

Dom frowned. This was all a bit cryptic. He let the old man light his joint, took a long draw upon it and waited for the familiar effects to overwhelm him. They did not. He was about to raise the roll-up to his lips again when Ezra laid a hand on his arm. 'No need to chase it. Let it come to you, like a wild bird.'

Dom was beginning to think the old man had given him some duff herbs, when his toes began to tingle, and a gentle heat suffused his body, and then his mind. It was like slipping into a warm bath, one that eased woes and muscles. He felt himself relax, without the usual sense of danger or need, and his frustrations begin to dissipate. Perhaps all *would* be well, one day.

The old man and the young lad were sitting there, together, in silence, perfuming the air with aromatic smoke – Ezra gazing up into the sky, Dom almost in a trance – when a movement amid the undergrowth caught Dom's attention, a movement that became a colour; then a shape, as an animal eased its cautious way out into the open.

A fox – russet, sleek as a twist of flame – blinked its topaz eyes at them.

Ezra, becoming aware of the boy's sudden focus, looked to their visitor, and an expression of bliss creased his wrinkly old face. He put a finger to his lips as he saw Dom was about to say something, and they watched as the animal walked nonchalantly past them, then made itself comfortable in a pool of sunlight a little distance away and, curling its long brush around its body, went to sleep.

'That's the greatest compliment a wild creature can pay you,' Ezra said softly. 'To say he don't fear you and regards you as part of his world.'

Dom's eyes were round with wonder. He couldn't stop staring at the fox, at the graduated fire of its pelt, at the lithe bunch of its muscles, at the graceful curve of its spine, at the long muzzle and delicate limbs; at the alert ears that flicked to let them know it still held them within its sphere of awareness. He had never seen anything so beautiful in all his life – not even Lindy Young's body revealed to him under the moonlight in Hector's back garden during a New Year's party, nor even Boris as a puppy. He had called both 'awesome' at the time, but it was only now that he comprehended the true definition of the word. Having the fox extending its trust to him as well as to Ezra, with whom the animal was clearly familiar, made him feel as if he had been given a gift, as if a magical door into another aspect of the universe had been opened to admit him. It was a gesture of fellowship and love, transcendent, and humbling. He wanted to cry. He also wanted to leap up and dance crazily around. But he sat there, taking in the pure loveliness of the fox, feeling the utmost joy and gratitude for this moment.

After a while, though, he did yelp, for the rollie had burned down to his fingers and his sudden motion of panic made the fox lift its head, then get to its feet and lazily stretch out its front, then its back legs in an exaggerated yoga pose.

With a last glance at the humans, it loped to where the half-rat lay, slyly caught it up between its jaws, melted into the hedge and out of sight.

Dom suddenly burst into tears. Its absence felt like a bereavement, but also a tension he did not realise he had been holding within himself, not just for these past minutes, but these past months, had been released.

Ezra said nothing, did nothing. He just sat and waited until, at last, Dom rubbed fiercely at his face and said, 'Sorry. Don't know where that came from.'

'No shame in it,' Ezra said softly. 'Just proves you're alive.'

Dom sniffed. 'Everyone's alive,' he observed.

Ezra shook his head. 'Not everyone.' Some people were dead behind the eyes.

Dominic took to visiting their neighbour regularly, and not just for the occasional smoke. Most often they just pottered around Ezra's vegetable patch or the orchard, and Dom showed far more interest in horticulture than the old man had expected. He couldn't help but be reminded how he and Arthur had tailed their father around the estate (though they'd been much younger than Dom), poking their heads into potato sacks, learning about all the different types of compost, making nettle and comfrey feeds, asking a million questions. Dom told him about the abandoned orangery, and was surprised when Ezra said, with a small smile, that he knew it well.

Light dawned in Dom's brain. 'Was it you who planted the strawberries and stuff we found growing there when we moved in?'

Ezra looked aside. 'Miss Eliza always did like a strawberry,' was all he said.

'I bet you could grow stuff there all year round,' Dom went on. 'You know, like you do in your greenhouse.'

Ezra fixed him with a stern look. 'I don't think that would be wise at all.' And when it seemed the lad was going to argue, added, 'That glasshouse is special. You should have seen it in its heyday when my da took care of it. Peaches and figs, grapes and melons, oranges and lemons, cucumbers as sweet as apples. In summer it were fair tropical in there. My brother and me used to hide in it and pinch stuff when he weren't looking.' He chuckled quietly. 'Da kept things growing all year round. Between the glasshouse and the vegetable beds, the chickens, the bees and the farm, Trengrose was pretty much self-sufficient.'

'Bees?'

'Come with me.'

Ezra led Dom and Boris through the orchard. Boris tried to chase Daisy and got a good pecking that made him a lot more circumspect around the chickens. They moored the Labrador to a tree a little distance from the hive and then Ezra beckoned Dom to approach with him. He knocked formally three times on the wooden front and said, 'I bring a visitor to the Queen of Trengrose. This here is Dominic, the young master from up at the big house.'

Dom grinned, thinking this a rare old pantomime. Then a bee drifted out of the hive and landed on his hand, making him jump.

Ezra made a calming gesture. 'Let her scent and taste you, then she'll know you and will return to pass the knowledge to her queen and the rest of her folk.'

They both watched as the bee walked slowly across the boy's skin, its feelers twitching. Then, with a flicker of diaphanous wings, she hovered into the air and returned to the hive.

'I thought she was going to sting me,' Dom said softly. 'Dad got stung recently, right on the neck. He made a right fuss about it.'

Something approaching pleasure suffused Ezra's mind. Trust a bee to know its enemy. Then sadness replaced the momentary glee: that small honey bee would likely be dead now, her abdomen ruptured as the barbed stinger remained embedded. He explained this to Dom, who was shocked.

As Ezra absently stroked the roof of the hive, the lad asked when the honey would be ready.

Ezra shook his head. 'I may not take any this year.'

'Why not?' Dom could hardly believe it. 'I mean, it's like farming, having a beehive, isn't it? You're farming for honey.'

'Time was, we had many hives on the grounds, but now there's only this one. Bees are in decline, lad, even here. Those that remain belong to Trengrose, not to me. They're its life and soul. Sometimes, when they have a good year, I'll take a jar or two, but they've had a hard time this past year.'

Dom stared at him. 'But there are flowers everywhere.'

'T'ent that. There's been too much change.' He wouldn't say any more, but those words preyed on Dom.

On the way back towards the cottage, they passed the old bathtub, and beside it a stump serving as a table that bore a bar of soap and a flannel in a plastic bag.

Dom gazed at this arrangement, bemused. Then it dawned on him and he asked, aghast. 'Don't you have a bathroom?'

'This is a very pleasant place to take a bath,' Ezra told him.

'But—' Dom looked around. 'It's outdoors. I mean, anyone could come upon you, it's not very private.'

'Aye, well, it *were* private,' Ezra mumbled. He showed the boy the arrangement of charcoal in the trough beneath the bath, and explained how he heated the water.

Dom picked up a plastic bottle in the grass beside the small table. 'Lavender bubblebath?' he laughed. 'Are you kidding me?'

Ezra said nothing but took the bottle back and set it in its place. 'Here, you may as well take it,' Eliza had said to him. 'I can't be doing with baths at my age.' Then her fingers had closed around it once more. 'Oh, I forgot. You have no bathroom, do you?'

'Not as such,' he'd admitted, but he hadn't let go. He'd had the sense she wouldn't live too much longer. In the end, she'd surprised him by lasting another eighteen months, and he'd kept it unopened till she'd died. Now, the scent of lavender, even artificial, would always be how he remembered her.

'Is all this yours then?' Dom asked.

Ezra's mouth set in a hard, straight line, his wrinkles that bit more pronounced. He didn't say another word till they got back to the cottage.

Dom knew he had crossed an invisible boundary, so he said after a while, 'I don't care if it is or isn't. The orchard, I mean. In fact, it's much better if it is yours, because it's exactly the way it should always be, whereas...' He trailed off.

'Whereas what?' Ezra growled.

Dom squirmed a little. 'Well, if it was ours, it'd get changed. Spoiled. Like the camping field.' He refused to call it 'glamping'. 'Dad would love to build a swimming pool outside the house and extend the grounds into the orchard: landscape the lot.'

Ezra could hear Toby Hardman's tone in the casual brutality of those three words. A man who knew the cost of everything, and the value of nothing, as his father would have said.

'Dad said on the plans the orchard was a "grey area". Don't really know what curtilage means, but he said it's in the curtilage of Trengrose—' Dom went on.

'Everything here is part of Trengrose,' Ezra interrupted. 'It's the way it's always been. But pieces of paper don't make owners.'

Dom looked away. His father was up in London right now, trying to acquire a bit of paper that said it was *all* theirs – orchard, cottage and all. It seemed very wrong, suddenly, that this should be the case, and he found himself hoping that his father would fail in this endeavour. He wanted to go on being friends with the old man, to smoke with him, to see his bees and his chickens, and his mad old particoloured cat, and Merlin the jackdaw, and the magical fox. To have found something worthwhile and then see it destroyed would be too much to bear.

18

Sam and Miranda, both back in London now, met up for a drink in a bar in Soho. It was full of rowdy rugby fans – there had just been a big match which Sam had failed to factor in when suggesting what he hoped would be a suitably modish venue.

It was hard work having any sort of conversation over the noise of the crowd, so they downed their drinks and wandered the West End streets, making small talk, dodging puddles and tourists taking photos of anything that moved.

Ran gazed around – at the neon lights, the theatregoers emerging from their entertainment, at the Cantonese signs, at the edgy boutiques, and yelled into the night sky, 'I love London!' She looked back at Sam and grinned. 'Sometimes, anyway. A bit less so when the rent's due, or I blow my nose and it all comes out black.'

Sam wished he felt the same. It had been a difficult few months for him. He found himself less and less engaged by his course, by the people around him, whose goals and interests seemed so at odds with his own; and now here was Ran, high on city life, just as he was feeling so out of tune with it. But he couldn't say any of this. Instead, he pointed to a noodle bar across the road and suggested they get something to eat.

Under its brutal strip lighting, he scanned Miranda's face. She really was the loveliest person. Her enthusiasm lit up her eyes, and for a while he was content to sate his hunger with the spicy noodles and listen to her talk about bands she had seen, political protests she had been on, about a ground-breaking installation at Tate Modern.

'You really should go! We'll go together – I'd be happy to see it again. Well, not really "see", but experience it. It's by this Cuban artist – Tania Bruguera. She's created a giant heat-sensitive floor in the Turbine Hall. If you lie down with the other visitors to the gallery, your body heat makes these ghostly shapes on the floor, and if enough of you cooperate, you can reveal the hidden portrait of a Syrian refugee called Yousef. Honestly, it's amazing. The artist refers to the experience as "forced empathy".'

Sam tried to form some sort of intelligent response to something that seemed a million miles out of his realm of understanding. Really, he was wondering who Ran meant by 'we', and to his shame, he wasn't entirely sure where Tate Modern was. Art exhibitions had not thus far ranked highly on his agenda for what little spare time he had. But he agreed at once to go with Ran, of course he did. Any excuse to be in her presence, because being with Ran made everything better, made him believe he could weather his course, get through to the end, survive in this inimical city.

'I've got tickets to Chelsea's Europa League game next week,' was all he could offer in return. His mate Will was a steward at Stamford Bridge and sometimes was able to get cheap tickets. 'Would you like to come with me?'

Ran gazed at him, her expression so inscrutable that he had no idea whether he'd been crass, had overstepped, or been in some way an idiot.

'I didn't know you supported Chelsea.'

'Gamps supports them, so I started to because of him,' he said, oddly defensive. He still couldn't quite read her reaction.

He felt his toes tensing against the floor tiles as if they were transmitting flight messages from his brainstem.

'I love football!'

Well, he hadn't expected that.

'Do you? That's amazing.' He gazed at her, even more smitten than he had been.

'Fabregas is just the most brilliant playmaker, and whenever Willian gets the ball, I get so excited: he's so fast.' She paused, then grinned. 'Plus, I love his hair.'

This observation made Sam swallow too hard, and a particularly hot noodle writhed out of his control and slapped him on the chin, raising a welt.

Ran laughed and handed him a napkin, but he felt like a total fool.

Even so, at the bus stop later with the rain pelting down so hard that it bounced back up off the pavement, Sam girded his courage and leaned in for a kiss, his heart thumping. Not only did Ran kiss him back, but when her bus came, she took him by the hand and pulled him onto it with her.

When they went to the match the following week, she turned up in a vintage 2012 Chelsea Champions League winning jersey, with DROGBA 11 printed on the back, and Sam squeezed her so hard she could barely breathe.

The following weekend Ran took him to Tate Modern and he gazed in awe at the immensity of the Turbine Hall. Just being there made him feel he suddenly owned a little bit more of a London he hadn't realised existed, and that was so satisfying he didn't really need anything more out of his visit. But when he and Ran lay down on the floor with all the other young people, he felt as if he were participating in the work of art. And when a powerful low-frequency sub-bass boomed around the hall, rumbling in his bones, the sound filled him up and he began to feel really odd; a bit sad, larger than himself, joined to the other visitors and especially to Ran. Seeing the image of the Syrian refugee revealed made his heart clutch. Another young man a long way from home who had somehow fetched up in London. He realised it was a bit of a stretch to compare himself to a refugee, but still, he felt a degree of commonality with Yousef's displacement. Maybe the city had been a haven for him; but it made Sam suddenly miss Cornwall so much that he almost sobbed.

'See,' Ran said, squeezing his arm. 'I told you you'd love it.'

Toby came storming out of the solicitor's office in a fury. It was the first time he had spoken face to face to the woman in months, and it was clear that he and Philippa Pidcock were never going to be on the same wavelength.

In the end, she had simply spread her hands and said, 'Mr Hardman, I did explicitly warn you that if you didn't manage to acquire a degree of clarification over the matter of the occupied dwelling in the Trengrose grounds before the purchase, your legal position would be weakened by the fact that you had nonetheless proceeded, and by that very action had accepted the matter as unresolved, and very possibly unresolvable.'

At which point, Toby had said something quite unforgivably rude about capitulation, cowardice and easy money, and had barrelled his way out. He stood now on the pavement outside Pidcock, Pratt & Jones on Holborn Lane, trembling, with the sun beating like a hammer on the top of his head, his nose full of exhaust fumes and his ears assaulted by the constant roar of traffic punctuated by car horns and shouts.

He felt – it was pointless to deny it – humiliated. The same way he had felt when caught cheating at a maths test at school by Mrs James.

Toby did not like being told off by women, and this had certainly been a factor in his rage; neither was he looking forward to admitting his error to Araminta, a prospect that was at least as excruciating as it had been admitting the cheating to his parents. He would have to sort it out, and if not by fair means then by foul.

He took out his phone and scrolled through his contacts till he found the one he had in mind. He walked into a doorway, not to be overheard – for this conversation would not be *entirely* above board – selected the number, and waited for his call to be picked up.

19

Ezra had avoided visits from Southwest Water, the electricity company, and others.

Luckily, his ears were still good: he could tell the difference between a car and a van at a hundred yards, and anyway spent most of his time outdoors, so that he was able to see what new torment was coming his way. He watched various service providers slide letters and cards under his door. These serried messages then ended up in the compost bin, shredded and unread, but at least contributing some practical use.

The only one who caught him out had been the TV licensing man. This was because Ezra had been on the loo as the vehicle had approached and the flush had drowned out the sound, so he was greatly surprised when, upon rounding the cottage, bog roll in hand (he couldn't leave it in the outhouse, because of the depredation of slugs), he found a young man walking up his path. Their eyes met: there was no escape.

'What do you want?' he barked.

The lad, who looked barely more than nineteen, given his pimple outbreak and razor nicks, quailed; then collected himself and tried to sound authoritative. 'Mr Curnow? My records tell me you have no television licence.'

'That's right.'

The young man was briefly thrilled to have extracted such an easy confession. 'So you admit you're in breach of licensing regulations?'

'No.'

'What?'

'Ent got no television.'

The young man looked dumbfounded; then his frown cleared. 'The regulations also cover watching the BBC on any other device – a computer or laptop, tablet, or smartphone.'

Ezra's eyes gleamed. 'Ent got none of them either.'

A look of such horror came over the lad's face for a moment that Ezra thought he was suffering some mental health crisis as the whole foundation of his world came crashing down.

'Surely that's just not possible!'

'Calling me a liar, are you?'

'No, not at all. Would you mind allowing me entrance to your property so that I can ascertain that this is, in fact, the case?'

Normally, Ezra would have point blank refused such a request, but he took pity on the youngster. What a crappy job to have. 'Help yourself.' He waved towards the front door.

The licensing man stopped on the threshold to remove his shoes and Ezra chuckled. 'No need for that, son. Just be careful not to tread on the cat.' He paused. 'Unless you fancy a trip to hospital.'

The visitor's face froze in panic and his eyes darted left and right, scanning the tiny quarters, taking in the threadbare rug, the well-worn furniture, the ancient range, the oil lamp, the utter lack of modern amenities. No television. No laptop, tablet or smartphone on view; just a book of poetry splayed face down on a knackered occasional table, beside a half-empty mug of coffee. And, in the gloom beyond, a dark puddle of fur punctuated by two hostile golden eyes and the merest sheen of bared fang.

With a yelp, the boy backed out again, almost cannoning into Ezra, who felt a tiny twinge of guilt, but not for long.

'Oh my god, it's like... going back in time. I... I had no idea anyone lived like this.'

'Pity they don't,' Ezra said placidly. 'Seems to me there'd be a deal less trouble in the world if they did.'

Bucca came to stand at the old man's ankle as the TV licensing lad fled the scene. Ezra bent to stroke the cat's head.

'Another one seen off, eh? I wonder who's been sending these folk my way?'

This was, of course, a rhetorical question.

Unusually early one morning, a man with a clipboard turned up at Ezra's door before he'd had a chance to escape.

The old man opened it warily. 'Ar?'

'I wonder if I might step inside, Mr Curnow.'

'No, you may not.'

Ezra stuck his feet into his wellies and joined the suited man outside.

'Nice little place you've got here,' the man said, smiling insincerely.

Ezra waited for the fellow to identify himself and tell him the reason for his unexpected appearance. Never trust a man with a clipboard, he thought to himself.

The visitor seemed unflummoxed by the old man's hostility: he'd been warned about it. 'So,' he looked down at the form on the top of his pad, 'just a few questions for you to answer, on behalf of the local council. Firstly, sir, we can find no record of you having ever paid council tax for this property. Indeed,' he paused, running his finger down the page, 'I don't appear to be able to find this precise address listed in our records.'

'And what address would that be, precisely?'

'The Lodge, Trengrose House, Trengrose Lane, TR19 6X—'

'En't no such place.'

'Could you please tell me your correct address and postcode, then, sir?'

'Nope.'

Ezra pulled the door shut behind him, put his hands in his pockets, started to whistle a few bars of 'Trelawney', walked past the bemused official, out of the gate, across the widened lane and into the trees on the other side. He kept on walking till he was in sight of the layby where a dull grey boxy vehicle had been parked, close to the new sign. He watched as the disgruntled-looking official got back in the grey car and drove off in the direction of Penzance. Then he walked down to the junction, took out his penknife and went to work on the 'Glamping' sign.

20

It took over a week for the reason behind the campsite's decline in passing trade to become clear. After the novelty of seeing her handiwork every time she drove into the lane, Minty had become blind to it, and in the end it was Toby who spotted the amendment when she picked him up from Penzance station.

'Clamping?' He craned his neck to look back at the sign as Minty swung the car into the lane and they rumbled past the lodge cottage.

'What?'

'Clamping. It says "Clamping", the sign. I thought you said you painted it yourself?'

'I did. And it most certainly does not.' Minty had clear muscle-memory of the paintbrush swooping that looping G.

'Stop the car.'

Furiously, Minty slammed the brakes on, selected 'park' on the automatic gearshift, flung the door open and stalked down to the junction. When she saw the subtle vandalism, she gasped, then swore.

Toby joined her. 'Some stupid little toerag. I'll call the police.'

Minty rounded on him. 'Are you joking? You think they don't have anything better to do than react to a minimally vandalised sign?'

He held up his hands. 'Okay. Just repaint the sign, no big deal, right?'

So she repainted the sign.

Minty was at the top of the house in her new study, which was finally equipped with the luxury of internet. She had made a habit of escaping to this little haven to get away from the chaos downstairs, and from her husband, who was driving her nuts with his booming Skype calls with clients and colleagues. This was where she came to watch ASMR videos that calmed her when she felt herself getting stressed. She had moved on from the simply sensory variety – rain falling, leaves rustling, fires burning – to more visual pleasures: painting walls, cleaning floors, pressure-washing filthy carpets, anything that achieved a clear goal, an obvious improvement. There was nothing Minty liked better than a Before and After comparison.

Lately she had become addicted to watching beauticians applying their skills to cleaning out pimples, feeling a cathartic rush of satisfaction as their instruments extracted blackheads that looked just like maggots, hardened debris like grains of rice, or even extravagant excrescences like Mr Whippy ice cream out of blocked pores. Her toes braced with tension as the beautician applied her tools to the afflicted clients' faces, and she felt instant relief as the debris was extruded almost as a sexual release. Much like sex, it felt shameful. (Minty had never much enjoyed sex: it was too messy, and left marks on the sheets.)

'Minty?!' Toby was roaring for her.

'Someone at the door. I'm on a call!'

She pursed her lips, closed the laptop lid and ran two flights of stairs... in time to hear the crunch of gravel as a car reversed and then headed for the lane. On the steps outside the front door was a cardboard box. Minty bent to examine it. There was no label, and the vehicle she had seen driving away had not been a Royal Mail van. Frowning, she picked it up and took it into the kitchen, where Toby was sitting at his laptop, chortling away, with his feet up on the table. He hadn't taken his shoes off.

Minty gave him a hard stare, then thumped the box down beside him, ripped the tape off the top of it, opened the cardboard flaps and stared in. Then she screamed.

'What in god's name was that?' came a voice through the laptop speaker.

Toby turned a furious face to his wife. 'I'm trying to have a meeting here, do you mind?'

Minty had backed away from the table until her back was up against their enormous refrigerator.

'So sorry,' Toby said to the client. 'Can you hang on a moment while I sort this out? Minor domestic crisis.' Both men laughed, as if domestic crises were faintly amusing.

Toby rounded on his wife. 'What the hell's the matter with you?'

She pointed wordlessly at the box.

Sighing theatrically, Toby leaned across to stare into the carton. For a moment he looked bemused, then he looked closer, did an almost comical double-take, and let out an unmanly squeak. 'What did you bring that in here for? Get it away from me!'

'I didn't know what it was!' Minty protested. 'Someone left it on the doorstep, then drove away. I thought it was a delivery...'

'Who the hell would deliver a dead cat to us?' Toby ran a hand through his hair till it stood up like a cockatoo's crest: he looked demented.

'I don't know!' Minty wailed. 'You didn't run a cat over somewhere, did you?' Her husband's driving could be aggressive.

'Of course I didn't run any cats over. Who do you think I am, Jack the Ripper?'

'Jack the Ripper didn't...' She thought better of the correction and, mustering herself, closed the box up with a shudder, then took it outside and put it back on the steps.

When she went back into the kitchen, her husband was back

on his Skype call. 'Some dead cat...' Toby was saying, and the client chuckled loudly.

'Made some enemies down there already, have you?'

The two men guffawed.

'Horse's head in the bed next!' Toby joked, his equanimity apparently restored.

Minty glowered at the back of his head. Clearly he was going to be no use at all in sorting this out. She retrieved the handset and went into the now-elegant drawing room, with its moss-green walls, restored cornicing and re-tiled fireplace, to sit on one of the off-white velvet chesterfields with her iPad. Scrolling through the Google entries, she found the listings she needed and called the first number.

All this first call rendered was a bolshie woman who offered no helpful information and cut the conversation short. Did people down here have no manners?

When she explained her predicament to the second respondent, they asked, 'Can you bring the cat in? It'll cost around £135 for the cremation, depending on what sort of container you'd like for the ashes.'

Minty explained patiently that it was not her cat, that someone had left it in a box on her doorstep.

'You must think I'm a mug!' the person at the other end said. 'People claim this sort of nonsense all the time to try to get out of paying to have their pets disposed of.' And they put the phone down.

Seized by righteous anger, Minty dialled the next number and repeated her enquiry. This time the person on the other end of the line listened, then asked if the cat had a collar, or any unusual identifying marks.

'I don't know!' Minty wailed, then calmed herself. 'I'll go and have a look.'

She went out and opened the box. Now that the initial shock had passed, she could see the inhabitant was an elderly tabby. Tentatively, she parted the lustreless fur at its neck. No collar, but whoever had placed the animal in the carton had clearly done so tenderly, for it was arranged carefully on a folded tartan blanket, and a felt toy mouse had been placed between its paws. But if this was a beloved pet, why had it been abandoned on a stranger's doorstep? It made no sense.

Minty went back inside, wiping her fingers on her jeans, and retrieved the handset. 'No collar,' she reported. 'Quite an old tabby cat, by the look of it.'

The vet was very nice but understandably unable to identify the animal or owners from such sparse information.

Minty thanked the vet, replaced the handset on its base and went back into the kitchen, where Toby had finished his Skype meeting and was hammering out emails. He had never come to the realisation that modern keyboards required only the lightest of touches. Light touches were not Toby's style, and he had wrecked laptop after laptop, first erasing the keys, then wearing them to breaking point. She knew how that felt.

'No one knows whose cat it is,' she said after a while. 'And no one wants to take it off our hands and dispose of the body.' She stared meaningfully at Toby's forehead until, reluctantly, he raised his eyes to hers.

'What do you expect me to do about it?'

'There will be a spade among the workmen's things,' she said, gesturing in the direction of the outbuildings. The builders were waiting for materials to arrive, or she'd have asked one of them to do the job. 'Just... bury it somewhere out of the way.'

'I'm busy,' he retorted, 'earning money to keep this bloody roof over our heads.'

Minty's eyes narrowed, and her lips firmed into a straight line. With an exaggerated sigh, Toby closed his laptop, pushed back his chair and got to his feet.

He buried the cat, cardboard box and all, in a shallow grave on the edge of the lane, among the soft earth where the big pine's stump had been dragged out, and congratulated himself on his quick thinking at saving himself more back-breaking work. Even so, the effort brought him out in a sweat. He patted the earth down, placed two stones on top to mark the spot.

Dominic, looking out of his bedroom window, saw his father stalking purposefully towards the trees with a spade in his hand, and for one irrational moment wondered if he had finally murdered his mother and was about to conceal the body.

Days later, Minty was watering the terracotta pots of tumbling pelargoniums outside the house when an orange streak caught her eye, disappearing into the dark eaves of the trees. Curious, she put down the watering can, and went to investigate. By the time she reached the lane, there was no sign of whatever it had been, but a putrid smell hung in the air. She walked a little further and then gasped. Amid a tumble of displaced earth lay a leg. A tabby leg and hindquarters, complete with tail.

Araminta Hardman turned away, retching, then fled back to the house.

21

Over the course of the next few days, two further cartons appeared mysteriously at the bottom of the steps. One contained a dead white rabbit; the second the corpse of a small black poodle.

Minty stood in the hall, wailing. 'What is happening to us? It's like being in a horror film!' She burst into tears.

Toby, at his wits' end, tried to console her, but she pushed him away.

'Just sort it out!' she yelled at him. 'Because if another dead animal turns up here, I'm moving into a hotel!'

That afternoon, a shiny Audi came crunching up the drive and pulled to a halt in front of the house. Toby, who had set up a work station at the window as a lookout for precisely this purpose, immediately leapt to his feet and was out of the house before the motorists had even managed to exit the vehicle.

The couple emerged slowly, looking forlorn. When they saw Toby barrelling towards them, they straightened up, making an effort to smile.

'Eliot's in the back,' the woman said, her voice catching. 'I wonder if you could help me to move him?'

'I rather did my back in getting him in there,' the man said ruefully. 'Bloody three-door cars, eh?' He paused, then added, 'He's quite a lump, the old boy.'

The woman sniffed fiercely.

Toby came down the steps with thunder in his heart. 'Why are you here?' he demanded.

The man looked perplexed, then gestured towards the car. 'For Eliot, as we discussed earlier.'

'No one has discussed anything with me,' Toby said grimly. Glancing past the man's shoulder he caught a glimpse of pale fur on the back seat, the shape of some large creature.

'For a woodland burial,' the woman added. 'You said to bring him this afternoon.' She spread her hands. 'So here we are.'

Toby began to feel as if he was going mad. And if he wasn't, *they* were. 'No one has telephoned me,' he reiterated. 'We don't do woodland burials. Why would you think such a thing?'

'But Betty and Julio had their Bluebell buried here,' the woman said tremulously.

'And Clarice and Mel recommended you,' the man added.

'I know no Betty, Julio, Bluebell, Clarice or Mel!' Toby rumbled. 'And we don't bury anything.'

'Aren't you the pet cemetery?' the man asked, bemused.

'No, we bloody well are not.'

'But that's what the sign says.'

'What sign?'

'At the entrance to your drive.'

'It most certainly doesn't!'

'It does...' the woman started. She looked to her husband.

The man said, 'Perhaps there's another property served by the lane, and we missed a turning? I'm awfully sorry to have bothered you if so.'

'No, this is our lane,' Toby enunciated slowly. 'It's the lane to Trengrose House.' He indicated his imposing dwelling place. 'There are no other properties along here, so please take Eliot and kindly bugger off.'

'But—' the man began, but the woman, furious now, caught his arm. 'Come on, Rory, I don't want this horrible man laying a single finger on Eliot.'

And they got into the Audi and drove slowly away.

Toby stomped back up to the house, grabbed his car keys, and drove the Range Rover down the lane so fast that he caught up with the Audi as it reached the junction, coming so close to its back end that he could see the panic in the driver's eyes in the rearview mirror. The Audi slid out onto the main road at such speed that it almost hit a van coming the other way and there was a cacophony of horns.

Toby pulled into the layby, leapt out of the vehicle and ran back to the entrance to his lane. And there, instead of the 'Trengrose Glamping' sign his wife had so carefully painted, was a different sign entirely.

HAPPY PAWS PET CEMETERY

it read, followed by a phone number and the instruction, 'If we're not in, please leave your beloved animal on the steps. We're only ever moments away'.

Toby ripped the sign down with such force that he broke the post. The glamping sign lay in a bed of nettles just to the side. Swearing as the ferocious plants stung him, he retrieved it and propped it awkwardly against the broken post. Yet another job for the builders when they returned tomorrow. Then he stuffed the 'Happy Paws' sign into the back of the Range Rover and took it roaring back to the house.

Minty heard her husband bellowing into the phone. Going into the hall, she could see that he was red in the face and his free hand was balling and unballing with pent-up violence.

'Why the hell is your sign stuck on our signpost?'

Pause.

'What? Oh. Trengrose House.'

Pause.

'Yes, we're your neighbours.'

Pause.

'No, I agree, this isn't the ideal way to make one another's acquaintance...'

Minty's gaze lit upon the discarded signboard, and everything fell into place. She tugged at her husband's arm. 'Just say sorry to them, and that we'll drop the sign back to them and say hello properly,' she informed him sharply.

Fifteen minutes later, she found herself on the steps of Happy Paws House, handing over the errant sign.

'Sorry it's a bit battered; my husband pulled it down with rather more force than was necessary. It has been a rather difficult few days, with people leaving dead animals all over our property.'

The couple who ran the pet cemetery were what Minty knew Toby would refer to as 'a pair of old hippies'. The man, who must have been going on seventy, had a huge, grey-blond handlebar moustache, a bald pate and a long ponytail, and his petite wife wore multicoloured woollen tights with a pair of lime-green boots, her waist-length brown hair the startling orange that comes only from the over-application of henna. Once she had got over her surprise at their appearance, Minty found them delightful – funny, irreverent and kind. They all laughed about the mix-up. 'Probably some local lads, having a laugh,' Stella offered.

'It seems a rather cruel joke to play on bereaved pet owners,' Minty said.

They pressed welcome gifts upon her – home-made herbal teas, flourless chocolate cake and a bottle of 'last year's sloe gin' – a virulent-looking purple liquid that she tried, and failed, to refuse.

As an afterthought, as they said goodbye, she asked, 'What can you tell me about our mutual neighbour, Mr Curnow?'

The couple looked confused for a second, then Stella said, 'Oh, you mean Ezra? He's a darling. We love him to bits.'

'An absolute trooper,' Max added enthusiastically. 'Proper salt-of-the-earth, tough-as-old-boots Cornishman.'

'To your knowledge, has he always lived in The Lodge?' Minty asked.

'The what?'

'The property at the end of Trengrose Lane.'

'Oh.' Stella looked perplexed. 'We've always called it Ezra's Cottage.'

Minty smiled thinly. 'I guess that rather answers my question.'

22

The Furnivals had driven down from Leamington Spa that day, a trial that had involved a fiendishly early start, since they had had to drop off Letty, their Maine Coon cat, at Juliet's mother's on the way. This had added a good forty minutes to their journey, as well as a great deal of psychological stress, since Letty had resisted their efforts to stuff her into the cat carrier with every fibre of her not inconsiderable being, drawn blood, and had then howled and hyperventilated the whole way. With two fractious children in the back – Marcus, ten, and Clover, eight, one of whom was intermittently carsick, and the other generating loud bleeping noises and explosions on his game console – by the time they finally crossed the border into Cornwall, then endured horrendous nose-to-tail traffic all the way down the A30, got lost and missed the Trengrose sign (unsurprisingly, given that it wasn't very visible, being propped up at barely knee-height against a broken signpost), everyone was in a very bad mood indeed.

Their spirits rose, however, once they had been shown to their adjacent glamping pods – a small one for the children and a much larger and more luxurious space for their parents – unpacked and had a cup of tea, which they brewed without incident on the efficient butane stove supplied as part of the field kitchen.

The children wandered around the campsite, investigating possible animal burrows, and were fascinated by the herd of grazing Friesians in the adjoining field which, curious about their visitors, mooched over to examine them.

'They're so big!' Clover was awestruck. 'Do they farm cows for their eyelashes?' Their mother never went anywhere without wearing a full set of false lashes. 'Do you think that's where Mummy gets hers from?'

Her brother screwed his nose up, then grinned. 'Yeah, they come complete with cows' eyeballs.'

Clover was appalled. 'No they don't! They just harvest the lashes and new ones grow back.'

Marcus scoffed. 'You're so gullible. Who the hell would remove cows' eyelashes one by one? That'd take ages. They just cut them off the dead cows at the abattoir.'

His sister burst into tears. 'I hate you! You spoil everything!'

Clover was so distraught that it was decided that an early night was called for, so after a meal of hotdogs and an apple (well, at least the apple was a healthy choice and surely the tomato sauce and onions counted towards their five-a-day, Juliet told herself), the kids were packed off to bed, and their parents sat outside their pod with a glass of wine and counted their blessings.

There were just a couple of tents at the other end of the field, and an elderly couple called Phil and Ruby in the next pod over who were drinking cocoa (they knew this because they'd been offered some). But other than that it was pretty tranquil, and Juliet could feel the tensions of the day – so long and fraught – drain slowly out of her. This was also helped by the fact that there was no mobile signal, so she wasn't tormented by endless glamorous Instagram photos of Rhia and Felix on holiday in the Caribbean, or James and Pippa eating their way across Tuscany. She could relax. They had got to Cornwall, the kids were asleep, and they had a week of paradise ahead of them.

She and Ben had another glass of wine (a rather good Rioja), and then he leaned in and whispered to her, 'Fancy a smoke?'

Juliet's gaze darted to their children's pod. All was silent. She grinned back at her husband. 'Go on, then.'

Surreptitiously, Ben lit up one of the joints he'd so carefully rolled yesterday in anticipation of this occasion, took a long draw on it and passed it to his wife. They giggled, feeling transgressive, like naughty teenagers. The buzz of the weed on top of the Rioja was quite something.

Juliet leaned back in her deckchair and wiggled her toes, blissfully at ease. This was exactly what a holiday should be – a new experience, a proper escape from everyday life.

Ruby and Phil had packed up and gone into their pod, so now it was just her and Ben and the stars, just like the old days when they'd gone on camping holidays to Pembrokeshire and Snowdonia, walking by the sea and lazily making love for hours. It wasn't just her toes that were tingling now.

She shot a sideways glance at her husband to see if he was feeling the same vibe, and that was when she saw it.

Out of the corner of her eye, a dark shape, but not just dark – something large, black and white and... terribly *wrong* – caught the moonlight and moved quickly out of view. Juliet's head whipped around, trying to locate it. 'What was that?' Her voice sounded squeaky.

'What was what?' Ben barely moved a muscle, just sat there with the end of the spliff burning down, looking contented.

'Something just there.' Juliet pointed into the darkness. 'Something big, really tall. It moved weirdly.'

Ben sat up. 'I can't see anything.'

Juliet interrogated the darkness around them, then shook her head. 'Maybe I just imagined it.' Perhaps it was the weed. It did have an odd effect on her sometimes, could make her a little paranoid. But she'd never hallucinated before.

They each took a final puff and Ben put out the stub carefully: it wouldn't do to set fire to their glamping pod, not on the first night.

There was a rustle, followed by a strange rattling sound, and then something ran out of the darkness towards them.

The air was split by a high-pitched scream that Juliet realised was not her own, so therefore, much more frighteningly, must be Ben's, and she felt a breeze on her face and the thing's weird head clacked at her, and then the figure was gone, vanishing among the trees.

Ben leapt to his feet, his face as white as bone.

'You saw it then?' Juliet whispered hoarsely.

Ben nodded. 'Holy shit,' he managed at last.

'It looked like a massive skull...' Juliet's voice faltered. She waited for her husband to laugh at this ludicrous statement, or at least to correct her, but he did neither.

Not much sleep was had that night, by the Furnivals or by their neighbours, the elderly couple who had come out to see what was going on after hearing Ben scream and had packed up and left first thing the next morning, having decided the place had a peculiar aura, which did not make Juliet feel any better.

She decided to walk up to the farm shop where the campsite owners had told them they could get all their essential supplies, to restore her sense of reality and rightness in the world, and was relieved to find it open, and well stocked with all manner of delicious and wholesome goodies. A solidly built man bustled around behind the counter, chatting as he did so to a wiry old gentleman in a holed Guernsey sweater, cord trousers and a pair of wellies. The latter tipped his head to Juliet with what she thought of as old-fashioned courtesy, and said, 'Marn.'

Processing this quickly, she managed to reply, 'Oh, good morning,' before taking a basket and browsing the shelves. At last, she approached the counter again and waited for the bustling man to return so that she might order some of the items in the chiller cabinet beneath the till.

'Staying at the campsite?' the elderly gentleman asked as they waited.

'Oh, yes,' Juliet replied. 'It's very nice.'

'Had a good night's sleep, then?'

'Well...'

The old chap raised an eyebrow encouragingly.

'I mean, the beds in the pods are very comfortable, but there was this odd thing, in the night.'

'Ar?' He leaned in conspiratorially.

'You'll think I'm mad. But I saw this... well... apparition.'

'Apparition, you say?'

'It was horrible. Big and tall and, well, floaty, but then there was this...' She darted a look towards Bob Hockin, but the farmer had his back turned and was stacking bread into baskets on the shelves a distance away. 'It had this big white head. Like... like a skull. Not a human skull, either. It was much, much bigger than a human skull.' She made a face. 'I know, it sounds crazy, doesn't it? But it clacked. The skull, I mean. The jaws went up and down and it clacked its teeth at me, and then it disappeared into the night.'

The old fellow nodded slowly. 'That's not good,' he said. 'Not good at all.'

'What do you think it was? I'm not going mad, am I?'

'Not mad, no. I think...' His voice lowered. 'That field there, where they got the campsite, it's said to be haunted by the shade of Ol Penglaz.'

She repeated the name questioningly, then asked, 'But what is it?'

'Nobody rightly knows. Some call him Old Greyhead. He's a figure out of legend that often appears in the form of a giant skeletal horse with a swirling black cape that comes out when the moon is high. I've heard it said that those that see Ol Penglaz... well, let's say he don't bring luck.' He straightened up. 'So you take care of yerself, bird, and hope you don't see him again.' He paused for effect. 'Trouble is, once he's seen you, he'll remember you.' And he tapped his nose.

Juliet looked aghast. She took the items out of her basket and replaced them one by one on the shelves where she'd found them. Then she said a hurried goodbye to the old man and fairly pelted back down the hill.

Ezra watched her go. He felt mean to have spoiled her holiday, but he had to hold his nerve. One battle didn't win a war. He finished his conversation with Bob, gave him back the key to the barn where the Golowan and Montol guisers' costumes – including the mast-oss known as Penglaz – were kept, and loped back down the lane towards his cottage. One of his shoulders was aching: he rolled it back and forth to ease the muscle. That old horse's skull was damned heavy: he should have remembered he wasn't a young man any more.

The door to the big house opened at long last, and a harassed-looking woman, very slim and neat and rather Sloaney, to Juliet's judgmental eyes, in tailored shirt, jeans and smart sandals, stood before her.

'Can I help you?'

A posh accent too. Juliet felt her hackles rise. She summoned up her best telephone voice: two could play at that game. 'I would like my money back,' she said.

'I'm sorry?'

'You *should* be sorry. That field is *haunted*.'

Minty frowned. 'What, the glamping field? Haunted? How do you mean, *haunted*?'

Juliet explained what had occurred the evening before, though carefully avoiding any mention of recreational drugs. 'We didn't get a moment's sleep, we were so spooked. And then when I went up to the farm shop this morning, I was told that what I'd seen was—' she quoted with her fingers, '"the shade of Ol Penglaz".'

'I don't have the first idea what that might be,' Minty said icily.

'It's a giant skeletal horse, a legendary figure, that's what the gentleman said. And he also said that once it had seen you, it would never forget you, like a curse or something. So you see, we can't possibly stay.'

Minty narrowed her eyes at the woman. It sounded like a put-up job. 'I'm very sorry that you haven't had a good night,' she said carefully. 'But I'm afraid I can't just hand out refunds on the basis of curious stories. We're trying to run a business here.'

'Well, perhaps don't situate your *business* on a haunted site?' Juliet suggested furiously.

'Honestly, I'm sure it's not—'

'We're moving off it today: I'm not staying here another bloody night. And,' she pointed an aggressive finger at Minty, 'if I don't get my money back, you'll be getting the sort of review on Tripadvisor that will put off anyone else even thinking of booking your so-called glamping pods.'

Reluctantly, Minty gave in. She still thought the woman was pulling a fast one, 'Ol Penglaz' functioning as a self-administered hair in the soup, but they couldn't afford bad publicity when they were starting out.

She watched the Volvo exiting the glamping field sometime later, then walked up to the farm shop to chide Bob Hockin for his unhelpful fabrications. Honestly, the resident Cornish really did resent incomers, she could feel it. Resented them having the money to buy a place the size of Trengrose; resented them renovating it, even though it had fallen into rack and ruin. Sometimes, she thought they would rather see their entire heritage fall down around their ears than suffer 'foreigners' coming across the Tamar and throwing their ill-gotten money at the problem. She was quite sure that attitude would have been different if they'd been wealthy local types: old farming stock, county aristocracy. There was, she had observed, a sort of feudal mindset down here – Tory counsellors, Tory MPs; not to mention the entire Duchy of Cornwall thing.

She sighed and marched up to the counter.

Twenty minutes later she was out again, and none the wiser. Bob Hockin swore blind that he didn't know what Minty was on about, and although his tone was polite, his expression was stubborn, and in the end, Minty decided that a good relationship with her neighbours was more important than getting to the bottom of this particular mystery.

23

If Toby Hardman had ever read any Greek mythology, he would have taken one look at his wife, who had pulled her hair out of her bun with such force that her curls snaked out in an angry mass, immediately thought of Medusa, and felt suitably terrified. But he hadn't, and didn't, because when confronted with an inconvenient truth (in this case, that Minty was the one shouldering all responsibility here at Trengrose), rather than reflect that it might have been his behaviour that had caused the spousal meltdown, he went into denial, and then on the attack.

'I'm the one financing this family at the moment!' he raged. 'Of course I have to be up in London most of the time: that's where I work.'

'But we have internet now. You can FaceTime and Skype clients.'

'Online chats don't get them all fuzzy round the edges and willing to trust you the same way a three-hour boozy lunch at Hawksmoor does.' *Followed by an evening watching the girls gyrating at Platinum Lace*, he thought, but did not add.

Minty sighed aggressively, since years of passive-aggressive sighing had got her precisely nowhere. 'For god's sake, Toby, we hardly ever see you! Who had to sort out engineers when the heating system failed? Who had to deal with the glampers' cancellations after those weird events in the summer? Me, that's who. I had to calm them down and arrange refunds and get the negative reviews taken down from the website!'

'To be fair,' Toby pointed out, 'it was Dom who sorted out the website.'

'Well, he shouldn't have had to! Someone's playing us for fools, and they think they have a free hand because you aren't here to see them off.'

'Do you think if I were in residence you wouldn't have locals terrorising the campers? What do you think I'm going to do about it, patrol the grounds with an AK-47?'

Minty glared at him. 'I think you don't want to be here at all. It was just a great big lord-of-the-manor fantasy for you, and now that it's happened, and throwing up all sorts of real-world problems, you just run away and leave me to deal with them.'

Toby's face flushed a deep and dangerous red. 'Run away? I've never run away from anything in my life.'

'How about when I found out about you and your so-called account manager – bloody Chrissie – and you swanned off to bloody Hong Kong!'

'That trip had been planned for months—'

'You ran away and hoped all the fuss would have died down by the time you got back six weeks later.' Her voice rose to a screech. 'Six weeks! Who goes to Hong Kong for *six weeks?*'

'Someone handling a very big and delicate multi-million-pound contract!' Toby yelled back. 'For Christ's sake, Minty, you were all right about it at the time, why are you having such a go at me now?'

'Believe me, I haven't forgotten or forgiven you for any of it,' Araminta enunciated furiously.

Toby scowled at her. 'You think I like being stuck up in the city, living in a broom cupboard on my own, working round the clock? This place is costing a bloody fortune. It's never going to pay its way at this rate. At least if we can get the old bastard in The Lodge out we can do the place up, flip it quickly, and fill the coffers a bit. Property is going for a small fortune down here at the moment.'

'What, now you want to sell it off? I thought the whole idea was to give Dom a project.'

Toby looked mulish. 'Circumstances change.'

Minty gave him a hard stare. 'Have you got the title sorted yet? What about your meeting with Philippa Pidcock? Didn't you tell me it was all in hand?'

'It *is* all in hand. These things just take time.' He felt aggrieved, glanced at his watch. 'Look, I'm going to get on my way now, rather than drive up tomorrow. Get a good night's sleep and an early start in the office.'

Minty made a sound that started as a growl and ended as a banshee wail. 'You see? Running away again! Don't you DARE go anywhere until you've had a proper conversation with the old man and found out exactly when he's going!'

In a sort of frenzy, Toby made a terse phone call and a little while later drove into Penzance, parked with difficulty at the top of Causewayhead (these damned parking spaces were too narrow!) and went into the handsome, domed bank in the centre of town where he had made an appointment. Fifteen minutes later he was stomping back up towards his car with a purposeful expression and a black neoprene laptop case clutched tightly to his chest, head down against the driving rain.

By the time he approached the entrance to Trengrose, the rain had gone to mizzle. Toby pulled into the layby just before the turning, got out and closed the car door furtively, then padded past the restored glamping sign and up to the gate of the lodge cottage. The old man's wellingtons were by the front door. Toby's eyes gleamed. Got him! He lifted the latch on the gate, strode up the path and rapped on the front door.

Silence.

He knocked again. 'Hello!' he called. The old codger was probably deaf. He raised his voice. 'Are you in there, Mr Curnow?'

Still no answer. Toby moved around the side of the cottage to peer in through the kitchen window, pressing his nose so close to the pane that his breath blossomed on the glass. It took a while for his eyes to adjust, but when they did, he could see that there was no one in the living area. He waited, trying to decide what to do. He couldn't disappear up to London before he'd had a conversation with the old man. Minty was exceptionally talented at knowing when he was lying. His gaze roved over the dingy interior. He could see from a dull glow that the stove was lit, one of its iron doors being slightly ajar. On top of the hotplate sat a fat copper kettle of the sort only ever seen in antique shops and junk markets. His eyes scanned for modern appliances, but he could see no toaster, no microwave, no fridge. Did the man even have electricity?

A wave of almost-pity washed through him. His grandparents had once lived in similar circumstances in a tiny, terraced house in Rotherhithe, cheek by jowl with the neighbours, all of them just getting by. He remembered his pride at being able to move them out of their slum and into a smart new flat in one of the modern low-rise blocks. How joyfully he had shown them the gleaming utility room, complete with washer and dryer, where once they had only had a mangle; the pull-out larder and built-in fridge-freezer.

When his granny had burst into tears he had beamed benevolently, only to hear his grandfather, arm around her for comfort, say, 'Don't take on, Eunice. I know it's not what we're used to. It's all very modern. But it's a very generous gesture.'

And she had warbled, 'But I'll miss the neighbours! What if I never see them again?'

For a moment Toby had felt rage at her ingratitude. His father had taken him aside. 'They'll get used to it,' he said. 'But it's a whole new life for them. That's a lot to get your head round when you're as old as they are.'

People generally didn't much like change, but Toby rather despised those who couldn't adapt. 'Survival of the fittest' was his maxim; grab your opportunities and keep moving. Working in the City hadn't encouraged him to develop much in the way of nuance or empathy. People who dug their heels in when faced with altered circumstances were obstinate and obstructive, unevolved. Like Ezra Curnow.

His eye was caught by a flicker of movement, and a figure emerged through the doorway on the far side of the living area. Toby ducked away from the window, slipped around the side of the cottage and once more knocked on the front door, as if he had just arrived.

This time, the door opened, and he found himself almost nose to nose with his antagonist. Toby took a polite step back: sometimes you needed to move backwards in order to move forward. He forced his contempt for the pathetic old git away and managed an insincere smile. 'Good day, Mr Curnow. I hope you're well, despite this rather soggy weather. If you have a moment I have a proposition for you, one I think you'll find both welcome and generous.' And he unzipped the laptop bag, bent down and placed it in the space between them as gingerly as if it contained a bomb.

It might as well have done.

Ezra Curnow stared at the wads of banknotes within the bag and then back up at Toby, who held up a hand.

'Now, before you say anything, let me explain what I have in mind. There's five thousand pounds in there—' (this was not strictly true, since Toby had skimmed three hundred or so off the top, thinking it highly unlikely the pensioner would be counting it out there and then), 'and it's yours right now, no questions asked, if...' he paused for effect, 'you agree to vacate The Lodge within the month. And then I will – cross my heart,' he made the gesture, 'bring you another 5K to seal the deal. Ten thousand pounds in all, to leave this—' he waved his hand at the meagre dwelling, and only just managed to stop himself uttering the word 'hovel', 'and find yourself somewhere much more comfortable. A nice little place in Penzance, maybe? Coffee shops right outside your door, cafés, supermarkets, a church – if that's your sort of thing. All mod cons, right? I could even,' he tapped his nose confidentially, 'back you up if you were to tell the council you'd been evicted and made homeless: then they would be duty bound to rehouse you, and you'd be quids in!'

He waited expectantly, scanning the old man's face for a reaction, but the Cornishman's expression was stony.

A moment later Ezra bent to pick up the bag, and Toby's heart leapt. It was going to be that easy! Why hadn't he done this in the first place? Of course, he had no intention of giving the old wretch another penny once he had cleared out, but he was happy to play the part of kindly benefactor for now.

But then, suddenly, unbelievably, the money was tumbling all around him – mostly in blocks still bound by the elastic bands the bank teller had placed around them in the private room behind the counter, but some rebelliously breaking their bonds and fluttering gaily around the scrubby little garden, settling in puddles, on and under bushes, and even in the old man's wellies.

For a moment Toby stood rooted, shocked to his bones. Then compulsion kicked in – *the old bastard had thrown the money away!* – and he found himself running around, scooping up notes here and there, getting smeared with mud and god knew what else.

Ezra watched the rich man's antics, contempt swelling inside him like a hot air balloon until at last it burst right out of his mouth.

'You can take your filthy money and stick it where the sun don't shine! I ent got no use for it. This is my cottage, as it were my father's before me and his father's before him, and to me it is beyond price. You can't buy birdsong, or the sight of your bees visiting your own flowers, or the sun through the leaves of the apple trees, or the smell of ripe tomatoes you've grown from seed, or the knowledge that the old Cornish range that warms you and the cat that has chosen to share its life with you has been there since the cottage was built, maintained with love and care and a sense of history and continuity, and every time you light it you think of your father telling your mother "at home by the fire, whenever you look up there I shall be – and whenever I look up, there will be you" – that's a quote from a book which I'm sure you haven't read by the way – and you eat your meals at the table that your grandfather made, into which he carved his and Gram's initials…'

Breathless, Ezra stuffed his feet into the wellies with some violence, feeling bits of paper crumple beneath his soles, which felt like a small, grim victory. He straightened up.

'People like you don't understand the value of anything which doesn't have a price-tag. You think everything and everyone can be bought, that you can snap your fat fingers and people will dance to your tune. Well, I got news for you, you great tuss: your money means nothing to me. Ten thousand pounds? Do you know nothing about Cornwall? Even if I were tempted by your "generous" offer,' he curled his lip, 'it wouldn't profit me anything to take it. I heard what you said about renting out my cottage to emmets: what was it, fifteen hundred a week? So what you'm offering here is less than a couple months' rent, since near all the houses down here is gone to rent to bleddy tourists. And if there was anything going for a long let it'd be no more than a one-room flat in a dingy block in some rundown bit of town. No view, no garden, no nature, no soul, no history. I got no use for coffee shops and cafés! Just a place to die quietly out of your sight, that's what you'd like, ent it? All of us inconvenient "peasants" to stop spoiling your view.'

He watched Toby chase down the last of the errant bills and laughed bitterly.

'You bought up all the old cottages, all the places with history and soul, and stripped it out of them, made 'em over like London houses and then added a bit of Cornish "charm" – seashells that ent never seen a Cornish seabed, wooden seagulls on sticks, glass fishing floats no fisherman has ever used; sea urchin lamps from China; and called 'em stupid names like Mermaid's Flippers and Ocean Froth and Holibobs Cottage and Frolicking flaming Dolphins. Pushed all the prices up so there's nowhere locals can afford to live. Soon you'll have the whole county to yourselves and no one to do your cleaning or grow your food or repair your roads or collect your bins or patch up your wounds or catch your fish or mend your bloody enormous great cars. And maybe then you'll learn your lesson and see that you've poisoned everything you touched. But then you'll just sell whatever you got to some bigger fool and go destroy somewhere else!'

Ezra stood there panting as if he'd run a marathon, chest heaving, the final words uttered so hoarsely they were almost inaudible. Almost.

Toby bent to pick up the laptop bag to stuff with the money he held cradled to his chest – at the same moment that Ezra launched a classic 'up and under' at the bag.

Foot and face collided catastrophically. Toby Hardman's teeth met with a crunch, and he suddenly found himself lying on his back, staring into the rain-dirty clouds, wondering if he had died, then realising he hadn't because he was in so much pain.

He lay there, stunned and disoriented, and was just about mustering the will to try to move when his vision was obscured by feathery blackness, and something light but scratchy landed on his forehead, pricking his scalp. A pale-blue eye – far too close – regarded him with what seemed calculating interest, and a wicked-looking beak came sharply into focus.

Toby mewed in terror and suddenly found he could wriggle (that was good, then – no spinal damage) even as his more primitive reflexes were telling him that some fearsome predator was about to eat his eye.

'Come along now, Merlin,' someone was saying, 'have some mealworms instead: much more wholesome.'

And then the monster was gone.

Toby scrabbled backwards and pushed himself into a sitting

position. Warily, he investigated the damage to the throbbing red planet that was his head. He worked his jaw, palpated his cheekbone and chin, ran his tongue over his traumatised teeth. Amazingly, he seemed to be in one piece.

Ezra Curnow stood over his fallen foe like some ancient spirit of place, crowned by the jackdaw, Merlin. He watched as Toby Hardman got to his feet and stood, swaying a little, looking exactly like a man who had been booted in the face. Ezra thrust the laptop bag at him, which he had retrieved and filled with the spilled banknotes. There had been a brief temptation to pocket a few of them, before disgust at the very idea had kicked in: bad enough that he actually had to touch the tainted stuff, but so much worse if he were to take any of it, which would render him in some degree complicit in the filthy bribe.

'I don't want your money, or anything to do with you,' he enunciated with grim clarity. 'Get off my property and leave me alone.'

Toby Hardman had, for a wonder, complied. But as Ezra latched the gate behind him, he growled, rather indistinctly, since his face was beginning to swell, 'I'll make you sorry for that, you bastard. Now, it's war.'

Ezra watched him go. War, eh? He didn't think a soft city man like Hardman knew much about war. But Ezra himself? That was a different matter.

24

CYPRUS 1957

Ezra and Arthur's troop was driven up out of the coastal plain into the foothills of the Troodos Mountains. A relatively benign landscape gave way to a sort of bleak majesty as the road switchbacked up tree-clad hillsides, passing villages clinging to the rock faces, or cradled between verdant strips of almond and carob, pistachio and olive. They stopped in a village, and a girl with beautiful dark eyes ran over to offer them fruit and flowers from her basket. Arthur gave her a coin, and suddenly they were beset by clamouring children flourishing handfuls of nuts, onions or cigarettes, pulling at their sleeves, chattering in Greek, '*Kopiaste, kopiaste!*'

'What are they saying?' Arthur asked.

Only Corporal Hollis spoke any Greek. 'It means come with us, share with us. Lying little bastards: you can't trust any of them. They'll lure you away and their big brothers'll be waiting for you in a back alley.' He paused. 'Or their big sisters.' He made a lascivious gesture. No one liked Hollis: he was sly, with a nasty sense of humour and a mean streak, but he had been in Cyprus since '56, so added necessary experience to the group of rookies.

'Back in the truck!' Sergeant Gunn barked.

Arthur looked down at the flower the girl had pressed into his hand: a perfect marigold. He sniffed it. 'Da plants these in between the tomato plants to deter whitefly, dun he?' he said to his twin.

Ezra concurred. 'Don't know how much good it does. I like the smell of 'em though, bitter and earthy. Smells like Cornwall.'

Thinking of Cornwall made Arthur go weak at the knees. Carefully, he tucked the flower into his top buttonhole.

'For your little sweetheart?' Baps teased, leering at the girl who had sold Arthur the fruit.

'Sweetheart? He's a married man. Got wed just before we went for training, left her with a bun in the oven.'

Arthur's face went very still at the mention of Gwen. He wanted to punch Ezra; but at the same time, he didn't want to make a scene, especially in front of the children.

Baps punched him lightly on the arm. 'There's a good lad,' he said approvingly. 'Didn't hang around, did you?'

The camp outside Platres on the slopes of Mount Olympus was even more basic than the Polymedia camp. Standard rations were meagre, and largely unappetising: the tinned sausages came out square and skinless, the tinned bacon was so salty it was barely palatable, though the steam puddings and custard were okay. Ezra and Arthur were able to find and identify edible plants and were skilled with rabbit snares, both of which supplemented the rations and increased their popularity.

Their first covert watch-and-report operation was to keep an eye on a remote village on the far side of the mountain that was reputed to be an EOKA terrorist hotspot. 'Keep out of sight, don't get caught, give me a sit-rep,' their commanding officer Captain Smart (known, predictably, as Thicko) ordered. 'There's only one road up to there, and I want to know who comes in and out – got it?'

Sergeant Gunn picked his squad: Ezra and Arthur, Tubbs, Ashes, Tails, Alphabet, and Corporal Hollis, because he spoke the language.

They climbed the western flank of the mountain then trended eastwards, following animal tracks through the cover of trees until they came to a position above the village they were to surveil, and before nightfall were in their LUP – lying up position. Three hours on, three hours off, in teams of four; two pairs of binoculars, one crotchety radio that kept losing signal and was not to be used at night, and about a million insects that got in their eyes, ears, mouths, clothes and absolutely everywhere else. The ground was hard, hot by day and cold at night; Sergeant Gunn was a tough taskmaster, and Hollis was worse, constantly taking the piss out of Ezra and Arthur for their bumpkin accents and country ways. They were not much enjoying their first taste of 'action'.

Movement in and out of the village was minimal. People walked the streets and went out into the fields and groves, but nothing seemed out of the ordinary, despite the defiant displays of Greek flags, and EOKA slogans around the village.

Hollis translated for them:

ENOSIS AND ONLY ENOSIS.
LIBERATION OR DEATH.
BLOOD WILL BE SPILLED!

'Yeah, *your* blood, scum,' he muttered.

On Monday market day, things got busier. Men on donkeyback, boys carrying sacks or driving livestock; women come to shop in the square. A motorbike appeared, sending up plumes of ashy dust. Tails was sent to track it as it disappeared on the far side of the settlement, but came back to report it was propped against the side of a house where the rider seemed to live. However, they could all tell that out of nowhere there did seem to be more young men around, with their gaunt cheeks and huge moustaches. Gunn radioed back to Platres to report their sightings and was informed that they had picked up word of a village wedding. That there was also intel that General Grivas had been spotted, but it was just a rumour, and they hadn't been able to confirm the information with a reputable source, and though it seemed unlikely that the general would risk such a dangerous sortie so far from his usual stamping ground, they couldn't help but feel exhilarated at the prospect.

Ezra whistled. 'Imagine, capturing the head of EOKA!'

Ashes said, 'We'd all get medals!'

Taking turns with the binoculars, the patrol watched more people arrive. 'Not many women,' Alphabet noted. 'You'd think if it was a wedding there'd be more women.'

But shortly afterwards a cart came rolling up the hill into the village, drawn by a mule and driven by a grizzled man in a beret. It was brimful with flowers – boughs of almond and orange blossom – and Arthur could almost smell it from where they lay in wait: honeyed and heady, and just a little dirty. In the back of the cart, crowned with a garland of flowers, was a girl. They all fought over the binoculars. She was lean and laughing, with tangles of long dark-blonde hair and a white smock-dress that did little to hide her shape.

'Lucky bridegroom. I'd give her one,' Hollis said appreciatively.

'Now then, Corporal: respect for the local women, and all that.' Gunn sat back, resting the only other pair of binoculars on his thigh. 'Perhaps it's a wedding after all, then.'

The cart trundled off towards the other end of the village, but although they did not see where it stopped, by the time it came into view again, the girl was no longer aboard.

Sergeant Gunn made a decision. 'Some of us will track that cart, see where it fetches up: the rest will make their way down a bit closer to the village and monitor what's going on there. Twins, you can do bird calls, right?'

'Yes, sir.' Ezra was eager.

'What sort of birds are there round here? They all look like LBJs to me.' Little brown jobs. The troop laughed.

'Oh, there are all sorts!' Ronnie 'Tails' Tailor piped up. The twins had been educating him as they went and he had developed a passion for bird-spotting, to the extent that no one trusted him with the binoculars.

Arthur said, 'Most are the same as back home, sir – buzzards and kestrels, blackcaps, ravens, robins, goldfinches, chaffinches, jays, jackdaws, magpies; but then there are black redstarts and hoopoes and shrikes and black-headed buntings and crested larks and—'

Sergeant Gunn held up a hand to cut him off. 'Just pick one distinctive call, right?'

Arthur whistled an eerie flight of notes. 'Warbler, sir.'

Hollis snorted. 'Wouldn't catch my attention, that.'

Ezra offered a blackbird's alarm call, and then a kestrel's piercing cry.

'That's the one,' the sergeant declared. 'And what about at night – not that it's likely, since we're only going for a recce, but just in case?'

'Plenty of different owls around, sir,' said Arthur, who found it astonishing that people didn't notice such things. 'And this…' He uttered a musical tumble of sound. 'Nightingale, sir.'

'It's not the Royal Opera House: let's stick with the owl. Twin Two, Ashes and Tails, you come with me. Tubbs, Alphabet and Twin One, you're with Hollis. Two calls for something untoward; respond with a single call.'

Hoisting their packs, the sergeant and his patrol picked their way carefully along an animal track heading further east, till they disappeared between the rocks and trees. Hollis and the rest spread out and made their way down the hillside, keeping one another within signalling distance. Meadows and citrus groves reached upwards from the village and as the slopes steepened, these gave way to acacia and myrtle, and then to pines and scrub similar to the landscape in which the patrol had been holed up these past few days.

The sun was dipping as they crossed a dried riverbed full of tamarisk and prickly jujube. Birdsong and the chirring of crickets was loud here: Arthur worried that if he were called on to sound an alarm it would go undistinguished from the ambient noise. They moved together to settle behind a fallen tree that gave a view through the cloaking trees to the main square of the village, where men in loose plaid shirts and baggy trousers stood in groups, smoking and chatting, or sat outside the two cafés, no doubt drinking ouzo or coffee. Children rough-and-tumbled in the streets, and a group of boys kicked a ball around in a patch of ground. But there was something wrong: Arthur felt his skin prickle.

'I don't like the sound of those birds, sir,' he said to Hollis, plucking up his courage.

The corporal stared at him. 'I thought you yokel-types were keen on wildlife.'

Arthur tried not to let his annoyance show. 'It doesn't sound right, sir.'

Hollis sighed but he listened, then shrugged. 'Nope, no idea what you're on about.' But Tubbs said suddenly, 'They sound afraid.'

'Yes!' Arthur was relieved. 'There's something going on down there.' He pointed a little way down the slope and to the left, where the low-spectrum light limned the outlines of an acacia grove.

Hollis sighed. 'Alphabet, you're reasonably light-footed. Go with Twin One here and check it out.'

Keeping the trees between them and the mule cart, Sergeant Gunn led Tails, Ashes and Ezra up the flank of the mountain, beneath a waterfall that burst out of the cliffs, and into a stand of pines. The mountain reared up, thrusting its bald, craggy head into the sky. They were forced to drop down onto a goat track when the trees ran out and by the time they were able to move east again, there was no sign of the cart.

'Bollocks!' Gunn swore.

'It's unlikely that cart would get this far up,' Ezra said. 'We'd have heard it. It must've turned off somewhere down there.'

They dropped down again until they hit a viewpoint that looked down over the east side of the village and saw, far off, the cart, heading towards an isolated whitewashed farmhouse. The ground was too open for them to follow it without being seen. The sergeant adjusted the binoculars. 'They're unloading the flowers,' he commented. 'Perhaps it is just a bloody wedding after all.' He sighed and handed the binoculars to Ezra, who refocused them, then said, 'Look: there's an orange grove just there—' He pointed down the hillside where tiny white blooms punctuated the glossy green leaves. 'Wouldn't it be easier to cut those boughs rather than transporting them all the way up the mountain?'

'Perhaps they had to bring the bride, so they brought the flowers too. Might just be a tradition, like our Maying Queen,' Tails offered.

Ezra shifted his focus. 'Unloading them from the cart, and not that carefully.' He looked to the sergeant, who took the binoculars back and brought them to bear.

'That's odd. Hold on—' He refocused once more. 'Looks like guns under there!' He turned to Ezra and Tails, his eyes gleaming in the light of the setting sun. 'Better call the others.'

Before he had gone a dozen paces, Arthur knew what they were going to find. The cries of the birds had become louder and shriller, and they could hear their wingbeats disturbing the still air. And within a few more steps, he swore he could hear voices. 'Get down!' he hissed to Alphabet, but the soldier just stood there, mouth gaping at the sight of a dozen or more birds – blackcaps, robins, warblers, even what looked like a golden oriole, his first sighting of such an exotic species – stuck by their feet to sticky rods or caught in nets strung among the trees, flapping desperately and crying out in fear. Then he let out a yelp that fell into an unfortunate momentary lull in the bird-noise.

Suddenly three figures appeared between the trees, carrying sticks and sacks. Seeing the two British soldiers, rather than turning and running away, they came charging at Arthur and Alphabet. The first of them clubbed Alphabet to his knees before he'd had a chance to go for his weapon. Arthur didn't have time to whistle the alarm call, so he just yelled, and launched himself at one of the youths, taking his feet out from under him as he'd been taught, then twisting and hitting him with a powerful uppercut till he went limp. The other two villagers were on top of Alphabet, raining blows down on him.

Arthur dragged a net out of the trees and threw it over them, tangling their arms. One escaped and ran off, but then suddenly Hollis was there, smashing the man on the head with a rock so that he fell bonelessly, without sound, clearly unconscious; maybe dead.

The third villager lay tangled with Alphabet, winded and panting, trapped in the net as thoroughly as any of the little birds, his frantic thrashing only making matters worse.

Hollis knelt and said something to this prisoner in quiet Greek, holding a knife that glinted in the gloom, and Arthur realised with a start when the captive replied in a tumble of unintelligible syllables that it was a girl. In fact, it looked a lot like the girl who had been in the cart, lanky and brown-limbed, dark-blonde hair under a cotton scarf; though up close she looked younger, maybe only fifteen or sixteen, he thought from the grand age of his own nineteen years.

Hollis pulled the net away and got her off Alphabet, who scrambled to his feet, looking bruised, dishevelled and embarrassed.

'Go and finish the other one off,' Hollis ordered. 'Can't have him raising the alarm.'

Alphabet and Arthur exchanged a horrified glance.

'But, sir, he's unconscious, and unarmed—' Arthur started.

'I'm sure you'll both be delighted to explain to the high-ups how you managed to be overcome by unarmed youngsters.'

'I'll do it,' Arthur said quickly, and ran to where the lad he had knocked out lay among the acacias, spattered now with guano from the birds trapped above; they were still shrieking out in panic as their feet were stuck in whatever foul gum had been smeared on the poles and branches. For a moment, rage came over him. He almost wanted to kill the villager for this barbaric practice, for the suffering of the little creatures. Instead, he knelt and, after ascertaining that the boy was still alive, untied the bandana he wore and wrapped it tightly around his mouth, knotting it carefully so that it did not restrict the nostrils, then returned to the sergeant. 'He won't be making any more noise, sir.'

'Good lad,' Hollis said approvingly. He looked down at his captive. 'She said they came to net birds to make *ambelopoulia* – some traditional dish made with songbirds.'

'For the wedding?' Arthur asked quietly.

'Special guest, I reckon.' The corporal looked triumphant. 'Really special guest, maybe.' He resumed speaking in Greek, and Arthur made out the word 'Grivas' among the babble, and the penny dropped; but now the girl wasn't talking any more, just staring at Hollis with big, dark eyes. 'Come here, Twin One, hold her down for me.'

The corporal began to undo his belt buckle: it was obvious what he was about to do.

Arthur backed away, appalled. He didn't want any part of this. 'Just going to check on the other one,' he said desperately, though there was no need: the man's skull was halfway caved in. He felt like doing the same to Hollis. Perhaps he should…

He strode quickly away before he could give in to the urge to murder his senior officer, glancing back to see Alphabet, who appeared to be crying, holding the girl's arms while the sergeant positioned himself over her gloatingly, like a hawk mantling over its prey. The visual image triggered a thought, and an idea came to mind: he could stop this! He formed his lips to make the kestrel call they had agreed on, but just as he was about to utter it, a piercing cry sounded from the other side of the mountain, hung in the air for a couple of seconds, and then was followed by another, and then a third. Arthur shivered, feeling his brother's thoughts trembling on the sound: it felt uncanny to him.

Hollis's head came up. His eyes looked like black holes, barely human.

'Alarm call, sir,' Arthur said, unnecessarily.

'I'm not fucking deaf.'

Alphabet let go of the girl. He wouldn't meet Arthur's eye, but pushed himself to his feet and took off running back up the slope to where they'd left Tubbs and the equipment.

Hollis stared at Arthur. 'Go on, get after him.'

Arthur just looked at him. He couldn't leave Hollis with the girl: he couldn't. A challenge swelled between them; and then suddenly the girl writhed like a snake and, catching Hollis off-guard, got a knee sharply up between his legs so that he crumpled, groaning, retching, and she was off down through the trees, fleeter than one of the native goats, vanishing into the falling darkness.

There was nothing to be done about her: she was gone. Hollis caught Arthur by the arm. 'One word about this and you're dead, you hear me?' He was a big man, menacing, tough; he had experience, and though he wasn't much liked, Arthur knew whose word officers would take. He nodded once, feeling self-loathing.

Hollis caught up with Alphabet before they reached the fallen tree; and from his body language, Arthur could see he was intimidated by the corporal; he wouldn't say a thing anyway. He was implicated.

They found Tubbs waiting, looking scared, laden with the radio and as much kit as he'd been able to carry, and together they headed east, trying not to twist an ankle or fall in the dry river gulches as darkness came for them.

★

On the other side of the mountain, Ezra floated a little owl's *'kiew kiew'* into the night to guide the rest of their patrol in, and it was answered by Arthur.

Before long, Hollis's troop was joining up with Sergeant Gunn's contingent, and the sergeant called in the information back to Platres that activity in the village suggested a guest of some importance was staying, based on the corporal's report of a young man trapping birds in the acacia grove.

'But don't worry, sir, he won't be talking, will he, Twin One?' Hollis tapped his nose and held Arthur's gaze, daring him to say more.

'No, sir.'

'Good lad.'

'That's right, outside Agros, on the eastern track,' Gunn said into the receiver, then listened to the response, and cut the connection. He turned to the troop. 'We're to make our way down the hillside and hole up somewhere we can watch the farmhouse.'

Before dawn flooded the area with its apricot light, the farmhouse was surrounded by British troops from the Troodos camp. There was a brief, fierce gun battle in which five EOKA militants and a cart full of weapons were captured. Captain Smart was happy to take full credit for a successful operation. But if there had been a 'special visitor', there was no sign of him, even after the farmhouse and the village were searched. Smart, knowing his reputation as a hard man, put Corporal Hollis in charge of questioning the prisoners; in turn, Hollis selected his team, including the twins.

'Now the real fun begins,' he declared with relish.

Ezra grinned, envisaging pints of Mansfield Bitter; but his brother frowned. 'What sort of fun?'

'It's our job to find out what they know. They're tough men; proud. They won't give up Grivas easily. That's where a bit of imagination comes in handy. You lads have shown the makings of good soldiers today. Tomorrow we'll start interrogating the fuckers; then we'll see what you're really made of.'

25

November 2018

With the glamping season well and truly over, it should have been the perfect time for Araminta Hardman to get to grips with her writing project, but life kept getting in the way. First, there was a problem with the drains, which she only realised when a terrible smell filled the house, and fouled water backed up in the downstairs loo. In panic, she had run to fetch Toby, who had simply stared in disgust and said, 'What do you expect me to do about it? I'm not a bloody plumber!'

A bloody plumber had been called – at exorbitant emergency rates, since it was, typically, a Sunday – and had spent several hours trying to fix the problem. 'These old places with no mains drainage – the cesspit can get overwhelmed, especially if you don't empty it regularly, or if you put stuff down the loo that you shouldn't.'

Minty had stared at him. 'What do you mean, "no mains drainage"?'

The man had seemed surprised. 'Should have shown up on your survey,' he said. 'You're too far off the beaten track up here: your waste goes into a cesspit a little way from the house. I pulled a load of stuff out of it that shouldn't have been there, including a load of wood shavings and chicken feathers. But it'll need to be emptied, and repaired – there's quite a significant crack in it, and I'm afraid the contents are leaking into your camping field.'

She was aghast, and even more shocked by the size of his bill, which she put under Toby's nose. 'You didn't even get a survey done when you bought the place? It's got an ancient cesspit and no mains drainage.'

Her husband shifted uncomfortably, shrugged. 'I'm not really a details man, darling: that's your area of expertise.'

She had an almost overwhelming urge to do him violence. It had taken weeks and six thousand pounds to deal with the problem, and she just couldn't stop thinking about how their bodily waste had been seeping into the field for months and months and months. The chicken feathers were a bit of a mystery, though.

And to top it off, her project at Misbourne House had been encountering all sorts of issues, too – the usual final fix irritations with electricians not showing up on time and the decorators waiting around or having to rearrange their schedule. Alexei had not been happy about the delays: and Alexei Antonov was not a man you wanted to disappoint. She'd had to take on a few other design projects – the sort of fiddly, lower-paying jobs she would never usually have bothered with – in order to maintain cash flow.

All this had detracted from her Civil War book. Even when she found some time, she just didn't seem to be able to settle to it. Something about it wasn't grabbing her imagination; the seventeenth century felt somehow too removed and unknowable. Even though she'd read dozens of books on the period, she couldn't seem to gain any purchase on either her subject or characters. Truth be told, her family members appeared to have been rather dull: not the flamboyant Royalist cavaliers she had imagined, but minor gentry with no scandals and no daring tales, even apocryphal ones. Perhaps, she reflected grimly, she just wasn't cut out to be a writer, and should stick to interior design.

She bent to her task once more, but now found the position of her chair wasn't quite right: if she stretched her legs at all, her toes butted up against the side of the drawers, but if she pulled the chair back, it was too far away from the desk to be comfortable.

With a growl of frustration, she hauled at the davenport. Just a couple of inches should do the trick. God, the thing was heavy! It didn't help that she had laden it with stationery; lovely, pristine little notebooks with marbled covers that she had found in the bookshop in Penzance, all thus far untouched because she had barely even used the big Moleskine, but having started to write in it felt duty bound to continue until it was full, leaving the pretty notebooks as a gift to her eyes. There were stacks of loose paper littered about, too: for letters and printing; envelopes, paperclips, pens, pencils, a ruler for her to-do list; stamps, wrapping paper, Sellotape. No wonder it weighed a bloody ton.

Damn. The thing just wouldn't budge. She pulled out one of the two larger drawers and tried again, but it was still too much for her. Should she call Dom for help? The idea of going downstairs, knocking on his door, and waiting interminably while he either deliberately ignored her or simply didn't hear her through his headphones was enervating.

Minty reapplied herself to the problem, removing the other big drawer. Now at least she was able to get a good grip on one side of the davenport – but all it did was skew a few millimetres and drag off some of the paint she had so lovingly applied to the floorboards.

Enraged now, Minty removed all the other drawers, large and small, till just the frame of the wretched thing remained, a baleful wooden skeleton. 'Sorry, sorry,' she said, patting it, then felt absurd. It was just a desk.

She levered it up a little and slipped paper under each of its feet one by one, and finally managed to pull it out from the wall without ruining the floor. Now she was knackered. She sat back on her heels, then allowed herself to tip over backwards onto the rug so that she could stretch out her back. God, there were cobwebs up in the beams! She'd have to deal with those as soon as she'd repainted the scrape on the floorboard, or she'd never be able to concentrate.

She was just raising herself onto her elbows when her gaze fell on the underside of the stripped davenport. It looked damaged; askew. Had she broken it? Panicking, she pushed herself up onto her knees to examine it, pressing her hands up against the underside of the desk. Nothing seemed loose, but the left-hand side was definitely lower than the right. Funny how she'd never noticed that before. Crabbing beneath the frame, she ran her fingers around the edges of what felt not like a breakage, but a discrete wooden unit with a sort of small, flat metal roundel on the front edge. When she pressed it (how could she resist?) she was rewarded by a click and the tiniest sensation of movement.

Oh goodness: a secret drawer! It was like something out of a gothic story! Minty manoeuvred the drawer gently, and it glided smoothly on its invisible mechanism and eventually into view.

It was shallow – more of a tray than a drawer – and in it lay an object. She lifted it out. It was a notebook, a bit smaller than A4, with a dark-blue marbled cover, remarkably similar to the miniature faux-Victorian versions she had bought in Penzance. Opening it, she found it was full of beautiful copperplate italic script.

A deep shiver ran through her, and she pressed her hands down onto the pages, as if by osmosis, she might absorb its contents before they fled.

The flyleaf read:

Catherine Rosevear-Glynn

in fine, black ink. The hyphen and the 'Glynn' appeared to have been added in a bolder penstroke, followed by

Trengrose House
Penwith
Cornwall

'Oh my goodness!' Minty said aloud. Catherine Rosevear: the portrait in the hall, the woman glancing back over her shoulder with that knowing, rather judgmental look. And this was, what? Her diary? A journal?

She looked for a date. There was none.

Flicking forward, she read:

I love Trengrose dearly, but upon occasion the darkness of the winters and the emptiness of this big house oppress me. Elsie, with her rheumatism, complains all the time, and Matty is worse than no company at all, for she cannot hold any conversation beyond details of the weather or the daringly contrasting lapels on the dress Mrs So-and-so wore to church last week. I have got into the habit of setting my own fires of a morning, for if I did not, they would doubtless find me one day frozen to death in my own drawing room.

Knowing that J is close is my soul's ease, though I know I should not depend on him so greatly.

Well! This was quite intimate in tone. She wondered who 'J' might be. Such poetic emotion in those three words 'my soul's ease'. She turned pages of prosaic notations of bills due and accounts paid, columns of figures and mundane entries, till she came to:

Captain Henry Glynn came calling again today. It is pleasant to share a cup of tea with such a gentleman, but I fear my heart does not leap as I have read it should at the sound of his carriage wheels coming up the drive. Neither do I become all of a dither and worry about the state of my hair as women seem to do in novels. We have agreeable conversations about the wider world, about our government and its frailties, the suffrage movement and industrial strikes. He was at first visibly surprised that I should take the least interest in such matters, but we have progressed beyond that unhelpful preconception and now enjoy some lively discussion. His visits do break the monotony of these winter days and I have not discouraged them. Perhaps I should.

Minty smiled. A gentleman caller; a captain, no less. That sounded promising, though the words 'agreeable' and 'perhaps' gave little hint of passion. But then, her eye snagged on:

I can hardly write today for fear my emotions will wash away the ink in my journal. Indeed, I shall not commit my misery to paper: my heart may never mend.

Had Catherine fallen in love with this Henry Glynn, only to have her heart broken? How faithless men could be!
Minty felt her heart beating faster and read on.

I have accepted Henry's proposal, yet even within hours of doing so I find myself wracked with indecision. It would be good for Trengrose to have a master again, after the sad loss of my father so many years ago. I have done my best for the old place, as have my trusty estate managers, but maybe stronger hands than mine should now take the reins.

A proposal! Minty grinned; then frowned. A proposal, but not received with a thrill of delight; rather, one angled towards the good of the estate. That Catherine should be considering marriage as an economic prospect spoke of Victorian times, or Jane Austen novels.
There was a fair bit about the farm and the upkeep of the house:

Maintenance of the house must be carried out: we lost tiles in the last storm, and there is damp and rot to be addressed. It is not for lack of income, for the estate remains productive, but there is no one but myself to organise repairs, for it would not do to entrust my estate manager with overseeing work in my living quarters; and the handymen who come to carry out work here take small notice of my opinion as a woman but talk over me as if I have suddenly turned invisible.

Poor Catherine, to be left alone (bereaved?) in charge of so much, feeling overlooked and underestimated. Minty bridled at the thought of the workmen not paying attention to her, felt a small rage building inside her as she remembered how one of the carpenters had talked over her while the kitchen was being reconstructed, even going so far as to consult Toby about a questionable measurement – as if Toby would have the slightest understanding of such details!

She read on.

Little wonder that the suffrage movement is gaining force. Poor Emily, such a courageous act, leading to a terrible death. Matilda brought me the Daily Sketch with its graphic account of the poor woman's violent demise. 'Right or wrong she had the courage of her convictions and gave her life for the vote.' I was struck by that, for as a rule the newspapers are less than charitable in their accounts of suffragette exploits. However noble the cause, though, I cannot help but imagine the terror Emily must have felt as those hooves thudded down upon her.

Minty read this entry again. Then she went to her laptop, Googled 'Emily suffragette death' and read the Wikipedia account of Emily Davison's death at the Epsom Derby after she had walked out onto the racetrack and was hit by King George V's horse, Anmer. It had happened in June 1913, and with that she had a date for the diary entries, and possibly for the portrait downstairs. Edwardian, rather than Victorian. Feeling a sudden boost of energy, Minty selected one of the little marbled notebooks from the drawer, took it to her reading chair and went back to the beginning, making occasional notes as she went.

Although Henry's name appeared intermittently, it was always in the context of practical matters: repairing the trap before Sunday service in Paul, or the reception of visitors. There did not appear to be many lines dedicated to Catherine's marriage – Minty read carefully back and forth to make sure she hadn't missed anything. Was her interest prurient? She would have expected to find some sort of entry about the wedding, the tenderness shared between bride and groom, Catherine's delight or shock following their first conjugal night together, but it seemed the writer had not entrusted such intimate details to her journal. Minty's own wedding had been a beautiful service at a village church outside Amersham, followed by a reception in a smart hotel. The best man had got falling-down drunk and passed out in a bed of hydrangeas, and Toby had nearly started a fight with a waiter. She didn't recall anything much about their wedding night other than that the mattress had been uncomfortable and that Toby had snored. Hardly details she would have chronicled for posterity – but surely Catherine's wedding had been more momentous?

Jottings about redecorating Trengrose House Minty read with interest, noting that the drawing room had been repapered in the spring of what must have been 1914, since there was also talk of gathering primroses from the local hedges to place in jugs around the house; and after that some mention of calving and the '*spreading of muck on the grazing fields for sweet summer grass*'. How she wished Catherine had been more specific in the details about the colour schemes she had chosen for the redecoration. Minty had chosen a deep moss-green for the drawing room, and some extravagantly expensive but extremely beautiful hand-painted wallpaper, giving the room the luxurious feel of a place to which to retreat, where elsewhere in the house she had chosen a palette of historic greys and paler greens. The style of the drawing room felt to Minty, somehow, authentic and fitting; but really, it would have been wonderful to know how Trengrose had looked a century ago.

Reading on, quite out of nowhere, she came upon a cryptic entry declaring, '*I can hardly breathe for joy!*' But with absolutely no context or explanation. What could have inspired such an ecstatic declaration?

A couple of pages further on came the stark exclamation: '*Today we have declared war on Germany!*'

Minty didn't need to look that date up: 4th August 1914.

Now the entries came thick and fast. Captain Henry Glynn had been summoned to the barracks at Bodmin and then deployed with the Duke of Cornwall's Light Infantry to the Western Front. The diary revealed the writer's natural concern for her husband's well-being, mentioned letters referring obliquely to his active engagement. A bit of Googling suggested to Minty that Henry might have been involved in the Battle of the Marne. There were references to the receipt of letters, which unfortunately had not been kept with the journal; but Minty was surprised to find that the bulk of the entries that followed had to do with the running of the estate, down to feed costs and the sale of livestock at the local cattle market, the quality of the milk and cream produced at their dairy, and how she had fought to keep her staff at Trengrose, since so many young men were leaving to join up. She wrote: '*I cannot lose J! I think if he were to go for a soldier, I would die.*' Such a curious phrase '*to go for a soldier*', like something out of a folksong or fairy-tale. And such passion in that pronouncement, passion that was nowhere in her thoughts about Henry, about whom she never seemed to feel deep anxiety.

It had been a hard winter, the winter of 1914. The house had suffered burst pipes, there had been frost on the inside of the windows, and they had been out gathering fallen branches after a storm to cut up for firewood. Catherine complained about her back paining her and supposed it was concomitant with her condition.

Condition?

Minty read back over the preceding pages but found no overt mention of a pregnancy, nor any act that might have led to such a thing, although Catherine and her dashing captain must have consummated their marriage. She pictured Captain Henry Glynn as looking much like her own great-grandfather: ramrod straight in his uniform, dark eyes impersonal under the peak of his military cap, handlebar moustache dominating his stern face.

She turned more pages and something frail and papery slipped from the journal and into her lap. Petals. Dried, pressed petals. The flower to which they had once belonged had left a ghostly impression on the page, and in confirmation a tiny pencil entry read:

J brought me the first rose of the season today, and this sweet gift delighted me. A symbol of new beginnings, new life: our very own spring. We kissed in the shelter of the courtyard, and he told me he loved me, despite the barriers between us. My heart is so full. How can it be that something society would deem both shameful and sinful should feel so perfectly right? He is Trengrose; and Trengrose is mine.

A kiss! An illicit affair! And J had told Catherine that he loved her. There was no doubt that she loved him. Who was he? And to what barriers did Catherine refer? Her conclusion – hard to avoid – was that 'J' was of a lower social class. Her skin prickled. Minty's parents had constantly chided her for marrying below her (indeed, her father had once memorably referred to Toby as an oik), and she had yelled back that this was a ridiculously outmoded, old-fashioned concept – yet here was that very situation being played out in Catherine Rosevear's secret journal. And at that time, such comparisons would have been much more stark.

Such contentment came over me that if I could have died at that moment, my life would have been complete. But at the instant of that unworthy thought, my unborn child came into my mind, and I chided myself for such egotism. This little one will be the master or mistress of Trengrose after me and will bring us all such joy.

Minty found herself doing some mental arithmetic. The old lady, Eliza Rosevear, whose demise had led to Trengrose coming on the market, had been – what had the agent said, over a hundred? Was Eliza the baby Catherine was referring to here? How extraordinary if so. Now Minty was gripped by the desperate need to know more about the woman to whom Trengrose had belonged. She felt, suddenly, a fierce connection with her, for this was Minty's house too. It was her family money that had made the purchase possible, and she was the one who ran (it seemed) every bloody thing. Her own husband might as well be away at war for all she saw of him.

She retrieved the papery petals and restored them to their place in the journal; had Toby ever picked and presented her with a flower? She laughed aloud at the very idea: no, of course he hadn't. Did she mind?

Minty sat back and reflected on this and found, after a little introspection, that she did.

26

The tower belonging to the church of St Pol de Leon was the one Araminta Hardman had spied from the attic window, looking out across the fields and hills, on her first viewing of Trengrose. It was situated in the hamlet of Paul, less than a mile uphill from the fishing village of Mousehole, looking out towards the sea.

Now, all these months later, she stood beneath it, neck craned to take in the handsome beacon turret poking up into the winter clouds. Following her reading of the journal, she had been researching the Rosevear family online – marathon internet sessions that had led her down a hundred fascinating rabbit-holes – and discovered that this was where they had worshipped and been christened, married and interned.

Seeing the head of the Celtic stone cross protruding over the front wall, she was jolted by its similarity to the tall granite marker Toby had so arrogantly removed from their lane, and once again she was filled with anger and disquiet. She had told him it was an ancient monument and that tampering with it in any way was a crime against culture and heritage, despite the council's permission. She ran her hand over the rough, lichened granite with a cross carved into it and felt a frisson at the deep history it represented. A straight line ran from here to the Trengrose marker stone, and both had probably stood sentinel for well over a thousand years. It was awe-inspiring. London was full of history – in its street names, the remains of Roman wall, old guild houses, Hawksmoor churches and the like, but here, in rural West Penwith, she could feel the prehistory of Cornwall. It outcropped everywhere – in stone circles and burial chambers, Iron Age forts and ancient villages. Something would have to be done about the Trengrose marker stone, she decided. Toby was currently up in London on business dealings, so she would arrange it herself, maybe for after Christmas. She would get someone to clear the brush and bramble where it now lay and re-erect it a few feet from where it had stood. The decision felt satisfying, filled her with a sense of power. She could do this, and damn Toby.

There were a couple of people in the doorway to the church, so Minty made a slow perambulation of the churchyard, examining the headstones, reading their inscriptions, noticing the little pots of cyclamen recently placed on the graves of the long dead. It was touching to know that people still honoured their ancestors and kept the chains of family love unbroken despite the passage of time.

Around the back of the church, she came upon a raised tomb for the Rosevear family, and found four generations buried there: John Rosevear (born 1810, died 1870) and his wife Elizabeth (born 1818, died 1844); Thomas Rosevear (born 1855, died 1909) and his wife Mary 'dearly missed'; and then, with a skip of the heart, she read 'Catherine Rosevear, born 1881, died 1961: "Love everlasting"'; and, more recently and sharply inscribed, 'Eliza Rosevear, born 1915, died 2017, "From my body, flowers will grow"'. And indeed they did, for someone had planted roses and bulbs all around the grave site. The old lady had been one hundred and two! Dying just last year, and within a turn of the sun, Eliza's family home, so long entrusted to the Rosevears, had become the home of her own family. For a moment, she thought *the Hervey family*, rather than *the Hardman family*, before silently correcting herself.

She brushed her fingers across Eliza's name, then Catherine's, and willed a connection to both dead women through the stone.

'I'm so sorry,' she apologised to Catherine, 'for reading your secret diary. I wish you were here to tell me your history. I want so much to know who "J" was.'

But the stone remained obstinately silent. Minty had chased lead after lead on the internet, on genealogy sites, online parish records, local history pages and blogs, census records, and had even made a fruitless journey into Truro, only to find the Cornwall Record Office temporarily closed as it prepared to move its files to a new home. She had not gleaned much information – it was a hidden gem. For such a fine old historic house, very little had been written about Trengrose, as if it somehow existed out of time. There appeared to be no legends or ghosts attached to the place, no scandals or triumphs. No one of any great renown ever appeared to have lived there, which, if she were being one hundred per cent honest, Minty would have admitted was just a little bit disappointing. All this time, in the back of her mind, she had rather hoped a story might emerge, like a butterfly from a chrysalis, that she could write up as a magazine article, or even a book; or at the very least on the Trengrose website to help with marketing the glamping business, and the cottage, once it was acquired and done up.

Now, when she went back to the entrance, she could see that the interior of the church was, splendidly, empty. She was able to take in at her leisure the magnificent long, arched arcade with its nine bays (she counted them), the white painted vaults, and the scorched pillar on the north side, testament to (she read) the fire set by the Spanish raiders in 1595, who had ravaged much of the village of Mousehole, the hamlet of Paul and this very church in retribution for the English victory over the Armada a few years before. Minty couldn't help but grin. How she loved this sort of historical detail.

She took her time to admire the handsome stained-glass windows, the ancient font, the lovely old encaustic tiling in the sanctuary, and came to a halt beneath the commemorative plaque honouring the fallen dead of the parish whose bodies lay not here but far away in Flanders Fields, with the rest of the heroic dead who had fallen in that terrible and bloody war.

The hairs on the back of her neck rose, one by one.

There, among the Blewetts, Bolithos, Madderns and Thomases, was

GLYNN, HENRY, CHARLES. Captain, Duke of Cornwall's Light Infantry,
2nd Battle of Ypres, 22nd May 1915

The handsome captain from the journal: Catherine's husband, Eliza's father. And he had not even survived to see his daughter. Minty stood for a moment with her head bowed. What a tragedy – for Henry, obviously – and for the country and this small part of it, to lose so many of its finest men for no good reason; but most of all for Catherine, widowed so young, and for little Eliza, never even to know her father.

Eventually, feeling melancholy and a little disrespectful, she snapped a photo of the memorial with her phone, took one last, lingering look around the pretty church and went back outside to the Rosevear family gravesite. There they all were:

John and Elizabeth; Thomas and his wife Mary; their daughter Catherine – 'Love everlasting' – and Eliza Rosevear.

Wait a minute. Just 'Rosevear'? Not Rosevear-Glynn, as inscribed on the flyleaf of the journal? That was odd. But then, Minty thought, perhaps it was simply the done thing when interring family members together; after all, the maiden names of Elizabeth and Mary were not listed, as if the Rosevear name subsumed all else.

But all the way home this curious omission niggled at her, and when she got back, she went to the filing cabinet and pulled out the paperwork regarding the sale of Trengrose House. Everything had come through the Duchy solicitors, but yes, there was the mention of the prior owner: Eliza Rosevear. Like her mother before her, Eliza appeared to have dispensed with her father's name.

Minty frowned. Captain Henry Glynn was a fallen hero, one of the glorious dead of the Great War. Surely his widow and his daughter would have wanted to honour his memory by retaining his name? Catherine had not, as far as her research had shown her, remarried; and Eliza had, strangely, remained single all her life.

There was a missing puzzle piece here somewhere, and she was sure it began with the letter 'J'.

The next day, Minty checked the census records for 1911, and found under the entry for Trengrose House:

Catherine Rosevear, head of household, female, aged 30 years, single

Head of household. No mention of parents or guardians, brothers or other male relatives. And, goodness, thirty was old to be single back then, wasn't it? Catherine would have been – what? – thirty-three when she was married? – and thirty-four when she gave birth to Eliza: a positively geriatric mother for the time.

There appeared to be only two other entries for 'every Person, whether Member of Family, Visitor, Boarder, or Servant who 1) passed the night of Sunday, April 2nd, 1911, in this dwelling or 2) arrived in this dwelling on the morning of Monday April 3rd, not having been enumerated elsewhere'. These were Elsie Hockin, aged 61, listed as Cook and Housekeeper, and Matilda Penrose, aged 22: Maid.

No males listed at all. What about the Curnow family? What had Toby reported back from his conversation with Ezra, that the old man's father and grandfather had lived here 'on an understanding'? Yet they were not listed as part of the household, and try as she might, Minty could find no records for them in the area, and no mention of the lodge cottage at all.

After much persistence, she managed to get through to the local parish records clerk, who gave her a list of useful links and sites, and she worked her way diligently through them till she was going cross-eyed. Even so, online coverage was patchy and incomplete.

She scanned the census record again. *Elsie Hockin*. Wasn't Hockin the name of the farmer up the road? It seemed more than coincidence that someone from the Hockin family should have been working at the big house right next to the farm...

Minty closed her laptop with a decisive click. Time to do some in-person research.

She donned her Ilse Jacobsen raincoat and Hunter wellies and walked up the track to the farm shop. There was a woman behind the counter today, a stout lady in late middle age. Minty smiled at her, and the woman acknowledged her with a stern nod. Not the most promising start. Making a few purchases seemed the best way to establish a chance to ask a question or two, so she took a basket and selected some home-made jams and chutneys and a bottle of local wine. At the counter, she perused the offerings behind the glass front: some divine-looking cakes, bread, sausages, packets of beef, butter and cream, all labelled with the Hockins' Farm logo.

'Goodness,' Minty said, trying not to sound too posh. 'Do you produce all this yourselves?'

'Course,' said the woman. ''Tis our farm.'

'All these lovely cakes, and all the bread?'

'I make the bread, Ma makes the saffron cakes, and Christine makes the rest.' She didn't elaborate on who Christine might be.

'Well, I'd love one of the saffron cakes,' Minty said, placing her basket on the counter. 'Are you Mrs Hockin, by any chance?'

The woman frowned. 'Who else would I be? Can't find any staff these days.'

Minty mulled this over and couldn't find anything useful to say. At last she managed, 'Sorry, I'm being rude,' and held out her hand. 'I'm Araminta Hardman – Minty – from Trengrose House.'

'I know who you are,' Mrs Hockin said darkly. She made no move to shake the proffered hand but set about ringing the items up on the till, businesslike and not at all friendly.

'Perhaps I could have some of your butter as well? I'm sure it's much nicer than supermarket butter,' Minty pressed on ingratiatingly.

'Course it is. Best get it while you can, though, cause my hands are playing me up something awful, and there's no one wants to learn to make cream or butter the traditional way any more.'

'That's such a shame. Tradition is so important, especially in rural communities like this. I'm sure your farm has been in the same family for a long time?'

'Hockin? Ar, it's been worked by Bob's family for generations. Hockins go way back round here. Penroses too.'

'You're a Penrose?' Minty remembered the name of Catherine's maid: Matilda Penrose. 'I was walking around the churchyard at Paul and saw lots of Penroses there.'

'Oh, I'll be joining them soon enough. That'll be £42.59.'

Minty gulped. She really should have put the wine back, but it was too late now. She fed her debit card into the device Mrs Hockin held out to her and keyed in her pin number. 'I saw on the 1911 census records for Trengrose House that Catherine Rosevear had a maid called Matilda Penrose,' Minty said quickly, trying to sound nonchalant.

'Matty? That'll be my great-grandmother.' Mrs Hockin brightened. 'She worked up big house most of her life. My nan and ma too.' Pride in her bloodlines suffused her thin skin, pale blood drowning her freckles.

Minty felt her heart beat faster. 'Your mother and grandmother as well? How amazing. They must have some tales to tell.'

'Nan's been dead a few year now, though she held on to her

hundredth. Women in these parts are long-lived, just like Miss Eliza. Something in the Trengrose soil, I reckon.'

'And your mother? I hope she's still doing well.'

Mrs Hockin cast a glance at her. 'Well enough. Still helps me with the baking, though she can't stand too well these days.'

'I'd love to meet her sometime, when she's feeling well enough for visitors,' Minty said eagerly. 'I'm so interested in the history of the house and estate.'

'I heard you been making a lot of changes down there,' Mrs Hockin said disapprovingly.

'It was in a bit of a state,' Minty said, feeling defensive. 'I've done whatever I can to honour the history of the house and to keep the renovations within the parameters of the original design and feel. You should come and have a look sometime.' She paused for a beat. 'Maybe bring your mother for a cup of tea?'

Mrs Hockin's eyes lit up with the natural curiosity of all neighbours. 'Well now,' she said consideringly, 'that would be grand. How about this afternoon?'

Minty watched the battered Land Rover traverse the gravelled driveway, not entering from the lane in the usual way, but from the opposite direction. Good grief! They must have driven the vehicle cross-country from the farm and across the glamping field! She felt a wave of proprietorial rage, then allowed it to ebb away. It wasn't as if this was going to be a regular occurrence. Even so, it had rained for days, and the Land Rover was liberally splattered in mud. She could imagine the deep ruts it would have left through her carefully maintained camping field. *Don't say anything*, she warned herself, and was glad that Toby, not known for his diplomacy at the best of times, was away. In fact, she knew she would never have invited their neighbours here this afternoon had her husband been in residence: he would bluster and show off and thoroughly alienate them and she'd never find out anything.

She ran down the steps to welcome the visitors. Mrs Hockin clambered down from the driver's side, came around to the passenger door and hauled a very elderly woman out and onto the ground as if she were a sack of potatoes.

'This here's my mother, Gemma,' the farmer's wife said. She looked at Minty. 'Sorry, I forgot your name. It were something foreign, weren't it?'

'Araminta, Minty for short. It's not at all foreign though, you know. It's an old English name first used by the dramatist Sir John Vanbrugh...' She trailed off, for the farmer's wife was regarding her suspiciously.

'My name's Thurza,' Mrs Hockin said. 'Proper old Cornish name, nothing to do with any dramatists or "sirs".'

As Minty followed the pair up the steps, she rolled her eyes so hard that they hurt.

In the renovated kitchen, the neighbours gazed around in wonder.

'Well,' Gemma said, collapsing into Toby's chair at the head of the kitchen table. 'This has changed a bit.' She and her daughter exchanged a confirmatory glance that clearly conveyed each to the other *told you so*. 'Still got the old range then,' Gemma continued, nodding towards the massive iron cooker that Toby always referred to as *that monstrosity*.

Minty nodded. 'It's the heart of the home, isn't it?' And was gratified to see the old woman's face break into a huge smile.

'The hours I spent stirring pots on that thing! All the hundreds of loaves I cooked in that bread oven.'

Minty ran a hand over the warm iron of the range. 'I love that,' she said quietly. 'That sense of continuity, of real, lived life. I'm not much of a baker myself, but perhaps you could give me some tips?'

Thurza snorted. 'Can't be doing that: I'd be losing a customer!'

The atmosphere grew warmer as Minty produced a pot of tea and slices of their own saffron cake, along with clotted cream, as instructed.

'That be the proper way to eat un,' Gemma dictated. 'Young people nowadays got no idea.'

'Probably watching their waistlines, Ma,' Thurza sniffed, patting her own respectably solid torso.

Minty, who had always been naturally thin, laughed nervously, and helped herself to a large dollop of cream. They chatted about the kitchen decor, the old woman being particularly fascinated by the various appliances like the enormous Gaggia: *oh, I don't like coffee, we were raised on good, strong tea*; the blender: *nothing wrong with a bit of elbow grease*; and the microwave: *I heard they fry your brain…*

'So you worked here, and your mother and grandmother, too?' Minty brought the conversation back to her agenda.

Gemma went misty-eyed. 'I were here during the war, you know, as a little girl. Those were good times. I was let to run wild, used to ride on the pigs, I did. Fell off once, ah the state of me! Miss Eliza, she washed me down and gave me fresh clothes that were hers when she were a child; oh, they were so soft. She were a lovely woman.'

'But she never married?' Minty asked.

'Never married. Such a shame.'

'I suppose it's hard when all the young men are away at war.'

Gemma looked down with a sly smile. 'Not all the young men.'

'Mother—'

Gemma shrugged. 'Well, it were just a rumour.'

Minty was desperate to press this point, but a dampening silence had fallen over the conversation like a blanket draped over a canary's cage. Eventually, she said, 'I'm thinking of writing an article about the history of Trengrose.'

'What, for a magazine?' Thurza asked. 'Like *The People's Friend*?'

'Sort of,' Minty said tactfully. 'I've only had a few bits and pieces published, mainly in design magazines – that's what I do, interior design – but I'm really interested in the spirit of the place and the people who have lived here. For example, I saw from the 1911 census that Catherine Rosevear appeared to be running the whole house on her own, despite being an unmarried young woman, with just a cook – Elsie Hockin – and a maid – Matilda Penrose. No men mentioned as residing here at all.'

Thurza laughed. 'Well, course not: the estate managers lived in Ezra's cottage. The Curnow men have always run the estate.'

'I couldn't find them in the census listings anywhere.'

'I don't know about censuses and stuff, but that's how it's always been.' Gemma sighed. 'I remember Mr Ethan: he were proper handsome. Ma said he took after his dad; he were a right heartbreaker, she said. Dearovim…' Her gaze drifted wide.

'What was his father's name?' Minty tried not to sound too eager.

Gemma shook her head. 'Afore my time, maid.'

'I read that Catherine Rosevear got married just before the Great War,' Minty said carefully, 'to a Captain Henry Glynn, but then her husband was killed a year later at Ypres.'

'Not even that. Nan said poor Miss Catherine was cursed: met him, married him, lost him in less than the turning of the seasons. Never had any luck with men, that family. Poor Miss Eliza—' She seemed about to say more when her daughter patted her on the shoulder, a little too sharply.

'Let's not bore Mrs Hardman, now, Ma. I like what you've done to the courtyard,' she said to Minty brightly, making it clear that there was to be no further discussion of the romantic affairs of the residents of Trengrose.

And so Minty explained how they had opened up the kitchen and installed the big glass doors – 'I won't show you how they work, or we'll all freeze to death!' she joked, but inwardly, as she took Thurza Hockin around the rest of the house, she was seething with frustration.

Thurza was clearly awed by the renovations. She kept stroking throws, curtains and tub chairs, sighing at colour schemes, and exclaiming over the ensuite bathrooms, and how much it all must have cost. But as they started up the stairs to the attic she stopped suddenly and turned back. 'No, no, I'd rather not.' She rubbed her upper arms as if she was cold, though the central heating suffused the house with warm air. 'Can you smell lavender?' she asked, as they made their way back along the corridor.

And now that she'd mentioned it, Minty could.

After that, the visitors left quite speedily. Minty helped the old lady down the steps towards the muddy Land Rover. Parked next to their own, rather newer, iteration of the marque, the difference struck Minty forcibly. On the one hand, here was old Cornwall: utilitarian, practical, down-at-heel, a truck that must be a good forty years old and had probably never in its life been driven further than Truro; on the other was smart London – an unnecessarily huge, shiny black tank of a thing with tinted windows, alloy wheels and a sunroof, for god's sake – far too large for the local lanes, imposing itself on foreign territory. Just like all the Little Greene and Farrow & Ball paint, the bespoke wallpaper, the OKA chairs and antique French wardrobes that had colonised Trengrose House. For a brief, hot moment, she experienced the disparity through the eyes of the farmer's wife: such ostentatious consumerism; such imposition. The cost of it all would probably be more than the farm's income across several years. She felt slightly sick and headachy.

'Well, it's been lovely,' Thurza Hockin was saying as she opened the passenger door and prepared to lever her mother up the tall step into the cab. 'You must come over to us for a drink some time.'

'That would be very nice,' Minty replied, collecting herself.

'I'll write down your phone number... Oh, my handbag! I must have left it in the kitchen.'

'I'll go and get it,' Minty offered, but Thurza was already stomping back across the gravel towards the steps, leaving Minty in charge of her elderly mother.

'It'll take her a while,' Gemma said, leaning against the grubby side of the vehicle, her small eyes gleaming. 'I tucked un down the back of a sofa cushion.'

Minty gazed at her in bemusement, and the old woman started to chuckle.

'Best tell you this quick, before Thurza gets back and gives me another sermon about gossiping.' She plucked at Minty's sleeve. The lightweight cashmere was remarkably efficient at keeping out the cold of this Cornish winter, but even so, Minty shivered.

'Tell me what?'

'I heard Ethan Curnow broke Miss Eliza's heart. One minute, they was all lovey-dovey, always in one another's company; the next, she shut herself away, barely even spoke to him again, in private, at least. Word is things got better, once he married Tamsin and had Ezra—'

Minty's sharp interest prompted her to interrupt. 'You know Ezra Curnow, then?'

'Course: we all played together as children.'

'And the cottage at the end of the lane, it belongs to him, does it?'

Gemma regarded her with a narrowed gaze. 'Course it does. Curnows have always lived there.'

No point in pushing that, then. Quickly, Minty asked, 'So do you think Eliza and Ethan had an affair?'

Gemma pursed her lips. 'Maybe it didn't get quite so far, but they say her mother put a stop to it, whatever it was.' She looked over Minty's shoulder and promptly shut up.

Thurza was approaching, red-faced and sweating, clutching her handbag. 'I can't imagine how it got where I found it,' she said, shooting her mother an accusatory glance.

For her part, the old lady was all innocence, apparently uncomprehending. 'Best geddon, dear,' she said to her daughter. 'Got a fearsome urge to pee.'

★

Minty watched the Land Rover disappear into the glamping field without even a thought of the damage it would be doing. All she could think of was the thwarted love between Ethan Curnow and Eliza Rosevear.

27

Dom pottered around the orangery, dodging the miniature cascades from cracked panes in its roof as the rain battered down. He cleaned out some flowerpots and stacked them away, swept the tiled floor, and picked and ate the last two tomatoes, without the least idea that having fresh tomatoes to pick in November was a rare treat. The orangery was warm and tranquil even on such a grey day, and Dom found it calming. Some of the seed trays he had found when they moved in had produced all sorts of salad leaves, just like the ones in the posh packets they used to get at Waitrose. They'd eaten them all summer, and for the first time he'd actually enjoyed eating salad, which his sister had teased him about. Ran loved lettuce, seemed to live off it, so to impress her, he'd bought a selection of salad seeds in Penzance and had sown them in trays, using compost he'd found in a huge tub. Against all odds, all the little plants were thriving, pushing up red and green leaves of all shapes and configurations – spiky and frilly, smooth and jagged-edged, round and long. He couldn't wait to show them to Ran when next she visited. He was extremely proud of them, had even rigged up a rudimentary hydroponic system to keep producing fresh salad all year round. It gave him more satisfaction than any other project he'd ever devoted himself to. Even the weed-production in his biometric dome at school. There were lots of other things he thought he'd be able to grow in the orangery, and he knew who to ask for advice.

When the rain eased from downpour to drizzle, he quietly opened the door that led into the courtyard and let himself into the kitchen. There was no sign of his mother: he guessed she was upstairs in her writing room at the top of the house, and of course his father was away working. He fetched a carrier bag, raided the pantry, slipped some items into it, then put on his wellies and his Finisterre waterproof, and was about to sneak out when Boris suddenly nosed around the corner and turned a wet-eyed, hopeful gaze upon him.

'Oh, all right,' Dom said, taking down the lead and clipping it to the dog's collar. The Labrador would give him an alibi. If his mother spied him creeping across the gravel, at least he would now be able to claim he was taking the dog for a walk, even if that was only partially true.

The 'walk' lasted all of five minutes, just as Boris was getting into his stride. Ezra's gate was closed, but the old man's boots stood by the door. Dom unlatched the gate, pulled a nervous Boris up the garden path, and knocked with the six staccato raps he and Ezra had agreed on for such visits. He wasn't sure exactly why such subterfuge should be necessary – it was hardly as if the feds were likely to raid the cottage – but he rather enjoyed the intrigue.

There was a long pause, and then the door opened just a crack.

When Ezra had visual confirmation of who his visitor was, he opened the door fully, then looked down at Boris. 'Sorry, he can't come in. Bucca's rule, not mine.'

Boris was secured on a long leash to the damson tree round the side of the cottage, so that he could snuffle and explore, though Dom suspected this would result in him winding himself to a standstill around the trunk, and in not very many minutes.

'I just put the kettle on,' Ezra said, indicating the giant copper vessel on top of the old iron range. 'If you'd like a cup of tea.'

'Okay,' said Dom, grinning. He had never actually been inside the cottage before, and to be welcomed into the old man's secret sanctuary and offered a drink made him feel warm inside. He emptied his pockets onto the kitchen table. 'I brought a few bits and pieces I thought you might like. I was hoping you might tell me something about growing fruit and veg in our big greenhouse.'

Ezra's eyes gleamed. As they talked, he picked up and examined in turn: a packet of chocolate Hobnobs, a jar of crystallised ginger and a bottle of curry sauce. Treasure, indeed! He went off to fetch Dom a couple of books about growing under glass – he had quite a little collection of gardening books, picked up from charity shops and library discards.

Dom gazed around him. The interior of the cottage was the exact opposite of the renovated Trengrose House, which was light and bright and minimally furnished with large, expensive modern pieces in neutral colours punctuated by occasional splashes of colour: an accent wallpaper of hand-painted Oriental lilies; velvet cushions, Tabriz silk rugs; abstract paintings that his mother referred to as 'good investments'. Ezra's cottage was stuffed to the brim with furniture that had been sat on, rested on, worked on, and lain on, for what looked like a hundred years. The rug was threadbare to the extent that it seemed to be a natural excrescence of the underlying floor, and every knick-knack was freighted with decades of significance, weighed down by love and history. And yet it wasn't dusty; it was spick and span, the wood waxed and buffed, the floor swept, and no cobwebs festooned the darker corners. It surprised and pleased Dom to think of Ezra meticulously cleaning this little space.

His searching gaze was snagged by an old-looking photo by the window, sepia-tinted, faded by long years of Cornish sunlight, and showed a man and woman in formal clothing. The man was tall and dark of hair and features, and there was something both striking and recognisable about his direct gaze. And there he was again, with straw in his hair, but this time in a much less rigid pose, looking as if he had just stepped out of the pages of a GQ fashion shoot.

Dom took the photograph down and scrutinised it. The frame was more ornate than the rest, shiny and silver, and when he turned it over an inscription in pencil read, 'To my dearest Jude, forever, your C.'

Beside it was a photo of another man, a sharper, more modern image, but with just the same expression as the first, recognisably from the same genetic stock, wearing a jaunty kerchief. The image felt familiar in some way. Dom was about to turn the frame over to see if it, too, bore an inscription, when Ezra took the photo from him proprietorially and returned it to its position.

'T'ent polite to come into people's houses and start touching their things,' he said.

The admonishment was gentle, but Dom felt stung all the same. He went and sat down at the kitchen table, pointedly ignoring the grotty old gardening books Ezra had dug out.

'Interested in old photos, are you?' Ezra asked.

Happy to be offered this olive branch, Dom said, 'Yes, ever so. I collect vintage cameras.'

'Any good at mending them?' Ezra asked.

Dom experienced a deep twitch of interest. 'Sometimes,' he said quietly.

Ezra didn't say any more, but set out the tea things: teapot, cups, saucers, a little lidded china pot and jug with roses on them, a tiny silver spoon and, like a potentate dispensing rare gifts, the packet of Hobnobs the boy had brought.

It was all so dainty, a tea party from another age. Dom thought of the sturdy Design House mugs and teabags with cotton strings in their own kitchen. He watched Ezra spoon loose leaves into the teapot and stir them through. He even used a strainer to catch the leaves when he poured the tea out.

Ezra noted the boy watching what was clearly to him an arcane ceremony. 'Gram Cecily never used a tea strainer. She used to tell people's fortunes by looking at the tea leaves in the bottom of the cups.'

Dom stared at him. 'Was she a witch?'

'Cecily?' Ezra laughed. 'Oh no, not she. She were a proper countrywoman, though, knew all the right plants and herbs to make you well. Time was, doctors were expensive: only the rich could afford them.'

'Before the NHS?'

'Long before.'

'Talking of herbs...' Dom said, and fixed the old man with a beseeching gaze, rather like the one Boris would use on you if you went anywhere near the fridge.

'Mebbe later. Let's just have a quiet cuppa, eh?'

They drank their tea and Ezra ate a Hobnob. Dom ate two.

'Are those people your family?' he asked his host after a while. 'In the photos over there?'

'Ar.' Ezra did not offer further information.

'I miss my family,' Dom said. 'I mean, my grandparents. Dad's parents, they're in the East End of London, and Mum's mother is in Buckinghamshire, and now we're down here, they seem a really long way away.' He paused. 'Well, I suppose they are. I expect they'll visit, though. We've got plenty of room for them. They could all come at the same time, and Ran, too, and we'd still have two spare bedrooms.' He thought about this for a moment. 'That seems really wasteful, doesn't it? I mean, we don't use half the rooms in Trengrose, and there are people...' He trailed off, looking around at the cottage.

''Tis enough for me,' Ezra said.

'But when you were growing up?'

Ezra gave him a lopsided smile. 'Ar, well then... five of us under this one roof for a time at least: Gram Cecily, Ma and Da, me and... my brother. Gram had the little spare room, and the rest of us were all in the bedroom with a screen between us. Then when we got older, we was up in the loft with the bats.' He shook his head. 'People expected less back in those days.'

'Where's your brother now? Did he move away?'

Ezra's gaze became shuttered. 'He'm long gone.' And he didn't add any more even though Dom waited expectantly.

'I wish I had a brother,' he said at last. 'Ran's lovely and all, but she's a girl. And she's older. And... not here.' He looked at Ezra. 'I get pretty lonely sometimes. I mean, this really is the back of beyond. There's no one my age for miles!'

'Didn't used to be like that. There was kids up at the farm, and the workers' families at Trengrose, and in the cottages downalong. But the cottages're all second homes now and they'm empty most of the year, and even Bob Hockin's lad's left the area: ent no jobs, see, and locals can't afford to buy with the prices pushed so high.' He sighed, then added, rather against his better judgment, 'Your da wants me out of here an' all. Wants to rent the place out to tourists.'

Dom looked pained. He'd heard his parents arguing about 'The Lodge'. 'I'm really sorry about that. My dad... he gets kind of obsessed about making money. But you aren't going to leave, are you?' There was a pleading note in his voice.

'The only way I'll be leaving here is feet first.'

Having delivered this emphatic declaration, Ezra pushed himself out of his chair and poked up the fire in the range. As the flames leapt, Bucca came oozing out of the shadows and arranged himself on their visitor's lap, where he sat rhythmically flexing his needle-sharp claws in and out of Dom's jeans and purring like a small engine.

Soothed by the silk of the cat's fur beneath his hand, Dom felt his head begin to nod, and he must have briefly dozed off, because when he came to it was to see that a small, battered cardboard box had manifested itself on the kitchen table.

'Oh!' he exclaimed so sharply that Bucca leapt up and took a sentry position by the stove and stared back at Dom in a recriminatory fashion.

Ezra patted the box. 'You take un,' he said. 'I don't want these old memories here any more. There's a small world of pain in there, but I never been able to bring myself to throw un out. Seemed disrespectful. But if you like old photos and cameras, maybe you'll find something of interest in there to take your mind off the loneliness.' He pushed the carton across the table to Dominic in a gesture that spoke of both regret and a hard decision taken.

Dom opened the flaps enough to glimpse the camera inside and almost shouted with excitement. 'Oh my god! I think that's a VPK!'

Ezra shrugged. 'No idea.'

'A Vest Pocket Kodak! But they were discontinued in 1926.' Dom lifted his gaze to Ezra's granite face. 'It's really, really old.'

'Ar, tis that. Belonged to my Gamps, and then my da, and he give it to us to take to Cyprus.'

'Cyprus?' Dom almost yelped, this information was so unexpected. With the self-absorption of the teenager, he had been under the impression that Ezra had never existed anywhere than right here, at Trengrose. 'Was that a holiday?'

Ezra laughed bitterly. 'No, lad. A holiday it most certainly wasn't.' He had barely been older than Dom when he'd been sent to serve out there, and what he had seen during those months – the violence and hatred, the desecration and inhumanity – was seared upon his soul, had changed him completely. He had come home a very different man.

28

Sam waited nervously at the entrance to the zoo on the Outer Circle, scanning the passers-by for the first sight of Miranda Hardman, wondering if he had somehow got the day or time of their rendezvous wrong. He had checked his phone a dozen times in the past ten minutes, enough to realise it only had three per cent battery left, since he had failed to charge it this morning. Honestly, he just wasn't made for modern life: he was hopeless at it.

Just when he was convinced she wasn't going to turn up, he spotted her signature cloth cap and striped woolly scarf between other pedestrians, and his heart went nuts, rattling the bars of his ribs. There she was! Warmth suffused his entire body at the sight of her; warmth, and a sense of wonder that this glorious woman was giving up her day to be with him, that she had shared her bed and body with him and told him he was a lovely, lovely, lovely man, and that she adored him. Trouble was, he had the sense that if he had responded with *I adore you too* he would have been overstepping some invisible mark between them, since the way she had said it was cheery and blithe, but for Sam it was deadly serious. So he had buttoned his lip and tried to be suitably nonchalant, but it was the hardest thing in the world.

Ran threw her arms around him. 'Sorry I'm late! Bloody Northern Line.'

And after that, everything was all right. They walked around the zoo hand in hand, and Sam stood for long minutes watching the gibbons swinging energetically across their enclosure, admiring their effortless technique.

'You look as if you want to join them!' Ran teased, and he grinned and told her how he'd run away from home to go climbing with his great-uncle Ezra and was remembering the sense of exhilaration he had felt tackling the overhang of Xanadu in the Great Zawn on a bright October morning.

'Will you take me climbing?' Ran asked, and Sam remembered the girl he had met who owned no sensible outdoor footwear, and made a shocked face.

'No, really, I'd love to have a go. Friends of mine go to the Westway Climbing Wall and say it's brilliant fun. Perhaps we could go with them sometime.'

Sam felt a little stab of jealousy wondering who these friends might be, but he said, 'Sure – indoor walls are great for getting to grips with some of the technical moves.' He had been to the Westway once but had been put off by the sight of overly muscled guys showing off to their clueless mates on the biggest overhangs, as if climbing was all about brute strength and Lycra. All the gear and no idea: put them on a sea cliff and they'd wet themselves. 'But there's nothing can beat padding your way up a sunlit slab of Cornish granite with the sound of the sea in your ears.'

They wandered on, around the cages and enclosures. Ran's favourites were the pygmy hippos, and the Sumatran tigers. 'They've got five types of whiskers,' she told Sam. 'To pick up all the different types of vibrations in the jungle. And yet still they're critically endangered, despite being so adapted to their environment. It's so sad.' She had been reading up on them, she said, though she didn't add that she had done so to impress Sam with her understanding of the natural world.

'And here they are, trapped in cages, with people staring at them,' Sam said quietly. 'It's not right, is it? Everywhere humans go, they wreck it. Pillage the land for whatever profit they can make out of it, without giving a thought to the consequences for any other living thing. Then, when they've almost died out, people put the last few specimens in zoos and charge other people to come and look at them.'

Not so long ago, Miranda would have teased him for being a mood-killer, a downer; but today she put her arm through his and said, 'I know. Zoos are weird places: I get that. Like people in the past paying to go and look at the mad people in the Bethlehem Hospital, pointing fingers and laughing at their antics and going home. It's so wrong, so vile.' She thought about this for a while. 'But then there's conservation and raising awareness. If you don't see animals, you don't connect with the environment. Kids who grow up in urban areas go to zoos and see wild animals in the flesh for the first time in their lives, and they fall in love with them. And as they grow up, they want to do something about the damage we've done—'

'Are doing,' interrupted Sam, and Ran nodded.

'Keep doing. But emotional connections make a difference. Because we love stories, and we're a collaborative species, humans, for all our flaws. And I really, truly believe there are more good people in the world than bad – and maybe there's no such thing as bad, just uninformed, so it's all about education really.'

Sam remembered how he had felt, lying on the floor of the Tate's Turbine Hall, making art come to life, and began to think he might have understood something fundamental about the world.

It dawned on him that Ran had stopped talking, which was unlike her. He shot her a look. Her gaze was averted, and she looked so pensive that Sam's heart stopped beating. Had she decided he wasn't up to scratch, wasn't clever or sensitive enough to be with her? 'What?' he asked softly, in some dread. 'What is it?'

Ran shook her head. 'Nothing, really. Or maybe something really big! An idea I had.' She laughed. 'Perhaps it's a totally stupid idea.'

The way she looked at him reassured Sam that whatever idea Ran had had, he was not at the heart of it. But whatever he tried, she would not be drawn on it.

Outside the zoo once more, with an hour or so to kill before Ran went back to work at her latest temp job, they strolled through Regent's Park. At the café by the lake they watched a heron scrutinising the still waters for prey like some throwback from the age of dinosaurs. Then they carried on down through Marylebone and Hyde Park, stitching London's green spaces together. A passing shower of freezing hail caught them as they were crossing the big roundabout at Hyde Park Corner, and they took shelter beneath the Wellington Arch and kissed for such a delirious ten minutes that Sam felt lightheaded, until at last Ran broke away, crying, 'I'm going to be late!'

The hail had turned at last to gentle rain, and they ran out onto Piccadilly, passing Green Park Tube station and knots of American and Japanese tourists taking selfies outside the Ritz. Ran was exclaiming excitedly about an exhibition that was on at the Royal Academy when Sam suddenly said, 'Isn't that your dad?'

Ran stared, then cried, 'Shit!'

She started to speed up. Sam kept pace with her, unsure of what to say or do, rather wishing he hadn't said anything. Because Toby Hardman was not alone. He was with a petite woman laden with Fortnum's carrier bags, holding an umbrella solicitously over her head; and that woman was not his wife.

Miranda started to run. 'Dad?'

Her voice was drowned out by a double-decker bus roaring through the puddles, but it wouldn't have made any difference, for the couple had flagged down a taxi and got into it.

Sam stood with his hand on Ran's shoulder as the taxi sped past them, heading west, and all they saw was the blur of two heads close together in the back seat. He felt her tremble beneath his touch, then break away from him, and he could tell from a tremor in her chin and her rigid jaw that she was trying very hard not to cry.

'Perhaps it wasn't him,' he offered, but Ran shook her head fiercely.

'It bloody was, and it was that bloody Chrissie woman with him.'

Sam was at a loss, not knowing who Chrissie might be, though the couple's body language had given him the sense of something intimate, probably illicit.

'He's cheating on my mum. Again! I can't believe it. All that hurt last time, all those lies. Spending his money on her, too – *our* money! I saw the shopping bags. Champagne and truffles and bastarding foie gras, I bet!'

Sam had never seen her so furious. In this moment, she seemed wilder than any of the zoo animals, ready to rend and tear. 'I'm really sorry,' he said.

They walked in silence down towards Waterstones. Just before they reached the entrance, Miranda roared into the darkening air, 'Fucking, fucking, fucking men!'

29

Early one Sunday morning, as the first light was just a greying of the sky, Ezra was woken by a loud banging at his door. In his dream, he had been back in Cyprus, watching men move stealthily between the trees like cats in a jungle. He wanted to cry out a warning, but his throat had closed up, and when he tried to run, his legs would not obey him and all he could do was watch.

The loud noise at his door became a part of the nightmare, and in life again he could not find his voice.

The banging continued. Cursing his arthritic knees, Ezra stumbled out of the bedroom to the front door, his thoughts now fixed on Sam and catastrophe. But when he opened the door, it was not to find a policeman outside, but a burly-looking man with cold eyes and a mean little mouth.

'You Ezra Curnow?' he growled, looking the scrawny old man up and down, and his lip curled in disdain. Far too easy.

Ezra immediately recognised his early morning visitor for what he was. He knew the type only too well. Ex-services, bully; not very bright.

'Who wants to know?'

The man gave him a smile, showing uneven teeth as yellow as a rat's. 'Eviction order for you.' He thrust a large manila envelope at Ezra, and when the old man merely stared at it, threw the envelope contemptuously at his feet. 'Consider it served. Pack your stuff and get out. Leave this property within the week.'

'On whose authority?'

'The owners of this estate and their legal representatives.'

'They don't own this cottage and I ent leaving.'

The man jutted a prognathous jaw at him. 'You'll be leaving all right. Or else.'

'Or else what?'

'Or else I'll be back.'

'I know your sort: you don't scare me, son.'

The man's face flushed. 'Don't you "son" me, you old tosser.'

Ezra said coldly, 'Off you go, and take your eviction notice with you.'

His visitor snorted. 'I been nice, but you going to be begging me for mercy if I find you're still here when I come back.'

'If you come back,' Ezra told him, with steel in his voice, 'you better bring a bleddy army. And make sure you've written your last will and testament.'

The bully raised a meaty fist.

'See you then,' Ezra said cheerily, and shut the door in his face.

From the kitchen window he watched the man jog back to the Transit van that was blocking the lane. Then he thought about the things that he had, and the things he would need, before heading up to the farm.

A few days later, Ezra was poking up the fire in the range first thing in the gloom of the morning when something shattered the kitchen window, bounced off the sink and skittered over the stone floor, arriving almost at his socked feet. He looked down. It was a new-looking house-brick. He took in the jagged hole it had made in his living quarters, then picked up the big stick he now kept by the front door and went outside. There were footsteps in the dewy grass on the kitchen-side of the garden – big footsteps.

Ezra, stick raised in readiness, patrolled his domain, but there was no sign of any intruder. He bet if he'd reacted faster, been a younger man, and simply sprinted outside after the brick had made impact, he'd have caught sight of the perpetrator driving away in a Transit van.

Ezra boarded up the window in a rudimentary fashion. It made the interior even more cave-like than it had been before, but it was winter, and he would manage. At some point he'd find an old window in a builder's skip and scavenge some glass with which to fix it. But that was not his priority right now. Right now, he needed to be on his guard.

30

Minty closed the laptop lid with a sharp snap. Another unexpected bill, plus certain anomalies in their bank accounts had required some investigation and the illicit use of Toby's passwords. She was exhausted. The problems with the cesspit had led to knock-on effects, for rats had got into the pantry and made free with her packets of nuts and rice, before – unbelievably – managing to gnaw their way through the lid of a jar of Nutella and scoff the contents. The pest control man she had called out in panic had assured her this was all quite normal for Cornwall, and that rats, no doubt displaced by the drainage problems she had described, had swum up into the house and entered via the downstairs loo, for they were capable of holding their breath underwater for several minutes. She hadn't slept for several nights between discovering their depredations and the eventual success of the rat-man's electronic traps: even now, she found her ears reaching after every tiny sound in the night, interpreting each creak and rustle as a return of avenging rodent hordes.

As a result of all this, she had hardly seen her son in days.

It was not that Dom had vanished, just that he seemed to have gone to ground, appearing only to raid the fridge or grudgingly share a meal she had prepared. She worried about this. Was it because of the rats that he was spending so little time downstairs, she had asked? He had scoffed at that. Of course not. He had things to do.

She'd had to bite her tongue on 'What with? Online gaming and social media?'

To be honest, she had no idea what Dominic was doing in his room. He could be constructing a meth lab in there for all she knew. *Breaking Bad* gone Far West Cornwall. The thought of this alarmed her so much that, on the pretext of taking him a mid-afternoon snack of tea and fruit cake, she went upstairs, knocked deliberately quietly on his door and, with the excuse of having received no answer, entered his room... only to find no sign of him. Which was odd, because it was raining, and she was certain he hadn't gone outside.

Having intruded into Dom's inner sanctum, Minty decided to have a good look round. She wouldn't touch anything, wouldn't open drawers, search under the bed or do anything invasive, she promised herself, just, well – she had the right to check on her son's well-being, didn't she? A duty, really.

Dom had inherited her own need for order, so this was not a stereotypical teenage boy's bedroom, full of strewn clothes and clutter, food wrappers and mouldy mugs on every surface. In fact, the tidiness of the room was quite unnerving. He had even made his bed.

But one thing that struck her immediately was that the walls were papered with images, some arranged apparently at random, others in vague groupings. Most appeared to be black-and-white photographs that had been aged to look antique. She put down the tea tray on his desk, examined the set of images that had been Blu-tacked above it, and was surprised to see that far from being faked to appear old, they appeared to be genuine. You could always tell the difference between fancy dress or even film costumes and the real thing. It was the ill-fitting nature of old clothes, the lack of tailoring, and wear that had bagged the knees and elbows and bobbled the wool.

Here was a group of agricultural workers with pitchforks and rakes and – good grief – scythes. It was such a timeless image it could have been an illustration straight out of Thomas Hardy – from *Far From the Madding Crowd* or *Tess of the d'Urbervilles*. No, not *Tess*. Those were forlorn, flint-pocked turnip fields over which a cold wind yelled and whistled. These images were, if not joyful, then at least gentle and communal: proud snapshots of shared work, people gathered for haying in some field. She blinked. Not just any field either: that was the land behind Trengrose, on the way up to the Hockins' farm; and this one was the glamping field!

'What are you doing?'

Dom stood in the doorway of his ensuite bathroom. His mouth was set in a grim line.

Minty stepped guiltily away from the pictures and indicated the tray on the desk. 'I did knock but you didn't answer.'

'I was in the bathroom. You can't just barge into my room and snoop around, you know.'

They stared at one another. Unspoken between them lay the scene back in Chiswick last year when Minty had indeed been snooping around her son's bedroom and had discovered a cache of baggies under his bed, stuffed with his home-grown weed and ready to distribute to his customers, even after he had assured her the incident at school had been a one-off.

Minty forced a smile. 'Sorry, darling. I shouldn't have invaded your space. But you know, I'm glad I did. These photos are fascinating.' She gestured to the displays on the walls. 'Where did you get them? Did you find them here somewhere?'

'Sort of.'

He was being shifty. Minty wondered why. 'Do you know who these people are? I'm pretty sure this is in the glamping field.' She indicated the group of workers.

'I'm not sure yet. I was sorting them into groups. Those are the oldest ones, I think.'

Minty scrutinised the faces, but the shots were blurry and

indistinct, hazed by the sun, the sepia tint gone to sand and apricot. It was hard to pick out any distinguishing characteristics. Except for one: a dark-haired woman in a long, fitted dress, where the other women all wore aprons or smocks, the men in flat caps and serge. She leaned in close. Wasn't that Catherine? So hard to tell with old black-and-white photos: they lacked the definition and immediacy of modern images, but there was something about her expression. That fierce, penetrating gaze; the sensual mouth quirked in a half-smile. And then she thought she recognised another figure in the captured image: a young man in a flat cap. Dark eyes, the shape of them, the – what was the word? – epicanthal fold of the eyelids, struck her as familiar somehow, but she couldn't think why.

'These are more modern,' Dom said, pointing to the next set of photos, which also showed agricultural workers. This time, the snapshots were clearer and darker, printed on a grained paper.

There was the dark-haired woman again. But no, it couldn't be – for most of the workers appeared to be young women in breeches and baggy trousers, and she wore a dress that ended at mid-calf. Their attire was too modern to fit with the previous group. Women working the land, in what appeared to be uniform. 'Oh!' Minty said. 'They must be Women's Land Army, you know: the Land Girls, during the Second World War. Dig for Britain, and all that. I think that first set would be from around the time of the Great War, or maybe the early 1920s.'

She peered at the dark-haired woman again, then recoiled. She didn't appear to have aged...

'I don't think she's the same person,' Dom said, following his mother's gaze. 'I noticed her, too. She's very striking, but look—'

He unstuck the faded sepia image of the dark-haired woman and held it beside the more modern photo.

'You're right,' Minty agreed. Such a bold, forthright expression these two women shared. 'But they look very similar, and both photos were taken at Trengrose. Are there any other pictures of them?'

Dom showed her a formal portrait of the first woman in a hat and cinch-waisted dress, looking askance at the camera, and then another beside a man in army uniform. She was, unmistakably, the woman in the hall.

Minty's heart clutched, then leapt. 'It's Catherine Rosevear,' she said. 'She owned Trengrose in the early part of the twentieth century. And that must be her husband, the captain.' She gazed at the pair, thrilled, even a little awed, at last able to put a face to the name of Henry Glynn. Seeing the woman in the hall portrait was different to seeing her in a photograph, as if paint interposed a layer of distance and the artist's interpretation between subject and observer. But here she was, captured in an instant, leaping suddenly to life: her passionate exclamations, interest in politics, unconventional views, beautiful handwriting.

'How do you know?' Dom looked, she thought, a little disappointed that the mystery he had been piecing together might not be such a mystery after all.

Minty explained about the journal she had found in the davenport they had carried up to the attic, and Dom shouted, 'I thought that thing was heavy! Was there treasure in it as well?'

His mother grinned. 'There was a secret drawer, but sadly no treasure.'

'A secret drawer!'

'I'll show you later.'

Minty was too fascinated by the image of Catherine and Henry, taking in every detail of their faces and stance. Not a millimetre of them touched, she noticed that, but she supposed this was usual for formal portraits of the time. The captain was handsome in that typically Edwardian way: stiff, unsmiling, moustached. But Catherine looked… well, unhappy. Did it take a woman's eye to interpret that expression? The thought flickered across Minty's consciousness – did it maybe take an *unhappy woman's* eye to recognise it in another? She quashed the idea. Of course she, Minty, wasn't unhappy; just frustrated and annoyed. Not unhappy at all.

The memory of Toby's affair flickered and sent up a hot flame of resentment and anger that was suddenly fed by details in Toby's bank statements. Surely he wouldn't? Not again. She pushed the thought away, tamped the fire down, focused on telling Dom what she knew. 'Catherine and Henry were married just before the outbreak of war in 1914, and he died less than a year later, at the Second Battle of Ypres. He's listed on a memorial at the church in Paul, just down towards Mousehole.'

Dom was impressed. 'You've been doing a bit of digging, have you?'

'Not literally!' she laughed. 'But the Rosevear family grave is in the churchyard: they're both buried there, Catherine, and Eliza – the old lady who died last year, which is why Trengrose came up for sale.'

'Wow! Will you show it to me?'

This was the most engaged Minty had seen Dominic in months.

'If you'll show me your pictures in return. I'll trade you.'

'Deal!'

They made their way together around the other sets of images, which were more haphazard in composition and subject matter. Groups of people at what appeared to be some sort of celebration, in their best clothing: women in tea dresses, men in suit trousers, but with their shirts opened at the neck.

'1940s, definitely,' Minty declared. She leaned in closer. 'Look, this must be Eliza!'

The dark-haired woman was standing with a group of workers, her expression solemn and engaged. Dom held the sepia photo of Catherine Rosevear alongside. 'I think you're right. So, Eliza is Catherine and Henry's daughter?'

'Yes, I'm sure of it!'

Minty scanned the other images in the group until her attention was captured by a man and woman dancing among other couples, she with her head back, laughing; he thin and dark, she curvaceous and fair. There was one of the same young man on his own, leaning against an apple tree in blossom, one knee bent, the sole of his foot pressed against the trunk, looking solemn and intent, though he wore a jaunty-looking kerchief. And here, also in the orchard, was the man again leaning into the camera, hands outstretched as if to grab it back from the photographer, his eyes half-moons of mischief.

'I've seen him before,' Dom said, tapping the picture of the handsome young man.

Minty felt sure she had too. She turned to look at him. 'Where?'

Her son looked aside. 'Promise you won't be cross?'

She looked at him steadily, her mind running through all sorts of unlikely scenarios. 'Tell me?'

'At Ezra's.'

'Ezra Curnow? At the lodge cottage?' Minty frowned. 'I didn't know you were friendly with him.' Though she recalled now the summer day when they had walked Boris to the cottage and Dom had stayed behind to talk to him.

'I go and see him sometimes.' He paused. 'I like him, he shows me things.'

'What sort of things?' Minty was alarmed.

Her son shrugged. 'You know, nature stuff. Did you know that bees communicate with one another by dancing?'

Minty did not.

'Or that if one bee finds another one in trouble – like if it's been caught in a spiderweb or something – it'll go back to the hive and fetch other bees to help, and they'll all work together to clean it off and get it home?

'Or that you have to tell them all the important news and secrets or they'll leave the hive, or die. And if that happens, it's like a curse on the land. He tells them everything important: he told them about Eliza Rosevear's death – he calls her 'Miss Eliza' – and about us buying the house and moving in, and he introduced me to them. He showed me his chickens too, and his jackdaw, Merlin. He's really cool, like a figure out of legend.'

Cool. That wasn't a word Minty would ever have associated

with their elderly neighbour, and she found it hard to believe he had anything to offer in the way of companionship to a teenage boy. She hoped there was nothing nefarious going on.

Her scepticism must have shown, for Dom went on, 'He doesn't say a lot, but that's kind of relaxing. I saw the photos in his kitchen: there was a really old one, very faded, and also one of the man in this picture. I think he might have been Ezra's father. They have the same eyes.'

Minty peered closer at the image, the insouciant posture, the laughter in his regard, his fine, dark features, and remembered the little painting that hung behind the door in Eliza Rosevear's room. 'So this is Ethan Curnow,' she said. 'The people from the farm told me a bit about him.' What was it the old woman, Gemma, had said? That whatever had been going on between Ethan and Eliza, *Miss Catherine put a stop to it.* And she could clearly see that he bore a resemblance to old Ezra Curnow, with his dark eyes, the fold of eyelid, the fine-boned skull. This picture of him was a very candid photo if it was taken by Catherine's daughter Eliza. *All lovey-dovey,* that's what Gemma had said. Minty could believe it: there was a lot of emotion in the subject's face, and it did not look in the least repressed or reined in. Interesting…

'Anyway, when I was there last time, he gave me this broken old camera. Come and see.' Full of enthusiasm now, Dom led her into the ensuite bathroom.

Minty stood in the entrance and stared. Dom had turned it into a sort of darkroom, the window taped over, sombre drapes strung here and there; the smell of chemicals in the air, developing trays in the bath. And then she remembered his school report before all the trouble, praising his skills not just with a camera, but with developing, and how proud she had been at the time, thinking that he had inherited her artistic streak. He must have kept all his equipment.

'Look.' Dom held out a small black object to her.

It felt weighty and cold in her hand. Like a small bomb. She walked to the door to examine it. *–ak Bearing Shutter–* the brass lettering read over the arch of the lens, which was cracked.

'It's a VPK,' Dom said. 'A Vest Pocket Kodak. Ezra said the camera had originally belonged to Catherine Rosevear, and that her daughter Eliza had learned to use it, and she gave it to Ezra's dad, who then passed it on to Ezra. So I know the camera's really old. I checked it online and I reckon it's from 1915 or so.'

'That's a proper antique,' Minty said. 'But it looks in really good condition, apart from the lens and the marks.' She turned it over. 'Oh, a lot of scratches on this side.'

'It was an awful lot worse when I took it out of the box. It was completely seized up and covered in rust,' Dom said. 'At least I thought it was rust, but when I wiped it down with WD-40, it looked...' He paused. 'It was probably rust.'

His mother handed the precious object back to him. 'It's really a beautiful thing, even if it is broken,' she said. 'It was kind of him to give it to you.'

'Oh, it's not broken now. I took it apart and cleaned it and put it back together again by following a YouTube tutorial. I don't know if it'll still take pictures – that's the next experiment – but I managed to get the old film out and develop it.'

'What?' Minty was having to revise her concept of her own son and his abilities moment by moment.

'Come and see.'

He showed her a line of pegged images: young men in uniform, shorts and short-sleeved shirts and caps, rifles slung across their backs in a mountain landscape that looked arid and rocky. Two young men, an arm around each other's shoulder, grinning into the lens. Was it a trick shot, one side mirroring the other? They looked identical; but no – one held a hand behind his back; the other a cigarette. They were the spitting image of the handsome young man standing against the apple tree in the 1940s photos.

'One of them is Ezra,' Dom said from behind her. 'Doesn't he look like his father? You can see the resemblance around the eyes, and the way he holds himself. He told me he had a brother, but he never said anything about having a twin!' He seemed excited to share this bit of information. 'Look, here they are again, playing football; and here, a bit closer up.'

His mother gazed at the pair of young men.

'Look—' Dom pointed to the photo. 'Ezra's got the same scar.'

Minty, who had vaguely noticed a jagged white mark on the old man's forehead when they met, was startled. So Ezra Curnow had a brother: a twin! She couldn't help but wonder what had happened to the unnamed one, and whether he, too, had a claim on the lodge cottage. That would complicate matters even further. Toby wouldn't be happy to hear about that, not happy at all. A little tremor of dread ran through her. For some reason, she didn't want to think about Toby: embers were glowing, threatening to ignite. Minty pushed these intrusive thoughts aside and concentrated on Dom.

'You've done a brilliant job developing these old photos,' she said, beaming at her son. 'It must have been terrifically tricky. What else did you find?'

Dom beamed at this unaccustomed praise, and Minty suddenly experienced a stab of guilt. Had she and Toby been too bound up in their own troubles to give their son the attention and encouragement he so clearly needed?

'It *was* really tricky.' His smile gleamed: even in the half-light of the improvised darkroom, Minty could tell he was proud of his achievements. 'I've no idea when these were taken, though, or where. It's definitely not Britain. It looks like somewhere abroad. Is that some sort of British Army uniform they're wearing?'

Minty agreed that it did look like some kind of hot weather uniform, though she was ashamed to admit that she had no idea where or when the Army might have been deployed in – she tried to work it out, what? The late 1950s? Early 1960s? A bit of a hole in her historical knowledge. 'We'll have to look it up,' she said, 'see if we can work out where it might be.' She paused. 'Or you could just ask Ezra.'

Dom shook his head. 'I don't think he'll tell me. He pretty

much shoved the box at me and when I looked inside and said there was a load of old photos in there as well as the camera, and asked did he want them back, he just waved it away. "Having a bit of a clear-out," he said.'

Minty wondered at this. Was the old man preparing to move out after all?

Dom looked pensive. After a long, quiet moment, he added, 'I think Ezra's had a hard life. Sometimes when he thinks I'm not looking and his face relaxes, he looks really sad. I think he's almost as lonely as me. I mean, he's got his chickens, and bees, and Bucca and Merlin, but...'

'Oh, Dom!' Minty's hand flew to her mouth in shock. 'Are you really so unhappy?'

He shrugged. 'I don't know. There's no one down here to be friends with, apart from Ezra. And it's all pretty different to what I'm used to.' The darkness of the bathroom made for a confessional atmosphere. 'I know you worry about me, Mum. You know, the drugs and all that. I'm not an addict, though. I like a little bit of weed every so often, but I wouldn't try anything worse, you know, harder.' He pondered for a moment whether to come clean about smoking with Ezra and decided against it. 'And I don't drink or do anything else. I'm pretty much a saint compared to some of my friends.'

Minty laughed and ruffled his hair. 'Okay, St Dominic. Let's go downstairs and I'll make us some fresh tea, and then I'll show you the journal I found.'

Dom retrieved the tray from his desk and carried it out into the corridor. Minty lingered for a moment in the doorway, gazing around at the images on the walls. Curnow men had been Trengrose estate managers for over a century. It was a whole lost way of life. That thought made her feel mournful, but something else as well. The puzzle she and Dominic had just shared, putting the pieces of a historical jigsaw together, was enjoyable, enlivening. Trengrose history springing to life in front of their eyes. Wouldn't it make a fascinating shared project, finding out whatever they could, Dom working on the pictures, she on the words? All at once, her Civil War book receded and she felt a sort of buzzing in her brain, like a busy bee at work, bringing pollen to the hive, starting the process of making honey, bright and gold and vibrant. The more she entertained this thought, the more the buzzing became a kind of music that thrummed right through her, until at last it felt as if the house was the hive, and she and Dom were constituent parts of its history, its community. They were, she thought. They were the present and the future of Trengrose!

But so was Ezra Curnow. And here they were, trying to evict the old man from his cottage, breaking an unbroken link with Trengrose that went back generations. Ever since she had started delving into Catherine's journal and the history of the family and the estate, she had begun to feel rather more equivocal about trying to oust Ezra Curnow from the lodge cottage. Toby was dead-set on evicting him, and her husband was tenacious when it came to any business dealing in which he felt someone was trying to put one over on him or take him for a fool. He was a point-scorer, her husband: it was, she supposed, something that made him so successful in what he did; but his instinct for winning at all costs often blinded him to rights and wrongs. Though the old man was turning out to be an indomitable foe.

She had suspected for a while that Ezra was the source of the troubles that had beset them these past months – the wrong trees felled, the dead animals turning up on their doorstep, the vandalising of the signs, maybe even their recent drainage problems. And possibly even the rats? But that seemed too dastardly even for such a determined old man. And now it seemed that he and Dom were friends. Might that turn out to be another chapter in his campaign of harassment?

That was a disturbing thought. She would have to get to the bottom of it.

She pulled Dom's bedroom door behind her, but it wouldn't quite close and made a quiet grating sound, as if an object was caught between the bottom edge and the bare floorboards. Someone must have dropped something, she thought, bending to retrieve whatever it was, and picked up a bit of metal that glinted in the dull November light.

It was an earring. And not one of hers. Nor was it Miranda's style.

At once, the banked embers in her brain roared to life as her suspicions caught fire; but no, that was ridiculous. She was here all the time: it would have been impossible for Toby to have sneaked another woman in here. Unless, of course, it had fallen out of his pocket. She looked more closely at the jewel. It was elegant, a simple curl of gold enclosing a small dark stone. Onyx, she thought. For patience and determination in the face of all odds.

Another thought struck her. She pocketed the earring, pulled Dom's door to – this time it closed snugly and silently – and followed her son downstairs into the hall. Then, instead of going straight into the kitchen, she went to stand in front of the portrait of Catherine Rosevear and there confirmed her guess. Holding the earring out on her palm before the painting, she said softly, 'I believe this is yours.'

She could have sworn she heard the whispered reply, 'No, my dear: it is yours now. All of it is yours.'

31

Dear Gamps,
I'm coming home for Christmas!

Sam paused, then put his pen down. No, 'home' *was* the right word. The house in Kent where his mother lived alone after the failure of her latest marriage was a house and nothing more.

He and his mother had a difficult relationship. He found Sylvie self-absorbed and mercenary, more focused on social status, a fashionable wardrobe, golf club membership, the latest model sports car. His upbringing had been fraught with difficulties adjusting to new places, new 'fathers', new schools. It had been hard to make and keep friends when his mother upped sticks every few years, pinning her hopes for the perfect life on a different husband. Three now; and surely a fourth would be along sometime soon: Sylvie's complex nature, combined with her striking looks and sophisticated style, was like honey to bears. Her repudiation of Cornwall and her denigration of everything to do with it gave him an almost physical pain. He wondered, now that he had some distance from her, if this might have something to do with his passion for the county and all it represented to him: it offered a sense of freedom in counterpoint to her smothering rules, suburban ambitions and focus on money as the answer to all things.

His great-uncle Ezra was her opposite: gruff and unkempt in his wellies and ancient corduroys, living off his little bit of land in a ramshackle cottage that had changed very little in the hundred-odd years it had existed; and Trengrose – semi-wild, historical, lost in time, remote from the rest of the world. It was where he retreated to in his mind when he was far away from Cornwall: a haven, a place of safety and repose when the press of the great city became too much for him.

Christmas in Cornwall beckoned. It wouldn't be the first time. He had pretty much lived with his great-uncle during his teens, at least out of school term. He remembered nut roasts and crispy potatoes, Ezra's home-made Christmas pudding alight with blue flame, rich in his mouth with clotted cream from the farm, the brandy-soaked sultanas bursting between his teeth; the door of the old range open so that the light of the flames danced across the polished wooden table, in the curve of their glasses, across the family photos and Bucca's patterned fur. He recalled Ezra reading poetry to him by the light of the oil lamp, which sent little twists of black fume spiralling into the rafters; sleeping so soundly that he wasn't even aware of the window breaking in a storm when a flying branch from the old damson tree cracked the pane.

But this time would be different. He took up his pen again and wrote:

I've been invited by Ran (Miranda) Hardman to spend Christmas with her family up at the big house. You remember her, Gamps, from that day I took her for a walk, and you said to take her to the Fox Dance? It must have worked...

When Ran had invited him to come to Trengrose for the festivities, he had said yes without a beat of hesitation, then immediately felt guilt-wracked. His first thought had not been of his mother, but to wonder how Ezra might react to him staying with the family at the big house, who were, Ran had awkwardly confided to him, trying to persuade Gamps to leave his cottage. And then, rather belatedly, he tried to imagine exactly how he would break this news to his mother. He had still been wrestling with the form of words he might use when – as if magically summoned – Sylvie had called him to let him know that she would be spending Christmas with her French family: she accepted at face value his excuse that he couldn't afford the Eurostar fare.

It wasn't as if he disliked spending time with the French side of the family. It had always seemed strange to Sam that his grandmother Gwen, who had been married to Ezra's brother Arthur, had fled Cornwall for a foreign country where she knew no one, but Sylvie had told him that his grandmother was a headstrong woman who had suffered a great tragedy, and had, just as so many young men had done for centuries before her, run away to sea. The *Marguerite*, a Breton crabbing lugger, had put into Newlyn for repairs and, job done, had carried Gwen off across the Channel just like a pirate abandoning a community of fishermen working on luggers for another community of men doing the same, but in a foreign language. And there she had married again, to a lovely man, but had died tragically, oh so tragically, in the throes of having his child.

Sam had visited Le Conquet once with his mother, and had been nonplussed to find it remarkably like Mousehole: a picturesque fishing village also in the remote and farthest west of the country. He had liked its unspoiled atmosphere and the unfussy practicality of the crabbers. But the language was beyond him, it was far away and hard to get to, and the similarities just made him yearn for Cornwall all the more. He would though, he thought now, love to take Ran to meet them one day.

If he survived Christmas under the scrutiny of her parents.

And so long as they left Ezra and his cottage alone. Doubt gnawed at him. Surely they wouldn't turf an old man out of his home, the place he had been born? Where would that leave him and Ran? Would they end up staring at one another from opposing sides of a battlefield? Surely it wouldn't come to that. The Hardmans weren't monsters, were they? Thus far, apart from Ran, he'd only met Toby, who had seemed decent enough, up to the time they'd spotted him with that woman outside Fortnum's. But Ran seemed to really love her mother – 'she can be uptight, even a bit OCD; but she drives herself really hard to make life better for everyone. And she's writing a book – she's really creative: she was an artist, you know, before she met my dad.'

No, he couldn't believe that anyone who had brought into the world a being as bright and beautiful as Ran could possibly do anything so wicked.

Well, he would cross that battlefield when he came to it. Before then, he needed to explain to Ezra the extraordinary change in his emotional circumstances.

You see, this amazing thing has happened. Ran and I are going out – you'd probably say courting, but it's not that serious...

Sam stopped again. It *was* serious for him. He could hardly think about anything other than Ran, could barely concentrate on his studies, tripped over things in the street, gave the wrong pizzas to customers. He had never felt this way about anyone in his life. Instinctively, he knew that his great-uncle would understand this, and not tease or belittle him for saying so.

Well, actually, that's a lie. I love her, Gamps, I really do. She's amazing, full of fire and principle, clever and funny too. When I'm with her, it's like being at the epicentre of an earthquake, or the stillpoint of a tornado. Or in the middle of the ripples caused by dropping a pebble in a lake. All that energy, creating waves that spread out right to the banks. Did you know those ripples echo the shape of the object thrown into the water? So if you throw a straight stick in, it'll cause straight waves, and if you throw a ball in it'll create round waves. If I'm that object, and Ran is the lake, imagine all those Sam-shaped waves spreading right across the reservoir at Drift!

He stared at this odd pronouncement, but rather than screw the paper up to start again, he decided to leave it be. He could imagine Ezra reading it and muttering 'Daft tuss' to himself, and cheering up the old boy seemed worth the ridicule.

Anyway, enough of my nonsense. Hope to see you on the 20th. We're coming by train (a luxury!) so I should see you later that afternoon. Really looking forward to it: if it weren't for Ran I don't know how I could stand London a day longer.

Hope you're well, Gamps. Give the chickens an extra handful of feed and Merlin some titbits for me. Rub Bucca under his chin, if he'll let you, and tell the bees I'm coming.

Lots of love
Sam

32

Dom was more interested in the secret drawer in the davenport than in the old journal. Minty sat beside him on the floor in the attic with the diary in her lap as he crawled under the desk and examined the mechanism.

'How clever people were back then to make this!' He seemed astounded.

His mother grinned. The younger generation always thought people in history were less savvy, less inventive, more backward, than their contemporaries. She caught herself in this thought, recalling how she had thought about old Ezra Curnow, called him a peasant, probably illiterate, and her cheeks flamed. She'd been reading a lot of historical sources, originally for her Civil War project, more lately about old Cornwall, and one of the things that had struck her forcibly was that, essentially, people did not change, but shared the same motivations and emotions, the same hopes and dreams as every other human being: for peace and stability, love, companionship and well-being. Yes, the nuances changed – the politics and the social mores, the fashions and circumstances; but underneath it all, people were people, no matter their upbringing.

Seeing those old photos of the agricultural workers, the estate managers and the mistresses of Trengrose, had made her aware that she was part of an ongoing tapestry of life here in this corner of Cornwall. Trengrose House had stood for hundreds of years; the fields around it had probably been cultivated for millennia: throughout everything – wars and plague, hard seasons and good harvests – the land persisted. People came and went, eking out a living; working, loving and dying, bringing new generations into the world to carry on the pattern. Each generation brought alterations to the stitches and colours, no doubt, and every life lengthened the tapestry of the place, weaving their threads through those of the animals and birds, the crops and wildflowers, and the ever-present trees, and she felt again sorrow for the felling of the big pine.

Even as she thought this, the scent of lavender bloomed around her, so much so that eventually she sneezed.

Dom, startled, hit his head on the underside of the davenport, and squirmed back out. He scrutinised his mother. 'Are you all right?' He thought she was looking rather dazed.

Minty blinked, coming out of her trance. 'Yes, I think so.' Her nose wrinkled. 'Can you smell that?'

'What?' Dom frowned. He concentrated. 'Oh, sort of like flowers? I thought that was a room spray, or your perfume.'

'No...' Minty said slowly. The scent of lavender was still strong. Her skin prickled as if someone were standing just behind her. A tremor ran through the centre of her: a sort of warning signal?

Dom had gone back to his examination of the drawer mechanism, and the rest of the davenport.

As if under a sort of compulsion, Minty opened the journal at random. The chaos of the past few weeks had interrupted her reading, and she felt a sense of joy at returning to her research.

The page it fell open to was not in Catherine Rosevear's exquisite italic hand but dashed off in a less controlled and decorative style which immediately snagged the eye. Not a variation of Catherine's hand, and in black rather than dark-blue ink, using a thicker nib, the lettering more upright, the descender lines of the 'g's and 'f's curtailed in comparison to the previous elegant cursive. How curious! She read:

Watching those Curnow lads fighting again today. One had the other by the neck and had already struck him by the time I caught his arm and wrenched the weapon – a shard of one of the old clay pots that broke during last winter's frost – from his hand. The injured twin was bleeding freely. 'Why do you two fight like this?' I raged. Arthur (the injured one, as I later found out) was on the edge of tears and couldn't speak, but Ezra glared at me. 'There can't be two of us,' he said, then ran off, still in a temper. This remark stayed with me. I know the Victorians used to think that twins were like one soul divided, but I think that's nonsense. It's not as if the boys are opposites: one meek, the other dominant, two halves of a whole. They are very like in far more than looks, but Arthur is generally the sweeter of the two. I see Ethan so clearly in them both.

There was a line at the end of the entry, but it had been crossed out. Minty held the page to the light and was able to make out the last sentence.

How I wish they were mine.

Oh. Poor, poor Eliza, unmarried and childless. For a moment, Minty felt quite choked with emotion.

There followed notes about items required from the market and about the need to source a new cockerel.

'Oh, listen to this, Dom!' Minty read the next passage. '*Ethan came up to the house this afternoon to thank me for patching up poor Arthur. The boys had had a fight,*' she explained to her son, 'and Eliza gave him first aid.'

Dom did not look impressed. He had come out from beneath the davenport and was now fiddling with the little drawers arranged along the back of the desk.

'Then it goes on: *The pair of us were polite and proper, though his hand shook when he pressed a small, paper-covered parcel into my hand, then left swiftly. I unwrapped it after he'd gone and found inside a small bottle of Yardley's English Lavender.*'

Dom stopped what he was doing. 'Lavender?' Suddenly, he had remembered Ezra's bubble bath, set beside his bathtub in the orchard. Well, that was weird.

Minty was feeling those shivers again. Was it just a coincidence? She didn't think so. She read on: '*I burst into tears, which is very unlike me, because I never, never cry. But I remember telling Ethan how much I loved the lavender eau de toilette Mummy used to wear. How had he got hold of this little bottle? And how much had it cost him? I waited till I'd been into Truro to give myself a plausible provenance for the perfume before wearing it. Mummy complimented me, so I dabbed her wrists too. I think it helps her failing memory. Now we both wear it, which is bittersweet: not just because of the scent, which is in itself melancholy and nostalgic, but for the emotions we share when we smell it. Our separate loves and secrets are knotted together like two threads of the same colour, but in slightly different shades.*'

What did that mean, '*two threads of the same colour*'?

Minty asked the question of Dom but got no answer: he was so absorbed in his task that he appeared to have stopped listening to her altogether.

It was clear that Eliza had been in love with Ethan Curnow, and that he had also had tender feelings for her; but he'd married someone else – Tamsin, wasn't it? – and had the twins with her. Ethan had, Gemma said, broken Eliza's heart. She'd also said, *Miss Catherine put a stop to it.*

The twins were so dark of hair and feature, and so was Eliza. But Gemma had been sure no affair had ever come to fruition.

Then she thought: *but Catherine Rosevear was dark, too,* and an idea blasted into her mind: shocking, scandalous.

No, it couldn't be.

Leafing through the pages of the journal, Minty reread the

entries leading up to and just after the period of Miss Catherine's marriage to Captain Henry Glynn, and the mention of the mysterious 'J'. She considered the dates of the events that she knew, but still nothing came clear. She could sense that the answer to the mystery was just out of reach, a ghostly shape hiding between the carefully formed letters on the page, but it remained elusive.

She ploughed on again, through diary entries about village fetes and carnivals, harvests, Tom Bawcock's Eve celebrations down in Mousehole, Christmas carol services, coal deliveries, the first snowdrops in the woods, and on through the turn of the seasons. Pride at Eliza winning a prize at school; a twenty-first birthday party at the house.

Catherine's handwriting became, she noticed, less precise and firm as she turned the pages. There were long gaps of empty paper, followed by a dated entry weeks or even months later, inconsequential notes, and once something was written that had then been entirely inked out. Spilled water had obscured one page and blotched the verso, but on the next leaf she read:

> *This is a note to <u>my beloved daughter Eliza</u> to whom I now pass on my journal. My dear, I have written and sealed a letter, addressed to you, and placed it in my bureau. It is to be read <u>only</u> on the event of my death. My mind is failing me, my heart too, according to Dr Tregenna: I shall write no more, Mummy.*

It was only after this entry and the two blank pages that followed it, like a polite pause or a mark of respect, that Eliza Rosevear's hand had taken over the journal, using it to jot down everything from her shopping reminders to lists of wildflowers seen, and estate accounts. More jottings, and a couple of pencil sketches of birds with such notations as 'Eastern Black Redstart' and 'Wheatear'; columns of figures and phone numbers.

Unlike her mother, Eliza did not appear to use the journal

much for personal reflection, which made the passage about the boys fighting and the lavender perfume stand out, as did a few short entries in swift succession. The first read:

That fucking, fucking tractor! I just can't take it in. I don't know which of us is most shocked and destroyed, me or Mummy. Oh, Ethan, Ethan. My god, how will we go on without you?

Minty's eyebrows shot up. This was a very different voice to Eliza's mother's far more modulated, elegant tone, and such forcefulness rather offended her sensibilities, but only for a moment. She began to revise her opinion of Eliza Rosevear.

And then:

I went to pay my respects to Tamsin, but she shut the door in my face.

Finally:

Mother's funeral. Paul Church, 11:30 am.
Order flowers.

Minty stared at these entries for a long time. She could feel the tragedy inherent in the stark words. Ethan Curnow, Ezra's father – dead in a tractor accident? That was what it looked like; his wife – his widow – refusing to see his employer; indeed, shutting the door in her face. Rude, or justified?

And then poor Catherine, dead not long after. How utterly awful. She remembered the grave in the village churchyard. *Catherine Rosevear, born 1881, died 1961: 'Love everlasting'.*

So Eliza had survived her mother for nearly half a century and had never married. What a solitary life she'd led, Minty thought, alone in this big old house – with the maid and the cook, and with her agricultural workers roundabouts, but even so: no Ethan, whatever he was to her.

It seemed rather a terrible fate, like being sealed up in a huge stone sarcophagus away from the rest of the world. Deprived of love. In a state of mourning. But then, as the scent of lavender assailed her once more, she began to revise her view. Trengrose did not have a tragic atmosphere, didn't seem to be imbued with dark and sorrowful events, with broken hearts and empty lives. There was something both homely and majestic about the house. Something crying out to be loved. And though it was large, it wasn't vast and unmanageable, especially now that the major renovations were underway, and they had a working kitchen and the plumbing and heating had been sorted out.

Her heart started to beat a little faster. It was hers: she could *feel* that. Her house: her home. And there was still so much more for her to do to it to make it her own. It filled Minty with anticipation when she considered the areas she had yet to get to grips with – the library, the drawing room, the three as yet undecorated bedrooms. To say nothing of the courtyard, the orangery and the gardens...

'Mum!' Dom's shout jolted her out of her reverie.

'What is it, darling?'

'This thing hasn't just got one secret drawer: look! I was fiddling around with this one up on the top, see?' He removed one of the little drawers that sat at the back of the desk part of the bureau and pointed into the shadows beneath. 'See this little catch-thing here? You push it in and sideways, just like for the drawer under the desk, and—'

A section of the back of the davenport now slid aside to reveal an object that Dom fingered out of its hiding place and handed to his mother.

It was a white envelope, addressed in a shaky version of Catherine Rosevear-Glynn's distinctive hand.

It read:

To my daughter Eliza.

When she turned it over, she saw a flattened blob of red sealing wax with, around the circumference, the letters

T R E N G R O S E

spelled out on it.

The seal was undisturbed.

33

Sam and Miranda boarded the train at Paddington Station. Ran could tell by the way Sam moved and stared around that it must be his first time taking the train here, and for a moment felt guilty. It was the expensive option, especially at this time of year, and it must mean he had had to dig deep into his reserves, but he had never protested or tried to persuade her to opt for the much cheaper coach from Victoria, which really she should have – in retrospect – suggested. It was one of the things she liked about him: a consideration that bordered on chivalry. It was old-fashioned, unusual in the circles she mixed in, where young men either wantonly sponged off you or made a fuss about lavishing their wealth upon you. She'd had her fill of both types – the wannabe artists, poets and musicians, who regarded it as beneath their dignity to take an unworthy job that might interfere with their precious creativity, but thought nothing of living off the paltry wages of their waitress-girlfriends; the businessmen who thought that because they had taken you to a fancy members' club and loudly ordered champagne, they also had purchased the right to take you home and stick their fat tongues down your throat and their sweaty hands between your legs.

No, Sam was nothing like that. As the rain-lashed countryside fleeted past, she found her mind gravitating to the night before last, when her flatmates had been away and she and Sam had had the place to themselves, and he had cooked for her – proper, delicious food involving garlic and fresh herbs – before picking her up bodily and carrying her off to her room where they had fucked for hours. Yes, *fucked*. Sam didn't like the word, except as an expletive, and that rarely, but Ran made no bones about it. Lovemaking was such a sappy term. She associated it with the slimy business types and languid poets, and rejected it fiercely. What she and Sam did together was what healthy young animals did, but with the glorious addition of imagination, awareness and humour. When at last he had fallen into an exhausted sleep, she had left the bedside light on for a while so that she could admire his body in repose: the remnants of his summer tan still colouring his arms, his legs and neck; the pale contrast of his belly and flanks vulnerable despite the muscles still so clearly defined even in relaxation, still firm beneath the velvet of his skin. Sam's weren't muscles gained by the endless lifting of weights while admiring his physique in the mirror of an expensive gym, but muscles acquired by constant use and movement.

She could imagine him flowing up a Cornish sea cliff like some species of big cat. Even on the climbing wall at Mile End or the Westway, surrounded by top-heavy young men in Lycra huffing up absurd overhangs, he stood out for the fluid way he balanced and reached and transferred his weight and ran his feet up and made every problem look effortless. She caught them watching him sometimes, envious, resentful, puzzled; no one wearing cut-off jeans and such battered old climbing shoes should be able to flash a 6a route. And the women, too: they stopped coiling their ropes and chalking their hands in order to look at Sam. Far from feeling jealous, Ran rather enjoyed their appreciation of him. Because he was hers. Even though that might be a bourgeois, materialistic concept, deep down she revelled in her ownership of him. For she knew how deep were his feelings for her.

What had really surprised her, given the unconventional free spirit she had always thought herself to be, was how completely and utterly and irretrievably she had fallen in love with him. This unsophisticated, decent, handsome, Cornish… She searched for a word and embarrassed herself by failing to come up with anything better than 'hunk'. Thinking this now, she failed to suppress a small snort of laughter.

'What's so funny?'

She grinned. 'Oh, nothing.' She knew he wouldn't press her – it wasn't his style.

Another thing she liked… loved… about him. In other relationships, she had often felt smothered, caged, pinned down. But Sam gave her space for her thoughts, didn't crowd her, didn't encroach.

He handed her the tail end of the pasty he had bought at the station. 'Go on, you finish it.' Despite her slenderness, Ran was always ravenous.

'Don't you want it?'

He made a face. 'Doesn't really warrant the name of "pasty",' he said. 'Wait till Gamps makes you one of his. Veggie, though, he don't eat meat.'

'He's an old hippie!'

'Well, sort of.'

Miranda applied herself to the pastry crust and its indeterminate filling, chewed, swallowed, found herself noticing for the first time the way it left a sort of lardy residue on her tongue and the roof of her mouth and washed this away with a swig of soda. 'Remind me what your mum's doing for Christmas?'

Sam's expression became shuttered and Ran regretted asking. Still, no one here was playing happy families. God knew she wasn't looking forward to telling her mother about seeing Dad outside Fortnum's with that woman. She knew about Sam's mother – how she had gone from one man to another as some women did, moving further and further from Cornwall and up the social ladder with each successive relationship or marriage. How Sam had changed schools each time, never really making friends, forever missing the only place he'd ever really been happy. She'd met Sylvie a week ago – at an awkward lunch at a little Italian restaurant off Carnaby Street, where Sam had invited them both and insisted on paying the bill. Whatever she'd expected of Sam's mother, it hadn't been what she'd got – coiffed and manicured and elegant in a formally cut navy blue suit and bright silk scarf. Where Sam was bluff and open, she'd found Sylvie rather cold and withdrawn, though she had warmed up a little on finding out that Ran's mother was Araminta Hervey – 'Oh, I've read her pieces in *Country House*, and didn't she do a marvellous article in *Tatler* about a mansion she was doing up for some foreign financier?'

Yes, Ran had said. That would have been about Misbourne House, the place her mother had helped a Russian called Alexei to restore. Sylvie's eyes had glittered covetously. 'How marvellous! And is this Alexei married?' Ran had replied in the negative, remembering how Alexei's gaze had lingered on her, how uncomfortable it had made her feel. He had the cold black eyes of a shark, a smile that never warmed his face. You wouldn't want to get on the wrong side of a man like that. She was pretty sure 'financier' was a considerable euphemism.

'Mum's spending time with her family in France,' Sam said now.

'And you didn't want to go with her? Don't you like them?'

Sam thought about this. 'They're okay. I quite enjoy going over there – I'll take you one day. But I'd much rather be with you and see Gamps and Trengrose.' And he started telling her all the things he wanted to show her. They would climb down the vertiginous path to Pedn Vounder, the golden-sanded beach just around the corner from the famous and beautiful Porthcurno. Pedn was more of a secret. It was also a nudist beach, and Sam, recalling their first swim together, when Ran had stripped off and eeled around him like a sleek selkie, knew she would be charmed by it. They would walk across the moors to Men an Tol and slip through the ancient, holed stone – for luck and health – then explore the ancient Iron Age village of Carn Euny; and offer up flowers and charms to the spirit of place at the sacred well at Sancreed. Walk down the steep hillside to Mousehole for a pint in The Ship, and into Newlyn to the smart little cinema that had recently opened there. His finances didn't run to the luxury of a meal in its bistro, at Mackerel Sky, or at lovely 2 Fore Street in Mousehole, but he knew enough fishing folk to get hold of a free monkfish tail to cook for her on Great-uncle Ezra's old stove, with a bit of saffron and some home-made bread.

Ran laughed. 'We'll never fit all that in on this visit!'

Sam blushed. 'Sorry, I suppose I was getting ahead of myself a bit,' he said gruffly.

She put a hand on his knee, squeezed. 'We'll have loads of time to explore Cornwall together.'

'We will?'

The way his whole demeanour changed, shone, gave her strength. 'I've been giving things some thought. Mum is going to need a lot of support at Trengrose once I've told her what we saw. This time she's bound to kick Dad out. So I'm going to stay on for a bit.' She paused. 'Maybe longer than a bit.'

She had poured out the whole tale about Chrissie and her father to Sam a few hours after they'd seen the pair getting into that taxi, when Sam had picked her up from work. How Toby Hardman had cheated on her mother with his much younger colleague, telling Minty he was working overtime or away on big deals, when in fact he was screwing Chrissie in her Walthamstow flat.

The thing was, she told Sam now, 'Mum knew about the first time. She'd seen his bank statements online, for meals out in the East End, even takeaways when he said he was abroad. Dad's a bit of a dolt sometimes, useless at covering his tracks, especially online. But she didn't kick him out: she said she'd let it run its course.'

'That must've been hard for her.'

'It was.' Ran bit her lip. She hadn't made it any easier for her mother: had had a massive tantrum and run off with Jez, who played guitar in a band that was just starting to get known, though not well enough known, somehow, for him to contribute to the bills she paid on the flat they shared. 'But there's no way she's going to put up with it again. I won't let her!' she said fiercely. 'This time, I'm going to stay put and do whatever it takes to support her.'

Sam nodded slowly. He looked her squarely in the eye and said, 'It will be all right. Whatever you need from me, you tell me, okay?'

His kindness caused her to promptly burst into tears. Eventually, she blew her nose noisily on the paper napkin that had come with the pasty and firmed her jaw. 'Well, that's got the weeping out of the way.'

'Onward and upward, eh?'

She smiled wonkily. 'Onward, anyway.'

34

Winter afternoons in Trengrose came in two varieties: sharp and bright, or wet and gloomy. That afternoon was the latter, and Ezra's arthritis was playing him up. He'd been out in the morning to a nettle patch he kept uncut close to the cottage and had liberally stung his swollen knuckles with the leaves, following the 'no pain no gain' principle. Tomorrow, the swelling and stiffness would subside, but right now they were tingling like crazy pins and needles and he was still finding it hard to form a fist or hold anything small, which had put him in something of a bad mood. So when he heard footsteps on his garden path, he was ready for a fight. Which was just as well.

More than one set of footsteps did not presage anything good, though he recalled Sam's letter and wondered whether maybe the lad was bringing that pretty girl from the big house with him, since the pair of them were due to arrive by train either today or tomorrow, unless he'd got his dates wrong, which did happen from time to time. Nothing to do with failing memory, just that dates held very little meaning in Ezra's world. He did know it was Christmas in a few days' time – it was impossible to avoid that knowledge since just about every radio programme seemed obsessed with the holiday, with its traditions and meaning, with family celebrations and gifts. But for Ezra, every Christmas would now remind him of Eliza's death, and it cast a pall.

He was pretty sure those footsteps did not belong to Sam, and absolutely certain the second set were not Miranda's – yes, that was her name: Miranda, daughter of Prospero, though Toby Hardman was certainly no sorcerer.

In the time that had elapsed since the visit of the thug who had come to try to serve the eviction warrant (which he'd used to light the range), and who had then – he was sure – put a brick through his window – Ezra had bored a small spyhole in his front door, and he now set an eye to it.

Two of them! He recognised the first as his previous caller and swore silently. The second was chunky, with high Slavic cheekbones and the pallor that comes from long stints inside. They stopped in front of the door, and he saw that they were both carrying what looked like police-issue batons. But he knew they were not police. 'Private security forces', wasn't that what they called themselves these days? Ex-military, skinning the gullible rich; out of uniform, out of shape.

The second man had now vanished from sight, no doubt to go round the back, cutting off Ezra's means of escape. The first had taken a device from his pocket – a lock bypass tool. Professional burglar, Ezra thought. Bet he'd seen jail time, too.

As the thug leaned in to apply the device, Ezra opened the door without warning, and the man almost fell inside.

'Bring your bleddy army, did you?'

The man opened his mouth to reply, and at that moment Ezra pulled sharply on the cord that hung by the door and quickly stepped back. The bucket, which had been balanced up on the roof by means of a cradle woven from hazel twigs, now inverted itself, cascading its foul contents over the man's head. Ezra was beyond satisfied to see that some of his bioweapon had even splashed into the mercenary's open mouth. The man recoiled, spitting and swearing.

Bob Hockin had supplied Ezra with the contents. 'What do

you want that for?' he'd asked, nose wrinkling. Ezra had told him it was good for the compost.

Now, he slammed the front door shut, and bolted it top and bottom. *Try using your lock-breaker on that*, he thought, and nipped round to the back door to attach the crocodile clip he kept waiting there for just this eventuality. He was just in time.

In the moment he stepped away from the back door, which was half glazed, he saw the second man set his hand to the old brass handle and then leap backwards, yelping like a stuck pig.

Ezra had wired the old car battery he used to power summer irrigation in the greenhouse to the handle and it still appeared to have a fair bit of juice left in it. *Surprise.* Still, it probably wouldn't stop the goon for long.

Ezra picked up the wooden stick he had set nearby and forced his uncooperative fingers to grip it tightly. Normally he used this fine length of hawthorn as a walking aid on the trickier parts of the coast path to Lamorna, but he had somewhat modified it.

The partially electrocuted thug was enraged and had recovered faster than expected. He kicked the door down and came at Ezra with a murderous expression, his baton extended, catching Ezra a painful blow across the shoulder as the old man ducked to avoid the head shot. Ezra spun and swung the club under the intruder's next blow, hammering his opponent on the upper chest. *Speed. Aggression.* Not so hot on the speed, but he'd tried to make up for it with the aggression. He heard the man's collarbone break, and with some difficulty extracted his weapon from the man's plaid jacket, where a couple of the nails with which he had studded it (an old Cyprus farmer's trick) were caught in the fabric.

Tears of shock and pain sprang to the man's eyes, and he swore in no language Ezra recognised.

Ezra's own shoulder was hurting like buggery, but he wasn't going to show it. With studied nonchalance, he examined the business end of the knobkerry, wiped some of the blood off the nails. His fingers throbbed as he rubbed the stick, for luck: hawthorn was the goddess's own tree.

He saw that the original thug had now arrived at the back door looking like an afterwalker out of one of the ancient Icelandic sagas, the ones who rose from the dead to terrorise the living. Cow urine and liquefied faeces dripped off him. The stench was eye-watering. In the moment in which the second man caught sight of this apparition, Ezra managed to hit him again, this time in the leg, making him stumble and impede the charge of the afterwalker, who had murder in his eyes.

Ezra nipped neatly around the corner and down the steep granite steps that led into the subterranean, pitch-black depths of the cellar.

The thugs followed. At the top of the steps, the first one searched for, and did not find, a light switch, so, with each hand braced against the opposing wall, he made his way down: one step, two steps…

He went flying, landing in a heap at the bottom of the steps with a howl.

The shape of the second man appeared at the top of the stairs. He gazed down into the gloom. '*Ty che blyad?* Can't see. What happen?'

'Tripwire, third step!' the other rasped back. 'Careful, the old tosser thinks he's James Bond or something. He's down here somewhere – there's some sort of cellar. We've got him now, but I think I broke my bloody leg!'

Pause. Then, 'I call ambulance?'

'There's no signal: you know that, arsehole.'

'*Schas po ebalu poluchish, suka, blyad!*' the second man swore. Picking his way past the tripwire he shouted, 'There no escape. Give up now!'

The first thug added, 'It'll be a shame when they find your battered old body washed up at Hell's Mouth, won't it?' He moved, testing the damaged leg; hissed with pain. 'Christ.' He hauled himself upright, the sharp smell of sweat mixing suddenly with that of the cow waste, and lurched into the cellar.

There was a moment of tense quiet as he assessed the space, then Ezra cried, 'Hell is empty, and all the devils are here!'

And something – god knew what – launched itself at the man, biting, scratching and yowling. Incoherent cries followed.

Such a fuss! Bucca had rarely provoked such a sound in another creature. There was something marvellously emancipating about causing a big human to squeal so, but it had tasted unutterably disgusting. Furious at the invasion of his space and hoping to clean the filth and feathers from his teeth and claws in the skin of the second intruder, Bucca launched himself again.

Ezra – who had excellent night sight, maybe as a result of being abroad at night so often in an unlit countryside, maybe from decades of proximity with other wild things – watched the two men stumbling around the cellar. One of them was feeling around the floor with his hands, sweeping them from side to side. '*Idi syuda!*'

'He's got to be in here somewhere.'

A moment later someone screeched, his fingers caught in the sharp metal jaws of a rat trap.

Ezra did not use rat traps to catch rodents – he left Bucca to do battle with them – but he had filched this one from Bob's farm, where the barn cats were fat and lazy.

'Fuck's sake. Hardman said he's just a doddery old man: we're not getting paid for this sort of thing!' The first man glared around the cellar as if the heat of his loathing could scorch the darkness away.

'Ready for Round Three, are you, you tusses?' Ezra roared.

A buried part of himself had risen, rampant to the challenge, but there was fear underlying the triumph: these men meant business, and he hadn't stopped them yet. If they did catch him...

He pushed the thought away: he had more surprises in store. 'Come and get me, then,' he goaded, and melted into the blackness.

'Where in hell he gone?'

Tarring and feathering was an established punishment for traitors and collaborators the world over, and Ezra had seen a particularly nasty case of a girl tarred and feathered by her compatriots for fraternising with an English soldier while he was in Cyprus. Ezra had no access to tar in Trengrose, but he was inventive by nature. When the man with the broken collarbone stumbled across the cellar floor towards him, down it came, a fine great bucketful of liquid honey mixed with chicken feathers, covering the man's hair and face, sticking his eyelids together, gumming up his reaching hands.

Ezra was tempted to stay and revel in the result of his booby-trap, but he knew his survival depended on getting ahead of these villains. Into the tunnel he fled. It had long fallen into disuse since its last employment as an air raid shelter during the Second World War, but Ezra had painstakingly re-excavated it over the past few weeks. Just in case. It was alarmingly unstable in some places, and you had to bend over in order to progress in others, but he had – with good mining practice – propped it here and there with sturdy timbers scavenged from the workmen's skips up at the big house, and he could pass along it in the dark, brisk as a night creature on its rat run. He knew this, because he had timed himself, and he was familiar with every outcrop of immovable stone and root in his path.

Behind him, he could hear noises of pursuit. He gripped his mace grimly and crabbed on through the passageway. There was light up ahead – or at least a paler shade of darkness – indicating the exit into the orchard. Normally this was concealed by the placement of his bathtub, but in preparation for this very contingency, Ezra had moved the thing. The task had taxed his muscles considerably, but now he was grateful for his foresight.

He came to a pinchpoint in the tunnel and squeezed himself through, as small and lean as a winter hare, his injured shoulder complaining as the bone grated against the side. It should slow his larger pursuers down, Ezra thought, but it was not his only line of defence.

He turned to see a sharp light some distance behind him. It shone in his eyes for a second, partially blinding him.

'There he is! Got you now, you old bastard!'

Ezra did not budge. The grey light indicating the emergence of the tunnel into the orchard beckoned him: clean air, room to move, but he made himself wait while the shambling noises and threatening voices came closer and still closer. The light sprang to life again, shockingly close, and out of the darkness behind it, a hand reached towards him. Ezra, horrified, whacked at it with the mace, but there wasn't enough room to get a good swing in, and the man kept coming. Had he misjudged? Ezra's heart began to hammer as he scrambled backwards, till he felt the prop behind him. Lying on the rough tunnel bed, he launched a rabbit-kick at the support that held up the most unstable section of tunnel and fled, almost doubled over, as the soil and stones came raining down.

By the time he reached the chamber at the end of the tunnel his chest hurt, and he was hardly able to breathe for all the dust. The noise of the blood beating in his ears obscured all other sound, so he launched himself fiercely at the steps that led up out of the underworld, wooden steps, just four of them, and clambered out into the world of the living. Then, with the very last of his strength, he dragged and pushed the old bathtub over the exit and leaned against it, thinking he might be about to have a heart attack. Which would be typical, after all the effort he had made to escape being murdered.

It was gloomy, darkness beginning to fall at this nub-end of the year, but Ezra knew every scrap of ground here, every trunk and fern, every rock and stump and stand of nettles.

As he made his way between the bare apple trees, he heard a voice up ahead. It was a voice he recognised. And then he heard the crack of breaking wood and a jolt of terror struck through him. The beehive! Someone was attacking the hive! He picked up speed, taking a direct path now, trampling dead bracken, stumbling over roots. He did not care what happened to him: he did not matter. His well-being, his very existence, was a small thing in the world, but he was damned if he would stand aside in the face of such horrific destruction.

The buzzing, the buzzing...

The pressure in his ears built and built, blood throbbing against the bones of his face, his eyes... He felt as if there were a storm approaching, felt his hair stand up as if he had been subjected to an electric charge...

And all at once he was back in Cyprus in 1958 after the attack on the farmhouse, where they had taken a number of prisoners, making his way to the buildings beyond the army camp at Troodos, the ones no one talked about, that were situated at the furthest extent of the boundaries. He had a damned good idea what happened in those buildings, especially since Corporal Hollis was in charge. It had to be the detention centre where EOKA suspects were held and questioned as to the whereabouts of General Grivas, leader of the terrorist movement.

His brother walked beside him: up ahead, Ash and Tubbs.

Lightning crackled over the mountains, followed some moments later by a rumble of thunder. He could feel the shockwave run through him, as if touched by the lightning, could feel his skin crawl and the electricity in his hair, his nerves. The sensation should have receded once they entered the detention centre, but it did not.

As soon as they set foot inside, they were assailed by noise. In one cell, they passed a man with a metal bucket placed over his head, a soldier raining blows against it, so it chimed like hellish church bells with a dull, empty resonance. Other soldiers watched on. No one asked questions or took notes; they just watched the beating of the pail and listened to the wails of the bound man as the metal reverberated around him.

In another cell, blindfolded men sat back-to-back, shackled hand and foot, or lay groaning and sweating on the bare concrete. Dark liquid glinted in runnels leading to a drain. Piss or blood? Probably both: the air was heavy with the tang of ammonia and iron.

Another man was being beaten, or worse, with a rubber truncheon: the backs of the spectators prevented a clearer view.

The men engaged in their gruesome tasks were men no longer, but rather beasts in the grip of some anti-human compulsion, revelling in the power that had been designated to them by their commanding officer, who went from cell to cell issuing orders.

And there he was, Hollis, directing his diabolical minions. When he saw them, he waved them inside.

'Just in time for the fun.' He gestured to the regulars. 'Prepare the prisoner!'

The regulars wrestled a slight, dark man, bare to the waist, down onto a chair. You could see each of his ribs clearly delineated as if he hadn't eaten in days; the hair on his chest lay in black whorls against the paleness of his skin, though his face and neck and forearms were sun-darkened.

'You – Tubbs – throw that water over the prisoner. Go on, don't hesitate, just do it.'

Tubbs shot an agonised glance at the twins, then picked up the metal bucket and upended it over the prisoner, who gasped, then shouted out, shaking his head like a dog coming out of heavy rain. Droplets of water flew everywhere, splotching the khaki of trousers and shirts.

Hollis looked at the other newcomers, then beckoned. 'Twin One, you can do the honours. The rest of you can watch to begin with. Don't worry, you'll all get a go.'

The corporal handed him a wooden wand with a bronze tip and an insulated handle that was connected by a thick wire to a rheostat powered by a large portable battery. 'This, my boy, is a picana, a species of cattle-prod. Delivers an electroshock that you can kill someone with – or simply hurt them till they're ready to spill their guts and offer you their sister. Michaels, ready?'

'Ready sir.'

The regular switched the control box on, turning the dial to regulate the voltage and a humming like a vast nest of enraged wasps filled the air.

Hollis leaned over the prisoner and tweaked a nipple till it stood out, pink and vulnerable within its nest of black hair. He took a step back. 'Apply the device, Private Curnow!' he ordered.

He looked down at the wand in his hand, then at the captive, and the captive looked back at him, his brown eyes full of terror. He said something quietly over and over in his language. You didn't have to know any Greek to understand the pleading.

'I can't do that, sir.'

'Can't?'

'Won't, sir.'

'You little fag, just do it.'

Silence.

'That's a direct order. Do it now!'

'I won't... sir.'

Hollis snatched up a baton, raised it and brought it down violently on the man's arm, where it was bound to the chair. The snap of bone echoed around the cell and the prisoner began to thrash and scream, making roaring, inhuman noises.

Bile was rising in his throat, and he could see his twin staring at him, Tubbs, Ashes beside him, but the tough Army regulars were laughing now, not at him, but at the captive, as tears ran down his face and he begged in Greek and broken English.

'Now fucking use the picana!'

Revulsion overcame him, and his thoughts spun. This was the British Army. They were not barbarians. There must be rules governing the treatment of prisoners, mustn't there? Perhaps Hollis, having already proved his implacable malice by breaking the man's arm, would start asking questions now about the whereabouts of General Grivas, about EOKA plans and weapons caches?

But Hollis's expression was demonic. He asked no questions at all, just said gleefully, 'You won't even be able to wipe your own arse after we've finished with you. Shit on a piece of shit. It's what you terrorists deserve.'

Private Curnow shook off his torpor and advanced on the corporal with the picana extended. 'This is torture, sir: it's wicked, just plain wrong.'

'Put that down, soldier.' There was a dangerous note in Hollis's voice.

He didn't let go. He looked around at the others, and one by one they looked aside. They knew it was wrong, but they weren't going to intervene. He was on his own.

He put up a fight when Hollis beat him with the baton till he dropped the wand, but there was little he could do when they held him down and Hollis broke three of his fingers, one by one by one.

Ezra's fingers ached now with the old arthritic pain as he forced them around the stock of hawthorn and advanced on the man destroying his beehive, for there stood Toby Hardman, a demonic expression on his face, hammer raised to strike down once more.

'No!' he screamed, just as he had screamed six decades before. 'No, no, no!' And he sprinted with the energy of a much younger man towards his foe.

35

'I'm dreading this. You will come up to the house with me, won't you?' Miranda pleaded.

She and Sam were in the back of Mickey Jewell's knackered Astra, which smelled of mildew and fish-scales. They'd just gone through a series of roundabouts leading out of Penzance and Mickey gunned the engine so hard out of every bend that his passengers were constantly shuttled from one side of the car to the other. The train had arrived later than expected and he was, he had explained, already late.

'Abi's going to give me hell, I'm supposed to be seeing to the kids' tea while she does some carol concert or something.'

Sam had already agreed that he should just drop them at the entrance to the lane rather than drive all the way up to Trengrose House. 'Course I will,' he said to Ran now.

She looked relieved. 'I thought you were going to abandon me, and I'd have to drag my case all the way through the woods in the dark.'

To Sam Rivers, who had wandered the Trengrose environs at all hours of the day and night, the woods in the dark were magical and unthreatening. He had been going to suggest that Ran go on ahead to talk to her mother and that he would follow in half an hour or so with her luggage once she'd had the chance to drop the bomb of her father's infidelity, but now he saw that simply wouldn't do: besides, he had pledged to do whatever she needed, and he wouldn't break his word.

Mickey didn't even turn off the engine when he pulled into the layby. He just waited till they got out, yelled 'Merry Christmas!' at them, performed an awkward and screeching manoeuvre, since there was a white Transit van taking up much of the turning space, and roared off back the way he had come, down to Newlyn to his young wife and two toddlers. Mickey's life seemed unimaginable to Sam – weeks away on the trawler far out in the fishing grounds in the Channel or the south of Ireland, deep in the Celtic Sea, times of feast and famine depending on how good the catch was, then supplementing his chancy income with temporary jobs at the ice-packing plant or driving for the local taxi company. Sam hoped he drove tourists rather more sedately.

'Just got to stick my head around Gamps' door first or he'll never forgive me,' Sam said.

The gate to Ezra's cottage was open and his great-uncle's wellies stood as usual beside the door, but there was no light on inside. And there appeared to be manure splattered around... and an empty bucket hanging overhead. What the hell?

'Hang on here a minute,' he said to Ran.

He shucked off his rucksack. Finding the front door locked, he went around the side of the house towards the back door, calling 'Gamps?'

The sight of the boarded-up kitchen window made his hackles rise. Something was not right.

Minty Hardman checked the online bank statements again and sighed. That final payment from Alexei still hadn't come through and things were getting pretty tight. She might even have to ask Toby to dip into his funds to cover some of the bills, which she hated to do, even though he was equally responsible for them. She had submitted the invoice weeks ago for the completed work on Misbourne House, and while she had not been on site in person to oversee the final finishes, she had been assiduous in keeping track of everything via FaceTime and Skype, and had had several conversations with Alexei's site manager, Helena, to ensure that everything went to plan, was up to scratch, and on time. From what she'd seen as Helena video-walked her around the manor house, the place looked spectacular, better than she had even imagined it would: she was proud of what they'd achieved and was sure Alexei was happy with the results and was not withholding payment over some niggle. So she'd been expecting prompt payment, as with every other invoice she'd submitted to Alexei over the eighteen months of their dealings. He was always so scrupulous. And now it was – she checked the calendar on her laptop – almost a month later. It must be an oversight, she told herself.

One thing Minty really hated having to do was chase payments. It felt so awkward, so infra dig, beneath her dignity; like being a debt collector, or petitioner. Perhaps her invoice had been missed in the frenzied approach to Christmas (goodness knows, that was one reason she had been so tardy in chasing it); or perhaps Alexei was having cash-flow problems: it happened even to the rich sometimes. But no: Alexei was an extremely wealthy man – Toby had boasted about having an actual billionaire on his books so often it had become painful – and forty grand was hardly going to faze him. Some people did renege on final payments, once all the work was done and they could dispense with your services and melt away, but she was sure even a tough businessman like Alexei wouldn't skin her like that. She laughed silently; who was she kidding? Alexei was not just 'a businessman' in any traditional sense of the word: she was well aware of the steel, even the suggestion of violence, beneath his gentlemanly politeness. You didn't get to be such a very rich Russian émigré without certain... connections. A dangerous man to cross. But surely not a dangerous man to chase for money he owed you fair and square?

In the end, Minty decided she would call Helena instead: she'd be able to check whether the invoice had been received, and if there had been a genuine glitch in the system, she'd be able to resend it and no harm done. She was just beginning to congratulate herself on this solution when she recalled a passing comment Helena had made the last time they had spoken, and that, alongside something she'd noticed in the bank statement, prompted a question.

She marched into the TV room, where her husband was stretched out on the velvet couch. With his trainers on, which compounded her annoyance.

Dominic could hear his parents arguing downstairs, and it sounded worse than usual. He sharpened his senses but couldn't make out any specific phrases. He turned his music up and went back to the job in hand, regarding his handiwork with no small degree of pride and wrapping it carefully in the most festive paper he'd been able to find in Penzance – robins in little red hats hopping in the snow. It seemed only right that he should give Ezra a Christmas present; after all, he was the only friend Dom had here. He hoped the gift wasn't too presumptuous, that Ezra wouldn't mind him taking such liberties, and that it wouldn't make the old man feel he had to reciprocate. He turned his music off and listened. They were still arguing. He sighed. It would be nice to have his sister and Sam here: perhaps their presence would put an end to the bickering. He had spoken to Ran earlier when she'd called to say her train had been delayed. She'd sounded pretty stressed about it and had asked if Dad was home, and when Dom had said yes he was, and did she want to speak to him or get him to pick her up, she had been very short with him and said one of Sam's friends was going to fetch them from Penzance station and give them a lift to Trengrose.

Voices suddenly rose louder – a door had opened downstairs – and Dom distinctly heard his father yell, 'Just stop it, Minty! You blame me for everything, but it's not my fault.'

He came out of his room and looked over the banister to see what was going on. He watched his mother come out of the television room and say something so quiet that he couldn't catch it, but his father became instantly incensed. 'Just watch me!' he shouted. 'I'm going to make damn sure that old bastard and everything to do with him is fucking obliterated!' Then he strode down the hall and out of the front door, banging it behind him so hard that the whole house seemed to shake.

Dom went cold from head to foot. Maybe it was the force of his feelings that transmitted themselves to his mother, but she suddenly turned and looked right up at him. He had never seen her look so coldly furious. She looked like a stranger: taller, stronger, her hair and eyes darker. She looked, he thought suddenly, like the woman in the photos, yet more like herself than she had ever been. Fierce, a matriarch.

He was about to say something, but she held up a hand. 'It's okay, Dom, just go back in your room. We'll talk later.' Then she stalked across the hall and into the kitchen and shut the door behind her: she didn't want to be disturbed.

That was good, because Dom knew he had to go after his father. He waited till it was clear his mother wasn't going to come back out again, padded downstairs, put his parka on, stuck his feet into the trainers he took from the hall stand, slipped out and closed the front door quietly behind him.

It was pretty gloomy outside, and there was no sign of Dad. Night was in the air, some way off yet, but he could feel it hovering, elemental; inimical. Trengrose was another country, and Cornwall another world.

As he walked as quietly as he could across the gravel he began to hear strange noises coming out of the wooded area near the edge of their driveway. He stood and trained his ears on the sound. A man was shouting. There was a strange reverberation.

And then a bird cried raucously, burst out of the trees, and came straight at him. He was sure it was going to strike him right in the face and had time to think what a bizarre way that would be to die, but then it landed with a thud on his shoulder.

It was Merlin.

Dom was so astounded that he couldn't speak or move. The jackdaw cawed in his ear then lifted off again, heading for the orchard. When the lad didn't move, Merlin flipped in mid-air and came back and forth until at last he felt compelled to follow.

He paused under the eaves of the trees, unnerved by the increased volume of the cries, until at last he realised that one of the raised voices belonged to his father.

Minty looked out of the window in time to witness the most uncanny sight: her son being attacked by a crow! But her phone call was important; she couldn't possibly cut it short, not now. Agonised, she watched until she saw the crow fly off into the woods, and Dom following. Strange, she thought.

When at last the call ended, she threw on a coat and boots and ran out into the dull winter light.

36

The attack had come out of nowhere, without warning, without any change in the atmospherics or other natural circumstances. No storm had struck, no tree fallen. All had been warm and orderly within their realm, and suddenly the world had broken apart and they were tumbling in cold darkness, disoriented, each alone. It was inexplicable: confusion reigned. Where was their queen? Some of their number lay dead and scattered amid the broken combs and parts of their house, which lay smashed upon the ground.

They hummed, communicated, spun, danced, exchanged what little information they had, sending messages into the air, messages that became an electrical charge.

Then the bees rose in a storm, a blacker cloud against the falling gloom, and their buzzing turned from individual fear to swelling, communal fury.

37

'Ezra? Gamps?'

Sam's voice rose in panic at the sight of the smashed back door. He made his way inside, finding no sign of the old man in the kitchen or living area. The range was lit: dull red light flickered over the furniture but gave no clue as to the whereabouts of the inhabitant. A slice of saffron cake sat discarded on a plate, two bites taken out of it. Beside it, half a mug of tea. Sam put a hand to the ceramic and felt a fleeting warmth within. He shivered. It was like being the first person to enter the galley of the *Mary Celeste*, there to discover that the missing passengers had left an eerie, half-eaten meal, the captain's boiled egg sitting in two halves in its shell, salt at hand ready to season.

'Gamps!' he called again, but the cottage gave nothing back: not an echo, not a groan.

Then something moved in the darkness and Sam felt the hairs rise on the back of his neck. The next thing he knew, it had brushed his leg. He reached down, and there was Bucca, visible only in patches where the ginger and white parts of him caught fragments of light. Sam's hand came away sticky. He sniffed his fingers. Honey and...

'Bloody hell, Bucca, where have you been?' Sam recognised cowshit when he smelled it.

The cat mewed piteously, in a very un-Bucca-like way. He didn't like being this dirty, not with stuff he couldn't rid himself of. Common or garden dirt he was fine with – the natural grime any hunting cat picked up: particles of earth and leaf, bug and burr – all that could be groomed away without disgust or peril.

'Where's Gamps, Bucca?' Even as he spoke the words aloud, he felt a fool: Bucca was no Lassie, to woof and wag and lead you to a missing loved one. But Bucca stalked across the room and, stopping at the top of the cellar stairs, gazed down in what seemed to Sam a meaningful fashion.

Panic gripped him. Had Ezra fallen down those steep, stone steps and cracked his head? Was he lying there at the bottom in a crumpled heap, clinging to life, or worse; his body slowly cooling after he'd broken his neck? Sam fumbled for his phone, found the torch function and shone it down the flight.

Nothing. He looked at the cat, its eyes lit unnaturally bright by the torchlight so that it looked more than ever like a minor demon, its fur standing out in spiky tufts, and then he started down the steps.

Part of the way down the torch beam snagged on what looked like a cobweb stretched horizontally across the span. Then he realised what it was, saw the screws that had been drilled into the wood on either side, the use of a nail as a ratchet to tighten the wire. That was one of Gamps's tricks: he'd seen him use it when mending the chicken run. Why would Ezra have fixed a tripwire across the steps down to the cellar? It was a death trap. Anxiety clawed at him as possibilities presented themselves, none of them good.

Sam stepped carefully over the tripwire and continued to the bottom of the stairs. In the cellar beyond he saw nothing immediately out of the ordinary. The sack of climbing equipment hung in its accustomed place from a hook in one wall, and the climbing ropes in their bags beside it. Shelves of tools and paint pots, a pile of logs stacked neatly in one corner. But what the hell was that? There was a bloody great hole in one of the walls where the wood panelling had been stripped away. And beyond lay darkness.

'Sam? Sam?'

Miranda's voice drifted down to him from the sitting room above. Sam almost broke his own neck in his haste to ensure she didn't start down the steps and break hers.

'Stay there!' he called urgently. 'Don't come down.'

A slim figure appeared at the top of the stairs.

'Why? What is it? Is Ezra down there? Did he fall? Is he okay? What can I do?'

'I'm not sure where he is, but Ran, can you have a go at lighting the oil lamp on the table in the kitchen? There should be matches right beside it, and if you can, get hold of Bucca, try and clean him up? Careful, though: he doesn't like being picked up.'

Ran laughed. 'He's here with me now, purring like a loon. He doesn't half stink.'

'I'll be back up in a mo', but whatever you do, don't come down these stairs – there's a tripwire across them.'

'A tripwire?'

'Don't ask – I don't know. Just give me a few minutes, okay?'

A long silence: Ran wasn't used to being given instructions. But then she said, 'All right. Just be careful, yes?' This last was issued in such a plaintive tone that Sam's heart twinged. She cared about him, she really did.

He disappeared back into the cellar and entered the tunnel. It was dusty and dank, and the smell of disturbed earth was strong and, in its way, comforting. He made his way thirty feet or so along it, marvelling at its very existence, unknown to him till this very minute, until he began to hear noises of distress up ahead, and he put his head down and hurried towards the sounds.

38

Dom stared as his father raised the hammer again, shrieking, 'You have to leave here! You have to go! Everything's gone wrong and it's all your fault!'

The precious beehive lay half-smashed, the little gabled roof demolished, and a distance away was a doubled-up, moaning figure.

'Dad! Jesus, Dad, just stop!'

Dom launched himself across the space between them and grasped his father's arm before the hammer fell again.

Toby turned towards him. It seemed to take him several seconds to register the presence of his son, and several more to allow the hammer to be taken from him. He looked completely insane, his eyes wide and his face already swollen from a dozen bee stings.

Ezra sat on the ground, rocking back and forth as if in unbearable pain. 'The bees, the bees,' he groaned. They were on his hands, in his hair, on his shirt. But they did not, Dom noticed, appear to be stinging him: they just landed on the old man as if he offered haven, as if he were a human hive.

For a moment, the thought stunned him, then he rounded on his father. 'Why are you smashing up the hive? These are Trengrose bees! They're like... like... the guardians of the place. They're special, like magic. What the hell is the matter with you?'

He looked at the bees that had given their lives when the hive fell, in protection of their queen, by stinging their attacker. He remembered that when a female honey bee stung someone, it could not pull the barbed stinger back out, so left behind not only the stinger, but also part of itself, and then would inevitably die from this catastrophic damage. The sight of such sacrifice seemed terrible.

Ezra groaned again, and Dom knelt and carefully placed an arm around the old man's shoulders. He was horrified when Ezra gave a gasp of pain and winced away from him. He stared up at his father. 'Did you hurt him? With your hammer?'

Toby blinked, rubbed a hand across his lumpy face, did his best to regain his habitual bluster. 'No, of course I didn't. What do you think I am, some sort of monster?'

'That's exactly what you are.'

Sam Rivers had come up behind them, emerging out of the darkness among the trees like a vengeful spirit. He was covered in earth and ash, had a gash on one cheek, and his eyes were blazing.

'I know what you did! You paid gangsters to rough up Gamps, to frighten him out of his cottage. One of them was a bloody Russian! I found them back there—' he waved behind him, 'and they were only too happy to talk if I helped them out of their predicament. And no, don't look around for them: they're not coming to help you. They ran – well, limped – off down the road back to their van. Told them to "Get rid of him, whatever it takes", didn't you? How dare you? He's an old man. He's lived in that place all his life. He belongs here, and you don't! I've a mind to beat the living shit out of you.'

'I'd rather you left that to *me*. I have much better ways of hurting him,' said a cool female voice, and Araminta Hardman came into view. Behind her was Miranda. Both looked dishevelled, upset.

Sam's fight reflex disappeared at the sight of her. 'Oh, Ran, I'm sorry. I know I said I'd only be a few minutes.'

'I was so worried about you. By the time I got Bucca cleaned up, you still hadn't reappeared, and I shouted and you didn't reply, and when I went down into the cellar you weren't there, as if you'd just... disappeared. It really weirded me out! And as I came running up the lane, these men ran past me, and they looked... the state of them: I thought they'd killed you or something. I don't know what I thought. And then Mum found me.' She looked beyond Sam and saw her father, and her expression changed.

Minty placed a hand on her daughter's shoulder. 'We found each other.' She turned to face her husband. 'And now I have a very good idea of exactly what you've been doing in London.' She paused, then added, 'And elsewhere.'

Toby looked flustered now, and the bee stings were really throbbing, disrupting his thought processes. He was usually adept at talking himself out of tight corners, but he couldn't seem to think straight. He knew that icy tone of Minty's, though, the uncompromising, adamantine hardness of it. London? Shit. He tried to brazen it out. 'Sorry, darling, I haven't the faintest idea what you mean, and whatever it is, I don't think this is the place to discuss it, do you? Let's get this poor old chap safely back to the cottage, and then you and I can talk.'

Minty folded her arms. 'Mr Curnow isn't going anywhere except up to Trengrose.' She glanced to Sam. 'Can you help him?'

Sam stepped to his great-uncle's side. 'Come on, Gamps, let's get you up.'

'Can't leave my bees,' Ezra said mulishly. 'I ent going anywhere.'

Sam and Minty exchanged a look. It was Dom who came to the rescue. 'Look, Ezra, there's the queen! She's still alive.' He pointed urgently towards the wrecked hive.

They all peered through the gloom.

The Queen of Trengrose sat quivering on a lip of splintered wood. She was long and lean, with an extended thorax that was smooth and gold, where the bodies of her subjects were short and fat. She crawled over and around them, her antennae signalling wildly.

The sight of the queen seemed to stir Ezra, and those of her subjects who had sought refuge upon him. They stopped pirouetting and waving their antennae, and all of them turned towards the monarch of the hive. Those bees that had been drifting aimlessly now flew back to the wreckage. 'Look,' he said to Dom, 'see how they're gathering. Her winter bees. They work for each other: she's telling them what to do. Come back and reform their society, make the best of what they have. Most importantly, they must guard her and fend for her if the hive is to survive. Fetch me the brood box, lad.'

Dom, having accompanied Ezra to the beehive many times over the summer as Ezra checked the bees, did as he was told and watched as Ezra gently picked up the queen and placed her inside the box with her progeny, then laid his hand on the edge of it so that the bees that had crawled on him for warmth could join her. Now they appeared docile, lulled by duty, as they marched down this human bridge and took up their accustomed positions around the queen.

'See, she's humming to calm them down, she's telling them to cluster around her and that the danger's past. She'll be sending out scent messages to them – see how they've already started to vibrate their wings? That's to keep her warm. They'll all work together as a group now, flapping and circulating the air around her and each other.'

Dom bent his head close to Ezra's. 'If I remove the broken bits, I can put the box back in the frame, I think. Then we can cover it for the night, till the hive is fixed.'

'Yes, best keep them warm, it's getting nippy.'

It was in fact, Sam thought, bloody freezing, as night fell in the orchard. Ezra started to strip off his shirt, but Dom was already out of his parka.

'Here, we'll use this. And I'll stay here for a bit to see if I can fix the hive as best I can.' Dom glared at his father. 'I'll see you all back at the house.' He patted Ezra's arm. 'They'll be okay now, I promise.'

'Right then,' said Toby, taking an authoritative tone, determined to get back in control of the situation. 'Let's get this poor old soul up to the house, get him warm and comfortable.' He stepped to the other side of Ezra and took his arm to help him to his feet.

Ezra shrugged him off. 'Don't you touch me,' he growled. 'You're an assassin.'

Minty rounded on Toby. 'Why on earth did you smash his hive?' she demanded.

'Those fucking bees have to go. They're on my land,' her husband muttered.

'It's not your land,' Minty bit back. 'It's Trengrose land.'

Toby wasn't entirely sure what she meant by that.

Sam stepped in, put an arm around his great-uncle's waist and got him to his feet. But Ezra had been on the cold ground for too long, and the events of the day had taken their toll. Once upright, his legs wouldn't support him. His knees wobbled and his thigh muscles refused to cooperate.

Sam felt the tremor go through Ezra's frame, forewarning collapse, and threw one arm under his knees and the other around his shoulders and picked him up in a dead lift. He could hardly believe how light the old man was! Alarm flooded him. He remembered Ezra belaying him on Bow Wall; how he had peeled off the crux, taking an absolute whanger of a fall that had lifted Ezra right off his feet from the force of holding him on the belay; but he had held it, and Sam at sixteen had already been six foot two and twice his size. Impossible to imagine he'd still be able to do that. Ezra felt barely larger than a child in his arms. Something about the old man's vulnerability and the weird events of the day now wore at him and he found himself on the edge of tears.

Thugs had brought violence to his great-uncle's peaceful cottage, interrupted his Gamps' afternoon tea, terrorised him;

perhaps even tried to kill him – and Ezra had escaped through a tunnel Sam hadn't even known existed! And he'd lived in that cottage on and off for *years*. He'd managed to move the old bathtub over the entrance – god knows how, because it had taken every iota of Sam's considerable strength to shift it. He must have been powered by fear and fury. And those thugs had been hired by the man who owned the big house because he wanted to steal Ezra's cottage. To forcibly evict the old man from the only home he'd ever known! The urge to put Ezra down and beat Toby Hardman to a pulp was an urgent, pulsing fire deep inside him, roaring to be let out. But the man was Ran's father. And no matter how furious she was with him, despite how disgusted at how he was cheating on her mother or how appalled she would be at what he had done to Ezra, he knew that if he resorted to violent retribution against Toby (no matter how pure and satisfying that might be), it would do nothing to help Ran. The best thing he could do was not to inflame the situation any further, and to look after Gamps. And so, although it was the hardest thing he had ever done, he tamped down his anger and concentrated on the old soul in his arms and carried him determinedly towards Trengrose House.

39

Back at the house, Ran and Sam settled Ezra into one of the huge, deep-piled velvet sofas in front of the fireplace, while Minty made mugs of cocoa, one with a dash of rum in for the old man, and distributed freshly made flapjacks. When Toby reached for one, she slapped his hand away. 'No, that's not for you. You're not entitled to anything here any more. Go and sit over there: I'll come and talk to you in time.' She pointed, her expression grim, the instruction enunciated as if she was talking to Boris.

Beside the chair at the end of the kitchen was the Labrador, looking up with large guilty eyes, as if he had also been caught doing something he shouldn't. And indeed, he had one of Minty's shoes between his paws, and it was chewed down to the sole. Boris and Toby exchanged a glance of fellow feeling: they were both in for it.

Minty took a tray full of drinks and snacks into the drawing room, where Sam was poking up the fire, and Miranda was tucking one of the very nice Shetland wool rugs around the old man. Back in the hall, she glimpsed herself in the long Georgian mirror: her unhighlighted hair dark and tangled, the hall light catching her earring, flecking the onyx with gold. She had had Catherine Rosevear's jewel copied by a goldsmith in Penzance and now she even slept in the earrings: they had become part of who she was, tying her closer than ever to Trengrose. There was a bramble-rip in her jeans and the sleeves of her Seasalt sweatshirt were pushed up to the elbows, showing off corded muscle. She looked pale and resolute, but tough as nails; practical and no-nonsense. This was who she was now. This was who she would be. Would have to be.

Re-entering the kitchen, she closed the door, sealing herself and Toby off from the rest of the world, sat down at the table and regarded her husband in disgust.

'Now I want the full truth. No meandering, no excuses, no half-lies. I spoke to Helena Petrova after you stormed out, and now I have a damned good idea of exactly what you've done. But I want to run it past you, and decide how to handle what could very well be an extremely dangerous situation.' She paused, watching the import of this drag Toby's laugh lines down into the appearance of a tragic mask. 'We'll get to the Chrissie situation as well, since it seems you've managed to mix business with pleasure,' she continued crisply. 'My business, and your pleasure. But let's start with the false invoice you submitted to Alexei.'

Toby Hardman's jaw dropped as if screws had popped out of its hinges. He stared at his wife, then sharply away. She could almost see the cogs whirring in his mind, trying to put together a plausible excuse. And failing.

'Let me help you,' Minty said quietly. She opened her laptop, tapped some keys, then turned the screen so Toby could see it. 'I gather you did not hand-deliver my final invoice to Alexei as you promised, though I see you did in fact go up to Buckinghamshire on 30th November, since you booked into the – ah – honeymoon suite in a rather nice spa hotel a couple of miles away from Misbourne House. I called them up and asked if they'd email me a copy of the bill, since I needed it to reclaim expenses: they were very nice, and very efficient – took less than a minute: they deserve their five stars, don't they? Apparently, you had one steak with Bearnaise sauce and one Dover sole, two side salads, two portions of dauphinoise potatoes, a chocolate mousse, a coconut sorbet and a bottle of Cristal delivered to your room. That's rather greedy, even for you, isn't it, darling?'

Toby said nothing, his mouth a hard, thin line.

'And then you delivered "my" final invoice by hand the next day. A very good facsimile of my header, even down to the same font. She's always been rather handy with computer technology, hasn't she, Chrissie? I know it can't have been you. Then, curiously, I came across this entry in your business account – don't look so shocked: you know you gave me all the passwords because you keep forgetting them. Did you really think I wouldn't look? Payment in, of £145,207, on 5th December.' She looked up at her husband, whose cheeks and neck had coloured. 'He's always such a prompt payer, isn't he? Alexei? And look, here's my original invoice.' She tapped a tab and there was her personalised header: Araminta Hervey Designs across the top of the page, an itemised bill for services rendered, ending in '£45,207'. 'That's a bit of a giveaway, isn't it, dear? Did your imagination fail you? You could have come up with an entirely different figure, but no… 207 remains unchanged. I had wondered why you offered to take my invoice and hand it to Alexei when you were here last month. It seemed such a surprisingly… chivalric gesture.'

She paused for effect.

'It's interesting that I'd noted a couple of weeks ago a payment from your business account for twenty grand going out to Marena Enterprises – which I happen to know is one of Alexei's companies. I was curious at the time, but didn't think much more about it, till it popped into my head that Marena was the ancient Russian goddess of death: she was featured in one of the online games Dom was playing and he told me about her. And when Sam said one of the thugs who'd come to threaten Ezra Curnow was Russian… well, things fell into place. He was obviously one of Alexei's men. Don't look like that: of course

I know exactly who and what Alexei is – but I can't believe you'd be such an idiot as to cross such a man.'

The colour had come and gone in Toby's face. Now he looked gaunt and drawn. At last he croaked, 'Oh god, Minty, please don't tell him.'

'I hate – absolutely HATE – being a party to such a fraud; and I really hate having my good name, and business, dragged into your criminal schemes. But I think if I were to tell Alexei exactly what you did, he'd probably kill you. At the very least have you beaten up. But probably disappeared. I'm sure Marena Enterprises are generally pretty efficient in all they do. Though they don't appear to have got the better of Ezra Curnow, so maybe you might fancy your chances?'

Toby shook his head frantically. 'No. No, I don't. Please, Minty. I did it for us. For the family—'

Minty cut him off with a look. 'Here's the deal.' She leaned across the table. 'You're going to grant me a quick and clean divorce... and Trengrose House and all that goes with it. And I will,' she gritted her teeth, 'resubmit the proper invoice to Alexei with a grovelling apology and a transfer of the erroneous hundred thousand pounds, blaming an administrative error. Oh yes, and you're going to cover that hundred grand. I want it in my personal account on Tuesday.' She drew a deep breath. 'Honestly, Toby, you are a fool. I should have divorced you the first time you cheated on me.'

Toby Hardman looked down at the tabletop. Some flapjack crumbs lay scattered there, fallen in the transfer between cake-tin and plates. Absentmindedly, he licked his finger and dabbed them up. Fleeting sweetness on his tongue, here, then gone. Like those moments of passion with Chrissie that he'd thought were so special. He had fucked everything up. He saw that now.

'There must be something I can do. To make things right?' he said plaintively.

Minty leaned back in her Ercolani dining chair. 'There is no "right" between us now. You've betrayed me on every possible level. If you want to make it right with Dominic and Miranda, I won't try to stop you, but I suggest you leave it a while before talking to them because I think they are both, rightly, extremely angry with you now, and they don't even know the half of it. I hope you can make a go of things with Chrissie. No, really I do. Now, do we have a deal?' She stretched her hand across the table towards him.

Toby stared at it as if it might contain tiny hidden razors. Then he said, rather unwisely, 'You know you'll never make a go of this place without me?'

'I beg your pardon?' His wife withdrew her hand, stiffened.

'I mean, how much did you make out of the "glamping"?' He made the very word sound ridiculous. 'About fifty quid? Maybe not even that?'

Minty showed her teeth. 'From here on in that's none of your business. We will – somehow – make it pay its way. Even if I have to go out and clean other people's houses.'

Toby stared at her, then burst out laughing. 'Well, okay, have it your way. You haven't got the grit to do what I did, to get that old bastard out of his winkle-shell. That cottage is about the only extra revenue stream you've got here. But if you're too soft-hearted to take it, you've got no one but yourself to blame when it all goes tits up.' He pushed himself back from the table and stood up. 'You can have your blasted divorce, and this money-pit of a house, and good riddance to both of you. I'll sort things out with Alexei, man to man. Honest mistake, all the rest of it. You don't even have to get your pretty hands dirty.' He shook his head. 'Cleaning? You? Araminta Hervey, grand-daughter of baronets fallen on hard times, hoity-toity socialite designer, down on her knees scrubbing floors? Don't make me laugh.'

Minty shot to her feet, flaming with fury. 'I've changed,' she yelled at his retreating back. 'But you never will!'

The front door banged, feet crunched across the gravel, and a few seconds later, the Range Rover roared to life.

40

Ezra gazed around in wonder at the drawing room in the big house, taking in the wallpaper painted with Oriental lilies, the restored cornicing, the bold artwork, the huge brass candlesticks, the vivid tribal rug, the bookcase, the handsomely refurbished fireplace, and blinked rapidly. Some colour had come back into his sunken cheeks and Ran had rubbed his poor cold hands till the feeling in them returned; then his feet, after gently peeling off his shredded, filthy socks.

'They're not usually like this,' he had been at pains to assure her. 'I lost my slippers in the tunnel.'

The ruined socks had been replaced by a pair of Dom's. No chance to ask his permission: he was still out there in the darkness, dealing with the broken hive.

Ezra wriggled his toes: he'd never worn anything so soft in his life. He took up his mug of cocoa and smelled the alcoholic vapour boiling out of it. He hadn't touched a drop in a while, but he drank it down without protest, and luxuriated; he might even have dozed.

After an indeterminate time, footsteps sounded in the hall; voices; a banged door. Minty came into the drawing room, looking determined and a little red around the eyes, but with her retouched make-up meticulous, with fresh mugs of cocoa, and a few moments later was followed by Dominic, beating his arms to warm himself up. There were crystals of ice in his hair.

'Where's Dad going?' he asked.

'Back up to London,' Minty said briskly, handing her son one of the mugs she carried. 'He has things to do up there.'

'At Christmas?'

'I'm afraid so.'

'But that's going to ruin our first Christmas here.' Dom looked devastated.

Ran hugged him. 'I'm so sorry, Dom. I should have called Mum immediately after Sam and I saw Dad and Chrissie together in London. I shouldn't have put it off.'

'What?' Dom stared at her, putting two and two together. 'That woman he works with? Is that why he's gone? He's been cheating on Mum again?' He looked to his mother. 'Is that why you were arguing earlier?'

'Part of it.' Minty cradled her mug against her chest, the residual warmth radiating from it oddly comforting. 'It's all right, Dom, I already had a pretty good idea. Women usually do. There were all sorts of little clues, changes in behaviour – he was harder to get hold of, never left his phone around, put a lot more effort into his appearance...' She paused, deciding against cataloguing other more intimately telling details. 'And, then there was the small matter of buying a huge great crumbling house as far away from London as is physically possible to get...'

She saw her daughter's eyes widen as this sunk in.

Dom stared at his mother. 'But he said it was all about *me*! I used to hear you talking. About how we needed to get me away from London because of the drugs. I felt really guilty about that, about making you all move to the arse-end of nowhere, as if all your problems were my fault, but it was all a lie. I hate him!'

Minty's gaze flitted to Ezra. The old man's eyes were shut, but he was still holding his mug, which was almost but not quite empty. Was he asleep? Was he listening? She was torn between the deep urge to take the mug from him in case the remnants spilled on the upholstery and bundling him out of the house so that she could have a full and frank discussion with her children. But of course, she couldn't do that, not after what Toby had done to him.

As if he felt the weight of her regard upon him, Ezra's eyelids flicked open, and he and Minty exchanged a glance. In it was a magnitude of understanding.

Minty looked back at Dom. 'Darling, we'll talk about it later. It will all work out, I promise. Do you trust me?'

Dom considered this, and at last said dolefully, 'I suppose so.'

Minty hugged her children. Toby was an encysted pustule, he had to be excised, and she had had to wield the scalpel. But there was a lot of talking to do, a lot of explanation, none of which should be done in front of the neighbours.

She gazed down at Ezra and Sam, seated close together on the huge velvet sofa. 'I'm so sorry. We shouldn't be washing our dirty laundry in front of you, it must all seem so sordid and paltry.'

Ezra shook his head and gave her a sharp, intelligent look. 'Ent none of my business.'

'Actually, some of it is,' said Minty, making a decision. She drew up a footstool and sat down on it so that she was on a level with him. 'Ezra, you are owed a huge apology for what my husband did to you. He was very, very wrong to try to oust you from your home, let alone in such an unforgivably violent way. And I'm extremely sorry for my part in that. I did genuinely believe that The Lodge was part of the estate and that we could factor it into our plans to make some income in the future.' She saw that Sam was about to speak and held up a hand to quiet him. 'There will be plenty of opportunities for recriminations later,' she said. 'Can I just say, Ezra, that I forgive you for the vandalism of the glamping sign and redirecting the pet cemetery customers to us?'

Ran stifled a laugh. 'He did what?'

'It was nothing,' her mother said, determinedly trying not to recall the poor dead animals and their poor, bereaved owners.

She looked back at Ezra. 'I imagine you know something about the apparition in the camping field, too.'

Ezra Curnow's face was a mask, though mischief gleamed in his dark eyes, which shone brighter and brighter until at last, he let out a guffaw, which became a bellow of laughter, shockingly loud and unfettered from such a wiry old man. 'Lord of Misrule, Ol Penglaz: the Penzance obby-oss! Borrowed the costume from out of the farm shed. Scared the livin' daylights out of them!' The laugh broke out again as he relived the scene. He had surprised himself by his own nimbleness – swishing the black cloak, leaping over tussocks, all the while clacking the horse skull's bony jaws. He chuckled once more, then became solemn. 'Sorry about the old pine, though,' he said quietly. 'That were a shame.'

Minty looked shocked. 'I thought that was the tree surgeons' error.'

'Your husband shouldn't have moved the sacred stone. Sides, the tree would've had to come down. Miss Eliza and I agreed to leave it till she were gone. And, well, now she's gone. It were diseased, full of needle blight.'

'Yes, I know that now,' Minty said rather tightly. 'The tree surgeons told me that once they'd had a chance to examine it properly, said it could have caused considerable damage if it had been left to fall in a storm. Anyway, let's agree that's all water under the bridge, shall we?' She paused, thinking. 'Actually, speaking of water, may I ask you if you know anything about the problems we had with our drainage system, the cesspit stuffed with chicken feathers and wood shavings?'

Ezra looked down. Minty was sure she spied a fleeting smile on his seamed old face, but he said nothing, so at last she sighed and said, 'Well, never mind about that now: it's all sorted, and I dare say it would have had to be replaced sooner rather than later, so perhaps it was a bit of a blessing in disguise. I'd like to get on to what I found, or rather what Dominic and I found—'

'Hang on, Mum,' Dom said suddenly, cutting her off. 'Can I give something to Ezra first? You'll see why.'

Minty looked up at her son, so miserable and deflated, so disappointed in his father, in his hopes – for Christmas, for life. She reached up and touched his cheek. 'Go on, then, darling.'

Dom turned and fled upstairs, returning with a neat parcel wrapped in festive paper, which he placed in Ezra's lap. 'I made it for you,' he said quietly. 'I was just about to come and give this to you when...' His words trailed away. How could anyone summarise the madness of it all? 'Anyway, hope you like it and that you won't think I'm taking liberties, or anything.'

Ezra looked down at the parcel, then up at Dom. 'You already given me the best gift. You saved the bees. Trengrose's bees.'

Dom coloured, pleased. 'I talked to them too, just like you showed me. Spent a while with them telling them what we'd been doing to the house, and the orangery, and how the gardens would be better for them next year. Told them not to worry and that everything would be all right. And I said I was very sorry about their house getting damaged, but that we'll remake it better than ever. I did what I could, but it's not the best repair. I reckon if you and Sam help me tomorrow we can do a proper job – but it should hold for tonight and keep them safe and warm.'

Ezra looked down at the parcel in his lap, and with his brows knit in concentration, he picked carefully at the tape holding the paper closed. Yet, despite the nettle cure of the morning, his arthritis was making it hard, and at last he was forced to give up his lifelong parsimonious habit of saving and reusing wrapping paper and ripped it apart to reveal the object within.

They all watched as he turned it over and gazed at it wordlessly.

Sam moved closer and looked down at it. 'Oh! It's like a history of Trengrose. Look – there's my great-grandad Ethan, and that's his father, Jude! These photos are amazing! Isn't that Great-granny Tamsin? And that's Gram Gwen, isn't it?'

But Ezra wasn't answering. His eyes were fixed on a photo down in the left-hand corner of the collage: a group of young men in uniform, eyes squinting against fierce sunlight. He brushed the image as if his fingers might magic them off the photographic paper and into the room. 'He died,' he said with a sob. 'He died, and I killed him.' He closed his eyes, remembering that terrible, terrible day.

41

Two months after Private Curnow had disobeyed Corporal Hollis's orders in the detention centre, he had been court-martialled, shamed and fined, and then assigned to the worst task he could be given: sweeping for booby-traps, time-bombs and other devices, walking ahead of vehicles to look for signs of disturbance that might indicate where an explosive device had been placed. A patrol had been blown up a few weeks back: no deaths, but three casualties with life-altering injuries.

His fingers had healed, a little crooked still, and painful, but his mind had not. He cried easily, though he tried to hide it, and suffered nightmares that tormented his sleep.

The other men avoided him, as if his weakness and the shame of his punishment might rub off on them by association.

Tonight they were heading back to barracks after a wild goose chase into Limassol. They had found no insurgents, achieved nothing during the entire long day. And they had travelled the very same track, safely, on their way into the city: no sign of explosive devices or anything out of the ordinary. So when he had held up a hand to stop the two trucks, the mood was mutinous.

'For god's sake.' His twin got out of the first truck. 'What is it now?'

'Something odd about the road surface, there.'

'I can't see anything. We already swept this sector this morning and we want to get back to base: everyone's tired and hungry.'

They glared at one another, and Arthur swore. Ezra pushed Arthur. Just a little push of the shoulder, a small gesture of twin dominance.

'Don't do that.'

'Or what?'

'You'll be sorry.'

Ezra mimicked him, parroting the words so they came out high and feminine. The rest of the troop, leaning out of the two vehicles, laughed and whistled.

'Think you're the big man, don't you? Think you're better than me.'

'Don't think it: know it.' Ezra winked grotesquely. 'Ask Gwen.'

'Ask Gwen what?'

'Ask her which of us she prefers. *Ooh, Ezra, that's so good, you're so much better in the sack than my husband.*' He sighed histrionically, then gave his brother a nasty smile.

Something in Arthur broke then, even though he knew Gwen would never have lain with Ezra, and in that moment he hated his brother with a terrible, boiling rage. And in that rage he lunged at Ezra and the next moment they were locked in one of their demonic twin-fights, while the rest of the troop goaded them on. The twins scuffled, kicking and punching till they were down on the ground, rolling and biting and gouging, beyond caring what damage either was inflicting on the other.

And then they were engulfed by thunderous noise; fire, stones, dust, hot liquid, red agony, the world gone distant and muffled.

Then there was nothing at all.

'I woke up in hospital in Limassol,' Ezra told them. 'I were pretty banged up: head wound, broken shoulder, shrapnel… My brother died instantly, they told me. Stepped backwards onto a home-made bomb while we were fighting. Old biscuit tin packed with explosives. Really crude, but horribly effective. I... I pushed him, my twin.' He ran a hand over his face. 'Did I know the explosive device was there? I don't know. I'd spotted the disturbance in the earth up ahead, but I didn't realise our fight had taken us that close. Or mebbe my unconscious mind knew it were there and I wanted it to destroy us both.'

He gazed at them, his eyes hollow.

'He shielded me from the worst of the blast. Some of my injuries were...' He swallowed, remembering. 'Two of his teeth were embedded in my cheek, bits of his skull in my chest wall. It's like we were always meant to be together, two parts of a whole; and in the moment of his death, the broken parts of him flew back into me.'

Silence fell and no one dared break it.

Eventually, Ezra went on, 'They didn't tell me he'd died for some time. When I regained consciousness, I didn't remember the blast, or anything that led up to it. I didn't even know who I was.

'Some of the lads visited me. I were all wrapped in bandages: they said I looked like a sultan in a turban.' He gave a small mirthless laugh. 'I couldn't even remember their names. Spent months with them, day in, day out, and couldn't quite recall who they were.

'They sent me home when I were well enough for the flight, and then I were in rehab for months. Couldn't concentrate, couldn't think straight, had trouble speaking. Physically, I recovered quickly, but when it came to words—' He shrugged. 'Couldn't read, couldn't write, couldn't talk to anyone. I got letters: put them in the bin. The writing were just scribbles, couldn't make anything out of it, my head was so scrambled. Then one day my mother arrived to take me home. I never saw someone look so sad. She kissed me and then sat down and told me all the news from Trengrose.

'It had been a fair harvest; Eliza had bought a new tractor for use on the estate, and everyone were very excited about it.

Jordy Jago had drowned in the bay, fallen overboard in a freak accident, and got caught under the keel of his fishing boat and dragged under the water; a hoopoe had been spotted in the orchard and birdwatchers came from all around to see it; Libby Angove's daughter Molly had won the gymkhana at the Royal Cornwall Show.' He swallowed, blinked. 'Then she said, "I'm so happy to have you back. It's been so quiet in the house," and she took a photo out of her handbag and showed it to me. "Look, here's your little niece, ent she gorgeous?"

'Something in my head broke then. It were like someone had shifted a rock and let loose an avalanche of boulders and they all hit me one by one, memory by memory, and I knew it all.

'I remembered meeting Gwen, making love with her in the barns. Being conscripted; the training; Cyprus; seeing men tortured, dying. But most of all I remembered the rush of hatred I felt for my own brother, as if it were seared into my brain. What a shameful thing, to hate your own twin brother. That were the last thing I remembered. Not the explosion or the immediate aftermath. I started to howl.

'Ma, bless her, she weren't one for a stiff upper lip: she believed in men having emotions. "Let it all out, Ezra, my love," she said, and she put her arms around me while I cried like a baby. And at last when the tears stopped, she brushed my hair back from my face – it had got so long and shaggy in those months since I was discharged. And then she stared at me, and I saw something awful in her eyes. Shock; fear. She reached out and touched my cheek where my twin's teeth had been dug out of me. She ran her fingers across the scar on my forehead, felt the difference between the one I got in childhood and the new ones. And then she whispered, "Oh no. Sweet heaven. What have I done?"

'I had no idea what she meant, and I took her hands in mine, and said, "Don't take on, Ma. It will be okay."

'And she said, "Oh, Arthur. This is just a tragedy. How could the authorities have made such an error?" I didn't wish to make her aware of the disastrous effects of an explosive device, so

I said I did not know, but there it was. But then her face twisted as she realised how far the error had stretched. "Your little wife! Oh, Arthur, we let her go. Gwen, and your baby girl – Sylvia. It seemed only right when Gwen was grieving so badly. We should have waited, but when the telegram from the Army came through notifying us of Arthur's death, she were too distraught to stay with us, because you know how you boys resemble your da, and it was too much for her to see that every day. She went back to her family in Newlyn...'"

Ezra choked at this point and came to a halt, like a clockwork mechanism that had run out of energy, his eyes fixed on the intricacies of the tribal rug at his feet. No one dared break the silence, and at last he added, 'And then Ma said Gwen had got on some fishing boat, taking the baby with her, and gone off to France.' Sam was staring at him open-mouthed. 'Sylvie? My mother? With Granny Gwen?' *On some fishing boat and gone off to France.* And France was exactly where she was now, with her French family. 'But didn't you go after her?'

Ezra's face went still, his expression inturned. 'I just couldn't. Couldn't face her – couldn't face myself, I reckon. Blamed myself for my brother's death, for the whole damn mess. Thought I were entirely worthless, that she and the babe were better off without me, see? And then it weren't long before I heard she'd met someone else – a French fisherman – and settled with him. 'Twere ironic, with me working on the boats at that time. They would put into port sometimes to land their catch here in Newlyn, the French lads, and we would sometimes do the same there, but if we came into a French port I always made an excuse to stay onboard, and the rest of the crew were always happy to have their leisure. And the time just dragged out, and by the time I'd got things more turned over in my head it seemed impossible to go back and put things right. What right did I have to overturn her new life in a new country? Her happiness, and that of little Sylvia's – she changed it to the French way, I heard. That's the thing with the fishing community: you pick up bits and pieces of gossip ever so easily. And by the same token I reckon she probably heard that "Ezra Curnow" had returned and was working in the Newlyn fleet, but she never got in touch, and who could blame her? And then... then, it were all too late. She died in childbirth, was the word.' He looked at Sam. 'I'm so sorry, my lad, to have not told you all this. You of all people deserved the truth. But I'm a stubborn old bugger.' He shook his head.

Sam's eyes were bright with pain. He could hardly take it in. Sylvie and Ezra – no, Arthur! And poor Granny Gwen. But most of all, his abundant sympathy flowed out towards the old man. 'Oh Gamps, I can't believe what happened to you, and you never said a word.' His mouth turned down; then he said, 'You're my actual grandfather!'

'Wait, what?' Miranda was completely at sea, staring from Sam to Ezra.

Dominic showed her the photo of the troop, pointing out the twins. 'One's Arthur and the other...' He stared at the old man. 'I don't even know what to call you now.' Then his eyes went wide, and he exclaimed, 'Oh my god, your jackdaw is Merlin, and your wife was Gwen... like Guenevere!' He looked awestruck. 'Arthur, like King Arthur!'

The man they all knew as Ezra gave Dom a cock-eyed smile, then shook his head. He had a final swallow of the rum-charged cocoa, long gone cold, and took a deep breath. 'I've spent sixty years as "Ezra": three times as many as I was "Arthur". Arthur hasn't existed since my brother and me were blasted apart, so I'll not change now. It's a way of having a bit of my twin with me always, keeping his name, honouring it, if you like. It's just a name. Do it change the nature of a swift if you call it a swallow? Or a frog a toad? And I ent no legendary king. No. So, I reckon I'll stick with Ezra. Tis all too much trouble to unravel such a tangle anyway. Arthur Curnow is dead and buried, according to the official records. I'm an old man now, and I'd rather let sleeping dogs lie.'

'I reckon Catherine Rosevear knew, though, didn't she?' Minty said gently.

Ezra shot her a look. 'Why would you think that?'

'Now we'll get to what I wanted to tell you.'

Minty left the room, then re-entered it a few moments later with an envelope in her hand. She spoke directly to Ezra. 'Catherine wrote this letter and addressed it to her daughter Eliza. It's dated November 1958.'

'That's just after I arrived back in Trengrose,' Ezra said, looking shocked.

Minty nodded. 'The instruction on the envelope was that it was to be opened only in the event of her death, and that was a couple of years later. Catherine sealed it.' She turned the envelope over and showed them the flattened blob of red wax, which had been broken and unstuck.

Everyone stared at it, but Dom said, in a scandalised tone, 'Mum, you opened it!'

His mother gave him a regretful smile. 'I just couldn't resist. I opened it, and I read it. The only person to do so in all this time. How different things would have turned out if Eliza Rosevear had found it.'

At the mention of Miss Eliza's name, Ezra had become very attentive. 'Where did you find this letter?' he asked quietly.

Dom explained about the secret drawer in the little writing desk, becoming increasingly eager as he relived their discoveries up in the attic room, a welcome distraction from their family dramas.

'It's like being in a novel!' Ran exclaimed. 'You must show me the secret drawer,' she urged her brother. 'But come on, Mum, what's in the letter? Tell us before we all die of curiosity!'

'Let me read it to you.' Minty opened the envelope and took out the contents: two sheets of creamy-white, laid writing paper. Its slightly raised texture felt soft and warm beneath her fingers, almost alive. She brushed the pad of her thumb across the first page, almost a caress, and started to read.

I write this letter to you, my darling daughter Eliza, while I am still in sound mind. Life's many shocks and setbacks have afflicted me sorely, and I don't know how much longer I shall be able to keep senility at bay.

Ezra leaned forward. There was a light in his eye. 'Poor Miss Catherine. She knew she were beginning to get a bit... don't know how to put it politely. There's probably a correct way to say it nowadays, but we used to say people were senile, or losing their minds.'

'A touch of vascular dementia,' said Minty gently. 'Or maybe Alzheimer's.'

Ezra nodded. 'Poor old soul. She were a tough woman, Miss Catherine. Could be very severe with the staff if they did anything wrong. But they all loved her. Trengrose was her passion; the land, the people. She were always very kind to me and my family...'

Minty gave him a small smile. 'Yes,' she said. 'And there's a reason for that.' She read on:

There is much I must tell you, Eliza my dear, but I cannot do it face to face. Call me a coward – perhaps I am – but I would prefer to believe that the process of committing my thoughts to paper in the quiet of my own room, seated at my little davenport, will enable me to control the haphazard flow of emotions and memories and keep it all straight in my mind, and then on the page.

I must also make confession (as I have never done to any other living person) of my sins, not least among which has been to curtail your own life, dear Eliza. I should have told you the truth long ago, and released you from Trengrose, for I fear you have found yourself trapped here by the spell it casts upon its inhabitants by its particular beauties, its history, and its own secret nature. You should, dear child, have gone away out into the world to acquire an education, a career, a love to call your own, rather than be forced to follow in my own flawed and selfish footsteps.

So, out with it, Catherine. State it baldly and without equivocation.

This is going to shock you, my dear. Best take a seat; and try not to judge your mother too harshly.

In the years before the Great War I fell in love and counted myself the luckiest woman alive to have that love reciprocated. But our bond was forbidden and had to be kept secret. We would meet in a little underground chamber he had made for us, connected to his cottage by a passageway, while I would go in from an entrance in the orchard. It was our secret hideaway, and no one ever knew about it. We would meet there when we could, and lie together in the bed he made for us there, like a nest in the kingdom of the fey, a place away from the rest of the world. But magic could not prevent me from falling pregnant, and when I did, it was necessary for me to marry if I were to keep my good name, not to tar Trengrose with scandal, and to prevent my child being deemed illegitimate.

I could not marry my beloved, for he had recently married a local girl for the sake of respectable appearance; in addition, he was my servant. Of course, I mean Jude Curnow, the Trengrose estate manager.

Minty stopped here to let this momentous detail sink in, and she watched Ezra Curnow's face. His mouth had dropped open, showing the loss of two teeth in his lower jaw, and the skin around his eyes was pale, as were his knuckles around the mug. He looked as if he had seen a ghost.

'Are you all right?' she asked quietly. 'Shall I go on?'

Ezra nodded mutely.

You were that baby, Eliza; a child in desperate need of another man's name on her birth certificate. And that is why

I swiftly wed Henry Glynn, who had courted me on and off for some months. It was a terrible thing to foist another man's child upon him, and to withhold from him my heart; but I fear the worst injustice was to you, my dear girl. Not only in depriving you of your true father, but also of the truth, and then later, by inflicting the worst injury of all.

While Henry was away in Flanders, and then after his tragic death in the war, Jude and I recklessly continued our affair, and when once again I became pregnant, I found myself in a dangerous pickle indeed.

On the pretence of her being too old to run the house any longer, I was cruel enough to dismiss poor Elsie Hockin, for that woman had sharp eyes and would soon have pierced the truth of my widening waistline: a scandal, with a husband in the ground. My only other servant was young Matty Penrose, but once she was put in charge of Elsie's duties, she had no time to speculate when I took to my bed with a 'lingering illness'.

I then arranged for young Cecily Curnow, née Johns, now wife to my beloved Jude, to take my baby to raise as her and Jude's own. I pleaded my grief at Henry's untimely death and my inability to cope with a boy who would remind me of him. She and her husband were to raise the child as their own and never speak of it to anyone. In recompense, I would ensure that they received financial support by increasing Jude's salary.

Cecily had no idea that she was raising her husband's own child; but as the years passed, I believe she suspected, for a great coldness grew between them; besides, they had no children of their own. The Curnow family resemblance is powerful indeed. They are dark, as the Rosevears are dark, and there is a similarity around the eyes. I have often wondered if our lines were entwined long before living memory.

I should have known the allure that Ethan would cast

upon you, for he had his father's looks and charm. My
darling, this was why I forbade your burgeoning romance as
soon as it became obvious that it was about to move beyond
friendship: for Ethan is your own brother. I am sorry I was
never able to tell you this hard truth: in failing to do so, I
broke your heart; and I also deprived you of a brother you
could have loved truly and openly.

Tears were running freely down Ezra's weathered old face
now, gathering in the deepest wrinkles, dripping off his chin.
Onto his old corduroy trousers, Minty noted, not onto the
impractical pale velvet of the sofa, though she had had it treated
with a good stain-guard, then caught herself thinking this and
felt just a little disgusted with herself. It was only a thing, a sofa –
a beautiful thing, bought from a beautiful shop in Penzance, but a
thing nonetheless, with a practical purpose. Meanwhile, the
words she was reading were blowing an old man's world apart.

Miranda, Dominic and Sam were agog: no one moved, hardly
even breathed, caught in the spell of the lost letter.

Minty reached out and gently touched Ezra's hand. 'Shall I
finish it?' she asked. 'Are you all right?' Perhaps it was too much
all in one day – the attack on him, his escape, Toby smashing his
beehive… and now this.

But Ezra firmed his jaw and nodded stoically. Minty was glad
to see him set the mug down on the coffee table to his side, out
of harm's way.

'Yes,' he said. 'Yes, I want to hear it all.'

I ~~have been~~ am a wicked woman. For all my attempts to treat
others well and kindly, at the centre of it all is a black lie. So
I would like to try to make some amends, to the Curnow
family at least. Here you are, my darling girl, approaching
middle age, and having stated your firm intention never to
marry. What will happen to Trengrose when you are gone?
There will be no more Rosevears to carry on the line; but

there are Curnows, and we are all of this land. Well, maybe you will make a late marriage, and this will come to nothing; but whatever happens, I beg you will provide for my beloved son, Ethan, your brother; and for his surviving son. Such tragedy to lose a child, and in such terrible circumstances. Poor Tamsin broke down and told me what had happened on one of her visits to dress my ulcers. A kind, sweet woman: I don't know how she can bear it.

At the very least, I assign to the Curnow family in perpetuity the cottage they have always lived in, but as for the rest of the estate, I will leave the apportioning of its assets to your best judgment, for you have a good head, my girl, and I know you will be fair in your decisions, and will do your very best to be fair to the spirit of the house and the land.

And now I must lay my pen aside, for this has been a hard letter to write, and once more beg you, my dear, dear girl, to forgive your mother,

Catherine Rosevear

The silence that followed the reading of this extraordinary missive was profound and long-lasting. Ezra wiped his face and gave out a great sigh.

It was Miranda who broke the awed hush. 'That's the saddest thing I ever heard. Poor, poor Eliza!'

'Puts our own family disaster into perspective, doesn't it?' Minty said with bitter humour. 'How much of this did you know about?'

Ezra looked away from her searching gaze. 'Know ent the right word. There's always rumours in small communities, and people often looked sideways at us for having a cottage on estate land. But no one ever did say anything to my da – he was the estate manager, and he'd a knocked 'em down for it.'

He mused for a little while, and no one interrupted his thoughts.

'Jude and Catherine, eh? Now, that's a turn-up. I knew about the tunnel from the cottage to the orchard, and the little room at the end of it. We used it as an air raid shelter in the last war, you know. Never occurred to me it might've been for anything different...' Ezra shook his head sadly. 'Jude and Catherine... Jude and Cecily. Same initials. So when my Gamps were carving those entwined letters on the kitchen table it must have been like his secret code. He must have loved Miss Catherine something awful.'

One of his knuckly old hands took hold of the other, made a bony knot as he pondered this. 'Poor old dear. Poor Gamps, too. They should have married and be damned,' he said fiercely. He bent over the collage of photos Dom had made for him, tapped the image of a young man in a flat cap and kerchief, then one of a young man in the orchard. 'Like two peas in a pod. No one could ever deny Ethan was Jude's son – but poor Gram Cecily, what a thing, to raise another woman's boy and not have any of your own. She and my da never got on in later life, you know. She were difficult: bitter, and no wonder. But Tamsin and Ethan, that were a different tale: that were love, that were. Poor Miss Eliza, alone all her life with her heart breaking over it.' He shook his head. 'I adored her, you know. I won't say "like a mother" because Ma was a fine woman and a loving mother to us boys. Tamsin and Miss Catherine got along well, but now I know why she and Miss Eliza didn't at all. Well, well, well.'

He looked at Minty, his expression somewhere between sorrow and devilment. 'Strange, eh? Seems I be the lost master of Trengrose!' He burst out laughing. 'What a turn-up!' he said again and shook his head.

Minty firmed her lips. 'In all honesty, I don't know where this—' she flourished the letter, 'leaves us, you know: legally. As far as I can ascertain, the letter has not been notarised in any way, and then Eliza passed away without making a will, and without making any official provision for you—'

'Mum!' Ran was outraged.

Her mother touched her on the arm. 'Really, dear, let me finish.' She turned back to Ezra. 'I know that in a story, you would suddenly find yourself the rightful owner of the whole estate. Your father Ethan being the illegitimate son of Catherine Rosevear, and you the only survivor of the family. But Eliza made no will, so the entire estate went to the Duchy of Cornwall, who of course sold it to us. And I think it would be hard to make a legal challenge on that front. But – and this is what I was coming to – it's quite clear in my mind that the lodge cottage is yours and,' she looked at Sam, who appeared entirely overwhelmed, 'your grandson's, and that we have no claim on it. And the land around it, too – your garden, and the orchard. And I'd be more than happy to help you and Sam get that all straightened away with the solicitors – establish and register the title.'

Ezra took all this in silently. He thought about his little cottage, with its broken gate, and its broken window, and its ancient furniture; with the book of Gram Cecily's tinctures on the shelf beside the poetry books Miss Eliza had given him; with the quilt his mother Tamsin had stitched for a wedding gift to him and Gwen – 'it's not as fancy as I'd ha' liked, but you didn't give us much warning!' – on his bed, the bed his parents had slept in. (His mind shied away from remembering Gwen, though: maybe in time he'd come back to that, and to Sylvie... but that was for another day.) He thought about the old range, there since the cottage was first constructed; about Bucca snoozing in the pool of warmth in front of it. He thought about his vegetable garden, slumbering now other than for some brassicas and leeks, and his greenhouse, all the plants harvested, the glass panes and irrigation system cleaned, the kit and pots tidied away till the spring. He thought about the birds that frequented his garden: the robins and blackbirds, wrens and thrushes, the dunnocks and house sparrows, the warblers and tits, and of course

Merlin, and his chickens. He thought about the apple blossom and the wildflowers and how the winter light sparkled on the little stream when there were no leaves on the trees. The bats that came and went, sometimes nesting in his loft, the fox, the badgers, the rabbits and hedgehogs; and finally, the bees. In a hive they would remake, better than before, in the orchard that would at last belong to him in word as well as deed. And despite the powerful upheaval that had occurred in his world these past couple of hours, like a seismic shift of tectonic plates, he felt peace settle over him.

'That's all I want,' Ezra said quietly. 'All I ever wanted.'

'I'm so glad, Gamps,' Sam said. He felt as if an immense weight had lifted from his shoulders. 'And perhaps...' he hesitated, then pushed on as if through a briar hedge, 'perhaps I can get Mum to come down here to see you. We'll have to tell her that her dad didn't die – that you're him.'

Ezra frowned. 'I don't know, lad. What would she want with a worn-out old husk like me? Isn't she better off thinking of her hero-dad blown up on active duty?'

'But... but she's your daughter.'

'Blood isn't always thicker than water, Sam.'

His grandson's eyes were slick and bright. 'I reckon it is.'

They moved into the kitchen and Minty heated tinned soup for them all while Sam and Ran toasted and buttered bread and fetched bowls and spoons. Minty set a place for Ezra and Sam at one end of the table, and for herself and Ran and Dom at the other. She served the old man and his grandson first, and then she took Toby's accustomed chair, looked at Dom and Ran, took a deep breath and said quietly, 'Your father and I will be getting divorced.'

Ran, still furious, was already jumping ahead. 'But if you divorce, won't he try to make you sell the house? You know what Dad's like: he always wants to win, even at bloody Monopoly.'

'We've already had a brief discussion about... the future,' Minty said. 'Trengrose will be mine – ours. Your father will have no claim on it. It was part of the deal.'

Ran looked admiringly at her mother. 'Wow, Mum, you drive a hard bargain! You're like some sort of scary ancient matriarch – like Agrippina or Clytemnestra!'

'I'm not entirely sure that's a compliment,' Minty said, but she smiled. 'And it's not going to be easy, but I'm absolutely bloody determined to make it work.' She looked ferocious.

Everyone considered this, and no one made a sound. The silence was broken by Sam letting out a huge sneeze. 'Sorry, I'm a bit sensitive to scented candles.'

Ran was bemused. 'We never have scented candles – Mum says they leave soot on things.'

'Oh, okay, room spray or whatever.'

Minty looked very alert. 'Dom,' she said softly. 'Dom, can you smell that?'

Her son frowned. Then he salt bolt upright. 'Oh!'

Ezra raised a hand, then dropped it. He gazed around, stared past Minty, past Ran, into empty space. His nostrils flared and he opened his mouth just a little in the same way Bucca did when he scented something unusual. 'I'd know that perfume anywhere,' he said at last. 'That's Miss Eliza's Yardley's English Lavender. She wore it every day.' His eyes glittered. 'She's letting us know she's here and that she's pleased, very pleased with everything that you're doing to make her house beautiful and joyful once more. The house deserves the love she never had, was never able to give it.' A wide, beatific smile spread across his face. 'That's right, my dear,' he whispered. 'You can rest now. New Cornwall and Old Cornwall are coming together to bring Trengrose back to life.' With a great effort, he levered himself out of his chair. 'Come on,' he said to Sam with sudden renewed vigour. 'Give your old Gamps an arm and we'll leave these good folk in peace. There's a barn owl that hunts at this time of night in the orchard, and she's a sight to see. Best feed that old demon Bucca, too. He's earned his sardines today and that's no lie.'

Sam got up and awkwardly gazed around at what remained of the Hardman family. 'I'll get Gamps settled and then I'll bring your bag up,' he said to Ran, but she grinned at him.

'I'm coming with you. Better get used to the woods at dark if I'm going to live here, eh?' She linked an arm through Ezra's. 'Come on then, Mr Curnow, let's get you back to your cottage.'

42

The next morning Dom and Ran and Ezra and Sam converged at the site of the broken beehive, Sam carrying various bits of wood and Ezra a bag of tools. Dom's parka lay folded neatly on top of what was left of the hive as a makeshift roof.

Ran looked at it and then at her younger brother. 'That was a nice thing you did: I know it's your favourite coat.'

Dom, unused to praise from his sister, shuffled his feet. 'The bees would have died otherwise: it was cold last night.'

It was cold this morning too, but it was December-cold, not depths-of-winter, no-end-in-sight January-cold. Ezra put the tools down and squatted beside the wrecked hive. He looked ten years younger than he had the day before. 'Now then, my lovelies, we'm come to remake your home for you. Don't be alarmed. You know young Dominic here: he saved your lives last night and stayed with you till you settled. And you know my...' he paused, 'my grandson, Sam. Same flesh and blood and just as much a part of Trengrose as me. The young lady is Miranda, and just as Miss Eliza was the daughter of the big house, now Miss Miranda holds that title.'

'Gosh, I hope I'll be luckier in love than she was,' Ran whispered, and Sam looked up from measuring the wood to give her a lopsided grin. 'Reckon you will be.'

'So, my lovers, there'll be continuity here on the estate, and the seasons will turn, and spring will come. But till then, there's hellebores and pansies, cyclamen and daisies near my cottage.' He emphasised the word 'my' with a certain pride. 'And dead-nettles and yarrow are in flower down by the stream, and the butterbur is coming through and there's some cow parsley too, so you'll not do too badly for foraging.

'He who damaged your home is gone and he won't be doing you any more harm. So you can buzz and hum and dance to keep your queen warm and know that all shall be well.'

'All shall be well, and all shall be well, and all manner of thing shall be well,' finished Dom. 'Julian of Norwich,' he told his astonished sister.

They went back to Trengrose House for lunch, all of them together. Minty had been up to the farm shop and had delighted Bob Hockin by shelling out on various cold cuts, cheese, bread, olives, some of his wife's home-made sticky toffee pudding and a big tub of the farm's cream. She'd also come away with a couple of bottles of Bob's home-brewed cider, which made Ezra chuckle. 'That stuff's lethal!'

Minty grinned. 'I'm sure it is, but it was a very kind gift.'

'A gift?' Ezra could hardly believe his ears. Bob Hockin never gave anything away.

'I told Mr Hockin that I'd like to talk to him about ways we could work together in the future and that I'm quite sure there must be all sorts of revenue streams and grants to be had that would benefit us all. It appears he's keen to find ways to make the farm pay, just as we must be to make the estate work. And I think he's rather hoping that if we can come up with some viable plans, he might be able to persuade Davey and Kerensa to come home to work with us on them.'

Ran leaned forward. 'Sam's got loads of ideas about sustainable tourism and farming. I'm sure he could help construct some business plans, couldn't you, Sam?'

Sam blushed. 'It's nice you've got some faith in me, but—'

Ran grinned at him. 'Come on, you know you're dying to.' She looked at Minty. 'I've read some of the stuff he's been putting together for his MBA: honestly, I think he's a bit of a genius.' And when Sam squirmed, she laughed out loud. 'It's perfect. You hate London. You belong here at Trengrose.' Her eyes were shining. 'Finish your course, get your MBA, and then apply it right here: help Mum run the estate.' She shot a glance at her mother. 'Honestly, he'd be brilliant.'

Minty looked pensive. 'Well, that's a lot to take on board. But I will give it some thought, and we can sit down and discuss things properly in due course.' Then she smiled. 'I suppose it's what your family has always done: you'd be carrying on a long tradition.'

'Bob Hockin and I have never quite seen eye to eye on farm stuff,' Sam said softly. 'But I reckon I could try to win him over.' He looked at Minty. 'Do up the big barn, make it a hostel for walkers and birdwatchers. We're not far off the Southwest Coast Path and loads of people walk it, and there's a ton of other beautiful walks and ancient settlements and stone circles around here. Give them a kitchen and a shower block or they can share the facilities in the camping field, and you could have a stream of customers all year around.'

Ran cried out, 'And you could add nesting boxes for the swifts! They're endangered, you see, and we could help them.'

Her mother gazed at her in amazement. Her daughter had never shown the least bit of interest in wildlife before; but people were adaptable, women most of all.

'And we could sort out the little walled garden around the side of the house and put tables and chairs there – offer it as an event space, or just do cream teas and stuff,' Ran went on. 'I could run that. I've been thinking about it for a while. I mean, all I've been doing lately is serving tea and coffee and cake in cafés, earning a pittance doing it, and living in a shoebox that costs eight hundred a month, so I thought – why not do it for myself, for us?'

Minty's eyes welled up. 'But darling, your life's in London.'

Ran looked at Sam, then back at her mother. 'It's people that matter most, and all the people I most care about are going to be right here. Besides, you'll need another woman to balance out the patriarchy!'

Dom snorted. 'Hey, enough of that – we're in a post-feminist era now: we all have to work together, for the planet, and all. And it's not just you who's been having ideas. I found out there's a course at the local college about sustainable agriculture and stuff. I think I can do it part-time and get placements in the area to get useful experience – there's a vineyard just down the road that takes volunteers, and all sorts of other small ventures around. And until then Ezra can manage the glasshouse – the orangery – just like he used to. He's really good at growing things, and he knows all about seasonality, and he's going to need to earn some money if he's going to have to pay actual bills!' He turned to Ezra, who was looking slightly alarmed. 'What was it you said you used to grow here? Peaches and figs, grapes and melons, oranges and lemons, cucumbers and strawberries?'

'That were mainly my da,' Ezra said faintly.

'That would be Ethan Curnow?' Minty asked, remembering the sketch of the man in Eliza's room, seeing again the resemblance here in his son, though the ages were reversed.

The old boy nodded. 'He had green fingers.'

'You do too!' Dom crowed. He turned to his mother. 'You should see what he manages to grow in his—'

Ezra had a sudden violent coughing fit and shot Dom a fiery warning glance.

Epilogue

27 December 2018

Bucca, who had followed the old man through the orchard, moved through the gnarled apple trees, the orange patches in his fur almost fluorescing as the hivernal light of this December afternoon struck down through the denuded branches. He regarded the human steadily with his green-gold eyes as he knelt beside the mended beehive with his head bowed. Something formal was going on; something ceremonial.

Cats love ritual. So he set his feet neatly together and sat up straight.

'I come to make you an apology, my queen,' the man said. 'I ent always told you the whole truth, and for that I'm very sorry. It were just too painful: my mind closed over it like scar tissue. I got to tell you about my brother Ezra and what happened to him, and to reintroduce myself as Arthur: Arthur Curnow. Though I dare say you knew the truth all along, for you hold all the knowledge of Trengrose: you are the keeper of secrets.'

And he started to tell the bees the tangled tale of his life – his lost brother, lost wife, lost daughter (not so much lost as let go, he thought mournfully, and whether there was any way to patch that up, he really did not know).

The words flowed over Bucca, just like the mild electrostatic charge generated by the bees as they made their stately little

325

dance within the hive, transmitting knowledge, keeping the secrets. He felt it as a gentle trembling in the ether, the energy of the web of life that wrapped itself around Trengrose.

As the old man spoke on, he forgot his duty as witness and fell into a pleasant doze. He had discovered a new nest of fieldmice this morning, had watched as they scurried back and forth in the chill of dawn, foraging for anything that would get them through another day. He liked watching their industry. It was... restful. It was restful because he felt sorry for them, for the way they had to expend all their energy solely to continue the process of living.

He was lucky. He was no longer under any compulsion of necessity to hunt. The tall, younger human currently occupying the cottage and his occasional companion, the girl with the soft hands, did not eat only vegetables like the old man did, but instead would share with him delicious treats: the fatty skin of roasted fowl, salty rinds, pieces of hard cheese, all of which were a delightful change from tinned sardines and manufactured cat food. In fact, he was getting quite portly.

He licked his belly thoughtfully, and decided that he was of an age when a little extra round the middle was all well and good.

Even though the yellow kie was still in residence, it seemed that peace and plenty had been restored to Trengrose. He patrolled every inch of it, knew it better than any living being, other than the bees.

With his eyes closed and his head now resting on his paws, he listened to the gentle drone, amplified by the remade hive, and perhaps by the bone chambers of his own skull, and he understood the message they transmitted, not from the precise language they used, but instinctively, from the timbre of their discourse.

All shall be well.

Acknowledgements

This is a book I could never have written without being raised and living in Cornwall for most of my life. I've seen the county evolve, and change, and flourish, and fall back, and progress, and struggle. We're a long way from the rest of the world, which is in itself both a blessing and a disadvantage. The remoteness has saved a lot of our ancient history and monuments; its natural beauty has preserved – to some extent, in these times of threat and change – its wildness and creatures. So first and foremost, I must thank Cornwall, for all it has given me. Oddly, then, I must thank the pandemic, for making me a gardener and bringing me so much closer to the land – to the soil and the worms and the seasons, and of course the bees, for a friend offered me part of her overgrown allotment to work in early 2020 and that became both an obsession and a retreat, a place to work and think, to nurture and create. So thanks to Helen for that generous offer, and to Sarah, who is the guardian of that little coastal strip of land.

Thanks to Kimberley Atkins and Sophie Whitehead for their amazingly insightful notes and positive input, and to everyone at Head of Zeus for crafting the magical object of the book in both its physical and digital manifestations and helping it to reach its readers so that Trengrose can cast its spell. To all the bookshops fighting the good fight and serving their communities; and to the libraries, for making magical spaces containing thousands of worlds: without you, I would never have become a writer.

And most of all to my support team: to my wonderful agent Danny Baror, who is my sword and shield. To my beloved husband Abdel, who took one look at the tangle of brambles and blackthorn when I took on my allotment and said, 'Good luck with that,' then came back and helped me dig and dig, and collect seaweed and make compost, and grow, in all sorts of ways. To my sister Kate, who ran her experienced editorial eye over the first draft, and helped me with the legal research and the National Service history; and to my dear friend Philippa, who always reads my drafts with such care and good advice; to natural loremaster David; and to Dora, for letting me visit her bees.

About the Author

Jane Johnson is a novelist, historian and publisher. She is the UK publisher of many bestselling authors, including George R.R. Martin and Robin Hobb. She has written for both adults and children, including the bestselling novels *The Tenth Gift* and *The Sea Gate*. Jane is married to a Berber chef she met while climbing in Morocco. She divides her time between London, Cornwall and the Anti-Atlas Mountains.

SECRETS
OF THE
BEES

SECRETS
OF THE
BEES

Jane Johnson

HEAD
OF ZEUS

An Apollo Book

First published in the United Kingdom in 2025 by Head of Zeus,
part of Bloomsbury Publishing Plc

9 7 5 3 1 2 4 6 8

A catalogue record for this book is available from the British Library.

ISBN (HB): 9781804546260
ISBN (XTPB): 9781804546277
ISBN (E): 9781804546246

Cover design: Simon Michele | Head of Zeus

Typeset by Siliconchips Services Ltd UK

Printed and bound in Great Britain by
CPI Group (UK) Ltd, Croydon, CR0 4YY

Bloomsbury Publishing Plc
50 Bedford Square, London, WC1B 3DP, UK
Bloomsbury Publishing Ireland Limited,
29 Earlsfort Terrace, Dublin 2, D02 AY28, Ireland

HEAD OF ZEUS LTD
5–8 Hardwick Street
London, EC1R 4RG

To find out more about our authors and books
visit www.headofzeus.com
For product safety related questions contact productsafety@bloomsbury.com

For the bees and the wild things